Meg Hutchinson

Meg Hutchinson left school at fifteen and didn't return to education until she was thirty-three, when she entered Teacher Training College and studied for her degree in the evenings. Ever since she was a child, she has loved telling stories and writing 'compositions'. She lived for sixty years in Wednesbury, where her parents and grandparents spent all their lives, but now has a quiet little cottage in Shropshire where she can indulge her passion for storytelling.

The Judas Touch

Meg Hutchinson

CORONET BOOKS

Hodder & Stoughton

Copyright © 2001 Meg Hutchinson

First published in Great Britain in 2001
by Hodder & Stoughton
A division of Hodder Headline

The right of Meg Hutchinson to be identified as the
Author of the Work has been asserted by her in accordance
with the Copyright, Designs and Patents Act 1988.

A Coronet paperback

2 4 6 8 10 9 7 5 3 1

A CIP catalogue record for this title
is available from the British Library.

ISBN 0 340 73862 6

Printed and bound in Great Britain by
Mackays of Chatham PLC, Chatham, Kent

Hodder & Stoughton
A division of Hodder Headline
338 Euston Road
London NW1 3BH

My thanks to Sue Fletcher whose suggestion
this story was.

Also, my thanks go to that long-gone seaman
James Allen of Wednesbury who I found in
the archives. I feel he would not have minded
my jiggling a little with his birth date.

Chapter One

'They be going to 'ang me, don't they Tam? They be going to 'ang me . . .'

'No Benjie, they won't hang you, it will be alright, you'll see.'

Closing her arms about the small frightened figure, Tamar Hallam pulled her brother close, one hand holding the fiery red head against her cheek.

He was not yet fourteen. Tears she dared not shed in front of him clogged her throat causing her breathing to be as ragged as that of the boy clinging in terror to her skirts. Not yet fourteen and facing the gallows.

'I didn't kill him Tam, honest . . . and I didn't steal that package . . . I ain't never stole nothin' in my whole life.'

Sobs breaking up the words he buried his face in the rough shawl covering his sister's shoulders.

It had been three days ago they had come for him. Two police constables and Charlie Selby.

Bending her head, touching her face to the spiky hair, Tamar felt the same bewilderment she had felt that night.

Charlie Selby, a man they had known all of their

lives, had come to the house and accused Benjie of murder and theft.

'This be 'im, Constable . . .'

Charlie had stepped across the kitchen to where her brother had been sitting and placed a hand on his shoulder.

'. . . this be Benjie 'Allam . . .'

Tamar held her breath against her teeth closing off a sob. Accused by a friend . . . a hand on the shoulder . . .

The Judas touch!

The words brought a cry of fear from the boy in her arms and Tamar winced against the sting of his fingers biting into the flesh of her back.

'Please?' She whispered to the uniformed man stood watching from the doorway of the tiny windowless room.

'Can't be wench, I've given you more time than I should already; if the inspector should 'appen in then I'd be for it. Sorry wench, I know the young 'un be afeared but rules is rules an' they 'as to be kept.'

Both hands lifting her brother's face Tamar tried to smile, but the terror staring back from red-rimmed eyes swallowed her like some black nightmare.

'I will come back tomorrow Benjie,' she kissed his face gently, 'we will be together again in the morning. Until then I want you to be brave. Do everything the sergeant tells you to do and remember to say your prayers before you go to sleep.'

'I said my prayers.' The hands about her back tightened. 'I said my prayers every night like you taught me, but God don't listen Tam, He don't never listen; He's turned His back just like He did when father died . . .'

'God does not turn His back!' Tamar answered sharply. 'Father died because he was too ill to live any longer, but God did not forsake us, He let us stay together . . .'

'Come along now wench, say your goodnights.'

Eyes sympathetic beneath heavy eyebrows streaked grey as his bushy side whiskers the policeman rattled the keys strung on a ring of brass.

'Don't go Tam!' The frightened cry rang from the walls of the tiny cell. 'Don't leave me, I be feared . . .'

'Shhh!' She kissed his face again. 'Where is my brave brother, the one who protected me at the goose fair when that man tried to grab me?'

The pale face smiled briefly. 'I did see him off, didn't I, Tam?'

'Yes, love.' Tamar answered, her eyes flooding as they gazed at the boy she had mothered the last five years. 'You saw him off, and you will see this off. Remember Benjie, the innocent have nothing to fear, and we both know you are innocent. In a few days it will be over and you will be home again. Now, give me a smile so I can tell the Marshes that you are facing this just as bravely as you faced that man at the fair.'

'You will come?' Quiet as a shadow the words followed as she eased the hands from her body then turned away. 'You promise Tam . . . you promise?'

At the door Tamar glanced back at the thin figure,

his father's coat hanging down over his shoulders, the sleeves covering his hands.

'Have I ever let you down, Benjie?'

'No.' His voice trembling he looked at the ground, 'No, you ain't.'

'And I will not let you down now. You have my promise Benjie, I will be here tomorrow just as soon as I am allowed.'

The sound of the key in the lock reverberated along every nerve in her body shaking her like the toll of the church bell that had rung at her father's funeral. It was that sound more than anything else had told her that her father was gone for ever, and now . . . but she would not think the similarity; her brother would not be taken from her.

'You get yourself along 'ome. You need 'ave no fears for 'im.' Fastening the ring of keys to a broad black leather belt the policeman looked kindly at her. 'I'll be 'ere through the night and I'll keep an eye on the young 'un; a cup of cocoa and a bun will 'elp to settle him to sleep.'

'That is very kind of you. Benjie . . . my brother has never been alone before.'

'Well he won't 'ardly be on his own in this place,' the policeman replied, jerking his head in the direction they had come. 'Them other cells be full, men with too much of a fondness for taking what don't belong to 'em, or with a liking for using their fists. But don't you go fretting.' He caught the look that leapt to her eyes. 'That little lad ain't going to 'ave company of that sort, not while I be sergeant of Hockley Brook

4

police station he ain't! So now, you get yourself along 'ome, and take care, the streets about these parts be no place for a young wench to be on her own after dark.'

Thanking the bushy-whiskered man once more for his promised kindness to her brother, Tamar stepped into the street, black except for patches of grey shadow thrown by a dancing moon.

They would believe him; the magistrate and people of the court would believe Benjie, see he was telling the truth when he told them he had not killed Joby Turner.

Pulling her worn shawl low across her brow she turned the corner, stepping nearer the middle of the narrow road as the door of a beer house was thrown open and a man staggered from its smoke-filled depths calling loudly after her as she gathered her skirts to run.

'You need 'ave no fear for 'im . . .'

Tamar's heart jumped wildly as a hand closed over her arm, a scream rising to her lips as she was jerked to a standstill.

'Zeph . . . !'

The face of the man who had caught and now held her revealed by the capricious moon, Tamar gasped her relief.

'. . . Zeph, oh, thank God it is you, I . . . I thought perhaps . . .'

'That drunk!' Zeph Tullio made a scornful sound in the back of his throat. 'A boot to the backside helped that one on his way.'

Breath easing from her in a long relieved sigh, Tamar smiled.

'I don't know how you come to be here Zeph, but I am truly glad you are. There are a few more beer houses to pass between here and Vyse Street and maybe a few more men as intoxicated as that one; it will be a relief not to have to pass them alone . . .' she looked up, moonlight showing a sudden uncertainty on her face, '. . . but maybe you are not going in that direction.'

His smile wide, showing strong teeth white even in the dimness of evening, Zeph Tullio nodded.

'Not only that direction but right up to number fifty-one.'

'My house?' Tamar was perplexed. Why would Zeph Tullio be going to her house?

'That's right.' He took her elbow, turning her in the direction of Vyse Street. 'Cal Perry said you had asked to leave the workshop early so as to visit your brother at the station along of Hockley Brook. I knew it would be almost dark by the time you got to come home and that it would be best to have someone to see you safe there, so . . . here I be.'

'You came just to walk me home, that was very thoughtful of you.' Seeing a figure emerging from the gloom Tamar pulled her elbow free waiting until it was past before adding. 'Thank you Zeph, I really wasn't looking forward to walking back by myself.'

Drawing the shawl closer about her she hurried on, the tap-tapping of her boots seeming to hang in the evening quiet. She knew these streets well and the people who lived in them, trusting most of them implicitly, but the nearby canal wharfs and basins with narrowboats that came in from every part of the country, sometimes spewed up characters a woman might feel were best not met in a darkened alley.

'Has there been any news of the one who got old Joby?'

'None.' Tamar's answer was sad but grateful that he, like the rest of her friends, did not believe her brother to be guilty of the crime.

'There will be, it only be a matter of time afore the bobbies catch up with whoever it was.'

Halfway along Warstone Lane they turned right into Vyse Street, Tamar's steps quickening as they approached the newly erected public urinal nick-named by locals 'The Temple of Relief' and very much resented by women embarrassed at having to pass such a place.

'Somebody will 'ave seen something,' Zeph continued, 'and they'll come forward.'

The ornate wrought-iron edifice behind them Tamar lifted her head. 'If that is the case why have they not come forward before this . . . why let a young lad suffer?'

'Could likely be a cut man, if so it could be a week or more afore he be this way again.'

A week, a year, or maybe not at all! The thought twisting her heart Tamar looked up at him.

'Thank you for bringing me home Zeph, I appreciate your thoughtfulness.'

Her steps almost a run she turned into the covered

passage that led between the small line of buildings joined one to the other in a ragged ribbon.

'If you appreciate it, then show it.'

His own steps light and almost soundless he was behind her as she entered the yard shared by eight families.

'I believe I did, I said thank you.'

'Saying ain't enough!' His voice seemed to throb and his fingers were hard as his hands grabbed her arms. 'You 'as to show me you be grateful, you 'as to give me more'n words, I d'ain't go across to Hockley police station for words.'

'Let me GO!' Trying to shake his hands from her arms Tamar gasped as he pulled her roughly against him, his laugh soft and coarse.

'Oh, I'll let you go right enough, once you 'as thanked me proper.'

Thrusting her sharply backward he dropped beside her as she fell backward on to the cobbled ground, pushing her skirts up over her chest.

'This be the thanks Zeph Tullio expects . . .'

Breath hot and rapid against her face, he gripped the waistband of her cotton bloomers ripping them away.

'. . . this be what he come for.'

Clapping a hand over her mouth stifling her scream he fumbled with buttons of his trousers, his hard flesh touching against her stomach as he struggled to force her legs apart.

Twisting with all her strength, her fingers clawed into his greasy jacket, Tamar tried to throw him off, her efforts growing rapidly weaker as his hand kept the breath from her lungs. Then, miraculously, he was rolling away from her his angry shout filling the quiet night.

'What you expects and what you gets be two different things you dirty bugger!'

Vinny Marsh's voice rose over the shout as her foot lashed out finding its target for the second time.

'I had an inkling what your game was Zeph Tullio, an' when I 'eard the scuffling in the yard I knowed my idea was right; well, we in Vyse Street knows how to deal with your sort as my lads will show you once they 'ears what I have to tell 'em, so lessen you want your filthy back broke you'll get your bare arse out of Hockley altogether and this will 'elp you on your way!'

Swinging a large platter chamber pot she carried in both hands she threw the contents over the figure sprawled at her feet.

Tipping a handful of soda crystals into the empty chamber pot and covering them with boiling water taken from the kettle steaming over the fire, Vinny carried it into the minute scullery and scrubbed it with a hard-bristled brush before returning to the kitchen where she had sat Tamar beside the gleaming fireplace.

'I don't let the little 'uns go out to the privy after dark,' she glanced at the huge flowered chamber pot now scrubbed clean, 'I makes them piddle in the po' an' I must say that tonight I be extra glad I does, and that Tullio bloke won't smell no worse for the bath I give 'im.'

'I never thought . . .' Tamar's mouth trembled '. . . I never dreamed, he said he had thought it best I not walk home in the dark alone.'

Opening the door that gave on to bare wooden stairs Vinny set the pot on the second one. It could wait to be carried to the tiny landing where it sat every night to be used by any member of the family that might need it before the morning. That done she turned back to the quietly sobbing girl.

'I know what Zeph Tullio thought,' she said bustling with teapot and kettle, ''e thought to get his oats in our back yard. Well, he will lose that he wanted to play with if my Joseph catches up with 'im. There'll be no more sticking it up any wench whether 'er wants it or whether 'er don't, only thing he'll be stickin' it into once my lad be finished will be his jacket, he can put it in his lapel for a buttonhole.'

'I . . . I'm sorry you had such trouble.'

'Trouble.' Vinny's thin worn-out face tightened. 'Weren't no trouble to me wench, I enjoyed emptying the piss pot over that toerag; Zeph Tullio be no good, I knowed it the day his Gypsy mother brought him on that Liverpool barge: he be sly an' he be treacherous . . . Gyppo blood!' She spat at the fire. 'It be in his veins. He'll never do any good by any woman nor by any man 'cept the one that lets it out wi' a knife!'

Spooning sugar into a cup she had filled with hot strong tea she stirred it briskly before putting it into

Tamar's trembling hands. This girl had had her fair share of the knocks of the world with a mother carried off with the typhoid and a father dead of a broken heart not two years on.

Heartbreak! Vinny turned back to the table taking up her own cup. That might be what a doctor called it. But what did they know of working the gold, of the dust of cyanide, of the ammonia fumes taken in with every breath, of engraving so fine that a few years of it could send a man blind, and the fly presses operated by girls so badly nourished the throwing of it almost swung them off their feet. This were the real nature of the part of Birmingham so grandly labelled the 'Gold Quarter'. The beautiful shining baubles turned out here hid the squalor of tiny crowded houses many of them not fit for a pig to live in. The glitter of exquisite gold work that concealed the misery of its making, the long backbreaking hours that went into every piece; but the backbreaking and the blindness was not the heaviest price demanded by the gold, that was the slow, inevitable destruction of the soul.

It was that, and the knowing of it, together with the knowing that it was all life would hold for his lad and his wench that had like seen Ezra Hallam to his last rest.

Gulping angrily from the cup, the hot liquid burning against her throat, Vinny coughed, dashing moisture from her eyes with one hand.

It was the same for her and her husband and it would be the same for their children. They knew nothing but the working of jewellery, and if they did, what then? England in 1887 cared no more for its poor than it ever had. Her grandfather and his had laboured for naught other than his bread and for all the promises of gentry that was still the way of it.

Putting her cup on the well-scrubbed table, Tamar got to her feet, her nerves trembling at the thought of crossing the darkened yard to her own home.

'I thank you for the tea, Mrs Marsh.' She hitched her shawl over her elbows, 'I . . . I will be along home now.'

'Nay, wench.' Vinny shoved aside her thoughts. 'You will sup wi' us and then my Rachel will stay at the house with you tonight and each night 'til young Benjie be 'ome. Now no arguin', get that shawl off and give me 'elp with the plates.'

They had all been so kind. Tamar watched the cloud-driven shadows flicker over the walls of her small room. Even with Rachel asleep in Benjie's room fear kept her awake. He had come behind her along the entry so silently, she had not known he was there until he had grabbed her. What if Mrs Marsh were wrong, if the threat of her sons were not enough to drive him away?

A cry freezing on her lips she clutched at the bedcovers as an owl hooted in the nearby churchyard. Would Zeph Tullio leave Hockley, or would he stay to strike again?

'I be sorry Tamar wench, but there were nothing I could do. The warrant called for him to be taken to

Winson Green gaol and warrants can't be argued with.'

'But he was to appear before the magistrate here in Hockley at two o'clock this afternoon, you told me so yourself.'

The sergeant of Hockley Brook police station looked at the distraught girl standing beside the table that served as desk and file cupboard, as well as the place he and his one constable took their meals while on duty.

Hair held with a length of twine in place of a pretty ribbon gleamed like silken fire, tears adding an extra brilliance to eyes beautiful and glistening as any jewels to be found in those jewellers' workshops. Ezra Hallam's girl was beauty in the bud, and when that bud burst many a man would feel the desire of it in his heart.

'That were what were supposed to 'appen.' Reluctantly taking his eyes from that beautiful flower-like face he opened a ledger, pointing to an entry written in a flowing copperplate hand. 'It be 'ere.' He traced the words with a forefinger. 'Benjamin Hallam. Appearance before Sir Jerome Keithley, magistrate, on the twenty-third day of January 1887. That be today.'

'Then why take him to Winson Green? I don't understand.'

Closing the ledger the sergeant stroked a hand over bushy side whiskers. 'Seems somebody has come forward and is willing to testify.'

A wild surge of joy speeding along her veins, Tamar pressed both hands to her mouth.

'Someone saw?' she whispered. 'Someone saw what happened . . . saw it was not Benjie killed Joby Turner?'

Picking up the blue bound book the sergeant set it on top of the pile of similar books stacked to one side of the table, his hands resting on them several moments before turning to face the girl, hands pressed against a trembling mouth.

'Someone saw.' He nodded slowly his gaze steady as he met hers. 'At least that be what he be prepared to swear.'

Hearing the pent-up breath trickle like falling water between her clenched teeth the sergeant felt his own stick in his throat. Swallowing hard he forced the rest of the words to come.

'Only what he swears to ain't good for young Benjie. Zeph Tullio be prepared to say on the Book that he seen the lad strike the blow that killed Joby. That put a whole new complexion on things, a witness to a crime of murder. The authorities ain't prepared to risk the accused doing a runner so they've had 'im moved to Winson Green 'til his case can be 'eard.'

Hands dropping to her sides Tamar stared with unseeing eyes.

'It's a lie!' She breathed. 'It's a wicked lie!'

That was his reasoning too but he could not say as much. His kindly face reflecting his sympathy he said gently. 'Lies 'ave a way of showing themselves. Keep a good heart and with God's help the truth will soon come to be known.'

The truth! Head bent, oblivious of the irate calls of carters whose path she hindered, Tamar walked slowly through the warren of narrow tight-packed streets that formed the area of Birmingham commonly called the 'Gold Quarter'.

The truth was Zeph Tullio had seen no such incident, probably he had been nowhere near the workshop. Then why say he had?

But she knew why. This was his revenge. She had refused him that night, refused as he knew she always would and this was his way of paying her back.

Zeph Tullio was willing to see her brother hang to soothe his own pride.

Chapter Two

'You say it be Zeph Tullio be going to testify against Benjie?'

Philip Amory placed a small square of bullion on the shining brass scale, meticulously weighing it to the last milligram, then recording both its measure and the name of the craftsman waiting to take it to the stamping machine stood in one corner of the workroom, then turned to the woman waiting his attention.

'That be what his sister told me last evenin'.'

Vinny Marsh handed the bracelet she had just finished polishing to her employer, watching whilst he checked the original weight of the gold against that of the stamped out article and that against the finished weight. She could not read the words set down in black ink or comprehend the figures marked out in red but she knew it had to do with the sweepings, the dust on floor and work benches swept equally carefully every night, then filtered to recover the fine gold dust lost by chasing designs in the metal or by filing edges smooth. She smiled to herself. Philip Amory was one of a rare breed; he was a fair man to work for but not one grain of gold was allowed to pass unrecorded from his workshop.

'It's a bad business Vinny, a bad business alto-gether.'

'Ar, Mr Philip, it does that.' Vinny agreed as, passing a final careful inspection, the beautiful golden bracelet, worked like a circle of bamboo, was placed in the small hand-operated lift to be hauled to the office where it would be invoiced and prepared for dispatch.

In her younger years she had often indulged in day-dreams, seeing herself dressed in beautiful gowns and adorned with glittering golden jewellery; but that had been when she had time for dreaming. Returning to the work bench in the gilding shop Vinny sighed. Carefully measuring a quantity of the coarse-grained cyanide powder into a container. Adding salts of ammonia and water she mixed them together the fumes of the evil-smelling brew filling her nostrils and causing her to cough. Taking up another bracelet she dipped it into the gilding solution. Time for dreams was long gone.

Glancing at her mother from her own position on the polishing bench, Rachel Marsh leaned closer to Tamar, the slap of leather belt that operated pulley wheels coming dangerously close to her hair.

'You can't be going to do that, you'll lose your job.'

The sound of stamping machine, grinding wheels and the dull thud of fly presses all combining into one deafening crescendo Rachel mimed the words.

A spoken answer being of little use and much effort, Tamar lifted her shoulders as reply.

She had promised Benjie she would go to him today and somehow she would keep that promise. But how to get to Winson Green? She had no money for the tram. But that would not prevent her going to that prison. Holding an exquisite bangle against the revolving polishing wheel Tamar pressed her lips together in a determined line. She had two strong legs, they would get her to Winson Green. And if she could not get leave from the workshop to go? Taking the now polished bangle to the gilding shop she handed it to Vinny. If leave were refused then this job and her living must go too; but either way she would go to Benjie.

Zeph Tullio fingered the package deep in the pocket of his trousers. Nobody had seen him take it from that open three-wheeled basket. Errand boys were notorious for leaving bullion or finished jewellery in the road while they played a game of marbles or football using parcels of gold as goalposts, and young Benjie Hallam had proved no different. It had been easy, Zeph smiled to himself. One quick grab and a small parcel had been in his pocket and him off among the warren of workshops without so much as a whisper of a sound.

It was easier than slaving your guts out in a workshop and it paid better supposin' you found the right fence to pass it. But that were if what you lifted was gold, but this . . . he fingered the stone again feeling the hardness of it against his fingers . . . this wasn't

gold though it had to be of equal value, maybe more
or why send it here to the Gold Quarter?

How much more? Zeph breathed hard. And would
the Juggler buy it?

'You won't get a lot o' pleasure that way.'

Zeph glanced at the coarsely painted face of the
woman who sidled up to him, her stained teeth
yellow against vivid lip rouge.

'A man playing in 'is pocket don't get the satisfaction Polly Bell can give 'im. What say I shows you a
good time?'

It would cost him a shilling to get what he'd hoped
to 'ave free the other night. Zeph looked at the
woman again. But that 'Allam bitch 'ad said no, 'ad
screamed at 'im to let 'er go. Well, her would regret
that, regret it a hundred times over when seeing her
kid brother swing!

The thought somehow exciting, he smiled down at
the crudely painted face.

'I don't 'ave enough . . .' he began, hoping to
lower the woman's price.

Reaching a hand to his knee she trailed it slowly up
his leg cupping the bulge that pressed against his
trousers.

'You 'as enough of what it takes,' she squeezed
gently, 'an' Polly can take all of this. C'mon, give
yourself a treat, an hour in bed will give you a new
lease of life.'

'If it don't finish off the old 'un by givin' you a dose
o' the clap!'

The keeper of the beer house wiped a dirty cloth

over the counter as the woman whipped round, her look thunderous as it met his smirking face.

'If Polly Bell 'as the clap then you 'as to be carryin' it an' all the number of times you've grunted an' groaned atop of 'er. But then that's all you could do ain't it? You never could get it up; as I remember that precious piece o' your'n flopped about limp and useless as a body that's drunk too much of your stale beer, neither of 'em any bloody good!'

'And neither be you, you old whore.' The cloth slapped into a puddle of spilt beer sending droplets rising into the air like a miniature fountain. 'When he sees what you got once you be outta them stays an' bloomers a bloke goes right off, that's if 'e could stand the stink o' you long enough to get that far.'

'I wouldn't talk about seein' what *I* got Clancy O'Rourke, case I be tempted to tell what you *ain't* got. A shilling be 'ard earned by lying with you, and that the only thing as *is* got 'ard! For that three inches o' flesh you calls a prick, huh . . . I've seen thicker an' longer in a sausage, ar an' a lot more tasty at that! When it comes to talking about what other folk 'ave got then it will pay you to keep your big parish oven shut!'

'I can keep me mouth closed an' still mek me livin'!' Clancy smirked again, 'but with 'er legs closed Polly Bell don't 'ave no livin', and you've taken your last shillin' in this 'ouse. Show your painted face in 'ere again and I'll throw you out!'

Hands going to her hips Polly tossed her head, the

bedraggled red feathers of her straw bonnet waving pathetically.

'Pig sties ain't 'ard to find,' she spat, 'not as 'ard as it be to find your balls! C'mon, sweetheart,' she smiled again at Zeph, 'let's find somewhere where the beer don't be stale and the landlord be pleasant.'

His mind only half on the proceedings Zeph allowed himself to be pulled out of the beer house, the woman clinging to his arm as they walked together through the maze of narrow streets. One hand touching against the package in his pocket he followed the woman into a dingy-looking house pressed close in among a line of similar buildings.

The Juggler would buy it, but this time he would pay the proper price.

'So you see Mr Philip I have to go, I promised Benjie I would.'

Replacing a quill pen in the brass holder Philip Amory looked up from his desk. He had employed both father and mother of the girl now asking leave to go visiting Winson Green prison and understood the closeness that existed between her and her younger brother, but business was business and he must put that before all else.

'You were given time off only a day or so ago.' He tried not to sound unsympathetic. 'This is a sorry do all round and much as I believe that what happened was none of your brother's doing I cannot go on permitting you to leave your bench. With a worker absent production goes down and that means less pay for other employees.'

'I understand, Mr Philip, and I will work extra hours for nothing once Benjie is home and safe.' Fingers twisting anxiously together, Tamar watched her employer purse his lips.

She had never asked for time off before, not even when her father had died. The funeral service and the burial had taken place at nine o'clock at night as was the custom, folk being too poor to lose pay even for the one hour it took to lay a loved one to rest.

'I'm sorry, Tamar.' Philip Amory shook his head. 'Try to understand, I have other workers to consider and that forces me to say no to your request. I cannot allow you to leave your work. You can visit your brother on Sunday after church service.'

Work, the making of jewellery, and church worship. All of this was more important than her brother! Tamar felt the bitterness of it rise like gall to her throat. Forcing her hands to be still she looked at the man sat behind the wide oak desk. She knew that as an employer Philip Amory was very much one of a kind. He was fair and considerate of the men and women in his workshop and it was larger than the tiny wash house workshops attached to every house in the district, or as in many instances the cramped space allotted to working the gold in a family's living room. She would not find another job the same, maybe she would not find one at all. But her promise to Benjie must be kept, and if in keeping it she lost her living then that was a risk that had to be faced.

'Sunday will not do Mr Philip,' she said, a tremble beneath the words showing how well she understood the enormity of them. 'I told Benjie I would see him today and . . . and that is what I intend to do.'

'I see.' Above a heavily starched wing collar that held his neck in a vice-like grip Philip Amory's head bobbed slowly up and down as he looked at the pretty face set so determinedly.

'I cannot of course prevent you in this.' He drew a long breath, letting it out slowly before continuing. 'But should you persist in refusing my advice to defer your visit to your brother until Sunday, I shall have no option other than terminating your employment.'

The sack! Tamar's heart jolted. The words he used were lost on her but the meaning was not. Leave this workshop before time and she went with the sack! That would mean no money coming in at all, and like as not no house to live in.

Thoughts running like wind-blown leaves through her mind, Tamar tried to see the logic behind them. Without a home and the means to support them how would they manage once Benjie was freed? Mr Philip was right, she should wait until Sunday before going to that prison; Benjie would understand . . .

'You will come . . . ?'

Quietly as they had been spoken the words returned, bringing with them the pale frightened face and red-rimmed terror-filled eyes of a boy whose world had suddenly turned into a nightmare and as they seemed to look at her, to cry out to her, Tamar

23

realised that nothing mattered except she be with her brother.

Bobbing a respectful curtsy she nodded. 'I understand Mr Philip, but like you with your business I have something other than myself to consider. I thank you for the time I have been employed here but Benjie must come first. I will just get my tin from the bench and then I will leave.'

'One moment.' Philip Amory took the chased gold hunter from his waistcoat pocket flipping open the front and glancing at the time before slipping it back, a habit he had developed whenever faced with a situation he was not completely sure of. 'How are you thinking of getting to the prison? Do you have money to take a tram?'

Remembering the sixpence she and Benjie had hidden to be kept against an emergency, Tamar nodded. That would more than pay her fare on the horse-drawn tram but it would not be used for that, not while she could walk.

The girl had indicated she had the means of travelling by tram to that prison. Philip Amory glanced down at the closed ledger, his fingers fiddling with his watch. She had not taken the opportunity she must know he had given her, the chance to ask his charity. But begging was not her style, young as she was he could see that in the way she held herself; respectful but proud, her eyes unfaltering on his holding him until he felt to be the uncomfortable one.

'The world is not always what it seems, girl.' He twisted the watch in and out of his fingers. 'And

Hockley is by no means the extent of it. There are people you cannot trust.'

Across the wide-topped desk Tamar flinched, a shadow of fear crossing wide green eyes and for a moment Philip Amory felt a deep anger. Someone had already tried to harm this girl, someone had . . .

Forcing back an anger he had never felt before he flipped the watch into his pocket then reaching into a drawer of the desk withdrew a small cash box.

Taking out a sovereign he held it for Tamar to take. 'You may find this of help . . .'

'No, thank you Mr Philip . . .' Tamar's head came up sharply, 'I have no need, though again I thank you for the kindness of the thought behind the offer.'

She had not even looked at the money. Philip Amory's fingers closed over the gold coin, embarrassment touching a faint streak of colour to his cheeks. Any other man, woman or even child in Hockley would have snatched his hand off in eagerness to take it, but this girl . . . she had refused and her refusal somehow was a far more magnanimous act than his.

Not understanding his own almost driving need to help her, to protect this girl who was after all nothing more than an employee, a young woman who could be dismissed by the flick of a finger, Philip Amory took a ledger from the several stacked on his desk. Opening it he ran a finger down one page.

Tamar Hallam, he read, employed this fifteenth day of March 1882.

The Ides of March! Philip's glance remained on the elegantly written date. It had been so filled with destiny for Caesar, why did he feel it held as much for him?

Five years. She had come to work here when the firm was headed by his father and in the two years since his taking over he had hardly been aware of the flame-haired girl at the polishing bench; yet now, seeing her as if for the first time he felt an almost overwhelming urge to touch that lovely face.

Beware the Ides of March!

The favourite phrase used by his Oxford don whenever his work fell below par echoed in Philip's head. It had always served as a warning, putting an end to his dreams, so why was it he now wanted to ignore it?

'If it is all the same to you, Mr Philip, I will be going, but before I do, I wish to apologise for the trouble you have taken on account of my brother. I can only say what my heart tells me, that Benjie did not steal that stone, neither did he murder Joby Turner. I hope that your property will soon be restored to you and the true culprit brought to justice, and I hope one day to repay your kindness to me.'

Reaching for the quill pen, dipping the nib into the glass-lined brass ink-well Philip Amory wrote the words, Employment terminated, then with a stroke crossed them out.

Then, the pen still in his hand he looked up at the waiting girl. Her employment would not be terminated, there would be a place here for her whenever her business was done.

Replacing the pen in the holder he smiled.

'We will not say you are dismissed, we will say you have leave of absence. Come back quickly Tamar, until then take care, take very great care.'

'You can't be serious wench!'

Vinny Marsh had come from the gilding shop to stand beside Tamar as she reached for the tin in which she brought a sandwich every day for her midday meal.

'You can't go on takin' leave, 'ow the hell do you propose to live? I tell you, think on what you be doin', young Benjie ain't goin' to die cos you don't be there today, wait until Sunday and my lads will walk you to Winson Green.'

'I know they would Mrs Marsh, but . . .'

'Ain't no buts!' Vinny returned sharply. 'You go back in that office an' tell Mr Philip as how you 'ave changed your mind.'

'I'm not leaving and that is the truth of it.' Tamar collected her shawl from one of a line of nails. Taking it across to a chute that disappeared into the cellar she gave it a vigorous shake, the dust that rose from it glittering with sparkles of gold dust as it was instantly swallowed by the suction of large bellows.

Quickly folding the shawl so it would collect virtually no more of the gold-laden dust arising from every aspect of the workshop, she scraped the soles of her boots on the metal grid that also gave on to a collecting bin in the cellars where dirt would be sieved through water and the minute particles of gold re-

covered. The ritual that each of the workers per-
formed before leaving the premises each night almost
complete, Tamar handed her tin to Cal Perry who had
carefully overseen the process and now inspected the
lunch-box ensuring no speck of gold adhered to it.

'I 'opes you know what you be doin' wench.' The
man's eyes were kind as he returned the tin.

Her own glance misty, Tamar tucked the tin
beneath the shawl.

'I hope so too, Mr Perry.' She smiled.

'Then God be with you wench.' He walked with
her to the door but the ever-mindful care of gold dust
on his clothes or his shoes he did not step through it or
even touch a hand to hers. Instead he shook his head
his voice soft as he added. 'And may heaven be kind to
that brother o' your'n.'

Standing on the pavement Tamar felt her nerves
twist. She had given up her income. Watching the
errand boys running behind their three-wheeled baskets, loaded with parcels she knew contained a fortune
in precious metals, she felt the enormity of what she
had just done. This was all she had ever known!
Lifting her glance she let it rove over the medley
of buildings. Three storied they shambled upward,
each of their assorted rooms a home and workshop
combined, each struggling to support a family.

It was no heaven, no place to long for, but Tamar
longed to hold on to the safety it held for her.

'Hey up Tamar! Ain't never seen you out of
Amory's workshop at this hour, you don't be bad
do ya?'

'No . . . no I am not feeling ill.' Tamar brought her glance to a tow-haired boy watching her from a few yards further along the road. 'I am going to see Benjie.'

'Oh ar.' The boy grinned, his attention already caught by another basket being pushed in the opposite direction bringing with it a possible game of football. 'Tell 'im my regards will ya?'

'I will, thank you Billy.'

Which way was Winson Green? Listening to the screech of wheels as the boy raced away Tamar looked helplessly along the length of the narrow street. And how to ask directions? She had heard tales of the prison there, the awful stories told by those who had served time there and were willing to speak of it to any man who would pay the price of a tankard of ale; stories later passed like titbits around the gilding shop, the women almost too breathless to eat their dinner. But to ask the way, to admit to going there . . . Tamar felt a quiver of fear rub against her nerves. But it was the only way, she would ask the next person she saw.

The decision made she turned her head to look at a woman whose coarse laughter filled the street. Fingers clutching the shawl she had draped about her head Tamar felt the prick of fear turn into a long shudder that walked along her spine. Accompanied by a man, holding on to his arm while her free hand reached to caress his face the woman laughed again, the gaudy feathers of her bonnet bobbing up and down. But it was the face of the man held Tamar's gaze.

Rooted with fear she watched him bend over the

painted face then lift his head to look in her direction.

The movement breaking the hold on her she picked up her skirts and ran. But those black eyes had already seen her.

Smiling to himself Zeph Tullio watched the flame-haired figure disappear into the distance.

Chapter Three

Leaning her weight against a tall building Tamar gulped deep breaths of air. The pain throbbing in her side had pulled for several minutes but fear had driven her on, fear that Zeph Tullio had seen her and might decide to follow.

But there was no sign of him. She glanced behind her along a stretch of street she did not recognise. How far had she come . . . was it in the right direction?

Clutching her side she moaned softly at the pain that grabbed her as she tried to stand upright. She should have gone home, taken the sixpence and used a penny of it to take the tram. But she had not, in her fear of Zeph Tullio she had simply run and now God only knew where she was.

From inside the building where she stood the sound of feet clattering on bare wooden stairs sounded clearly through an open door.

Trying to move on she gasped again as the muscles in her side pulled like a tautened string.

'Be you poorly?'

Still sucking in breath, Tamar shook her head.

'Then if you ain't poorly, what be wrong for it's clear that summat be.'

Setting her teeth against the discomfort of it, Tamar stood upright. Beside her a woman, basket in hand and concern in her eyes, waited.

'I . . . I have just been running . . . that . . . that's all.'

'Looks like you run yourself to a standstill, ain't nothing that important, lessen you be runnin' from a man . . .' The woman stopped speaking, understanding taking the place of concern. 'That be it don't it? You be runnin' from a bloke, your old man is he?'

'No.' Tamar shook her head quickly. 'Not my husband.'

'Your father then, too 'andy with his fists I bet.'

Her breathing easier and the pain in her side less acute, Tamar straightened.

'No, nothing like that.'

'But it were a bloke you were running from?'

Catching the look that flashed across Tamar's eyes the woman nodded triumphantly.

'I thought I was right. I see enough of women running for their lives around here to know what it was had you doing the same, and if it weren't your husband nor your father then it has to be the other sort, the type as don't know how to keep his 'ands nor nothing else to 'imself; I'm right ain't I?'

She was right. Nothing to be gained by denying it. Tamar nodded.

'Bloody scum!' The woman's mouth tightened. 'They should be 'ung up by the parts they try to force on a wench then a knife took to it; cut the bugger off, that would teach a lesson they wouldn't forget in a hurry! But you runnin' away won't do no good.'

'I am not running away.' Tamar saw the quick glance shift to her lunch tin. 'I am on my way to visit my brother.'

Her mouth softening into a smile the woman hitched her basket high on her arm. 'Then could be we might walk part way together. Where be your brother livin'?'

How could she tell, how could she say Benjie was in that awful place? Tamar's glance fell.

'Oh, it be like that does it? Well you ain't the first to 'ave menfolk locked up in Winson Green, that is where your brother be ain't it?'

Drawing her shawl tight about her Tamar made no answer.

'I understands.' The woman swung her head sympathetically. 'It be hard to talk of and even harder to think of a man cooped up inside that hell hole.'

'Benjie is not a man, he is only a boy, he is only thirteen.'

The thought unwittingly turned to words rushed from Tamar's lips.

'Dear God Almighty!' The woman's hand lifted to her chest making a swift sign of the cross. 'Thirteen, that be no more'n a babby; why in the world 'ave they stuck him in there?'

'They say he stole a parcel from the basket.'

'Your brother be an errand boy?'

Tears pricking her eyes, Tamar nodded. 'He worked for Amory's.'

'Oh, I've 'eard of them,' the woman interrupted again, 'they 'ave that proper workshop along of Warstone Lane, bet that be a better place to work than in your own 'ouse. So, your brother worked for Amory.'

'We both do . . . did.' Tamar corrected herself. Now the woman knew practically everything, it could do no harm to ask direction.

'Oh, I knows the way there alright.' Replying to Tamar's question the woman glanced to her right. 'I should do, I walked there and back once a month for almost ten years. It be this way on, I be going the same direction meself.'

Glad of company, especially of a woman who knew the way to the prison, Tamar fell gratefully into step as the woman began to walk.

'It were my husband.' Acknowledging the politeness of the girl's silence on the subject the woman talked on. 'He were done for putting a bloke in 'ospital, nigh on broke his back as well as both arms. Vicious assault the magistrate called it, grievous bodily harm . . . but never a word said about what that dirty swine of a man did to me . . . no mention of rape or the fact it were done to a woman five months gone; no charge were made against that one, not a respectable business man. I tell you wench, money talks, it can talk a man into gaol an' it can talk him out of it and them as has none stand no chance, no chance at all.'

'But my brother did not steal.'

'Huh.' The woman paused waiting for a cart to rumble past. 'I 'opes you 'ave the money to prove it.'

The cart having passed Tamar followed the woman across the road turning a corner into a street equally narrow as the other. She had no money, but that could not possibly affect Benjie's case. The magistrate would see he was telling the truth, and then there was the stone, when that was found . . .

'My man was paying back what had been done to me.' The woman continued. 'You would 'ave thought the law to be on his side, but the law teks no account of a man wi'out a shilling to his name. Ten years they give Abe Bryce, ten years of rotting in that gaol, leaving me with my babby gone and none to care about it.'

Glancing at the drawn face Tamar felt a deep pity for the woman. How could she have stood the terribleness of rape? She shuddered, the touch of Zeph Tullio's hands on her, the feel of his hot breath returning vividly to her mind. Then to lose her unborn child and her husband.

But she would not lose Benjie, that could not happen.

'This be Lodge Road, we crosses the bridge here and Winson Green be a way further up.'

Following across Tamar stifled a scream as a steam engine belched its black breath beneath them. She had heard the sound before but always from a distance and never had she allowed Benjie to coax her into going to actually look at the new railway trains. Now she clutched her skirts, wanting desperately to close her eyes as she hurried over the wooden planking that formed the road bridge.

The road was wider than those surrounding Vyse Street, and busier with laden carts making their way to and from the wharves and basins of the Birmingham Canal.

'That be your way.'

Some few minutes later the woman halted, a hand waving forward.

'But I thought you were going to the prison, your husband . . .'

'I be going to see Abe right enough, only not in the same place you be making for. Abe be here,' the woman gave a quick sideways jerk of her head, 'the fever 'ospital. They put 'im in this place when he got the smallpox. They don't let me go beside 'im but they lets me see 'im through a little glass window.' Her voice breaking, the woman glanced at the basket. 'They lets me leave bits for 'im at the gate, though he won't be wanting them much longer.'

'He is to come home?'

' 'Ome,' the woman laughed, a dry hopeless laugh. 'Yes, Abe will be going 'ome, only not to the one I 'ave made for 'im. Abe be dying, could be he is dead already!'

'Oh!' The word came softly on a gasp of sympathy. 'I am so sorry.'

'Ar well, that be appreciated.' Turning towards the gate in the high blank wall that closed off the hospital from the street, the woman cast a glance over her shoulder.

'Visitors must leave the place you be headed for in less than an hour, I will wait for you 'ere. Just ask at the gate for Letty Bryce, they'll tell you if I still be inside.'

Turning in the direction Letty had pointed, Tamar heard herself praying. Please God let them have found the true killer, please let this be the last time she would ever have to walk this path!

'He was not there!'

Sat in the one downstairs room of Vinny Marsh's house, Tamar stared blankly at her hands.

Vinny clicked her tongue, a sure sign of impatience. 'What you mean he weren't there . . . you did go to the right place?'

'He was not there!'

Empty of any emotion the words were repeated. Of course the wench had been to the right place, her weren't daft! Vinny chided herself silently. There were only one bloody Winson Green and everybody in Brummagem knowed of it. The wench couldn't have made no mistake.

'Did you say Benjie's name?' She sat heavily on the second of her only two chairs. 'Tell me again wench, tell me exactly what was said.'

Her voice dull and heavy Tamar said again what she had already told twice.

'I knocked at the gate, it was such a high wide gate. But that was not the one that opened, a smaller one set to the side was that which answered my knock. I told the officer what I was there for and he said to come back on the proper day as no visitor was allowed except on the first Saturday of each month. I said that would not be possible as I had to work. He laughed at that and said we all had to work and his work was to make sure visitors kept to the right day.'

'Then what?' Vinny urged.

'I . . . I said I was not familiar with the correct visiting times, that my brother had only been trans-ferred to the prison a day or so before. It seemed to make no difference for he only laughed and said to come back next month. Then he pushed me away and closed the door.'

'So?' Vinny urged again.

'I knocked again and when the gate remained closed I kicked it hard. That annoyed the gatekeeper and when he opened it again I think he would have struck me, but just then another officer came up and asked what the disturbance was. When I repeated to him what I had told his colleague he took a sheet of paper from a small office I could just see through the gate. He found Benjie's name on it. It was then he told me Benjie had already gone to trial and that it was being heard at Stafford . . . at the Crown Court.'

'Lord God help the lad!'

Vinny stared at the fire, the words she had heard before at last being accepted. Murderers and killers were sent to the Crown Court and once there most said goodbye to life!

'I don't know what to do, Mrs Marsh . . .'

As if Vinny's unspoken words had been heard Tamar turned to the older woman.

'I have to help Benjie but I don't know what to do!'

Resting her hands over those of the young girl, Vinny Marsh shook her head.

'Ain't nothing you *can* do wench, ain't nothing any of us can do 'cept wait and pray.'

'. . . *God don't listen, Tam . . . He don't never listen . . .*'

The words Benjie had sobbed beat suddenly against her brain. Life returning to her voice she looked with determined eyes at the woman who would comfort her.

'I do not intend to wait and I do not intend to pray, both are futile. I shall go to Stafford, no matter what, I will be with my brother.'

Her fingers tightening Vinny shook the smaller hands her own covered. 'That be crackpotical talk an' you knows it. Stafford ain't Winson Green, it don't be just up the road! 'Ow do you expect to get there, a wench on 'er own an' with no money, it be askin' for trouble. Wi'out money you'll get nowhere!'

Letty Bryce had said much the same thing. Poor woman, Tamar thought remembering the drawn face and almost silent walk across the city. Abe was dead, she had whispered, he could be hurt no more. But Benjie was not dead and nothing was going to keep her from him.

'I walked to Winson Green and I can walk as far again.' Tamar rose to her feet. 'I promised Father I would take care of him, that I would see no harm come to him and I shall keep my word.'

'Ar well, sick people don't always realise what they be askin'.' Vinny's hands kept their hold. 'You've done your best by that lad, God knows you've been mother an' father to 'im, but racin' off into the night will do 'im no good. At least wait 'til morning, a meal and a night's sleep will help you think clear.'

It was only common sense. Tamar allowed herself to be pressed back on to the chair. But come tomorrow she would go to Stafford.

'I wish you had come to me with this before.'

Philip Amory frowned as he looked at the woman standing before his desk.

'I didn't think as you would 'ave an interest Mr Philip, not in Tamar anyway.'

'I have an interest in all of my employees.' Philip Amory's face took on a tinge of pink.

'But Tamar be left from Amory's.' Vinny Marsh defended herself.

'That is correct.' Philip answered quickly, embarrassed by the woman's blunt but truthful reply. 'But whilst her brother stands accused of stealing my property I wish to keep myself informed of both of their whereabouts. You told Cal Perry she has gone to Stafford?'

Facing the man who with one word could take the very bread from her mouth, Vinny hesitated.

Sensing her fear Philip Amory gave a brief smile. 'I apologise for speaking sharply, Vinny. Of course you were not to know I had not already been informed of what has happened. Please tell me exactly.'

'. . . and then with the morning her was up and off

to the square in the middle of Spencer Street. I watched her go, seen her run past the Temple of Relief like her arse . . . like her skirts was afire.'

'Why Spencer Street?' He picked up the quill pen stood on the desk, hoping his query did not echo the feeling in his stomach. Vinny Marsh must already be wondering why his interest in Tamar Hallam. So was he? He twiddled the pen watching it roll between his fingers. But it was a question to which he had no answer.

'The carters sets off from there.' At last Vinny replied. 'I told 'er to ask if any were bound for Stafford and if so to ask for a lift. I thought that way her would be safer than walking the road by herself.'

'That was very thoughtful of you, Vinny.' Philip looked up all trace of pinkness gone from his cheeks. 'But why not advise her to take the train?'

'Eh, I wouldn't do no such!' Vinny was aghast. 'They don't be safe, great fire-breathin' monsters. They shouldn't never be allowed.'

'They are perfectly safe, Vinny; why even Her Majesty has travelled on one.'

' 'Er 'as?' Vinny's face took on a look of horror.

'Of course, and she remained perfectly safe.'

'Ar, well that can be understood. The Queen of England be of special importance in the sight of the Almighty, and that be only as it should.' Vinny shook her head. 'But the like of that young wench, young Tamar, well they don't be nobody special.'

No, Tamar Hallam was no one special. Philip glanced down at the pen still twisting in his fingers.

So why this feeling in his stomach, why the dread that something might happen to her?

'I were glad the wench didn't 'ave the money to pay for no train, I wouldn't rest easy knowin' her did.'

The pen instantly stilled, Philip Amory looked up.

'The girl had no money? But when I asked she said she had.'

Vinny frowned. 'Then her lied, but I has to say it be the first time I've known her to do that.'

'Thank you Vinny, you may return to your work now.'

Watching the woman leave his office, hearing her shuffle into boots that had been removed before entering, Philip let the pen fall to the desk. The girl had not actually answered when he asked if she had money, she had simply nodded and that no more than the merest movement of her head. Pride, pride had kept her from admitting the truth and from accepting his help; but pride sometimes led to a fall and he did not want Tamar Hallam to fall.

Taking the gold hunter from his pocket he glanced at the time. It was not yet ten. Returning the watch he glanced at the partition that closed his office off from the workshop. He could get to Stafford and be back before the day's work ended.

But to leave the workshop. Much as he trusted the people who worked for him that was something he had never done. It had been the one unbreakable rule of his father, his ultimate teaching. The successful goldsmith was one who checked every move made in his workshop and one who never left until the last of his workmen had already gone. It was a maxim he himself had observed with meticulous care.

Supposing he took the train to Stafford, supposing he found the girl, what then? He could not force her to return to Hockley.

The hearing had already been set. Even now it could be underway. Come evening the girl would be home.

Unconsciously withdrawing the pocket watch he turned it absently between his fingers.

'The stampers need more plates Mr Philip.'

Looking at the man standing at the office door Philip Amory flipped the watch back into place. Business here could not carry on without him and business must be his first concern.

Tomorrow he would have Vinny Marsh tell the girl to come to the workshop. Once she returned he would see she got any help she may need.

Chapter Four

That bitch wouldn't try that again, in fact her wouldn't try any tricks again . . . ever!

She had led him some distance, laughing and talking of the good time they would 'ave and it had been good considering he hadn't paid for it. But that trollop had paid, paid in full.

Hands in his trousers pockets Zeph Tullio sauntered past the Church of St Paul turning casually into Brook Street. This was not the quickest route to where he wanted to be but not being seen going direct to the Juggler's place was safer.

Keeping his pace slow and easy, acknowledging carters passing the time of day, ignoring the errand boys intent on their five-minute games, their barrows and parcels left unattended on the ground. That was the hardest part, walking past those parcels which he knew each held more money than a workman slaving his life away in the dingy little workshops could hope to earn in a lifetime. But he would not slave his life away in the gold, he would wear it; he would wear the trinkets made in the Gold Quarter, made by some who laughed and others who turned their backs on Zeph Tullio.

The woman had laughed. Zeph's fingers tightened on the stone in his pocket. All the time her was shedding laced-up stays and wide cotton bloomers. He grimaced now feeling the distaste of it, the smell of that cluttered room . . . and her! He blew down his nostrils trying to free himself of the memory but the aroma of that cheap perfume lingered. The afternoon was not one he would 'ave chosen and certainly not one he would 'ave paid for. A smile touching his mouth he crossed Warstone Lane into Spencer Street. A shilling! The smile widened then died. He 'ad given her more than a shilling!

They had rolled on that bed for an hour or more with her trying every trick of her trade, but her had found it was not easy bringing Zeph Tullio off; he allowed things to happen only when he said so. Perhaps he ought to 'ave paid the whore, her worked 'ard enough for it.

A swift picture of that coarse-painted face streaked with the perspiration of her efforts, the dishevelled hair, its carefully covered grey more obvious now than the black stuck in the tiny rivulets as if it had been plastered, flashed across his mind. It had been 'ard for her, but that was all her had found 'ard. He almost laughed as the mental picture faded. Then what amusement he had in the woman's contortions had become jaded, he wanted it over and done. But why leave with nothing? He had lain there as she clambered over his naked body, straddling him, watched that coarse face as she rode him, then he had finished it.

She had padded naked across the room to bring him a tankard of ale. The beer had been cheap and stale. Like her, Zeph thought, but Polly Bell 'adn't worked so 'ard for nothin' before! But cheap and stale as it were the drink 'ad put 'im to sleep and when he wakened it were to find her dressed and with the package in her hand.

She had laughed as he leapt from the bed, laughed as he snatched the package from her.

'I was onny lookin' at it darlin', but I could always look at summat else if you be ready again, Polly . . .'

But whatever Polly had been prepared to do would never be done now, not to Zeph Tullio nor any other man, the whore was dead.

He had brought his bunched fist hard to the side of her face and as her head snapped around had struck again on the opposite temple.

The heat of anger dissipated Zeph felt the twang of wrought nerves.

He 'adn't meant to kill her, he had only wanted to frighten the bitch; 'er shouldn't 'ave been thinking to rob 'im. But what magistrate would swallow that when what Polly Bell was taking 'ad been stole by 'im in the first place?

A trickle of sweat sliding coldly down his spine Zeph felt the urge to run, to get away from Birmingham as quickly as his legs would take him; but to run would draw attention. The woman would be found, that was inevitable, and Clancy O'Rourke knew her 'ad gone off with Zeph Tullio, that would be enough on its own for the bobbies to 'aul him in, to be seen runnin' would more or less seal the fact that it were 'im killed 'er!

Every cell of his brain concentrated on keeping his feet moving. In the same slow, easy pace he walked on towards the Jeweller's Arms. There would be men there taking a tankard of ale now the day's work was done. It would be beneficial to be seen. After all, a man who 'ad just committed murder would 'ave bolted, he wouldn't go wasting time in a public house.

Several heads turned watching the tall, lank-haired figure walk into the tap room coming to stand beside the smoke-shrouded bar, answering his greeting while not making room at their table. The Gypsy's boy had long been known in Hockley but never liked. Putting a coin on the stained bar top Zeph called for a tankard, nodding to the men who turned back to their ale and conversation.

They could turn their backs on 'im. Zeph grabbed the foaming tankard, drinking deeply. But one day they would laugh on the other side of their faces . . . yes, by Christ they would! Once the contents of that package were sold he would be rich, then see 'ow they treated the Gypsy's child!

The door to the street opened again, a group of five or six men crowding into the cramped room. Zeph felt his pulse quicken. Charlie Selby was not among them. But he would turn up soon, he would be wanting his share.

More customers crowding into the public house Zeph hitched along the bench seat as several, Charlie included, came to share his table. The Jeweller's Arms was a popular haunt for the men who worked the gold, and the more that came tonight, the more that saw him sitting relaxed and drinking, the better for Zeph Tullio should the hue and cry go up.

''Ow do Zeph, 'ow be you?'

One by one the men settled. Clay pipes in their mouths, the conversation centring on the day's work, but soon this gave way to talk of the theft of the package.

'I still says that lad d'ain't tek it, 'Allam's lad wouldn't pinch so much as a shake o' salt.'

'I reckons as 'ow you be right in that.' A second man replied, his pipe never moving from between his teeth.

'Course I be right!' The first man spat tobacco-stained saliva into the fire that burned day and night in the cast-iron grate. 'We all knows the errand boys be little buggers the way they goes leavin' parcels and baskets lyin' untended while they teks a game of marbles or kicks a ball across the street. It be summat we all of us done when we was lads; but pinchin', tekin' what don't belong of 'em! Then I says they wouldn't do that. The tekin' of that parcel were none of their work, I says it were a man done it despite what Charlie Selby says.'

Taking his time, swallowing a gulp of ale slowly, Zeph listened, wiping the back of his hand across his mouth. It had been said loudly enough for all to hear and as others nodded agreement towards the speaker, he nodded too but remained silent. He wanted no part of this conversation. Picking up his empty tankard he took it to the bar fishing a coin from his pocket as it was refilled.

'What you say Tullio, what think you on this robbery?'

Flat cap pulled over his brow, a crudely knitted muffler tucked inside an almost threadbare jacket, one of the men glanced up as Zeph returned to his seat.

'It be 'ard to know what to think. Cal Perry reckons the parcel were in the basket when it left Amory's.'

'Ar, so 'e do.' The man spat again sending saliva sizzling on the bars of the grate. 'An' Charlie Selby reckons it d'ain't never get to 'im, that he never set eyes on no parcel from Amory, but he do reckon as 'ow that lad pinched it, said he seen the kid run off wi' a bit o' brown paper stickin' from his pocket.'

'That don't be the all of it neither.' The first man cut in, unwilling to be left out of the conversation. 'Selby reckons 'e seen young 'Allam pick up a mould and crack Joby Turner on the 'ead when 'e tried to stop him gettin' away.'

'That be bloody moonshine!' His friend spat angrily. 'Selby might be willin' to tell the bobbies that but I doubt he 'as what it teks to say the same to any o' we.'

'Ar, I reckon that bugger's courage comes in one o' these an' when the glass be empty so be his mouth.'

Laughing loudly the men sank their noses into their tankards.

Selby would not be able to stand much of this. Zeph supped from his own drink. He would want his share so he could disappear, shake the dust of Birmingham from his feet for good and all.

Finishing his ale he returned the tankard to the bar. It would raise no eyebrows his leaving early. The men here understood that one with no job, one who depended on the odd bit of work, could afford no more than a couple of drinks.

Outside the alehouse Zeph breathed deeply, the cold air crisp after the smoke-laden atmosphere of the tap room.

It wasn't only Selby wanted shot of this place. One hand touching against the pocket that held the package, reassuring himself of its continued safety he turned the way he had come. Following narrow streets, their darkness deepened by grey-black shadows of tall, tightly packed houses, his eyes watching for every movement, his ears strained to the slightest sound, he walked as he had from childhood on the balls of his feet, each step soundless as the one before.

Coming to Charlotte Street he stood listening, the deep shadows swallowing his body. He would not be seen from any of the houses but he would wait, give anyone following the time to catch up.

A few streets away the bell of St Paul's Church chimed the hour. Zeph smiled. The Juggler would not be expecting him at this time, nor in this place.

Silence thick and undisturbed on any side satisfying him that no one was near to see his next move Zeph slid around behind the buildings whose rear bordered the canal. The buildings were old and rotting with damp, the people living in them riddled with the diseases of poverty. But here the Juggler stayed though he could afford the grander houses beginning to be built in Edgbaston or Handsworth; it was useful to his trade having doors and windows that came within feet of the canal. Many a parcel had been dropped on to a passing barge for delivery to secret destinations, and many a return of payment made the same way.

Drawing the slim-bladed knife that never left him even when he slept, he slid it expertly beneath the sash of a ground-floor window. Inside the room he stood still. He had not been heard. Pausing every few steps to listen for any sound he crossed the room. Instinct his guide and experience his eyes, he found the door that gave on to the stairs. He had not forgotten; nights spent alone in the darkness of this house whilst his mother earned their living the same way Polly Bell had earned hers had ground the image of each room on his mind as clearly as any engraver's wheel.

Reaching the landing he paused, holding his breath as the crying of a child and the shrill tones of a woman followed by the deeper shout of a man drifted along the damp, musty smelling corridor. Greed for money did not stop with the fencing of stolen goods, the Juggler had let half of his house. Zeph waited. If anyone should come out now . . .

But the doors he knew stretched away to one side remained closed and the commotion died as swiftly as it had been born. Moving with the agility of a cat he crossed the landing and seconds later stood smiling at a small thin-shouldered man, a jeweller's glass held in one hand.

'I told you never come here!' The thin claw-like hand lowered the glass on to a table covered with a shabby red chenille cloth. 'It isn't safe, someone might have . . .'

'Nobody ain't seen me!' Zeph snapped.

'Are you sure?'

'Sure enough. I come to bring you this.'

Reaching into his pocket Zeph drew out the bundle of crumpled brown paper placing it in the centre of the table.

'What is it?' The sharp ferret eyes reflected the light of the oil lamp, gleaming sharp and feral in the pale anaemic glow.

Peeling away the paper he breathed long and slow before looking up at Zeph leaning over him both palms flat against the table.

'I thought it would be you . . . you bloody fool, don't you have more sense than to lift something like this?'

Pulling the lamp closer he fitted the glass to his eye.

'What do you mean, 'ave more sense than lift that, it be gold don't it?' Zeph watched the other man scrutinise the object he had taken from the package.

Bent over the gleaming object Theo Blatt took several moments before answering.

'Oh, it's gold alright.'

'And the stone?' Zeph bent closer. 'Charlie Selby said it were the real thing.'

'It's real.' Theo continued to examine the large stone gleaming at the centre of a row of smaller ones.

'Then there ain't no problem.'

Zeph straightened. The money was as good as in his pocket and him as good as gone from the bloody Gold Quarter.

Removing the glass Theo Blatt rubbed his eyes with finger and thumb.

'There may be no problem for you.' He lowered his hand. 'As for me I wouldn't touch this with a bargepole.'

'Wouldn't touch . . . what you talking about! You said it were gold, and the stone, you said that was the real thing.'

'And so it is.' The long, thin fingers touched the beautiful necklace glittering against the red of the tablecloth.

Zeph's dark eyes flashed angrily. If the Juggler thought to get one past him then he could think again! Words bursting from him he brought his closed fist hard down on to the table.

'Then 'ow come you says you won't touch it?'

'Look at it.' The claw-like finger touched against the large white square-cut stone set around with ten smaller matching ones each gleaming like white fire in the exquisitely worked setting. 'Have you known the Quarter to work anything but gold? Have you known them work with gemstones before? No you haven't 'cos this be the first. Haven't you heard talk of what Amory and some of the others be planning to do?'

'I 'eard summat, but that be nowt to do wi' this.'

Placing the necklace back in the brown paper Theo Blatt pushed it away.

'It has everything to do with it.' He looked up at his visitor, eyes squinting in the light of the lamp. 'Trade in the gold be bad. It be so low some have gone from the business already and the rest be close to doing the same. For that reason Amory and a few more decided to have several items of jewellery made to present to Princess Alexandra. If she accepts and is seen to wear them, then it will give the trade the boost it needs, for what the Princess of Wales wears the world wears; and this,' he touched the necklace again, 'this is the major piece, the Alexandra Diamond.'

'So, if it be so special you will get more for it.'

'I will get nothing for it . . .' The thin hand drew back leaving the jewel lying like an island on a sea of red, '. . . 'cos I have no intention of trying and I doubt you will get anybody else to try.'

Anger pressing against his throat Zeph's mouth thinned, hands balling into fists at his side.

'If you be thinkin' to cheat . . .'

'I am thinking nothing of the sort. I tell you what I think . . . what I know. There be nobody will take that piece, it would be impossible to sell on.'

'Impossible?' Zeph laughed scathingly. 'There ain't a piece of gold been made yet as Theo Blatt couldn't deal. You can pass it in a dozen different directions at once an' never lose sight of it, that be why folk calls you the Juggler.'

'That is true.' Theo nodded. 'But even Theo Blatt could not juggle this.'

'Then take the bloody stones out!' Zeph's voice rose. 'Just pass the gold.'

The older man's head waved on his thin neck. 'I won't touch it, not this. Take it and go.'

'Go!' It was almost a shout. 'Go where? You be the fence in 'Ockley.'

Glancing nervously towards the door Theo bundled the necklace in its wrapping shoving it towards the other man.

'I don't care where you go, just get that out of my house!'

If the Juggler wouldn't touch it then it was a sure bet no other man would. Zeph breathed heavily.

'Every fence and every bobby from here to kingdom come will be on the watch for that, the safest thing for you to do is find a way to get it back to Amory. Do it before Selby sings for his supper.'

Every fence and every bobby. Before Selby sings! Zeph's eyes narrowed as he scooped necklace and paper into his hand. Charlie Selby was already twittering like a canary in a cage, a decent reward on offer and he would sing, he would shop Zeph Tullio without a second thought. But Selby weren't the only man knew where that necklace was, the Juggler knowed it as well and the Juggler 'ad a tongue.

Slipping the package in his pocket Zeph crossed to the small window looking out into the darkness. Below, the canal shone like a ribbon of silver in the moonlight. 'What about a barge?' he asked. 'That be the way you passes most things.'

'I've told you already . . .'

'Ar, you 'as.' Swift as a striking snake Zeph was behind the chair, one hand twisted in the grey hair, stretching the head back on Blatt's neck. 'And it be going to be the last you tells any man. Selby ain't the only one wi' a tongue, but a man 'as to be livin' to use it!'

Drawing the knife he slashed it across the Juggler's throat, wiping its slim blade on the man's woollen cardigan as he pushed the body forward to sprawl on the table. Red mixing with red the Juggler's lifeblood seeped into the chenille cloth.

A man had to be living to use his tongue. Zeph Tullio let himself silently out of the house.

Charlie Selby would be waiting for the pay-off.

Chapter Five

Every bone in her body aching, Tamar climbed down from the carter's wagon. The journey had taken the whole day. Stopping once only for the man to eat his midday meal yet they were still no more than halfway.

'It be more'n a two-day haul for to get to Stafford.'

Tamar's heart had sunk as the carter had told her that. But she would cover the distance no more quickly on foot. Wrapped in her shawl she had heard little of the talk the man made and looked at little of the fields and hedges, the stretches of wild countryside so very different from the close-packed buildings and narrow streets of Hockley, her thoughts only with her brother.

He would think she had forgotten her promise. Remembering the frightened face, the eyes stark with fear, she clenched her teeth on a sob. Maybe if she walked throughout the night, so long as she kept to the path she should not lose the way.

'You can bide the night along o' there.'

Clambering from the driving seat the carter pointed to a low building, a light shining from its single downstairs window.

'The widow Chorley will find you a bed and a meal

for threepence and that includin' a breakfast in the mornin'.'

'Thank you, but I will be going on.'

One hand on the leather bridle the man's weather-beaten face creased in deeper lines as he looked at her.

'Goin' on! Eh wench, you can't be goin' on in the dark! You don't know the way an' Stafford still be a ways off. Take heed of what I tells you an' bide the night 'ere in Little Wyrley. Tomorrow I will tek you on to where you wants to be.'

'No.' Tamar shook her head. 'I . . . I have to go on, I promised my brother.'

'Mebbe's you did.' Clicking his tongue the carter began to lead the horse towards a building, a lantern lit beside a board on which someone had painted a man holding a tankard in his hand. 'But did your brother expect you to walk the night through countryside you 'olds no knowing of? It be already grown dark, should there be no moon the way you go will be black as the devil's 'eart. You stray from the path as it crosses the Chase at Cannock and you will never find your way out, nor be there a deal of a chance of anybody finding you, leastways not with the life still in you!'

'But if I follow the path.' Tamar glanced along the road that within a few yards melted into the purple dusk.

'Ar, you can follow the path.' The carter did not turn his head as he led the horse towards the stable adjoining the inn. 'But what when you comes on the crossroads, does you head for Great Saredon or for Norton Green? Not that you will find sings wi' names painted on even for them as can read 'em; then there be turnings for Pye Green, Walton on the Hill an' Weeping Cross not to be talkin' of the many as lies between, 'ow will you be knowin' which of them to follow?'

Giving the horse into the care of the ostler who came shuffling from the stable the carter returned to where Tamar stood staring at the road shrouding itself ever more deeply into the deepening darkness. Touching her shoulder gently he said.

'Look me wench, I knows I you wants sore to be in Stafford along of the brother you speaks of, but you won't get there by swanning off into the night without the least knowledge of the road. Rest the night with widow Chorley and tomorrow I will tek you on.'

Holding back tears of frustration, Tamar nodded. Whispering her thanks she turned in the direction of the small low-roofed house. Threepence for a bed and a meal. That was half of the sixpence, half of all the money she had in the world! What if Benjie should need it? Drawing close to the hedge she guessed bordered the garden, she paused, turning to watch the carter disappear into the inn. She would wait for the ostler to release the horse from the traces and stable it for the night, then when he left she would creep inside, spend the night in the hay loft.

Hours later, her face hidden beneath the shawl Tamar listened to the snuffling of the horse below her, the unfamiliar creakings of beams and the rustling among the hay that left her too afraid to sleep.

Was Benjie too afraid to sleep? Was he lying awake somewhere, was he alone in some prison cell? The sergeant at the police station at Hockley Brook had been kind to them, he had promised to give the boy a mug of cocoa and a bun. Had the warders of Winson Green jail been as kind, and the people who had charge of him at Stafford, how would they treat him?

Burrowing deeper into the soft hay Tamar sought its warmth. What was this town of Stafford, why take Benjie there? Question after question ran through her mind until one brought a coldness that despite the hay sent a shiver the length of her body.

What if Benjie was no longer in that town, what if he were already left, taken to yet another prison?

But that was ridiculous! Tamar tried to stem the cold fear that shot along her veins. What reason could there be for taking him elsewhere? But there had been reason for taking him to Stafford! By tomorrow she would know these fears were groundless. Her whole body tense, she clung to the comfort of the thought. Tomorrow she would have her brother back in her care.

Beneath the shawl she twined the fingers of both hands together, bringing them to rest against her trembling lips.

'Please,' she whispered softly, 'please let morning come soon.'

He should 'ave known. The minute he seen what was in the package he 'ad lifted from that basket he should 'ave realised it was special. Keeping to the shadows Zeph made his way along the narrow streets, quiet now the day's work was done; the baskets of the errand boys, the handcarts and wagons pushing their way to the canal wharfs, the carters delivering to the various grocer shops gone for the night.

Why 'adn't he thought? The Quarter dealt only in gold, never with gemstones. He could prise the stones out, sell just the setting and throw them in the cut. But valuable as that rose gold was the stones must be more valuable. What had the Juggler called it? The Alexandra Diamond. Zeph's hand closed over the pocket holding the necklace. Was that why it was spoken of as the stone . . . was the stone *so* precious? If so he could be chuckin' away a fortune.

No fence would touch it, nobody would take it! That was what the Juggler had said. Dodging into a doorway Zeph pressed close against the wall waiting until the sound of heavy boots died away. The bobbies would be at their sharpest until that necklace were found.

Soundless as the shadows that swallowed him he moved out on to the street.

No policeman would find that necklace. Here in Hockley or anywhere it took, Zeph Tullio would find sale for it.

But the Juggler had been right about Selby; he was ready to sing. At least he *had* been. Zeph smiled. Like the Juggler he would never sing again!

There had been hints going around for weeks, murmurs in the Rose Villa Tavern and the Jeweller's

Arms of special items being made in the Quarter, only the very finest Britannia gold was to be used and the stuff was being made for the Princess of Wales herself. He had listened to the quiet talk of the craftsmen, their pride in the beautiful pieces they created warm in their voices. But they were fools, working themselves blind for a pittance; but Zeph Tullio was no fool.

He had waited for Selby to leave the beer house, following moments later. Selby had said the least, had sounded most disgruntled, Selby was the one he would talk to.

Footsteps coming towards him from the shadows he had slipped silently into a deeply recessed arch that housed the door of the Mint. He had guessed Icknield Street to be deserted at this time of night, but then he 'adn't guessed the value of the trinket in his pocket; from now on it wouldn't do to count any street in Hockley deserted.

A few yards on and he could cut through the cemetery, that way would be empty of folk, the living anyway and the other sort would give 'im no trouble.

His cold smile hidden by the turned-up collar of his jacket he had stood listening to the footsteps fade into the night.

'All you needs do is tip me the nod when one o' them trinkets be set to leave Amory's, I can do all the other and we splits the take 'alf an' 'alf.'

Selby had been doubtful at first, but a couple of tankards and a well-described picture of how he might live had soon had him changing his mind.

Moving as silently and carefully as he had on the streets, making use of cover afforded by tall grave-stones, he had made his way through the graveyard pausing halfway. To his left had lain the catacombs with the expensive coffins that held John Baskerville and his like in almost the comfort they had enjoyed in life. But the place had an aura, despite its special more costly tombs. It held the sort of stillness that pumped fear into many, only those that must went near and certainly no one at night. But it wasn't the dead he had needed to take account of.

They had arranged it between them. Selby would let him know when any special package were being dispatched, the rest was left to him; and that was all it was, except Joby Turner had seen Selby rummaging in the basket before the Hallam lad had fetched it.

'I 'ad no choosin' . . .' Zeph felt contempt for the man that had sought him out that same night, Selby almost piddlin' 'imself wi' fright. '. . . he seen me, Turner . . . seen me, I 'ad to do it!'

'All to the good,' Zeph had assured him, 'now there ain't nobody to query what you was about in that basket. So far as folk know the 'Allam lad pinched that package after killin' Turner and if you keeps your wits that be how it will go on, won't nobody guess no different.'

And they hadn't. Taking the branch of the path that wound past the catacombs he had continued on through the graveyard emerging finally into Vyse Street.

They had arranged to meet behind the Temple of Relief. It was a better choice than most, Zeph had said, nobody hung about that place longer than it took.

Selby had been there waiting, demanding his share of the selling price, calling him a liar when hearing the Juggler had not taken the trinket.

'There be talk of a reward.' Selby had muttered. *'Two 'undred pounds for information leading to the recovery of that stolen packet, two 'undred pounds! A man could live on that for many a month . . .'*

Zeph had listened, his fingers closing over the knife.

'. . . might be better to tek the reward . . .'

Selby had said no more. The slim blade had found its way beneath his ribs, burying itself deep in his heart.

The sound of the ostler leading the horse from the stable brought Tamar out of a fitful doze. Grey light streamed in at the open door illuminating dust motes that danced in its pale gleam.

Clambering from the loft she shook the clinging straws of hay from her skirts and shawl then ran her hands over her hair. The carter would not be out of the inn yet, she would not have kept him waiting.

'More comfortable than the widow Chorley's place?'

The question taking her by surprise as she hurried out into the yard Tamar turned to see the carter watching her.

He crossed to where the ostler was fastening the horse into the thick leather traces, checking them himself before they were attached to the wagon. Satisfied, he nodded to Tamar.

'Get yourself up wench, we 'ave a ways to cover afore dinner time.'

Pulling herself up next to the driver's seat she held the ends of her shawl tight over a stomach jabbed through with pangs of hunger. She had eaten nothing all day yesterday. The carter had offered her a share of his own dinner but she had refused, saying she was not hungry even though her stomach rumbled for lack of food. But the man was being kind enough by letting her ride with him for no payment, she would not take his food as well.

Climbing on to the wagon beside her the man dropped a small cloth-wrapped bundle on to her lap.

'I knows you took no meal last night same as I knows you took none this mornin'.'

He took up the reins clucking the horse into a steady walk.

'You need answer no question for I'll be asking none. What you be about be your own business, but I want no woman fainting on my 'ands, so you best get that down inside you; 'tain't no more than bread and a slice from the landlord's own bacon pig but it'll keep the senses from draining out of you afore we be a mile down the road.'

The cold sting of those long sleepless hours, the worry of not knowing what might be happening to her brother adding to the misery of hunger, Tamar had to fight hard to hold off the tears as she thanked him.

It was more than a two-day journey to Stafford. She chewed on the bread and cold bacon. That would be four days since she last saw Benjie, that was supposing she was allowed to see him as soon as she arrived.

Glancing sideways at the ruddy face enveloped in a bush of white side whiskers she asked, 'Do you know Stafford well?'

'Stafford be a bigger place than some. Can't say as I knows it well.' He answered, not taking his eyes from the road.

The Crown Court, the warder at Winson Green prison had said. They had taken Benjie to the Crown Court. That must be an important place, a well-known place, but would the carter know where it was to be found? Should she ask, if she told him where she wanted to be would he turn her off the cart, want nothing to do with the sister of a thief?

But Benjie was not a thief. No matter what Charlie Selby claimed, her brother was not a thief!

Shaking crumbs from the cloth she folded it neatly. Glancing across the wide stretch of land empty to the horizon she rested her hands on the folded cloth. If she spoke now, if he abandoned her here in the middle of heaven knew where, then it could be many more than four days before she found herself in Stafford. To-morrow, once they reached the town, then would be soon enough to ask, but would it be soon enough for telling this man the truth. He had shown her a kindness, she must show him respect.

Taking a steadying breath she turned to look at the man sat beside her.

*   *   *

'A man dead!'

Sat in the gilding shop Vinny Marsh stirred sugar into her midday cup of tea.

'A man killed and nobody knowin' the doin' of it.'

'They do say it be young 'Allam as done for Joby Turner.'

'They says . . . they says!' Vinny Marsh glanced at the woman who had spoken, her mouth filled now with bread and dripping. 'Some folk would say black was white when truth be they don't know t'other from which. I would bet my bloomers that young Benjie 'Allam played no part in that killing, no nor in no robbery neither!'

'Don't you go laying out stakes like that Vinny.' The first woman grinned, bits of bread and dripping stuck in the spaces left by missing teeth. 'We all knows the pair you 'ave on be the only pair you owns, lose them and your old man will 'ave a clear path to your 'appenny.'

'My old man forgot my 'appenny after I had our youngest, and so long as I can keep him with a quart jug every night then that be the way it'll go on. You should try it yourself, Dinah.'

'Ain't no need for her to go trying it.' Sat in the corner of the tiny room a younger woman smirked spitefully, as the chorus of laughter died away. 'Her bloke has been playing away for years, her ain't had the pleasure of him in bed since Lord knows when.'

Biting into bread and dripping Dinah Edwards nodded.

'That be true enough, and the Lord knows where

he took his pleasure last Saturday night and again last night and so do I Connie 'Arding!' Dinah swallowed before looking at the younger woman. 'You been opening your legs for Sim Edwards regular, in fact you took him a week or two after I chucked him out, a week or two after the doctor told him he had the clap!'

Taking her mug of tea Dinah laughed aloud as the younger woman, her angry face red as holly berries, paled visibly at the words and ran from the room, her sandwich falling to the floor.

Choking on the tea still in her own mouth Vinny swallowed noisily.

'Christ, Dinah!' she gasped. 'I didn't know your Sim 'ad the clap.'

' 'E ain't.' Dinah laughed again. 'But Connie 'Arding don't know that and her won't, least not until after Sim has give her a paling for claiming he has!'

'I would 'ave thought you to 'ave done that long since.' Vinny said, aware of the girls from the polisher's bench sitting with avid ears. 'Given that one the hiding her deserves.'

Dinah fished another slice of bread and dripping from the cloth spread over her lap taking a large bite before answering.

'What Sim Edwards does and who he chooses to do it with don't worry me that much; all he ever give me were babbies and them he left me to work to feed. Men and babbies!' She grinned, 'Dinah Edwards can do without more of either.'

'I knows what you mean.' A sallow-skinned dark

woman joined in. 'Most kids brings you grief at one time or another.'

Dinah's head swung in the woman's direction. 'Eh Bertha, you 'ave a sixteen-year-old up the stick and no man to say he done it, but her ain't the only wench be pregnant without a wedding day; it be hard for you to bear but think on it this way, it would be harder still to bear if you was mother to them 'Allam kids.'

'You be right, Dinah.' Vinny nodded agreement. 'Poor little buggers. One brought up for pinchin' and for murder and the other one chucking in her livelihood to go stand beside him.'

'You think the law will say he done it?'

Refilling her mug with tea Vinny reached for the sugar then tapped a finger against a jar filled with almost identical fine white crystals.

'I don't know about that Dinah, but this much I does know. If I had the toerag that really done for Joby here in this room I would feed him a spoonful of this, a swallow of cyanide and the law would be saved a deal of trouble.'

'Hold on Vinny, things ain't so bad you be about to sweeten your tea wi' that stuff?'

Holding the spoon in her hand Vinny grinned. 'I weren't thinking of it for meself Cal Perry, I were thinking of your cup and I still might if you says back to the bench afore another five minutes be up.'

At the doorway that boasted no door Cal Perry chuckled. 'Now would I do that to you, Vinny?'

Heaping sugar on to the spoon Vinny turned,

holding it so the workman could see it while her eyes danced with laughter.

'You might Cal Perry, supposin' you was daft enough.'

Waiting until the man turned away Dinah whispered. 'You suppose the gaffer might 'ave had any word of young Benjie?'

Vinny's shoulders lifted in a shrug as she resumed her seat. 'Who can say? But one thing be certain. Cal Perry won't keep we 'anging on. So soon as Mr Philip gives him any news then Cal will pass it to we. We will know soon enough . . . good or bad we will know.'

Chapter Six

'No wench, you keep your money. Your company be payment enough for the ride, and right glad of it I've been for the road can be lonely at times.'

Sat on the wagon Tamar smiled to herself as she remembered the carter's words of the day before. They had stopped for dinner and again he had passed her a cloth-wrapped meal. She had thanked him but before attempting to eat she had told him of Benjie and the purpose of her journey.

'I 'ad feelings it might be something of the sort,' he had answered when she eventually finished speaking. 'What else would 'ave a young wench so hell-bent on getting to Stafford her were prepared to walk through the night?'

She had apologised then for not telling him before the journey started. Placing the cloth-wrapped bread and cheese on the ground beside him she had stood up. Taking the sixpence from her pocket she had held it out to him.

'I hope this will be enough to pay my fare this far, I am sorry I have no more to offer except my thanks. I will walk the rest of the way.'

'Why?' He had not looked up nor paused in the

eating of his meal. 'Why walk, ain't old Betsy there good enough to pull you into Stafford town?'

'It isn't that.' Her face had warmed with the rush of blood that rose to her cheeks. 'But you . . . you might not want the sister of a criminal riding beside you.'

Pulling the cork from a fat-bellied stone jar he took several swallows of cider then squinted up at her against the autumn sun.

'But you just told me your brother never stole no package, that he didn't kill no fellah neither.'

Bending quickly she had placed the sixpence on the cloth beside the wedge of crusty bread.

Watching her as she turned to follow the track leading ahead he had called. 'Has that brother o' your'n been tried, has the case against him been proved and the law pronounced him guilty?'

'No.' She had paused to look back.

'Then you 'ave no cause to go calling him a criminal. As for who rides on my wagon then I 'ave the deciding of that, and you wench can ride beside me for as far as I goes.' He had patted the bank beside him. 'So sit you down and eat, and you can put your sixpence back in your pocket, old Betsy will get you there in her own time.'

But would it be time enough? Tamar's lids drooped; a second night spent in a barn had her almost exhausted. The carter had not remonstrated with her on that, he had shrugged his shoulders muttering something about her knowing her own way best then had walked off towards an inn.

She had slept no better in that barn than the first,

but it had kept her from the steady downpour that had drummed on its roof the whole night, and the lodging there had been free.

'This be the village of Weeping Cross.'

The carter's voice waking her Tamar glanced along the track that had widened into a path rutted with the deeply entrenched mark of wheels.

'I 'ave one or two calls to make here and the next place we comes against will be Stafford town.'

So close! Tamar's fingers fastened in her shawl holding it close about her. She could most definitely walk from here, she could probably be there before the carter finished his business in the village. Feeling that every minute was vital she turned to him.

'If it is alright with you I will make my own way from here. Thank you again, you have been very kind.'

'Weren't outta my way none to let you ride along of me, like I said, you been company for an old man.'

Jumping to the ground as he drew the horse to a standstill Tamar asked. 'Would you know where I can find the Crown Court?'

'I ain't never been there meself.' He rubbed a calloused hand across his chin and up over his crop of side whiskers. 'But I reckons the very name of the street tells where that place be; Gaolgate Street, and many a poor bugger has gone the way of that gate and never come back.'

The last of his words biting into her, Tamar could only half suppress the shudder they brought.

'If you be set on going the last of the way on your

own then you keeps to this road, don't go turning to one side nor the other.' Lifting the slack rein he clicked his tongue and as the wagon began to move away to the right he called. 'If you feels you be lost, or if you changes your mind then wait for me, I will be along this way again afore nightfall.'

By nightfall she would have Benjie with her again. For the first time since he had been taken from her Tamar felt happy. Perhaps the carter would let them travel back to Birmingham with him . . . and Mr Philip might even give him back his job.

Everything would be as it was, everything was alright now. But as the smile curved her mouth she heard the scream and what she saw as she turned her head had the blood in her veins freeze to ice.

Selby had been on the verge of claiming that reward. Zeph Tullio trod lightly. That would 'ave meant one going down the line and one swingin' on the end of a rope. Only now Selby wouldn't swing, Selby wouldn't never do anything again!

Across the street the light of the Rose Villa Tavern spilled through the window. This time of night the taproom would be filled with men having their nightly glass of ale. Should he go on as intended, leave Brummagem tonight? That wouldn't go unnoticed. He touched a hand to the pocket that held the necklace. Two killings in one night, couple that with Zeph Tullio's moonlight flit and the theft of a trinket meant for royalty and even the slowest bobby must suspect; and that would be enough, they would plague him like flies round a midden!

But not if he showed his face, acted as he did every night, taking a tankard either in the Villa or the Jeweller's; both taverns were used to seeing Zeph Tullio at their bar and seeing him there they wouldn't see as 'ow he could 'ave done for Charlie or for the Juggler.

But first he must hide that stone. Any glimpse of a package in his pocket would set a man's mind to workin', for everyone in 'Ockley knowed he owned nowt but what he stood up in. So where would Tullio get a paper-wrapped packet lessen he 'ad lifted it from somewheres?

Minutes later, stood with a pint of ale, he listened to the conversation around him.

'I tell you that be what I 'eard . . .'

'Then you been listenin' to rubbish as well as shiftin' it, that piece couldn't 'ave been meant for 'er.'

'Then 'ow come the gaffers 'ave slapped a two 'undred pound reward on the findin' of it?'

Zeph took a swallow of ale wiping his mouth with the back of his hand.

'I'll tell you why,' the voice resounded, the speaker raising his voice for all to hear, 'it be to stop any more pieces being pinched, stop it afore it gets started . . .'

'It be a bit bloody late for that don't it Bert? It already be started.'

'Well, you knows Bert Mason, he be late with everything, reckon Gabriel will 'ave to blow more'n one trump afore Bert realises he be dead.'

In the burst of laughter that followed Zeph glanced about the room, the thick bloom of grey tobacco smoke making faces of men sat in the corners difficult to define.

'So if that reward don't be aimed at stoppin' more thievin' then what do it be aimed at? C'mon, if you all be so much quicker off the mark than me then one o' you say . . . what be that money aimed at?'

The man named Bert glared indignantly.

'Don't tek it funny, there were no harm meant.'

'Nor a lot o' bloody good neither!' Bert picked up his tankard his face stormy as he strode to the bar waiting in silence for it to be refilled.

'There be plenty o' sense in what you says.' A third man spoke as Bert returned to his stool. 'A man would be more'n foolish to lift a piece wi' that sort o' money flying around. It would be like asking to be shopped, ain't many folk in these parts could resist the takin' of two 'undred pound, it be more' a twelve-month wages.'

A white clay pipe stuck between lips invisibly among a forest of whiskers the first speaker nodded. 'Ar, a man would be foolish not to tek it, but I reckons the real fool be the one that took that necklace, I mean, who will buy it from 'im? A necklace designed for the next queen of England! The man must be bloody daft!'

' 'Tweren't lifted by no man, not accordin' to what Charlie Selby says.'

Puffing a cloud of smoke the first man watched it curl upward, joining itself in the grey cloud that hovered close to the ceiling.

'I 'eard of what Charlie Selby said, an' if you believes that then you be dafter than the rest; it were no errand boy stole that package.'

'Then who?'

The stem of the pipe clamped firmly. It did not move as its owner spoke again.

'Buggered if I knows who. But this I does know, it be somebody as knowed what he were lookin' for, that means it were a body that works 'ere in the gold or failing that has an accomplice that works 'ere. Either way the cloud falls over all of us, we all comes under suspicion and that I don't like. I tell you summat, if I finds out who took that piece then he be as good as in gaol an' the gaffers can keep their bloody Judas money!'

At the bar Zeph kept his hand steady as he raised his tankard. These men had no idea who had taken the necklace but when that body behind the Temple of Relief was found it would be Selby took the blame.

But the necklace was not with the body. He lowered his glass wiping the line of creamy froth from his mouth. That meant the search would go on. He must get rid of it, he must find a fence who would take it, but there was none in Hockley.

'What I finds 'ard to swallow be that stone . . .'

'It ain't the swallowing Bert, it'll be passin' out the other end you'll find 'ard.'

He should go now while they were all busy laughing at Bert Mason. Zeph realised the advice he gave himself was sound yet somehow he could not leave, he must hear all these men had to say.

'Eh!' Bert joined the laughter. 'I tell you, if I 'ad swallowed that stone I wouldn't shit for a week and when I did it wouldn't be in no privy in 'Ockley. I would make sure I were far from 'ere.'

'And I for one would be glad, I wouldn't want the stink not for all of Amory's two 'undred pound!'

The banter flowing from one to another Zeph scooped the few coins from his pocket. Laying a penny on the stained wood counter of the bar he nodded to the landlord.

'Two 'undred,' Bert Mason shook his head. 'That be a mighty sum o' money, an' that sets me to wonderin' why them places like Amory's bring in an' sends out gold in them baskets an' nowt but a lad to see to it; me I takes and fetches for meself.'

Across the bar the landlord joined the talk. 'That be easy done when you deals with no more than a couple of ounces in a week, but goldsmiths like Amory that 'ave men working for 'em couldn't fetch and carry every single bauble for theirselves nor carry the weight of bullion, that be the reason for them baskets on wheels.'

'Reckon you be right.' Bert nodded before supping his ale. 'But it makes it easy for a lad to pocket what ain't his an' whether we believes or don't believe as young 'Allam done the pocketin' he be the one as will carry the can. Looks like the poor little sod'll do more than time, he looks set to swing.'

'Talk says the bobbies 'ave him across to Stafford.'

'Talk says true.' Removing the clay pipe the man scraped the inside of the bowl with the blade of a penknife while answering the landlord. 'That sister of his was away there a couple of days since. My missis said as nothing could stop her. But I reckon that be wasted effort, 'aving the lad to the Crown Court means he be for the drop and no mistake.'

Blowing air through his teeth, Bert picked up his tankard. 'Ar, what Charlie Selby says will be more than enough to weave the rope they sets about the lad's neck.'

Tapping the scraped bowl of his pipe against the palm of his hand before setting the stem back among the enveloping whiskers his friend nodded.

'Ar, Selby will 'ave set the lad off on his journey to meet his maker, but when Selby gets back from givin' his performance at Stafford he will sing longer an' louder to we. He will be only too ready to say what he truly knows about Joby Turner's death and the liftin' of that necklace, by the time the men of 'Ockley be done with him and any that be in it along of him.'

The chorus of assent loud in his wake Zeph Tullio walked from the tavern. Hockley was no longer safe for him.

Tamar stared across the empty heathland to where a group of trees formed a dark fringe. Fear solid in her veins she was instantly back in the shadowed yard of her home, Zeph Tullio's hand stripping at her bodice, tearing at her skirts, his body forcing itself on hers. The smell of his unwashed clothing, the rank odour of his stale breath alive in her nostrils she turned away running blind along the path.

But it wasn't Zeph Tullio, it wasn't happening to her. The sound of a second, more terrified shout bringing her back to reality she stopped running. Her head turning, sending her eyes immediately to the line of trees, she saw the tumble of limbs as a figure kicked out at a man dragging it into the shelter of the copse.

Her heart telling her to run, to get away to where people were in the streets, Tamar felt the blood pounding painfully in her veins as her brain shouted to her to help.

'No . . . !'

The cry died abruptly killed by the hard sound of flesh striking against flesh. An arm rising, the hand open for a second blow released the force that seemed to hold her feet to the ground and Tamar was running, the little sound her feet made on the thick grass-covered heath lost in the grunts of a man kneeling over the fallen figure of a young boy.

'I can get a good sum for you in any number of places . . .'

The thick laugh that followed brought Tamar to a halt. Hidden by the thick trunk of a huge oak she stemmed her own horrified cry with a fist wedged into her mouth.

'. . . they fights over who gets the likes of you in them foreign places, a lad with hair the colour of fresh grown wheat . . .'

Tamar watched dirt-ingrained hands snatch at the

boy's trousers pulling them down to his ankles before flipping him on to his face.

'. . . ar, you'll fetch a good price, but first Ike Biggs be going to 'ave 'imself a taste . . .'

Not believing what her eyes told her, Tamar watched as the man released the buttons of his own trousers.

He was just a boy! The small figure lying unconscious beneath that man was little more than a child, maybe not as old as Benjie!

The thought lending life to her horror-struck limbs she grabbed a fallen branch. Engrossed as he was in what he was about to do the man failed to hear the tiny sound of leaves crunched underfoot, the flickering shadow of pale sunlight filtering through leaves disguising the separate shadow of her arm as Tamar raised the branch above her head. Holding it in both hands as she stepped clear of the tree she brought it down with all her strength on to the back of the man's head.

Collapsing with a grunt that seemed to empty his body of breath, he fell forward, completely smothering the child beneath him.

Her hands shaking, her whole body trembling on the verge of collapse she stared at the figures lying at her feet.

Was the man dead, had the blow from that branch killed him?

A sob of terror drawing up from the very base of her stomach she stared at the branch still in her hand, a cry breaking from her as she saw the blood and small pieces of skin marking one side of it.

What had she done! Dear God what had she done!

A sound breaking from the boy's lips drowned out by the terrified clamour in her brain, the branch fell from her nerveless fingers.

She had killed him! She had killed . . .

The thought ended, snapped off as the light to her eyes was snapped off.

'I found you pair of bastards . . . I found you . . .'

Tamar felt the blow to her temple, the words following her into darkness.

'This is a full report?'

Philip Amory glanced at the neatly written script covering a sheet of paper.

'It is Mr Amory, sir. The lad was found guilty and was sent down.'

'But there was no conviction for murder?'

A little man with sand-coloured hair and glassy brown eyes, Sam Morton shifted uncomfortably on his feet. Philip Amory had hired him to report on the kid's trial but the report seemed less than pleasing to him. 'The truth,' Philip Amory had told him when handing him that railway ticket to Stafford, 'naught but the truth!' And the truth was what he had got but his face told he was not pleased with it.

Fingers tightening on the sheet, Philip Amory read the paper through again.

'. . . sentenced to receive ten strokes of the cat followed by thirty years imprisonment . . .'

Eyes held fast by the words he felt his insides turn at

the barbaric cruelty the court had described as lenient. Ten strokes of the cat o' nine tails, that instrument of torture that took the flesh from a man's back, to order such punishment for one so young when half a dozen strokes could finish a man.

Forcing himself to read on to the end, though he already knew every word contained in the report he had commissioned, gave him time to bring his emotions under control and when he glanced again at the nervous little man his face showed none of the revulsion he felt.

'The man Selby did not testify?'

Fingers fidgeting with black bowler hat Sam Morton swallowed.

'He never showed, sir.'

'Never showed?' Philip's tone was sharp.

'That's right Mr Amory sir, he never showed. He weren't in court when the trial started and he never come in afore it ended.'

Selby had not gone into court. It answered a dozen questions for Philip but not the one paramount in his mind, the one he had been wanting to ask since first reading the paper still held in his hand.

'I see.' He tapped the paper with one finger. 'But the lad's sister, you make no mention of her in this.'

A frown creasing his narrow brow seeming somehow to bring small close-set eyes even closer together, the nervous twitch of fingers spinning the bowler in his hands the man Morton swallowed again. He had been promised five pounds for his day's work but should Amory decide the job not suitably done he could kiss that fiver goodbye.

'Sister, Mr Amory?' His Adam's apple jigged in his thin neck.

'The boy's sister!' Philip tossed the paper on to his desk. 'She was there at his trial yet you make no mention of her.'

The promise of the five pounds growing fainter by the second Sam Morton searched his brain for the right use of words. It must not seem he called the goldsmith a liar, but how to tell him he was mistaken? Gaffers anywhere took exception to being told they were mistook and those of the Gold Quarter were no different.

'Could be the woman were present in the gallery, but not knowin' her nor having no likeness with which to identify her . . . if you could describe her then p'raps I would recall.' Sam chose the diplomatic route.

'Did any woman testify?'

Sam Morton's glassy little eyes took on an interested gleam and his brain clicked quickly into gear. Why the interest in the sister? Could there be something between her and the goldsmith? Might it be worth it to him to make up some tale of a woman taken sobbing from the court? He could always say he thought it just some female overcome at the sight of that lad sobbing in the dock.

'Well! Did a woman testify?' Irritation showing clearly, Philip glared at the man he had hired to bring him a full account of the proceedings at the Crown Court.

The bowler now unmoving in his fingers Morton held the creasing frown for just long enough, then as if only now remembering the fact looked up, his glassy eyes taking on a look of understanding.

'No woman took the oath Mr Amory sir, but there were one, about thirtyish I would say, with black hair . . .'

'Never mind!' Philip cut in, his tone sharper than before. The man was obviously lying. Pulling on a bell cord hanging at the fireside he reached into an inner pocket, withdrawing a crisp five-pound note from a Moroccan leather wallet.

'I trust the report were satisfactory, sir. If you should want that sister of the lad found . . .'

'No!' Turning his back to the man, Philip stared into the fire. 'The business is finished.'

Hearing the door close behind his manservant and the fellow he had hired, Philip Amory loosed a long slow breath.

'The business is finished.'

He murmured the words softly to himself. But why did they hurt so much?

Chapter Seven

'You'll touch no more kids you filthy swine . . .'

Feeling as though she was ploughing her way through turgid waters Tamar struggled against the blackness that had swallowed her.

'. . . I'll carve the black hearts from the two of you!'

Centring what hazy consciousness had returned to her on that angry voice she tried to pull herself upright, a loud gasp of pain breaking from her as a heavy boot caught against her ribs.

'. . . you lie there you bloody child stealer!' Shaking with rage the voice rang against her ears. 'I'll be dealin' with you after I've seen to your 'complice!'

'No Father, not the woman . . . her never touched me. It were nothin' to do with her . . . Father, listen! The woman helped me, it was her laid that swine out.'

Sick from the blow to her ribs and her temple Tamar had no strength to pull free of the rough hands that grabbed her, hauling her to her feet.

'Be that true, did you try to help my lad?'

'It's true father, I swear.' The boy answered quickly. 'He . . . he had me pinned beneath him when I heard this fearful smack and he collapsed. See here, this

86

branch has blood on it, it must be what the woman used to hit him with.'

'If that be so, if it was you truly sought to help my lad then I be beholden and I be sorry for raisin' my hand against you.'

Mists clearing from her eyes, propped against a tree for support, Tamar tried to focus on the scene before her. A tall spare-framed man, breeches tied round beneath the knee with string, a threadbare jacket over a collarless shirt, was drawing a wicked looking knife from the side of one heavy boot, using the other to turn the still unconscious form of the boy's attacker on to its back.

Still caught in the strange half awareness in which every movement was in slow motion she watched the knife rise, a sudden dappling of setting sun glinting crimson on its blade, watched the fingers of a weather-beaten hand reach down to fasten on the jacket of the unconscious man, heard the fury-injected voice snarling as the knife lifted higher.

'No!' Every ounce of will-power left to her went into that one word.

'Then you *do* be with him.' Turning his head the boy's father stared at her with venom in his eyes. 'You be in this thing together . . . well you'll be in hell together when I be through!'

'No . . . no we are not together!' Features drawn, from the pain in her ribs, Tamar stepped forward as the figure caught in the man's hand groaned. 'I . . . I saw from the road, I thought it might be Benjie, I . . . I hit that man on the head.'

'That's right Father.' The boy caught Tamar's hand

holding it in his own. 'If it weren't for her then he would . . .'

Lifting one foot the boy's father sent it driving into the bare flesh of the other man's stomach, his angry voice rising over the groan that erupted.

'I know what would 'ave happened, the evidence be clear for all to see, but it'll happen no more!'

'Please!' Tamar gasped as the knife moved. 'You can't kill him.'

'Why not? It be what scum like this deserves, what they does deserves no mercy; even vermin never treat their young that way. The world can only be a better place for the riddance of creatures that sell children into slavery, give them over to any whose lust leads them to buggering young boys, and if you ain't part of what he were about then like as not you would 'ave gone the same way as many another, on the first boat to slip her moorings from Liverpool.'

Her senses cleared Tamar looked at the angry face a question deep in her green eyes.

'Oh, it goes on wench, though I see by the look on your face you 'ave no notion of it; but believe you me, many a little wench and many a lad gets 'anded over at the docks for transportin' to the Orient. They fetches a price there that men be greedy for, so greedy they snatches children from the streets just to line their own pocket; and it ain't just riff raff like this one that does the sellin', some of 'em wears fine clothes and rides in fancy carriages. Them I can't serve up to justice but this bastard . . . !'

The man held by the collar of his jacket his trousers

still about his ankles, screamed as the knife rose again catching the glint of the watery January sun.

'No . . . no.' Ignoring the ache behind her eyes and the pain spearing her ribs, Tamar wrenched her hand from that of the boy, throwing herself forward. 'Don't kill him, he must be given over to the justices.'

Glancing at the figure squirming in his grip the boy's father nodded.

'You be right wench, he should be given over to the justices, but they won't be the sort as sits in a courtroom with a wig on their 'eads, this scum will know the justice of the people. I won't kill him, but there will be times he'll wish I had. The mark he will carry he will carry for life, a mark no whiskers will hide and one by which he will be known for what he be, a stealer and a defiler of children; every cut man on every canal, every man who works the wharfs and basins will know the reason for this.'

Snatching the writhing figure upward, at the same time slashing downward with the knife he sliced the man's nose laying it open to the bone.

A silent scream filling her throat Tamar fell once more into darkness.

Sat in his study, Philip Amory read again the report of the court proceedings. The man had been thorough, careful to write up each speech made by counsel and by the presiding judge, but trying to fabricate a story of Tamar being present . . . He laid the paper on the desk. It was immediately obvious what the man was about, but then could he really be blamed? He must have thought payment would be withheld if it was seen as a carelessness on his part by not mentioning a woman.

But why had the girl not been there? Had something happened to her?

Feeling the kick of his heart in his chest he closed his eyes letting his head fall backward against his chair. Why did he feel this way whenever he thought of that girl, why think of her at all? She was simply an employee, a paid worker. She should be nothing in his eyes . . . she *was* nothing in his eyes! So why the anger that filled him, why the fear?

He should have gone to Stafford, attended the hearing himself. It would not have been seen as extraordinary, the necklace was after all stolen from his premises and it was one of his own employees accused of its theft and of the murder of another man.

But Benjamin Hallam had not answered to a charge of murder. Selby, the man said to have seen the act, had not appeared in court.

Opening his eyes he looked again at the neatly written words of the report.

'. . . there being no witness to the crime and no
evidence it was the defendant delivered the blow
that killed the man Joby Turner, the court finds
the defendant not guilty of the charge . . .'

The boy had escaped the gallows. Philip Amory felt the same sense of relief he had on first reading those words. The boy would not hang.

'. . . *as to the charge of theft . . .*'

He read on, scanning the words as if seeing them for the first time.

'. . . given the seriousness of that crime, the stealing of so valuable a necklace, a necklace intended for Her Royal Highness the Princess of Wales, the court can only impose the maximum sentence. Benjamin Hallam you are hereby sentenced to ten strokes of the cat o' nine tails and thirty years hard labour in Her Majesty's prison at Winson Green. However, while the tenderness of your years is no excuse for your action and can certainly not condone it, the court is inclined to be merciful. Therefore you may serve out your sentence imprisoned here in this country or you may serve it in one of Her Majesty's colonies overseas. The choice is yours.'

The choice is yours! Philip's eyes ran over the last sentence several times. The court had offered no real choice. The deportation of criminals had been revoked years before but giving them the choice of serving out their time in the colonies amounted to the same thing. They would be handed over to any that would take them, handed over as free labour and in many instances be worked to death. Here or abroad young Benjamin Hallam would find little mercy.

The lad had chosen to serve his sentence in the colonies, he would be a middle-aged man before he was free to return to England, but chances were he would not live to see that day; penal servitude killed off more folk than ever it allowed to survive.

But why had the girl not been there? The same question returned to his mind. If she had reached Stafford at all she would have been present in that courtroom; someone like her did not throw up their living, leave their home on a whim. Tamar Hallam had been determined to be with her brother, so how come she was not.

Taking the gold hunter from his waistcoat pocket he flipped the lid clicking it closed before returning it. Would she return to Hockley, take back the job he had resolved would be given to her? He took out the watch, turning it absently in his fingers. To which colony had the court chosen to send her brother? If she knew of it would she try to follow?

The last question needed no in-depth enquiry. Tamar Hallam would follow her brother to hell if that was what it took, but which colony?

Tomorrow he would re-hire the man he had sent to Stafford.

'You be alright, me wench.'

Coming slowly from the blackness Tamar heard the words spoken gently.

'Vinny,' her face crumpled as pain flashed a light-ning bolt through her temple.

'I ain't Vinny, wench, but you need 'ave no fears, you be safe enough.'

The sharpness of the pain receding, Tamar opened

her eyes, a frightened gasp trembling on her lips as the darkness remained. That blow to her head . . . her sight!

The fear of blindness was even more terrifying than the sight of that man, his face covered with blood. She pushed upward but gentle hands pressed her back against a soft pillow, the gentle voice soothing as it spoke.

'You rest you there a while. You've 'ad a bit of a shock but it be over now.'

Swallowing hard on the sickness and fear threatening to carry her back into that world of silent blackness, Tamar closed her eyes. The woman who was with her was not Vinny, then who was she . . . and where was this place?

'You 'elped my lad.' The woman spoke quietly. 'You remember, you saved him from what that swine was about to do to him . . . if it 'adn't been for you . . .'

She had hit a man over the head, struck him with a fallen branch! Slowly the memories returned building the whole awful scene in minute detail. Then she had been struck on the temple, a blow that had knocked her momentarily unconscious.

'My Joe be sorry he hit you,' the woman resumed, 'but when he seen our lad spread face down his trousers round his ankles then he lost his rag. Joe don't be given to losin' his temper often but seein' what he seen, well to 'pologise be what he intends once you be feelin' yourself.'

Her eyes opening, Tamar watched shapes form

from shadows as the darkness released her eyes. Beside her a woman crouched on a stool, a smile lifting her mouth as she saw senses returning.

'You be feelin' better, wench.'

The pain in her head all too obviously present Tamar gave only half a nod.

'The court,' she murmured, 'I have to go to the court.'

'If it be the court in Stafford town you be on about, then it be closed.'

'Closed!' Ignoring the throbbing in her head Tamar sat up swinging her legs down from the bed set in a small alcove. 'But it can't be, my brother is there.'

'Not at this hour he ain't.'

Pushing back her stool the woman stood up to light an oil lamp whose glow showed the narrowness of the cramped room.

'The business of that place has been finished and done for the day some hours since, won't be in session again afore the morning.'

'But Benjie . . . his case . . . they said today . . .'

Shadows verging the pool of light hid the sympathy in her eyes as the woman lifted a kettle from the stove and poured boiling water into a flower-painted enamelled teapot. Could be this wench had seen the last of her brother for a very long time, if her ever seen him again on this earth. Stafford Court weren't exactly lenient in the judgments they passed.

'Could be your brother's 'earing were passed over, put back to another day.'

Knowing what she said was highly unlikely the

woman filled two enamelled mugs with tea, handing one to Tamar.

Her hands trembling as she took the mug, Tamar looked at the woman her fear blatant in her eyes.

'But if it was not . . . if Benjie's hearing went ahead . . . I promised him . . . I promised I would be with him . . .'

'And well you might 'ave been had you not stopped to 'elp my lad.' The woman shook her head, apology deep in every word.

Hearing her feelings of guilt, Tamar replied quickly. 'I am glad I was able to, though what I could have done had the man recovered his senses before . . .'

'Before my Joe come on the scene.' The woman's lips tightened. 'It don't bear thinking on! But one thing be sure, the dirty swine won't get his 'ands on the next child as easy, Joe seen to that alright.'

Remembering the knife slicing downward, the spurting of bright crimson as blood washed over that man's face, his awful cry before she fell into unconsciousness, Tamar shuddered. The whole thing seemed like some awful nightmare. Tea spilling over the rim of the cup with the trembling of her hands she set it down, her voice no more than a whisper as she asked:

'Is . . . is your son unharmed?'

'Ar, that he is, the Lord be thanked.'

Her bent head hid the apprehension in her eyes but the tremble in Tamar's voice refused to be disguised.

'And the man . . . is he dead?'

'No he ain't dead!' The woman snorted. 'But 'ad it been my hand holding the knife then he would 'ave been; the earth would be a better place without him and his sort. But the face he'll carry for the rest of his days will make certain he won't find his filthy ways so easy to follow in the future, and that future won't be stretching very far ahead lessen he sticks clear of the cut. Every narrowboat man will recognise the sign and too many will be willing to add their payment to my Joe's for that swine to live long.'

Setting her cup beside Tamar's, the woman rose. Her dark skirts brushing against a low chest of drawers that did double duty as a table, she bent to the stove feeding coal into its glowing stomach.

'I must be on my way . . .' Tamar sank back, pain once more vicious in her temple and her ribs.

'You best not think of going anywheres tonight. Ain't nothing you can do for your brother afore the mornin' so bide you there where it be warm for the look of you tells me you ain't got the means of buying a bed in no inn, same as it tells me another night under a hedge or in some barn will about see you off. Tell me if I be wrong but 'tis my guess that is where you've lain your 'ead these past nights.'

'You are not wrong.' Tamar's head remained bent.

'Hmmph!' The woman snorted again. 'It ain't often Kate Mullin do be, an' 'specially not when the trouble be with a woman.'

'But I do have money.'

Her head nodding slowly the woman looked at the small silver coin Tamar fished from her pocket.

'A tanner.' Lips pursed she looked at the girl sat on the edge of the small bed. 'And that be every last farthing you possess, that I warrant.'

Tamar's head came up, her glance meeting that of the woman. 'It will pay for a night's lodging.'

Hands rising to rest on almost non-existent hips the woman's eyebrows rose. 'Oh ar, it'll do that right enough, question is why ain't it bought one up to now, why sleep rough when you've money in your pocket?'

Her glance falling to the sixpence, silver glinting in the light of the lamp suspended from the low ceiling, Tamar thought of those nights spent in barns, the cold eating into her bones. The money she held would buy her a bed for two nights, a bed where she would at least be warm; and after two nights she could be home in Hockley.

But what of Benjie? After days locked up in prison he might need the comfort the sixpence could buy. Her fingers closing over it she held it firm in her palm.

'You don't 'ave to say.' The woman's head swung again. 'You be keeping it against your brother's release from that courtroom, so put it away wench, you can bide the night with the Mullins.'

'No, I can't.' Tamar stood, forcing herself to remain on her feet. 'It is kind of you Mrs Mullin but I have to find my brother.'

'There be little chance of your finding anybody out there, the night be black as an undertaker's 'at.'

Joe Mullin followed his son down the few steps Tamar now saw led from a waist-high door into the room whose sides seemed to have to bulge in order to contain them along with a cupboard, a chair and two stools. Only the small bed fitted into the alcove seemed to hold any space.

Ducking his head to avoid the lamp which swung gently with each step, he crossed to the chair drawn against the cast-iron stove.

'I 'eard what you said about looking for your brother,' he held his hands inches from the hot metal, 'but you should put the looking aside until the mornin', 'less of course you knows definite where he'll be, in which case I'll walk you there.'

The sixpence a tiny solid shape in her hand Tamar drew no comfort from it. 'I . . . I do not know where he will be.'

'Then there be no sense in your traipsing about the town, there be a few streets in Stafford and many a house and he could 'ave found shelter in any one of 'em.'

Or in none. Tamar's brain answered quickly.

'I told her that her best course be to bide here on the barge for the night.'

'That be my advice an' all.' Joe Mullin smiled at the lad come to kneel at his side.

She was on a barge! Tamar glanced quickly about the confined space that was filled to capacity, every stick and utensil glowing with the painted colours of flowers and vines. She had seen inside barges before, many of the cut folk welcoming her and her father aboard during their summer evening walks. There had seemed little enough room to her child eyes; it seemed impossible that a family could live and sleep in this one tiny cabin. Yet they were offering to share that cabin with her.

Easing her thin frame past her husband and son, Kate reached plates from a rack fastened to one wall of the cabin. 'I'll be taking no refusal!' She set them on the table, a determined thud echoing from each. 'A fine thank you it would be for 'elping our Davy should I set you to drifting through the night; you will bide with us and afore you says about space there be plenty. Davy and his father will take blankets up on to the deck, they will sleep warm beneath the tarpaulin.'

She could not see a man and a child out of their own beds, especially on a winter's night.

As if reading the thought the lad touched a hand to hers. 'Best give in, miss,' he grinned, 'Mother can be right stroppy if her don't get her way.'

It made a great deal of sense what these people said. She may not find Benjie tonight. He would have found somewhere. After being freed from the court he would have found somewhere warm to wait for her knowing she would come.

Thanking them quietly she let the boy take the shawl from her shoulders, accepting the stool the man pointed out to her.

Tomorrow she would find Benjie. Tomorrow they would go home.

Chapter Eight

'Two hundred pound! That be easy talk for you Amory, but there be others of us don't have money of that sort to give away!'

'Fisher speaks for most of us Amory, the fall-off in trading has some nigh out of the gold for good, finding money for the paying of a reward would like as not see their doors closing for good.'

'But two hundred . . . what is that when placed against five thousand already?' A small man, a round skull cap fixed firmly on the crown of his grey head shrugged his shoulders expressively.

'It be bloody five thousand two hundred, that's what it be Cohen, two bloody hundred more than it was to start with, two more hundred up the suff!'

'You don't know it will be wasted.' Isaac Cohen's steel-rimmed spectacles gleamed in the light of the gasolieres adorning the walls of Philip Amory's dining room. 'Could be it will lead to the recovery of the necklace.'

'Ar, and could be it don't!' Saul Fisher's face, irate and red turned to the Jew. 'You knows as well as me that necklace be long gone, handed to some fence who has the stones stripped from it and the gold melted down.'

Philip regarded the goldsmiths sat around his table. They had come at his invitation to dine and discuss what action, if any, were to be taken to recover the stolen necklace.

'I would not think so. Think of the beauty of that setting, the intricate design,' he said, all faces turning to him, 'even without the stones it would be worth far more than the melted down value of the gold.'

'Not if you can't sell it.' Fisher returned to the argument. 'Supposing a fence can't shift it? Then it be no good to him no matter how beautiful or how intricate; I tell you it'll be melted down.'

'And the stones, Fisher?' Isaac Cohen peered through the thick lenses of his spectacles. 'What will he do with the stones?'

Saul Fisher threw a disdainful glance at the men seated on each side of the table. 'Diamonds be diamonds, they can be got rid of any day of the week.'

'Yes . . . yes they can be got rid of already!' Isaac's shoulders rose again his hands turning palm upward as they lifted a few inches above the table. 'At least some of them.'

'What do you mean Cohen . . . some of them?'

'Think of that necklace, Summers my good friend.' Isaac peered towards another of the guests. 'Of the months we searched for perfect stones, stones that would be worthy of England's future queen, diamonds that matched each other exactly; and having found ten we searched for another – one large and so beautiful it would take the breath from an angel – and at last we found what we searched for and set it in that necklace. It is the Alexandra Stone and its flawless beauty may never be matched again. That is one diamond no fence could pass, it would be too easily recognised on any other woman whose throat it graced, therefore I say it will not be sold and the one who stole it . . . two hundred pounds when you might get nothing? That can seem like a fortune my friend.'

'Ar, an' it be a bloody fortune!' Fisher's face took on an extra depth of colour. '*Our* fortune. I tell you we've spent enough; I for one ain't throwing good money after bad.'

'What makes you think that diamond be one of a kind?'

Isaac Cohen smiled at the question. 'The goldsmiths of Hockley are not yet familiar with gemstones Summers my friend, but Isaac Cohen has worked with their fabulous beauty all of his life. I have set emeralds for the royal court of Persia, rubies as large as pigeon eggs for the sultans of Turkey, the maharajahs of India. Sapphires, pearls and diamonds. Isaac Cohen has seen them all. In Russia I was jeweller to the House of Romanov, the Tsar himself came to Isaac Cohen. Believe me my friends, if I say a gem is without comparison then it is so.'

'That might well be and we ain't denying it,' Fisher returned. 'But all it means is some toerag of a thief has a stone too valuable to chuck away and too bloody beautiful to sell! Either way we be stuck up shit alley!'

'Crudely put Fisher, but I must admit, accurate.' Matthew Summers shifted his glance from the scarlet face to the calm features of his host. 'We can only hope that someone be tempted to come forward. In the meantime we have lost a great deal. Philip and I cannot afford to use more money replacing that necklace even supposing a stone of matching quality could be found, and without the necklace the gift we propose to present to the Princess of Wales appears somewhat paltry.'

'Not paltry my friend.' Isaac Cohen shook his head. 'But I understand your meaning.'

Colour in his face still rating his vexation, Saul Fisher banged a hand on the table the force of it rattling fine crystal wine glasses. 'Then understand this an' all! I put all I intends to put to that gift, I ain't made of money and what I have left I'll keep.'

Touching fingers to the watch nestled in the pocket of his silk waistcoat Philip Amory listened to the murmured assents of his guests. They had all agreed on the plan to present jewellery to the Princess hoping thereby to increase the trade and thus better the living of everyone working in the Gold Quarter, some of them unable to afford the cost easily.

Withdrawing the watch he flipped the lid then reseated it in his pocket without looking at it.

'Gentlemen.' He tapped a fruit fork gently against the stem of a crystal glass, setting it ringing. 'I did not ask you to come here tonight to discuss replacing the necklace with another but to discuss the possibility of recovering it. That, it appears, might take some time.'

'Just about forever. The bloody thing be gone and our money gone with it, there be nothing else to say!'

'Except for this.' Philip went on, leaving Fisher's exclamation ignored. 'It was my workshop had the crafting of that necklace, my basket it was taken from and one of my errand boys convicted of the theft. I see the whole responsibility as mine and as such I shall make restitution for each man's loss. You will each and every one be reimbursed in full for every penny spent on gold and on stones. The responsibility, as I say, was mine, therefore the cost shall be mine.'

'We don't want . . .'

'It is what *I* want Summers.' Philip Amory's reply was instant.

'But not what Isaac Cohen wants.'

Behind thick-lensed spectacles the brown eyes of the gem setter stayed on Philip's face. 'I too have a responsibility, Amory my friend. Was it not Isaac Cohen taught the children of Ezra Hallam about stones, which were precious and which were not? Did Isaac Cohen not sit with them in the evenings showing them books, illustrations of how these stones were found in the earth, how they were polished to reveal the beauty held in their depths? If it were young Benjie took that necklace it is because I, Isaac Cohen, taught him the value of the Alexandra Stone, therefore I stand firm in its loss. Restitution shall be mine. No my friend,' Isaac's shoulders rose, his hands lifting palm upward in the gesture so well known by the others, 'what is money already! It cannot buy a man peace nor bring back loved ones claimed by the grave, but it can allow a man to feel respect for himself. I see my own responsibility in what has happened and only in repaying each man's loss can I feel vindication.'

Pushing from the table he smiled at the others. 'Please, my friends, do not deny me in this, believe an old Jew when he tells you this is what he wants.'

His supper guests gone, Philip Amory walked slowly to his bedroom, fingers twiddling absently with his pocket watch.

Had he done the right thing allowing Isaac Cohen to pay the entire cost of that necklace? The old man had claimed that was the only way he could regain his self-respect.

None of the others had made demur after that. *He* had made no demur.

Suddenly Philip Amory felt a deep sense of shame.

'Will you be wanting anything brought back?'

Tamar's eyes flew open. Benjie was calling, she must be late for work!

But it was still dark, there was no show of morning through the thin curtains that covered her window!

Puzzled she sat up, her head catching against the low ceiling as she did so.

'I've told you afore about bawling, now see . . . you've woken the wench.'

That awful man . . . the boy . . . the blow to her head and ribs! They all rushed in on her like some living thing sending the breath from her lungs in one gasp.

'Excuse my lad,' the woman turned to her, a ready smile on her lips, 'he still has much to learn about keeping quiet.'

Her senses still not fully together Tamar looked to where a broad shaft of watery light suddenly streamed through the low doorway, spilling over the few steps that gave into the cramped room.

The barge! Of course, she was on a narrowboat!

Memory fully restored she drew the bedcover up over her shoulders as the boy she had helped yesterday grinned at her from the hatchway.

'Come you in and leave that draught on top.'

Leaving the hatch to swing closed after him the boy jumped the few steps down to the cabin.

'Morning, Tam.'

Her heart twisted at the easy greeting. That was the way Benjie always greeted her when first getting out of bed.

'Father and me be going into the town, he said to ask if there might be summat as you was needing.' He held both hands to the warm stove.

'I be needing you gone. Now that your shouting has woken Tamar her will be needing privacy so as to get herself dressed.'

'Wait!' Tamar said as the boy's mother caught his shoulders propelling him towards the hatchway. 'Please, if your husband is going into Stafford town I would like to go with him if he will wait while I dress.'

'O' course he'll wait.' Kate Mullin gave her son a gentle push. 'Go tell him Davy, give we a two, three minutes, then you both comes down to the cabin. The morning be a sharp one so a mug of hot tea will warm the cockles afore you sets away.'

The boy gone, Kate handed Tamar her clothes that had hung all night on a thin rope strung above the stove.

'Get yourself into them and then you eats a breakfast. I'll not 'ave you carry an empty stomach, not from the *Brummagem Maid*.'

Dressing quickly, rinsing her hands and face in a bowl of water warmed against the stove, Tamar ignored the soreness of her ribs. Kate Mullin was so kind that the slightest inkling of pain and she would have her back in bed, and somehow she felt Kate was not easily denied.

Taking the bowl of water Kate handed it through the hatch for emptying over the side, at the same time calling her family to join them in the cabin.

'Lad tells me you still be set on going into Stafford town.'

Joseph Mullin took the plate his wife handed to him, settling himself in the one chair before biting into the thick slice of bread fried in dripping.

'I must.' Tamar answered. 'I told you why last evening.'

Setting a plate before the stool Davy had drawn to the makeshift table, Kate set a round of crisp, brownly fried bacon on it.

'Ar, you did wench, and we understands the need you 'ave to find that brother of your'n. Family be family after all.'

'What will you do if your Benjie don't be there, if he be gone from Stafford?'

Kate looked up quickly, her eyes flashing as they reached her son. 'Davy Mullin, if you can't fill your mouth with naught save questions then I'll be throwing your breakfast to the bank for the river voles to feed on!'

Chastened but not cowed, Davy grinned at Tamar as he sank his teeth into his slice of bread.

'Don't you go dwellin' on what the lad said. It will be as you said last night, your brother will 'ave waited on your coming.' Kate transferred bread from frying pan to her husband's plate.

'Kate be right.' Joseph drank from a steaming mug before attacking the hot bread. 'That brother of your'n will 'ave the sense to stay close to the court building, he'll know that will be the first place you'll look. Davy and me, we'll take you there then see you on your way back to Brummagem; we would take you on the *Maid* but we be bound in another direction.'

'Thank you.' Tamar smiled. 'Benjie and I will be alright once we are together.'

Walking over heathland crisp with frost, Tamar held her shawl close about her, a silent prayer filling her heart. Please God Benjie had found a friend that had given him shelter after leaving the court, kept him safe.

She would never let him out of her sight again. The cold of frozen ground biting through the worn soles of her boots, Tamar trudged beside Joseph and his son.

Once she and Benjie were safely home in Hockley she would keep him at her side. He would take no employment of errand boy, no job that would see him running the streets of the Gold Quarter even if that meant he had no job at all. She would work to keep them both. She shivered in the icy breeze that gusted over the empty ground. Whatever it took to keep Benjie from being accused of anything again, then that was what she would do.

'We be nigh on into the town.' Taking a hand from his pocket Joseph pointed to where the castellated turrets of a castle rose from a low hill. 'A few minutes will bring us to Eastgate Street, the courthouse be not far from there.'

Cold as she was Tamar could not help but stare as they came to the town; patterns worked by the oak beams of ancient buildings seemed to transform them into old paintings, the intricate stonework inter-mingled like the stitches of an embroidery. They were as beautiful as anything she had seen before, jewellery worked in wood and stone.

'That there be the Crown Court.' Joseph indicated with his head at the same time catching her arm and pulling her from the path of a horse-drawn tram. Schooling herself not to be diverted by the buildings and shops that lined the busy street, Tamar quickened her steps following after Joseph as he led the way to the other side.

'Davy and me will bide here 'til you be done.'

Glancing up at the face turned to brown leather by the constant buffeting of wind and weather, Tamar shook her head. Joseph had business of his own to see to, she must not keep him any longer.

'No.' Tamar's smile held all her gratitude. 'You and Davy must go on. I can find my way from here. Benjie will be close by and I have the promise of the carter who brought me from Hockley to take me back with him. I am sure he will let my brother travel with him also.'

'If that be what you want. But should you 'ave need then ask at the Bear Inn yonder.' He flicked his head once more. 'It lies in that direction, you won't miss its sign of a bear's head. Just you ask for Joseph Mullin, there'll be folk there as will tell you where I'm to be found. Failing that the *Maid* will be at her moorings 'til the morning, you will be welcome there wench.'

Watching the pair walk away, the boy striving to match his stride to that of his father, Tamar felt a touch of sadness. Like the Marsh family they had shown her kindness and friendship. It would have been nice to have known them for a longer time.

Drawing closer to the imposing building Joseph had pointed out as the court, Tamar could detect no entrance. It must be at the rear. Following the road she turned a corner into what a painted board fastened high on a wall named as Tipping Street, turning right once more as this led into Greengate Street.

Opposite the courthouse the market square with its ornate stone butter cross was already alive with people. Women, mostly dressed in black with baskets on their arms, boys running here and there between traders who loudly claimed their wares the finest to be found; and the wide road lined with buildings throbbed to the traffic of carts and horse-drawn trams.

How would she ever find Benjie in all of this? A moment of despair had her standing still until a man with several baskets balanced like a wicker tower on his head shouted none too politely for her to move.

Apologising to the market porter she walked on. Benjie would be close by somewhere, she had only to look.

She had only to look! Tamar fought back the tears pressing against her lids. She had walked the length of every street, looked in every doorway, beneath every arch where her brother might have taken shelter but there had been no sign of him. Back in Greengate Street she stared at the imposing structure that was the Crown Court.

Maybe someone inside would remember Benjie . . . maybe they could tell her where to find him.

Reluctance in every step she walked through the high arched entrance keeping her glance lowered, even the walls of the place creating a fear in her she found difficult to control.

Inside, hands gripped tightly together beneath her shawl, sounds echoing from the high ceiling adding to her nervousness she glanced about her. Men with black gowns flapping about their ankles, grey curled wigs sat on their heads hurried in every direction, none of them sparing a glance for her.

Away to the left a woman's high-pitched shriek heralded the opening of heavy doors.

'He never done nothin' . . . I tell you he never done nothin' . . .'

Struggling between two uniformed policemen a woman was dragged into the foyer, Tamar's eyes widening as one of the men pushed her roughly, sending her tumbling to the floor.

'You stop your blethering,' the man's mouth twisted in a threatening leer, 'that is unless you wants a taste of 'Er Majesty's pleasure along of your husband.'

'That be your strong point don't it, pushin' women about. But watch out for yourself. Step out of this place one dark night and you'll see what it be like to try pushin' a man; but by the time you steps back 'ere . . . *if* you steps back . . . you'll be more of a woman for your balls will be lyin' at the bottom of the river. Heed my word you lying bastard, for you be a marked man from now on!'

The fear still on his face the policeman turned away, ignoring the continuing threats of the woman as she straightened her bonnet and smoothed her patched skirt.

'Excuse me . . .'

Tamar propelled herself forward catching up with the departing constables as they came up to the same heavy doors. '. . . please, have you seen my brother?'

Half turning, the one who had pushed the woman ran a glance from Tamar's head to her feet before answering.

'Judging from the look of you it be more than likely

I've seen your brother, another bloody no-good vagrant no doubt.'

'Hold up a minute, Jed.' The second constable intervened, his voice kinder than that of his colleague. 'I take it your brother was fetched here?'

Nodding her answer Tamar was prevented from speaking as a black-robed man, his head devoid of wig, came flurrying toward the constables like an agitated crow.

'His worship is ready to hear the next case, he will not take kindly to being kept waiting by you.'

A hint of apology in the half nod he gave to Tamar the policeman turned away.

'Please,' she tried again as the crow-like figure made to move on. 'Have you seen my brother?'

'Brother . . . brother!' Beady eyes dartingly bright over a hooked nose the man appeared even more like a bird as he looked at her. 'I've see hundreds of men come and go here, what makes you think I would remember your brother supposing I had seen him?'

Tamar's hands clenched even more tightly together.

'He . . . he is very young, not yet fourteen . . .'

'And that makes him special?' The clerk scoffed. 'Not here it doesn't. I see boys that age and younger brought to court every day. I've no reason to remember any of them.'

There was nowhere left to look, nowhere else to try, this was her last hope. Gathering all her courage Tamar ran to catch up with the flapping figure.

'Please sir, my brother was here yesterday or maybe

the day before, no more than that. He is small in build with hair the same colour as mine. He . . . he was facing a charge of theft . . . the stealing of a diamond necklace but he didn't . . .'

'The Alexandra Stone!' He came to an abrupt halt.

Head thrust forward from hunched shoulders, eyes beady over the hooked nose the clerk looked at her with something almost like sympathy.

'The Alexandra Stone!' He shook his head slowly. 'Christ have mercy on the lad!'

Chapter Nine

'He would not tell me anything. He must have known but he would not tell me.'

Sat in the dimly lit cabin of the *Brummagem Maid*, Tamar looked at the man who had brought her from the courthouse.

'I don't understand. He must have known about Benjie, he named the necklace.'

'Yes wench, he knowed.' Joseph Mullin glanced at his wife.

'Then why not tell me?'

Glancing at the boy sat on the steps of the hatchway Joseph flicked his head with an upward motion. 'Go see to the hoss.'

'It ain't time . . .'

'It be time when I say it be time!' Joseph's unusually sharp return had the boy on his feet. 'Go see to the hoss and make sure he be tethered firm, he's felt the wanderlust a time or two lately.'

'Do you think the man I spoke to might have known where I could find Benjie?'

It was Joseph who answered, the momentary sharpness gone from his voice. 'I would say he knowed where your brother were took, though whether he be there still be summat else again.'

The bang of the hatch doors closing after the departing boy going unheard, Tamar frowned. 'Took? Benjie would not have gone anywhere without me.'

'Maybe not willing . . .'

'Tamar girl.' Kate Mullin reached forward touching a hand to those twisting restlessly in Tamar's lap. 'Joseph, he has summat to tell you, you best listen.'

'It were in the Bear.' Joseph began hesitantly. 'I 'ad seen to the business of getting a fresh cargo and left Davy eating his bread and cheese while I went into the Bear for a sup. It were while I was drinking my ale I 'eard men talking, but it weren't 'til they mentioned a necklace they said were intended for the Princess of Wales I took notice. Remembering what you 'ad told Kate and me regarding your brother, how he stood accused of murder and theft I asked the outcome of the 'earing. I were told . . .' he broke off, casting a glance at his wife who nodded '. . . I were told the lad were found guilty.'

Guilty!

Joseph and his wife, the cabin with its flower-painted cupboard and dishes faded into nothingness leaving Tamar stranded in an empty lifeless world.

Benjie had been found guilty of murder . . . her brother would hang!

'Tamar . . . Tamar girl . . .'

From an endless distance the voice called her name but it seemed that, held in an icy stillness, she had no strength to respond.

'Tamar, you ain't heard it all . . .'

A hand shaking hers, bringing her back to reality she heard the words repeated, Kate's tone heavy with sympathy.

'. . . you ain't heard the all of it. Your brother don't be going to the gallows.'

'Then he is free!' Tamar's voice trembled.

'No wench, he ain't free.' Joseph shook his head. 'There be more, but how to tell you.'

Benjie was not to hang, there was nothing Joseph could tell her now that would end the joy of hearing that, nothing to detract from the relief surging through her.

'There be a sentence still to serve.'

Eyes brilliant with happiness Tamar smiled at the man who had insisted she return with him from the town, almost carrying her when she refused to leave without finding her brother. A week or so in prison, maybe as much as a month, the prospect was daunting but not hopeless. Benjie would survive and she would be here in Stafford waiting for him to be released.

A month. Tamar's hands relaxed. It would pass. The days would be long but they would pass.

'The judge found him not guilty of murder seeing there was nobody to say they seen the doing of it.'

'Charlie Selby admitted he was lying?'

'Selby never showed his face.' Joseph answered. 'He didn't turn up for the trial. You can thank the Lord for that. If he had then it be more'n a fair chance your brother would have paid the price guilty or no.'

'I do thank God.' Tamar smiled as the tension of

days at last flowed out of her. 'A week or two in prison will be hard for Benjie but at least he will know I'll be here waiting to take him home at the end of it.'

Withdrawing the hand that had covered Tamar's, Kate Mullin got to her feet. Lifting the kettle from the stove she scalded tea leaves she had dropped into the teapot when her husband had returned with the girl.

'I fear it be more'n a week or two.'

Kate's fingers gripped hard on the handle of the kettle. She had seen from Joseph's face the news he carried home was not something would give joy to the girl who had saved Davy.

'Tamar, wench.' Joseph moved uncomfortably in his chair. 'What I 'ave to tell won't be easy for you to bear yet hear it you must. The sentence passed in that court were not one of a few days or even a few months in gaol. Your brother were give thirty years . . .'

'No! No that is not right . . . you heard wrongly.' Tamar smiled as if correcting a child. 'You have made a mistake.'

'I wish to 'eaven I had!'

Setting the kettle aside Kate turned, the pity so marked in her husband's answer setting her senses singing.

What had the judge served on that child . . . two years . . . three? Leaving the tea to mash in the pot she caught Joseph's glance. Dear God, it couldn't be more!

A slight tightening of his mouth displaying his distaste of what he must say next, Joseph began again.

'Listen to me wench, I thought like you just said, that there were some mistake so I questioned those men in the Bear, questioned them close; but there were no mistaking who it were they spoke of. A lad of no more'n twelve, p'raps fourteen year, a lad by name of Hallam. They said as 'ow the judge reckoned the sentence he passed were lenient seeing as the lad were young yet.'

'Lenient!' Kate's face was a mask of scorn. 'They calls giving a babby thirty year hard labour lenient!'

'The lad ain't a babby, not in the eyes of the law he ain't.' Joseph answered. 'You knows as well as I does it could 'ave been life.'

Ain't no difference to my way of thinking, a lad that age won't never survive no thirty year in gaol. Kate bit the words back taking out her disgust on the mugs she banged on to the table.

'Thirty years . . . thirty years . . .' Tamar's lips barely moved. 'He will never stand that . . . Benjie never liked being shut in . . . he likes to be out in the air, he likes to be free . . . Benjie will die in prison.'

'Hush wench, your brother won't die. You will see for yourself that he be bearing up when you sees him on the visiting day . . .'

Catching her husband's glance Kate broke off as he slowly swung his head.

'There be more yet,' he said quietly.

The girl could take no more. Enough was sufficient and the wench had had enough! Kate's thoughts ran quickly through her mind.

Lifting the bead-edged cover from a prettily painted jug she poured milk into the four mugs.

'I think we could all do with a sup of tea, then I think you should lie down a while Tamar, you've had a rough day.' Handing Joseph a steaming mug she added. 'No more Joseph, what be left can wait.'

'No.' He placed the tea on a cupboard set against the stove. 'It has to be said. The wench must hear it sometime and that time best be now, ain't no sense prolonging bad news, hear it all together you gets over it all together.'

It made sense in a logical sort of way. Kate placed a mug gently in Tamar's hand, her own holding on to it until the girl became aware of it. Picking up her own she looked pityingly at the young girl whose lips still moved beneath silent words. Common sense were not always the gentlest of ways.

His own sympathy solid in his throat Joseph coughed. Avoiding the censure of his wife's eyes he went on.

'Kate be right, you 'ave had a hard day but I thinks it best you hear all, hear it here on the *Maid* and said by friends; but if you wishes it left to another time . . .'

'No.' Tamar stared at the cup in her hands. There was nothing she could hear would hurt more than what she had heard already. 'No, if there is more then I prefer to hear it now. Tell me please Joseph, tell me everything.'

'It be as I told you, the charge of murder were dropped on the grounds of insufficient evidence but the charge of theft stood. Your brother were found

guilty and given a sentence of thirty years hard labour
. . . and,' he glanced at Kate, 'and ten strokes of the cat.'

'Oh my God! Oh my dear God!'

Tea spilling in trembling hands Kate gasped. How
could a lad live through that! How could this wench
live *with* it?

Setting her cup down she watched her husband lift
the girl who had sunk unconscious to the floor.

Zeph Tullio watched the playing cards being dealt
deftly around the table. He had joined these men
some hours ago playing the game of three-card brag.
He had won consistently, slowly building the pile of
coins lying beside his right hand. Watching the last
card fall into place and the rest of the pack laid aside he
felt instinctively he would win again.

'Be up to you Sol, you be first in.' The dealer
gathered his own cards.

Looking at the shillings with which each of the four
had bought into the game, a thickset man with a shock
of dark hair picked up his cards. Holding them for a
few moments as if memorising each of the three he
laid them face down in front of him. Taking a coin
from his pile he threw it with those already in the
centre of the table.

'Two bob.' He leaned back against his chair.

On his left Thomas Danks looked at his cards. 'I'll
bet two bobs' worth.' He threw in his coin.

Letting his cards lie untouched Zeph added his own
florin to the kitty.

'You playing blind?'

The dealer, whose turn to pay in followed Zeph's, reached for his cards.

'That means the rest o' we pays double the stake,' he whistled through his teeth, 'that be too steep for one 'and, reckon I be out.'

'Then you fetch the ale.' Danks held out a coin as the dealer threw in his cards.

Collecting a penny from each the man made his way to the smoke-hazed bar.

The man Danks looked at the cards held close to his chest. 'Four bob a brag be a bit rich don't it?'

'If it be too rich then chuck your cards in.' The other man answered sourly.

Danks looked again at the cards held between his fingers. Hesitating a moment he added four shillings to the money lying at the centre of the ring-marked table.

'What about you, be four bob too rich for you?'

A hand touching a chin that hadn't seen a razor in days the thickset man looked at Zeph with eyes sharp as twin blades.

Glancing down at his untouched cards, Zeph felt the other fellow's animosity. It had grown with every game he had lost and judging by his tone it was just about ready to break. An angry man made a poor card player!

Slowly raising his glance Zeph let it lock with the eyes challenging him across the table. Years of card playing telling him exactly which coin lay where, Zeph selected one, never shifting his eyes from that angry stare. Voice level as his look he dropped the coin in the centre of the kitty.

'I'll brag . . . or be that too rich for *you*?'

Seeing the gleam of the coin, Danks loosed a nervous gasp.

'That be a sovereign, Sol, he's bragged a sovereign! That means two quid if you wants to foller.'

The thickset man frowned, bushy eyebrows lying stiff and dark like two dead caterpillars.

'I knows bloody well what double a sovereign be.' Thick lips hardly moving Sol Burke surveyed the hand dealt to him. Taking less than a moment he banged two gold coins down on top of Zeph's.

'I knows 'ow much it be an' all, too bloody much. I ain't braggin' two quid on any hand.' Danks placed his cards on those remaining in the deck.

'An' 'ere be me thinking as you 'ad a good 'and.'

Returning with the ale the dealer grinned at Danks.

'So I 'ad an' all, but not one I be fool enough to brag two quid on.'

'But Sol done it.' He glanced at the ever-growing pile of coins at the centre of the table. ''Ave a runnin' flush, do yah Sol?'

'Could be Tonksy . . . could be.' The thickset man grasped his tankard, immediately swigging from it.

'Play be back wi' you.' He wiped a hand over his mouth spreading froth over the growth of whiskers. 'Be you still blind?'

One hand touching the coins remaining to him Zeph smiled, his Gypsy blood urging him on. Still not breaking his hold on the other man's eyes he put down another sovereign.

'Christ, Sol!' Danks shuffled on his stool. 'Throw in now afore he drags you too far!'

'Leave be!' Sol Burke laughed mirthlessly. 'I knows when a bloke be pissin' in the wind and this bugger gonna finish up well and truly soaked. It be me an' you Tullio an' I knows which will take the pot.' The smirk wide on his face he threw in two more sovereigns. 'Me and you Tullio,' he said, 'it be just me and you.'

Zeph saw the glance slide swiftly to his pile of coins. Burke was already assessing the next move of the game, already feeling the pot in his grasp.

'Think on, Sol.' Alfred Tonks watched over the rim of his tankard. 'You can't go on throwin' sovereigns in like they was bibbles. See his cards now.'

'Mind your bloody own bussiness, Tonksy!' Burke spat viciously. 'Never tell me 'ow to play cards lessen you wants your innards draggin' out and set round your neck for a scarf!' Grabbing at the coins he flung them to lie with those bet so far. Then, eyes blazing as they returned to Zeph he grated. 'Brag, you gypsy bastard!'

He had taken almost eleven pounds from that carter, hitched a ride then hit him over the head, robbing him of his takings before leaving him for dead. Eleven pounds. Zeph watched the face regarding him across the table, a face that sneered. What hadn't gone on food and beer lay in that pot . . . all except for the five-pound note shoved deep in his pocket. If he staked that and lost . . .

Wordlessly he felt for the bank note. Smoothing out the folds he placed it with the sovereigns, smiling inwardly as the caterpillars died once more.

'Christ Almighty!' Danks breathed slowly. 'You can't brag on that! Your stake would be ten pound, jack the game in now Sol.'

'Sol Burke don't give up that easy. The 'and I 'olds will beat the one he's got. The bastard be bluffin'.'

Would Burke brag again? Lay down ten pounds? Zeph felt a faint flicker against his spine. If the man took this pot then he would take almost the last penny of that eleven pounds. None of these thoughts showing in his face Zeph stood the remaining few coins in a neat column. His voice calm and even he lifted his glance to his opponent.

Opposite him Sol Burke's mouth tightened, the sneer fading. Resting on his unturned cards his hands balled into fists.

'How much you got Danks?'

'A couple of quid.' The other man retrieved a handful of coins from his pocket spreading them before him on the table. 'Tonight 'as near wiped me out, I ain't got anywheres near enough to top that.'

'Tonksy?'

Alfred Tonks started nervously. 'Same 'ere, Sol. I got almost nowt. Tullio cleaned me early on.'

Sol Burke swallowed noisily his fists remaining solidly on his cards.

'Then you'll tek my marker, Tullio!'

'Zeph Tullio teks no man's marker.' Zeph watched

the sharp eyes harden to ice. 'I plays for cash and pays in cash, I expects to be paid the same. If you can't match the brag then the pot be mine.' His answer was casual and though his nerves were taut as bow strings he reached both hands to the coins grouped in the middle of the players, scooping the heap towards him.

'I 'ad cards nothing would beat!' Anger red in his face, Sol Burke picked up his cards, skimming them face upward at Zeph.

'Christ Sol, Jack, Queen, King, an' all clubs!' Tonks whistled again through his teeth. 'That be a runnin' flush. It could 'ave teken the pot.'

'O' course it could 'ave teken the pot, teken the whole bloody lot an' I lost it for the sake of a few bob. I tells you it were a bloody good 'and, better than that the gypsy 'ad.'

He did not have to show his cards. The rules of the game said a winner who had played blind, had played without once looking at his cards to ascertain their worth, could replace them in the deck without showing them to the rest of the players. But the rogue element in Zeph was too strong, his bluff had paid off, the Gypsy in his blood was once more king.

'A good 'and I grant you.' He glanced dismissively at Sol Burke's cards, then slowly, tauntingly, he turned his own spreading them apart on the table. 'But is it good enough to beat this!'

'Jesus!' Tonks gasped again. 'That be a prial, don't nothing beat that!'

The men staring at the three aces, Zeph dropped the winnings into his pocket, not looking back as he left the tavern.

At the corner of the street he slipped into a shadowed doorway. How long would he have to wait?

You promised Tam . . . you promised . . .

Eyes stretched wide with fear stared at Tamar.

. . . you promised . . .

A sob in her mouth Tamar stretched her arms to the small figure as it faded into darkness.

You didn't come Tam . . . why didn't you come?

The voice was harsher now, hard and condemning, the figure staring at her from the opposite corner.

'I did come Benjie, I did come.'

She lifted her arms but once more the figure slid away, only to return as swiftly to stand beside her.

Don't leave me Tam . . .

The lips that moved were dry and cracked, the eyes that pleaded with her puffed and swollen from weeping. Don't leave me Tam, I be feared . . .

'I won't leave you Benjie, I won't ever leave you.' The words sobbing from her she stretched her arms to her brother.

You promised Tam . . .

The figure stepped from her reach.

. . . you promised . . .

'Benjie!'

Tamar's sob became a tortured scream as the figure

turned from her showing a back criss-crossed with blood-soaked slashes.

'Will her be alright?'

Davy Mullin looked on anxiously as his mother wrung out a cloth in the bowl of cold water he had been sent to fetch.

'Her will be well, given time.' Kate answered her son.

'It's been nigh on three days and her ain't woke not once. Father said if her still be like this tomorrow we'd best get a doctor to her.'

Placing the cool cloth gently across Tamar's forehead Kate nodded. 'To my way of thinking a doctor will be of no more help than we be, mebbe less. This wench be caught up in shock, and that weaves a web a body be sometime hard put to break'

'But when it do break?'

Looking at her son Kate read the genuine concern in his dark eyes. That encounter with the swine who would have defiled him had taught him something more than caution, something her and his father might have taken a few years yet to get so deep embedded; it had taught him responsibility. She had watched the way he was with the girl, so caring, so eager to help with whatever her might need. Many another would 'ave called it calf love, a boy's infatuation with a pretty girl, but in her heart her knowed it were more than that. He realised that but for going out of her way to 'elp him her would 'ave been to that court in time, been there to keep the promise her must 'ave made and in doing so none of this would 'ave happened.

But it would 'ave happened. Kate handed him the bowl. Only Joseph and Davy wouldn't 'ave been stood outside that courthouse in the 'ope of finding her. The shock would 'ave been just as cruel, just as mind swallowing but there would 'ave been no friend to 'elp.

'When it do break . . .' Kate paused in her answer. There was nothing to be gained by lying to the boy, truth was sometimes the bitterest herb but its balm had the stronger healing in the long run. '. . . when it do break then we will see, there be no other answer I can give. Now get that water tossed over the side and then 'elp your father, for we'll be coming up to the five bridges shortly and King will need to be loosed and led over the top.'

Turning back to the bed as the hatch doors closed behind her son, Kate smoothed the covers over the restless girl.

'How will you be when the web do break?' she murmured. 'Kate Mullin don't 'ave the answer; 'er can only pray, pray you wakes with a sound mind.'

Chapter Ten

'We'll be coming into Tewkesbury in half an hour or so, once there I'll go bring a doctor.'

'Ar, that be best, I can do no more for the wench.'

Who needed a doctor, what poor girl was ill?

Floating on a warm cloud Tamar listened to the quiet voices.

'I've 'eard tell that shock the like of what her suffered can do strange things, some say it can keep a body sleeping for months.'

'But folk can't eat if they be sleeping . . .'

Of course they couldn't. Tamar smiled.

'But if they don't eat they die . . . is her going to die?'

'Not if we can 'elp it. We just 'ave to keep her warm and comfortable.'

She was warm and comfortable. It was wonderful here, dark and cosy; she would stay here in this exquisite comfort forever.

'I don't want her to die.'

'Davy lad, that'll do! If your meal be finished go give King his feed bag.'

Davy. Tamar smiled in her intimate world. It was a nice name.

'You asked in Puckrup?' The softer voice spoke again, answered immediately by a deeper more resonant tone.

'Ar, and in Twyning. But it seemed nobody in them villages 'ad seen him nor even heard of a Benjie Hallam. If he's made his way along 'ere then he done it wi'out being seen.'

Benjie! Tamar's closed world erupted in a soft explosion, the gentle darkness consumed by a yellow glow that beat against her eyes. 'Benjie!' The cry broke from her lips as she was flung back into reality.

'Shh, wench.' Kate was beside her almost as her eyes opened.

'Benjie.' Tamar pushed against the hands that pressed her back to the pillows. 'Benjie, I didn't find him . . . I didn't find him . . .'

'Shh,' Kate soothed again, 'it be alright.'

Her vision focusing more clearly Tamar looked at the face bending over her.

'Kate?'

'Ar, it be Kate, and you be awake, thanks be to 'eaven.'

Blinking against the sudden light Tamar struggled to sit up. 'I was looking for Benjie, I . . . I don't remember . . .'

'Ain't surprising, but it will all come back soon enough, just give it time.'

Relief thick in her voice Kate turned to her husband. 'Reckon we don't be needin' no doctor. Go up top and let Davy know all's going to be well with the wench, he were right worried for her.'

'Tell me what happened, how did I come to be back with you?'

Taking the bowl of warm broth handed to her Tamar held it untouched.

'I'll tell you true enough, but only once you've eaten that broth. No . . . no argyin!' Kate's mouth set determinedly, 'You needs to eat and there'll be no word from me 'til you 'ave!'

Watching the woman remove the lamp that had hung above the alcove bed, blowing out the flame before setting it aside, then set to collecting dishes from the chest-top table and placing them beside an enamelled bowl, Tamar obediently ate her broth.

Kate's features were temporarily lost amid the cloud of steam that billowed up from the bowl as hot water mixed with cold.

Washing the crockery one piece at a time, setting each on a tray placed next to the bowl, Kate kept a wary eye. The wench would eat every last drop or her name weren't Kate Mullin.

'That's better.' Smiling her satisfaction Kate took the empty dish and spoon, setting them in the warm water.

Swinging her legs from the bed Tamar glanced around the dim cabin for her clothes.

'I should get dressed.'

Refusing would cause the girl stress and that would be of little benefit. Kate flicked her head towards the line of thin rope strung above the stove.

'Your things be airing against you waking. Get yourself into them while I dries the crocks.' Taking up a piece of scrubbed huckaback she proceeded to dry the dishes, stacking them away in the flower-painted cupboard.

'Anything you be wanting mother?'

Kate glanced towards the hatchway, an understanding smile relaxing her mouth.

'You can come say 'ello to Tamar, I knows that's what you be really asking.'

A quick shuffle and the boy had cleared the few steps to stand grinning at Tamar as she smoothed her skirts.

'We thought as you was going to sleep forever.'

'This be a narrowboat not some enchanted castle and you be no prince charming, my lad.' Kate flung the huckaback over the rope. 'You've seen what you come to see now get some fresh water so Tamar can wash her hands and face.'

Grin as wide as a Cheshire cat the boy grabbed the bowl.

'Be sure you gives that bowl a proper swill afore you puts fresh water in it.' The bang of the hatch doors her answer Kate shook her head as she turned to Tamar. 'Bear with the lad, he just be so glad you be woke in a sound mind, we all be glad; you had Joseph and me worried.'

'I'm sorry. I had no intention . . .'

'Course you hadn't wench, we just be thankful Joseph and Davy found you when they did. Tell me, how much do you remember?'

'I . . . I was in the Crown Court, I remember that. I asked if they had seen Benjie and a man in a long black gown shook his head and said "Christ help the lad". Then I remember Joseph taking hold of me.'

'You remember what Joseph said to you here on the *Maid*?'

Tamar nodded. She remembered it all now, it had returned to her mind as clearly as seeing a picture in a book.

Taking the bowl of cold water from her son, Kate shooed him out of the cabin. Adding the rest of the boiling water from the kettle she tested the temperature with a finger before stepping aside.

Her brief toilet finished Tamar reached for her shawl neatly folded at the foot of the bed.

'Joseph and you have been very kind and I thank you, but I must go find which prison Benjie has been sent to and find somewhere close by to live. He has to know I am close even though we cannot be together.'

'It ain't going to be so easy as that.' Seeing the quick frown hover over the girl's brow Kate loosed a long sigh. 'Sit you down wench, there still be summat you must needs be told.'

Waiting for Tamar to settle on a stool she went on. 'Your brother were given thirty years but them years was not to be served in no prison, least not one as you can visit.'

'But the law allows . . .'

'Ar, the law allows,' Kate cut in, 'but circumstances don't.'

Her frown deepening Tamar looked at the other woman. 'Kate, I don't understand, what are you saying?'

Drawing a quick breath, the words rushing to get out before she changed her mind, Kate answered. 'I be saying this. The sentence laid on your brother is to be served in the colonies, he be going to be sent abroad.'

Abroad! Tamar sat as if stunned. That was what Kate meant by circumstances preventing her visiting Benjie. She had no money to buy passage to the country he would be sent to, she would never have it; jobs paid little enough to live on even were you fortunate enough to find work, certainly she would not get it from Amory's polishing bench.

Eyes dulled with the heartbreak inside her lifted to Kate.

'Which country?' she asked tonelessly. 'Which colony have they sent my brother to?'

'But he must 'ave seen her or at least asked her whereabouts.'

'So he did, but as he said Stafford be a bigger place than 'Ockley and the wench could 'ave been in any part of it. He couldn't go traipsing round looking, indefinite like, he has his livin' to make like the rest o' we.'

'All the same . . . to leave the wench there on her own.' Dinah Edwards bit into her slice of bread and pork dripping.

'The carter waited longer than he told Tamar he would.' Vinny Marsh held her own thick slice of bread between her teeth while she reached two mugs of tea from the bench that held sugar and milk along with the chemicals used to give the gold trinkets their final lustre.

'P'raps if he hadn't he wouldn't 'ave got that knock on the 'ead there in Edgbaston and his pocket lightened of his money.'

Taking a gulp of hot tea, Dinah bit into her bread, a full mouth in no way impeding her reply.

'I don't know what the world be coming to, I'll be buggered if I does! First Joby Turner gets his brains bashed out, then they finds Theo Blatt with his throat cut – mind you I reckon he's been asking for it for years – everybody knowed he took on things stole by others then sold 'em on.'

Vinny nodded. 'Ar, he were well named. A Juggler he was when it come to gold, pity he couldn't juggle when it come to a knife passin' across his windpipe.'

'As if that weren't enough they finds Charlie Selby done in an' all.'

'If anybody deserves to be done in then that sod did!' Vinny chewed vehemently. 'He were ready to swear a lad's life away when he knowed all the time young Benjie Hallam be innocent as the day is long, that lad wouldn't drop his clog on a fly let alone bash a man's 'ead in.'

'Well he won't do no more swearing.' Dinah shoved the last of her bread and dripping into her mouth, shaking the wrapping cloth free of crumbs before folding it.

'Ar, the lad be innocent right enough.' Vinny nodded agreement. 'He killed no man nor do I reckon he took that necklace otherwise they would 'ave found it afore now. The law 'ave taken a scapegoat to cover the fact they don't know who be the thief or where that stone might be. When you don't know then blame some bugger else, that be the style of it; and if you ships the scapegoat overseas then nobody be like to find out.'

'Eh, poor little soul!' Dinah took up her mug, looking over the rim at her friend. 'He won't never see 'ome again.'

'And Tamar won't ever see him again. What a wicked thing to 'appen to them both. Like you Dinah, I begin to wonder what this world be coming to.'

'You won't 'ave to wonder for long if Amory catches you sat canting and the dinner break over five minutes ago.'

'Since when was you a bloody clock, Cal Perry?' Dinah glared at the man stood in the doorway of the tiny finishing shop.

'Since I were made chargehand 'ere.'

'In that case you needs get somebody to look at your workings, it were ten minutes into the dinner break afore Vinny and meself got to sit down, Amory wanted that job finished so we 'ad to finish it. That means we still 'as five minutes left for talking afore we needs start again.'

'Dinah be right.' Vinny refilled her mug then stared at the man stood in the doorway. 'And we would like them minutes in peace, so you can bugger off, Cal Perry!'

'Five minutes then.' Cal turned, then paused looking over his shoulder at the two women. 'But keep a north eye open, Amory has been irritable as a bear with a sore 'ead since hearing of young Hallam getting thirty years.'

'Reckon I knows why that be.' Vinny waited until Perry disappeared down the workroom. 'Philip Amory feels guilty for not going to that court hisself, for not speaking for the lad's good character, and now it be too late he feels the wrong of it.'

Reaching for the tin in which she carried her daily meal Dinah placed the folded dinner cloth inside it. 'He feels summat alright,' she replaced the tin on the bench, 'that be seen clear the way he be asking after the girl. It be the same every mornin'; have we 'eard from the 'Allam girl, has her come 'ome? Then 'aving his arse in his 'and when we says as we ain't.'

Philip Amory was not in the sweetest of tempers when told there was no word of Tamar. Vinny packed away her own cloth; anybody would wonder why that be, could he 'ave feelings for the wench? She were certainly pretty enough to take any man's eye – and it were not unknown for a master to take a wench on the side.

Vinny kept her thoughts to herself. If such talk should surface, as it very well might, then it wouldn't be her tongue it would roll off.

'Ar well, Amory might be 'aving more than his arse in his 'and, he might 'ave our tins in his 'and if he sees we still sitting. You 'eard what Cal Perry said.'

'Ar, I did. A bear with a sore 'ead and a sore arse don't be one to play about with; I reckon it be high time Amory took hisself a wife.' Dinah laughed.

Settling herself at the polisher's bench Vinny watched her friend shuffle to her own workplace. Did Philip Amory think that too, or were his thoughts more along the lines of taking hisself a mistress; and was young Tamar the mistress he had thought to take?

'Which colony?' Tamar asked the question again.

'I don't know wench, and that be the truth of it.'

The dimness of the cabin not enough to entirely conceal the emotions flitting across the girl's face, Kate watched in silence. If she thought the answer a lie then who could blame her after all she had been through.

Feeling the slight bump as the barge touched the bank Kate spoke again.

'This will be Tewkesbury or near enough. Joseph will ask again 'ere.'

'Ask?' Her voice dull, almost lifeless, Tamar watched the woman busy herself at the stove.

'Joseph has asked at every place we've passed through; he thought you would 'ave wanted that even if there be little point to it.'

How many places had they passed through? How far had she come from Stafford? How could Joseph know they were travelling in the same direction as Benjie?

'Sit you back down and wait for Joseph, he can better answer your questions than I can.' Kate placed the kettle on the stove, bringing it to the boil while she reached for mugs. 'They will both be down in a minute or two. I know you be wantin' to be away searching for your brother but to 'ave all the facts be better than running off with only half.'

Kate made sense as always. Tamar glanced towards the hatch as the doors opened and father and son came down to the cabin.

'Davy said as how you was awake and feeling better.' Joseph, his face pinched with the cold of early February, smiled as he set a bucket of coals beside the stove.

'Tamar been asking which it is of the places overseas her brother's been sent to. I've told her we don't 'ave the knowing of that.' Kate placed the cover back on the milk jug, pink glass beads jangling against the flower-painted china.

Holding both hands momentarily to the heat of the stove as Davy settled cross-legged on the clipped rag rug set before it, Joseph took his chair.

He took the steaming mug from his wife holding it between hands blue with cold. Watching him Tamar felt a wave of guilt sweep over her. How many nights had he and Davy slept on deck, how many freezing nights spent under a tarpaulin while she had slept in his bed?

'It's the truth Kate be telling.' He sipped several times at the hot liquid pulling the heat of it into his cold body. 'The men in the Bear spoke of his sentence, of the lash followed by thirty years 'ard labour in one of Her Majesty's dominions overseas. Christ, them judges makes it sound like they be presenting a bloke with paradise!' He sipped again. 'But we all knows it be no paradise, no heaven on earth, the few that 'ave returned testified to that, and it seems each be the same no matter the country. They was treated no better than the slaves of thirty year ago.'

'Joseph!' Kate's tone and frown halted her husband's invective. 'The wench asked only to be told the country he be sent to.'

'And I wished I could tell her, but I can't.' Joseph understood the silent message. 'I asked that question of them men but they claimed the judge had said he would announce that the following day; I see no reason not to accept that as truth. Why should they refuse to tell if they had knowed, they didn't withhold the rest.'

He looked apologetically to Tamar. 'But we couldn't lay over at Stafford any longer. We 'ave to get cargo to its destination on time or we gets no payment, and this time of year can see river or canal freeze over; if that 'appens then we could be at a standstill for days.'

'Joseph felt he couldn't leave you behind, not with you 'aving no place to sleep the night that be why he insisted on you returning to the *Maid*, then when you blacked out, well the rest tells itself.'

'How long since you left Stafford?' Tamar asked quietly.

'This be the fourth day.' Kate answered, handing her son a scone spread thick with butter.

'Four!' Tamar's face creased with alarm. 'Benjie could be anywhere!'

'Ar, he could. Ain't no use in denying that.' Joseph

took the scone handed him on a flower-patterned plate.

'Listen to the rest of it, hear it all afore you decides what we done be the wrong thing.' Kate set a plate at Tamar's elbow but made no comment as the scone went ignored.

'We don't get to every village we passes but it be safe to say that news reaches there quicker than might be thought, carters and packmen carries more'n goods and trinkets. That being so any news they brings gets to the inns alongside of the waterways.' Joseph chewed on the scone. 'Should it be that a convict be transported this way either by coach or boat then talk of it would be in them inns; but none had heard of a red-haired lad sent down for stealing a necklace.'

'So I *am* travelling the wrong way!'

'That might not be.'

'But Joseph, you said news of him would be in the inns, if it is not then that can only be because he has not been brought this way.'

'Not so Tamar, wench. Ways of doing things be changing. Convicts sometimes be sent their way on them new-fangled trains. They be shackled in what be called the guard's van. Trains be quicker at covering ground than does horses whether they be pulling a coach or narrowboat, and likely them prisoners has less chance of escaping when they be 'urtling along at twenty miles every hour.'

'I'd like to ride in a train. P'raps when I be grown I'll be able to.'

'God forbid!' Kate shuddered as she looked at her

son's upturned face. 'They don't be safe, people was never meant to move over God's earth at such a speed.'

'Train or coach it doesn't tell me where Benjie is or where he is being taken.'

'No, it don't.' Joseph agreed. 'But to send your brother overseas they first has to send him to a seaport and the nearest port from Brummagem be Bristol. By my reckoning that be the likeliest one them officials would choose.'

Bristol. Tamar clutched the shawl still held in her fingers. She had never heard of such a town, how far away was it and how could she get there?

'Me and Joseph guessed what you would do when you 'eard all he had to tell, that be another reason we kept you on board the *Maid*. We 'ave cargo for Bristol, you can travel there with us, and along the way Joseph can ask at every village we passes; it will be quicker for you than going on foot and safer too I reckon.'

Looking at their faces lined from exposure to all weathers Tamar felt the tears rise to her throat. These people were so kind, how could she ever hope to repay them?

'That be settled then.' Kate gathered the plates briskly.

She had found such good friends. Tamar rose to help as Joseph and his son disappeared through the hatch doors. But what had her brother found?

Ten strokes of the cat . . . thirty years hard labour . . . the tears thick in her throat spilled silently down her cheeks.

Chapter Eleven

Bristol was overwhelming, terrifying in its strange sights and sounds. Trying not to lag too far behind Joseph and Davy, Tamar's eyes were drawn to the high-built warehouses bordering the docks; the ships with sails furled, their masts standing like long fingers against lead grey skies.

Coming to a low building set between taller ones, a graceful carved and painted wooden effigy of a high-breasted woman fastened to the wall topping bow-bellied windows, Joseph paused.

'We be needing candles and one or two things for the *Maid*, this be the place to get them.'

Tamar glanced at a painted sign set over the door. Whatever a ship's chandler was it was here at this dark little shop.

'Be you coming inside?'

Though the cold bit through her clothes, feeling for her bones, she must wait here in the street. If Benjie should pass by she must be here to see. Glancing at Joseph she shook her head.

'I will wait here, if that is alright with you.'

'As you will. Davy will stay with you.'

Catching the quick look of disappointment flash

over the boy's eyes, Tamar shook her head again.

'There is no need. Besides, Davy would not know Benjie if he saw him so there is little point in his standing here.'

Knowing the pleasure his son got from seeing all that the ship's chandlers held, Joseph was not difficult to persuade. Warning her not to step away from the shop he went inside followed closely by a delighted Davy.

Which of those ships would be carrying Benjie, might he already be aboard? Tamar caught her breath. In mid-channel a ship spread its sails to a wind that filled them, billowing them like the wings of some fantastic bird. It was beautiful, the most beautiful sight she had ever seen! As if following its soundless call she walked closer to the quayside mindless of everything save the beauty of that ship. It could be sailing to some wonderful place, some magical paradise where there was never any hunger, never any cold, where every-one was happy . . . it could be carrying her and Benjie . . .

'Stand there and you'll be joining the bloody mermaids!'

Tamar swayed, a shove to her back sending her dangerously close to the edge of the dock. Below her, water lapping the side of a tall ship oozed black with slime and oil, its surface crusted with filth and floating debris.

'Careful man!' A hand caught her arm, yanking her away from the narrow chasm ready to swallow her.

'And you miss, surely you are not wishing to meet with Davy Jones.'

Steadier on her feet, Tamar pulled her arm free.

'No, I can see you are not, nor are you familiar with our ever-watchful friend.'

'I was not looking where I was going.' Tamar touched a hand to her hair, smoothing back fronds the wind had tossed over her brow.

'But Davy was watching, waiting for you with open arms, not that he is to be blamed, who would not welcome so pretty a girl with open arms.'

Tamar kept her glance on the ship gliding down-river on the wide swell of water sails spread like the wings of angels.

'You would like to be with her.' The voice at her side lost its mocking quality. 'You see her beauty, but it is a dark beauty, one that hides the miseries of so many men.'

'Miseries?' Tamar let her glance follow the tall sails.

'That is the *Swallow*. She is a convict ship.'

A convict ship! The breath caught in her throat. Could Benjie be on that ship?

'There are men on board her will embrace Davy long before they reach their destination, and many who will wish they had for it's a hard future they face.'

'Davy?' Tamar's question caught by the wind scuttled in the wake of the white sails.

'Davy Jones. Sailors believe he waits at the bottom of the sea to welcome the drowned, and there are those on convict ships who go willingly to meet him.'

A certain pity in the voice had Tamar turn. Eyes of grey steel were softened by the same pity she had

heard in the words. A close-clipped beard traced a
narrow band of black along a firm jaw, emphasising
the strength of a handsome face.

'I thought you too had meant to join him, but I see
I was wrong.' He turned away along the quay.

He had spoken of that ship as if he was familiar with
its trade, certain of the cargo it carried. Maybe he
might have news of Benjie.

'Wait . . . please . . .'

The wind caught at her skirts and shawl dragging
them out behind her as she ran.

'Wait . . . my brother, can you tell me . . . ?'

Catching up to the tall figure Tamar touched a
hand to the man's arm, her eyes wide with question
and hope.

'. . . please, you said that ship carried convicts,
would you know if my brother was among them?'

'Your brother is destined for the colonies?'

The trace of pity was back bringing a trembling to
Tamar's own lips.

'Which one?' he asked, as she nodded.

'I . . . I don't know.'

'Then how do you know he came through Bristol?
There are other ports carry Her Majesty's unwanted
from the shores of Britain.'

'Joseph said . . .' She broke off as he caught the
hand that touched his arm jerking her from the path of
a handcart piled so high with boxes the stevedore
pushing it could not be seen.

'This is not the place for questions.' He glanced
over her head, one quick look encompassing the busy

scene. 'There.' He pointed to a street leading away from the dock.

Holding fast to her elbow he propelled her along beside him, men stepping smartly from his path, their quietly spoken words respectful as he passed.

Sat at a table Tamar had no eyes for the pretty chintz curtains and white cloths or the people sat at other tables their eyebrows lifting as they stared down their noses at the girl in patched skirt and threadbare shawl her face pinched and blue with cold.

'Now.' He looked at a pocket watch as he spoke. 'I regret I have not much time to spare, I must be with my ship in a quarter of the hour, so if you will tell me quickly how you think I can help.'

'That ship . . .'

'The *Swallow*?' he said.

He nodded to the woman dressed in frilled cap and apron who approached their table, took his order and bustled away.

Tamar's glance fell to the hands clutched tight in her lap.

'I thought perhaps you might know if my brother were on board.'

She did not know the ship her brother sailed on, she did not even know if he was to sail from Bristol. Nathan Burford watched the hope in the soft green eyes that almost pleaded as they lifted to him. Why had she followed after him; and how far had she come? Her speech held none of the Bristol flavour.

Waiting while china cups and pot were set before them he gave a slight shake of the head.

'I have no business with the transporting of convicts, that is one cargo I will not carry.'

Seeing the sudden tinge of colour seep her cheeks and the swift dropping of her glance, Nathan Burford felt a touch of something he had thought long forgotten.

'I make no judgement of those men or women.' He spoke quietly. 'Only with their sentence. You are given the choice, is what prisoners are told, the choice to serve out your term here locked in one of Her Majesty's prisons or to serve it abroad working the land. But the truth is there is no choice. Here or in some other dominion the prisoner is shackled, forced to labour for his right to live; wrongdoers must be punished, that part of the law I have no quarrel with, but to hand men and women over to what virtually amounts to slavery, that I will never hold to. They are no longer termed penal colonies but that is the only respect in which those places have changed.'

'Those places, are they far from England?'

She did not need to look at him for him to know the tears that filled her eyes. He ought not to have spoken so forthrightly. Whatever that brother of hers had done the girl clearly loved him.

Ignoring the question and the speculative glances cast their way he filled both cups passing one across the table.

'Drink that down, then maybe we might enquire after your brother.'

The unaccustomed aroma of the hot liquid filling her nostrils Tamar pushed the cup away.

'I'm sorry. I should have asked what you would drink. Perhaps coffee is not to your liking.'

His hand half-lifted to summon the waitress, Tamar shook her head. 'I do not want a drink thank you, as for coffee I have never had that, we drink only tea or sometimes cocoa in Hockley.'

How many of the women he knew would have been honest enough to admit such a thing. Nathan smiled inwardly, and it was a smile that held no mockery.

'Tell me what your brother looks like, anything that would mark him out among others.'

He had been right about the tears. Glittering like sunlight on the sea her eyes lifted to his.

'He is not very tall, not yet as tall as I am . . .'

Small indeed for a man! Suddenly Nathan had a picture of her walking beside him, her head just clearing his shoulder.

'. . . but there is nothing to distinguish him . . . unless his hair, it is the same colour as mine.'

'Unusual enough but not exactly unknown.' He finished his coffee. 'Men with hair that colour have been seen here before.'

'But my brother is not a man, he is just a boy. He is thirteen years old.'

A coin halfway to the table Nathan paused. A boy of thirteen sentenced to the colonies, Christ Almighty, what had the child done to deserve that?

'Small build you say.' He placed the coin beside his cup then reached a hand to her chair. 'And with red hair. Maybe I know of someone who will have seen him.'

Retracing their steps to the dockside he swung a glance over the bustling scene.

'Wait here.' The words were terse, an order more than a request. Tamar watched him walk to where a ship rode gently on her moorings, men scurrying up and down the gangplank balancing sacks and boxes on their shoulders. At the foot of the gangplank a man in blue jacket and trousers touched a hand to his forehead.

'Tamar!'

The shout echoed over the bustling sounds of the wharf, the head of the man who had bought her coffee snapping at once in its direction.

'Tamar . . . we thought you lost, where 'ave you been? Father said not to move from the chandler's.'

A hand tight on her sleeve Tamar turned to the boy his grin wide with relief.

'I . . . I got to watching the ships.' She smiled apologetically at Joseph as he came up to her. 'I have never seen such a ship before.'

'Ain't hardly likely you would, living in 'Ockley.' He sniffed, his nose red with cold. 'But that don't mean you can go swanning off, the docks be dicey places at the best o' times but for a young wench on her own they be downright dangerous.'

'It was wrong of me Joseph . . .'

'Well we'll say no more about it.' Joseph cut in unable to hide the shiver a sharp blast of wind sent through him. 'Our business be done so we can return to the *Maid*.'

'Oh but Benjamin . . .'

'I found no news, wench. I asked about but seems nobody knows a word of him. But we can talk more when we be back to the barge and out of the cold, it fair cuts to the bone.'

'No, I can't . . . I mean . . . I must wait.' Tamar glanced to where a tall figure turned its dark head towards a full-sailed ship, small now in the distance.

'But you can't stay 'ere.' Joseph said, cold giving a firm no-nonsense edge to his voice.

'Just a few moments Joseph please, there is a man who may be able to help, he said.'

'You ain't been so bloody crackbrained as to go talking to some man! Ain't what you seen 'appening to Davy taught you nuthin'!' Joseph exploded. 'God Almighty Tamar, this aint 'Ockley, you can't go gettin' mixed up with the men you see round 'ere, it be asking for trouble.'

'Sound advice, you would do well to heed your father.'

More anxious than angry, Joseph turned to the man who had joined them. 'I don't be her father.'

'It is still sound advice nevertheless, and luckily for her I am no wharf rat. Captain Nathan Burford. I command the *Verity*.'

Joseph's mouth relaxed. He had heard of the *Verity* and her captain, the man had a reputation for fair dealing and an honest hand.

'No disrespect, Captain Burford, but Tamar be unused to the docks, I was worried for her.'

'Quite so.' His nod brief to the point of dismissive Nathan turned his glance to Tamar. 'I have enquired of your brother, my first mate has a talent for finding local news. Seems he spent some of last evening in one of the local taverns. There was talk of a young lad bound for the colonies, deported for thirty years on a charge of stealing something called the Alexandra Stone . . .'

'Benjie!' Tamar gasped.

'Would that be your brother?'

'Ar, that be him.' Joseph answered, Tamar's hands being pressed to her mouth. 'Young Benjie Hallam were given thirty years but he stole no necklace, that I would swear before the Lord God hisself!'

'Where is he?' Brilliant with tears Tamar's glance lifted to the strong face. 'Did . . . did they say where Benjie is now?'

'There!' Turning to where the river broadened on its way to the sea Nathan Burford pointed. 'Your brother is aboard the *Swallow*.'

Tamar took a few steps towards the edge of the dock her eyes crossing the span of water to reach the disappearing vessel. Benjie was on that ship, at last she knew where he was, at last she could be with him.

Her glance held fast to the white sails still visible above the horizon of the river she did not turn as she asked.

'Where is the *Swallow* going, how soon can I catch up to her?'

At her back Nathan Burford stared after the ship.

'She is bound for Australia, and the truth is you cannot catch up to her, the *Swallow* is a clipper built for speed, there are few vessels, if any, could overtake her.'

'But that does not mean I cannot follow.'

'No it does not,' Nathan answered, 'but you must be prepared for a long journey. Australia is on the other side of the world.'

Her glance once more towards the sea Tamar answered. 'I love my brother Captain Burford, and when you love someone no distance is too far.'

'You 'eard what that man said and he should know if anybody does him being a ship's captain, Australia be at the far side of the world, ain't no way you can get there!' Kate Mullin glanced first at her husband and then at the girl sat in the tiny living space of the narrowboat.

'There has to be a way Kate, and I intend to find it.'

Kate shook her head, a tiny perplexed movement. This argument had already been had. They had all three talked long and hard the evening before, the girl insisting she stay here in Bristol to look for a way of following after her brother; Joseph and herself insisting such a thing was madness, God knows what might become of a wench alone in that place.

'You far better come back with Kate and me. We can take you straight into Gas Street Basin, ain't but a few minutes walk from there to 'Ockley.' Joseph added his argument to that of his wife. 'Back among them you knows well, you can decide what to do.'

Tamar's pale smile touched each face in turn. This man and woman had more than repaid her for helping their son and that was what they wanted to do now. But they could not help with what she must do.

'I have already decided.' She answered quietly, 'I made a promise to my brother and somehow or other I will keep it. Other people have taken passage to that country, I will do the same.'

Kate's exasperated hiss held a measure of impatience.

'That be like roasting snow in a furnace, you can't never do it! 'Ave a bit of sense wench, you needs money afore you can take a boat anywhere and to go so far as the other side of the world will take quite a bit I fancy, and unless I be sore wrong you don't 'ave that kind of money!'

'No, I do not have that kind of money . . .'

The eyes that lifted to Kate's were dark with dejection but beneath it she saw the spark of hope. But it was more than just hope; it was defiance and determination. This girl would move mountains to find her brother, God grant they didn't fall on her!

'. . . I do not have the money to buy a passage to that country,' Tamar went on, 'but I will earn it. Believe me Kate, I have to get there, I have to go to Benjie.'

'I know wench, I know. A blind man could see the love you 'olds for the lad.' Kate held out her arms enfolding the slight form against her breast. ''Eaven keep you safe and if God wills we will meet again.'

On the deck of the narrowboat Tamar smiled at the

boy clenching his teeth to hold back tears already glinting in his eyes.

'Won't you give me a smile, Davy?'

Almost throwing himself at her he clasped both arms about her waist pressing his face into her shawl.

'I wish you wouldn't go Tamar, I wish you would be 'ere with we.'

'I have to Davy, you do understand?'

'Ar.' He sniffed. 'I understands and I 'opes you comes on your brother, but just as much I 'opes you comes back. I loves you Tamar.'

Gently releasing herself Tamar smiled down at the boy. Emotion quivering in every word she murmured. 'I love you too Davy Mullin, I love each of you and I would need to travel a lot further than the other side of the earth before I forgot you.'

Tears too thick in her throat to say more she jumped to the track that ran alongside the water's edge. Holding her shawl against a trembling mouth she ran without looking back.

Chapter Twelve

'The *Verity*? That be Captain Burford's boat. It be gone missy, set sail afore midday.'

'Thank you.' Tamar thanked the white-whiskered man sat on an upturned barrel, a rounded stump of wood stretched before him where a leg must once have been. Numb from cold she turned away as the old man replaced a long-stemmed clay pipe between toothless gums. Why had she asked for that man, why did she think he might help her? She had walked the streets all day, asking at almost every house if they could give her work, afraid to stop lest the fierce cold freeze her to the ground. But those of the houses that had not had the door slamming in her face they too had refused. Employment here in Bristol was every bit as hard to find as it was in Hockley.

Should she have gone home? Should she have returned with the Mullins?

Evening creeping over the sky, behind it a deeper veil of grey, Tamar tried to drive away the fear that had played for hours at the back of her mind. What if the sixpence in her pocket were not enough to buy her shelter for the night? There were no barns as she had seen, only tall warehouses and they were locked tight. But not to find a place out of the wind and cold would most likely be to freeze to death. Pulling on the shawl that already damp and night frost had clamped to her arms she tried to coax an element of warmth from it but the little it had to offer had long since been swallowed by the chill wind.

Each step becoming harder to take she stumbled back towards the maze of streets branching from the docks. There had to be a place, there had to be.

'Mind out where you be pushin'!'

Tamar reeled against a painted railing, one of many that adorned the line of houses. Head bent against the driving wind, she had not noticed the plump woman now staring angrily at her beneath an over-feathered bonnet.

'. . . spent so long sucking the gin bottle you can't stand straight, knock a decent body off her feet!'

Lips so stiff with cold they would hardly move, Tamar whispered an apology.

'Drunk as a fiddler's bitch!' The woman snapped again then as Tamar went to move on grabbed her arm flinging her back against the railing. 'Not so fast. Mebbe you ain't so drunk as you couldn't cut a purse.'

Planting her large body in front of Tamar the woman lifted her hand, glancing at the purse still looped to her wrist.

'So you didn't cut my purse. And I don't believe you to be drunk, so why career into a body like you have no control to your brain?'

Hearing her own voice, yet having no feeling of her mouth moving. Tamar asked, 'Please, would you know where I might find a shelter for the night? I . . . I have sixpence I can pay with.'

'So that's it!' Beneath folds of flesh the woman's eyes were sharp. 'You be another of them wharf rats. What's the matter, did no sailor fancy laying his money down for you?'

'I am sorry I bumped you.'

Too cold to feel disgust Tamar made to step aside but a plump hand to her middle caused her to pause.

'I be wrong again.' The ferret sharp eyes ran over her, taking in the patched skirts and worn-through shawl. 'You are not drunk and you are no doxy neither, nor listening to your tongue do you belong Bristol way. Sixpence you says. Well, get you a night's lodging it will but it will be one you shares with a thousand fleas.' She hesitated, then as if making up her mind and having to say the words quickly before changing it again added, 'You can have a bed at my house for the night, it be nothing grand but it be clean and you'll be off the streets.'

Tears glistening like frosted droplets along her lashes Tamar murmured the swell of gratitude that rose within her, following the woman's steps, so quick and agile for a body richly endowed with flesh.

'This be it.' Fishing a key from the pocket of her coat the woman opened the door of a two-storied house, its lights gleaming behind drawn curtains.

Handing her bag to a younger woman as thin as she was plump, she drew off her coat before turning to Tamar who stood shyly just inside the hallway.

'This young woman be going to stay the night.' She

held out the coat for the other woman to take. 'We couldn't leave her out there on the street to freeze, not and look the good Lord in the face we couldn't.'

Fat wrinkling around her eyes she smiled at Tamar. 'No doubt you could eat a supper and after it a warm bath will chase the chill from your bones. Nothing like a meal and a bath to settle a body to sleep.'

Waving aside Tamar's thanks she led the way to a kitchen glowing with the light of several oil lamps and cosy with heat from a well-fed fire.

'I be Mrs Sampson, Lena Sampson and this be Corrie Fletcher.'

Turning to smile at the thin figure that had followed them into the kitchen, Tamar felt the breath seize within her throat. Light from the lamps catching the woman's face showed a tight-drawn lid closing off the left eye while a jagged scar ran across her cheek dragging down the corner of her mouth before sliding away beneath her chin.

Seeing the horror Tamar could not immediately mask, the woman turned to the fire, swinging a large pot over the coals.

Sharing their meal Tamar told of the reason for her being in Bristol.

'So your brother were on the *Swallow*, poor little lad.' Lena Sampson cut three slices of cherry cake handing a slice to each.

'And did you tell Captain Burford of your intention to stay on in the town 'til you could take ship for Australia?'

Tamar picked at the cake her appetite suddenly

gone. She had not told Nathan Burford of her decision it was of no concern to him, yet somehow she
wished she had.

'No.' She answered, not looking at the women sat
with her. 'I did not tell Captain Burford, I said only
that I would follow after Benjie.'

'Well, I doubt he could have helped had you told
him. The *Verity* plies the West Indies run, brings
tobacco, sugar, cocoa beans and the like, then offloads
most of it on to barges bound for Birmingham and the
towns round about; I haven't known him to make the
Australia trip. He don't mess with the kinds of cargo
they sends there, not that it be all convicts; but Nathan
Burford be his own man, if he don't want the run he
don't make it, not for profit nor for government. But
you be shivering, girl.'

The woman got to her feet, chins folding back on
themselves as she smiled.

Turning to the other woman, the softness fading
from her voice leaving it hard and brisk she said sharply.

'Bring the bath from the scullery then come you into
the sitting room, there is an errand for you to run.'

Sat in the zinc bath, the heat from the water and
from the kitchen range soothing her aching limbs,
Tamar closed her eyes. It had been like a hand from
heaven had sent her stumbling into Mrs Sampson.
Things were not going to be so bad after all. Come
morning she would look for work again, perhaps if she
prayed very hard tonight then God might listen and
tomorrow she would find it.

A towel draped about her, another binding her hair,

she had scrubbed with soap that smelled of something sweet and pleasant. She looked up as the scar-faced woman came back to the kitchen. The initial shock of seeing such pitiful deformation now passed, Tamar had no difficulty in smiling as she was handed a heavy cotton nightgown.

'Leave your things afore the fire, they will air overnight. When you be ready give a call and I will show you the bedroom.'

A mouth tightened by its awful scar seemed if possible tighter than before, the eyes reflecting an anger they had not previously held.

Minutes later, her hair brushed and braided, Tamar thought of the thin woman who had shown her silently upstairs. What had caused such a horrible injury? Had she suffered some terrible accident as a child? What was she to the woman who had brought Tamar herself in from the streets? They could be mother and daughter, the names were different but the younger woman wore no wedding ring, and there seemed no affection between them, no love like there had been between herself and her own mother, between her and Benjie.

'Please God, help me find him.' Tamar's eyes closed on the whisper and already asleep she smiled at the face that watched her from the edge of her mind, smiled at Captain Nathan Burford.

'I tell you NO!'

The raised voice beating against her ears threw Tamar up from the depths of sleep. Startled, unsure whether she had dreamed the shout she lay with opened eyes.

'You'll do as I say!'

It was not the voice of Vinny Marsh.

Disoriented she stared about the unfamiliar room, a thin stream of early light touching against the window showing the tall chest of drawers, the washstand with its pretty marble top.

This was not her room!

'I've finished doing what you say to do. There'll be no more of it Lena Sampson . . . you hear me . . . there'll be no more!'

Ignoring the barrier of walls and door the answer came clearly into the bedroom.

Lena Sampson! Memory returning Tamar lay listening. Mrs Sampson and Corrie, they were shouting at each other, but for what reason?

'There'll be no more of you once Trader East gets wind of what you be about . . . no more self-righteous Corrie Fletcher!'

'You think that bothers me?'

'If it don't then it should, Trader has a nasty streak and it shows clear when he's crossed.'

The voices rang in the silence of the house followed by the sound of footsteps on the stairs and the door of her room being flung hard back on its hinges.

Breath loud as it left her lips, Tamar sat up.

'Get these on and get out!'

Cold and dead as that of a fish the one good eye in that scarred face stared as the thin woman threw a bundle of clothes on to the bed.

'Get dressed and leave . . . *now*!' She ordered again as, panting for breath, Lena Sampson came into the room behind her.

'Corrie, it be too late, I've already sent word. Be sensible, think of what you be doing . . .'

'I am thinking!' Corrie snapped. 'And I'm doing what I've dreamed of doing for so long.'

'But the money.' The plump woman almost whined.

Glancing at Tamar struggling into her clothes, Corrie's drawn mouth tightened pulling the ridges of the long scar into tiny jagged gullies.

'There will be no more money,' she said, not looking at the face of the woman stood behind her, 'Trader East has made his last deal at this house!'

The last word jerked from her as the heavy figure grabbed the back of her hair almost pulling her off her feet.

'It be you finished in this house.'

Fingers fumbling with buttons that haste made more elusive Tamar pressed back against the bed. She had seen women fight before, it was no unusual occurrence among the narrow tight-packed streets of the Gold Quarter where simply to live from day to day was a fight against poverty and squalor. But the anger of those women had been superficial, fleeting, over in moments but this – she caught a glimpse of the scarred face as Corrie stumbled – this was different; there was a coldness about it that grabbed at her limbs, holding her almost paralysed.

'I'll see you floating in the dock, you scarfaced bastard!'

The taunt within the threat added a vicious anger to the awful coldness of Corrie's features drawing them into a hideous caricature. Twisting round in Lena's grasp she struck out with one hand – her fingernails tracing a line of blood over the fat jowls – while the other fastened on a heavy brass candlestick ornamenting the shelf above the fireplace.

Tamar's mouth opened in a scream that caught in her throat as the candlestick crashed into the woman's skull.

'I told you . . . I told you there would be no more . . .'

The candlestick still in her hand, Corrie stared at the figure sprawled at her feet, blood oozing thickly from the gaping wound to the temple.

The blow somehow releasing her limbs from their unseen shackles, Tamar dropped to her knees beside the fallen Lena.

Her hand shaking, she reached to touch the figure lying so still and silent and when she looked up her eyes were wide with fear.

'I . . . I think she is dead.'

No flicker of remorse in her one good eye Corrie Fletcher lifted her twisted mouth in a smile.

'That's to the good for had it been other I would have hit her again.'

'But why?'

'Why?' The scathing laugh as thin as her body the woman touched a finger to her mutilated face. 'You can look at this, then ask why? It was Lena Sampson did this to me. I was no more than a girl, my age matching what your own must be. My father had married his prostitute lady friend and when I refused to follow her example I was thrown out of the house. For days I lived off the streets taking charity along with the kicks of those who gave it; then Lena Sampson offered me a room for a few nights. She brought me here to this house, treating me as she treated you; offering a meal, a warm bath and a bed. You don't need me to tell you it seemed the hand of heaven was being held out to me. She was kindness itself for a week or more and I thought I had found a friend, and so I had until the night Trader East called.'

Tamar rose to her feet but the other woman seemed not to notice, it seemed the one eye stared at a scene Tamar could not share.

'After being introduced and talking with them both for a while I went to bed, but Lena stayed on drinking with the man I had instinctively disliked. It was late when they came laughing into my room, bumping against the furniture, knocking over the lamp.'

A sob trembling from her twisted mouth the woman drew a long shuddering breath.

'Lena ordered me out of my bed, half dragging me when I was loth to do it. He laughed at that, laughed as he sat on the bed. Then Lena ordered me to strip and when I wouldn't she snatched the nightgown ripping it from neck to hem.

' *"How do you like that Trader?"* were the words she said, *"be them tits high enough for you, be that body to your tastes . . . what amount will that bring on your next trading?"* '

Pale light searching its way into the room settled on the thin face, highlighting the jagged contours of the scar turned whiter by the tension of clenching teeth. Pity thick in her own throat, Tamar made no attempt to interrupt, an inner sense telling her this woman needed to tell it all.

'He made no answer . . .' the twisted lips barely moved, the words no more than a breath '. . . made no answer as he stood up and stripped away his own clothes. Then it was I realised their intention. I tried to run but Lena's hands were strong. She pushed me to where he sat naked on the bed legs spread wide; kneel, she told me and when I cried out she twisted her fingers in the back of my hair, twisted tight pressing my face towards his jerking flesh laughing when I tried to twist away . . . and him' – she breathed again, a long trembling shuddering the length of her – 'he took my face between his hands, hands damp with sweat, pulling it into his crotch. I could smell the odour of him, cheap perfume mixed with perspiration and I heaved; but it had no effect on him, he pressed himself against my face forcing his flesh past my lips, shoved himself into my mouth. I felt the throb of him against my tongue, the kick of hard flesh in my throat and I bit down, bit as hard as I could. He screamed, at the same time punching hard against the side of my head knocking me unconscious. When I came round he was gone . . .' she paused, the lid twitching above that one staring eye, her mouth writhing as it fought to bring out the words '. . . he was gone but Lena was there waiting . . . waiting with a whip in her hand.'

'A whip, dear God she didn't . . .'

'I remember that whip.' The whispering voice went on, the dull, lifeless tone driving over Tamar's horrified exclamation. 'The end of it plaited into three separate strips, each tipped with a ball of spiked metal, remember the sting of it as it bit into my flesh, the agony as it ripped through my face. I've remembered it every day of my life, a life Lena Sampson put an end to.'

Breath trapped behind her teeth, Tamar bent over the still figure sprawled at her feet forcing her fingers to touch the dead face to close the lids over the staring lifeless eyes.

'No.' Straightening, Tamar looked at the tortured twisted face. 'Your life is not ended, you can get away . . .'

'Away!' The empty laugh mocked the silent walls, the staring eye at last showing recognition. 'Away to where? To where no one will look at this face without repugnance, without showing what your eyes showed when first you seen it?' She laughed again. 'There is no such place, I know for I've tried, only to have women turn from me in the streets, crossing their breasts as if for protection against some demon, to have children taunt and call after me in the streets. Men fresh from the ships laugh and point as I pass the docks. No, there is no place of peace, no life beyond the walls for Corrie Fletcher, and no life worth the living within them. But at least I stopped *her*.'

The candlestick still in her hand Corrie lifted it, staring at it with a wild delighted stare, her voice rising on a note of hysteria as she glanced down at the still figure.

'I told you,' she laughed, 'I told you, Lena Sampson, told you I wouldn't go along with it . . . not any more, I wouldn't. But you was not listening, you was busy with thoughts of how much this one would fetch, too busy to listen to Corrie Fletcher when I told you there would be no selling of Tamar Hallam to the Trader, no selling her as you have sold so many others.'

Perplexed, Tamar shook her head. The woman had suffered, was still suffering, her brain must be playing tricks.

'Corrie,' she said gently, 'Lena was not about to sell me, one person cannot sell another. It is against the law.'

'Not if the law knows nothing about it.'

The one eye lifted to Tamar and she saw instantly that it was clear of the smudge of madness that a moment ago had tainted the woman's voice.

'But the law don't always know.' She went on, her words clear and precise, every cell of her brain knowing what it was about, every nerve and twitch of muscle under control. 'Lena and the Trader were careful never to let their doings be known. Early morning, with the first breathing of the dawn, that were the time their business were done. There was none about at that hour to see the sacks carried aboard a ship bound for the East, sacks that held young women and girls, some no more than six or seven years, sold to the slave traffickers. Sold like cattle at a market, to be passed on to the highest bidder. Sold to gratify a man's pleasure no matter the form they might take. That be where Trader East takes his name, from selling to the Orient where his evil will be put to no question nor bring any restitution. But I told Lena Sampson he would not take you.'

This woman had saved her from a life so dreadful she could not hold thought of it in her mind. Her legs threatening to give way beneath her, Tamar sank to the edge of the bed. Staring at the unmoving body she felt an icy cold fear against her spine. The penalty for murder was death and Corrie had committed murder!

Corrie's hand reached to her shoulder snatching her to her feet and even in her confused state Tamar could not help but note the strength of it.

'You mustn't go sitting there.' A note of urgency now in the quiet voice the woman shook her. 'You have to leave afore the streets gets busy.'

Raising her head Tamar met the look on the scarred and twisted face, the tortured eye struggling to lift the gathered lid.

'I can't,' she said quietly. 'You did this for me, I will not leave you now.'

Suddenly the other woman smiled, the ghastly marks on her flesh writhing like white serpents. Devoid now of rage the eye held a strange look, one of cold satisfaction.

'You can do nothing for me,' she said, the whisper gentle on the blossoming dawn.

Tamar reached a hand to that which had dropped from her shoulder. 'You could come away with me, we could find a place well away from here, some-where where the law will never find you. Leave with me Corrie, leave with me now.'

Breaking free of Tamar's hand the woman lifted thin fingers to her mutilated face touching the jagged riverine line of the scar, and for the first time tears glistened their silver message along her lashes.

'To carry on the same way I have since getting this?' The fingers traced the scar again, feeling its depth tracing its length and behind the tears the twisted mouth smiled. 'To have the same existence I've had since Lena Sampson gave me this? I told you that woman put an end to my life and now I have put an end to hers. What happens to me now be of no consequence.'

'But it does!' Tamar cried. 'I can't leave you, I won't, but you have to come away now, the penalty for murder . . .'

'Is hanging.' The twisted mouth smiled more dee-ply giving an awful caricature to the deformed fea-tures. 'I know that but then death holds no terrors for me, it holds only release.'

What could she mean, why should she speak of death as a release, as if it were welcome? Her mouth starting to form the first of her questions, Tamar paused as Corrie threw the heavy candlestick at the body on the floor.

'I know what you be wanting to ask and I will tell you. Death will put an end to that whip, it will stop the rise and fall of it I see every time I close my eyes to sleep, ease the pain I feel whenever I see my face in a looking glass or feel my flesh when I washes it. Death is welcome to Corrie Fletcher for it will bring her release . . . release from the burden of carrying this!'

Snatching aside her hair she laughed low in her throat, a slow, hopeless laugh that illuminated the despair wrapping her soul.

White and livid, the scar travelled sideward from the twisted eye, bald lines like the beds of minute dried-up rivers reached across the scalp to a mound of ruched flesh drawn over the hole where the ear had been sliced away.

Despite herself Tamar caught her breath in a loud gasp.

Her hand falling, releasing the hair that hid the ghastly marks, Corrie gave a slow nod.

'Now you see, now you understands when I say death will bring me naught but release.'

She could run now, find a policeman and bring him back to the house, the law would believe when she told them what had happened . . . The law! Tamar checked her thoughts . . . they would believe it was an accident, believe Corrie had not intended to kill? Or would it be the same as it had been with Benjie? She looked at the thin figure, the early light playing over the scarred face. This woman had wanted only to save her. In a way this murder was all her fault. How could she turn her back?

'Corrie please, you did not mean to kill Lena, it was an accident.'

'Was it?' The open eye looked at Tamar and in its depth was the shadow of the despair that had echoed in that dry laugh. 'The only accident is that it did not happen sooner, soon enough to save more girls from the hands of Trader East; but at least Lena Sampson will supply no more and he carries my mark, the flesh he tried to push into my mouth lies somewhere deep in Bristol Channel and I thank God for it. No other woman will be subjected to sucking his filth. Now do as I say and go, the sun be rising.'

'No, no I won't go. Listen to me Corrie, together we could . . .'

'It's no use, girl.' The woman shook her head taking a backward step as Tamar reached a hand to her. 'You want to help Corrie Fletcher. I thank you for that and will carry it with me into heaven and lay it at the feet of the Almighty when He calls me to account for what I've done.'

'But . . .'

Taking the paraffin lamp from the tiny bedside table Corrie threw off the glass funnel tipping the contents over the body lying between them.

'No buts.' She spoke through tight-clenched teeth. 'This be the end of a house of evil. I deserve no pity and asks no mercy. I knew what happened to the women I helped Lena Sampson to procure, and God help me the children as well. I knew and still I did it. That can have no forgiveness.'

'But all that is over now.'

'Yes it's over . . . thank God it's over.'

Taking a box of matches from the pocket of her skirt Corrie struck one, holding it high between thin bony fingers.

Beneath its tiny flame her eye glinted with a look that was almost triumphant.

'Lena Sampson and me, we will both get our just deserts though the law will never give them, unlike your brother, God keep him. I hope you find him, Tamar . . .'

The rest was lost in an explosion of flame as she threw the match on to the body, the blast hurling Tamar aside.

'Corrie!' It was a scream as Tamar scrambled to her feet. A hand held to shield her face she started towards the blaze, then stopped.

Encased in its red gold heart the scarred face smiled.

Chapter Thirteen

He had guessed they would follow. Watching from the shadowed doorway Zeph Tullio felt his nerves tighten. He had seen the looks pass between those men he had played cards with, felt the growing irritation of the heavier one.

Peering from the shelter of the doorway he saw the door of the beer house open, the dense cloud of pipe tobacco smoke stretch long grey fingers into the frosty, moon-bright street. He had seen the three of them turn to look both ways, Sol Burke's arm wave as he positioned them into a triangle, himself the apex.

Sol Burke had not liked losing his money, was not used to losing, now he was looking to get it back.

'He couldn't 'ave got far Sol, ain't been but a minute since he left.'

'Shut your mouth, Tonksy,' Thomas Danks answered, 'do you want 'im to 'ear!'

Even from the doorway halfway along the street, Zeph heard the loud exasperated breath shoot from Sol Burke.

'If I'd known you two wanted a parade I'd 'ave brought a bloody drum! Now close your trap the pair o' you afore I closes 'em for you! If that gyppo swine catches sound of you he'll be off like a bloody jackrabbit and my money gone with 'em.'

'And mine.' The voice of Tonks was plaintive, carrying clear on the night air. 'That gypsy bloke took my money an' all.'

'He took each of our money . . . !'

Burke's answering snarl had the other man back further to the side of him.

'. . . and he be like to keep it if you keep sounding off like some bloody foghorn; one more word and I'll cut your wagging tongue from your 'ead!'

Sliding a hand to his pocket Zeph drew out the knife. Running a finger over the blade he smiled, brilliant blackbird eyes glittering in the shadows. Sol Burke and friends would lose more than their money if they came close enough.

The knife was sharp and he knew how to use it but three to one were not odds he would choose. Zeph pressed back into the shadows. One he could deal with, two at a push but three was one too many, better to let them pass.

Hidden in the doorway unable to see them now he listened to the footsteps, the slow purposeful tread as they shuffled closer.

He should have run the second he had stepped through that door, kept on running until he had put a distance between him and the beer house. Should he run now? His fingers clenching on the knife Zeph dismissed the idea. Those men had been no hand at three-card brag but it might prove a different tune when it come to running. No, he couldn't take that chance, he had to stay put until they were gone.

Tuned to every sound he listened to the steps drawing closer . . . closer . . . the first two men were level with him, now passing the doorway. In a moment the third would be passed and he would wait giving them a wide margin of clearance before leaving the doorway.

A film of perspiration, gathered despite the frost-cold air, trickled slowly down from his hair-line sliding into his eyes. Aware that any movement, even that of lifting a hand to wipe his eyes might give away his position he blinked rapidly. Damn! The moisture stung his eyes but worse it clouded his vision. Feeling the droplets gather again, beginning to follow the same course, he gave a quick jerk to his head the first move striking against a bell.

God Almighty! Zeph's breath snatched to a halt. He hadn't seen that in the dark . . . a bloody bell! He had rung somebody's death knell, Christ grant it wouldn't be his own!

All three stopped at the same moment.

Zeph's senses flared.

'He's in there . . . it 'as to be 'im.'

That was Tonks' voice, the nervous little Tonks. Zeph recognised the high-pitched tone. Little they might be but that makes them no less dangerous, poison comes in little bottles. The words his mother had often spoken came back to him now and he would heed their warning, Tonks would not be underestimated.

'Fetch 'im out,' Sol Burke's satisfied answer grated on the quiet night, 'fetch the bastard out. He be going to learn what 'appens to any bloke as makes off with Sol Burke's money, fetch the gypsy dog out 'ere!'

If they took him here in the doorway he would be finished. There was too little room to manoeuvre. Zeph assessed the situation, his brain working swiftly. If two came at him at once he stood no chance.

His own course of action determined with the thought he sprang from the shadows at the same time bringing the knife forward and upward, the movement slowing as it bit deep into flesh.

The scream of one man crashing against his ears he dropped low to his haunches, brilliant eyes fastened to the second figure as it drew back.

'Get 'im, get the bastard!'

Sol Burke had moved quickly, closing the distance between himself and the man still standing.

'He's got a bloody knife!' Danks' answer held a weight of fear. 'He's already stuck Tonksy, it ain't worth it Sol, it ain't worth getting a knife in your guts for a few shillin', I say we leaves it.'

'You leaves it now and one night you'll feel my knife in your guts.' Burke spat savagely. 'You knows I speaks no idle words, tonight might be the last you'll see of that gypsy but it won't be the last you'll see of Sol Burke.'

Crouched almost on his heels Zeph watched Danks turn his head to look at his companion then again to look at the other lying silent on the ground. That was his first mistake, taking his eyes away, his first and his last! Agile as any hunting cat Zeph launched himself into the air, the knife already finding its mark as his body bore the other man to the earth. Pulling the blade clear he plunged it into Danks' throat using the same moment to roll clear.

Now it was him and Burke. Zeph smiled as he hitched the handle of the knife more securely into the palm of his hand. He liked these odds better.

'Well?' He spoke softly as he leapt to his feet but the menace was heavy. 'Be you coming for the gypsy dog, or be you frightened of his bite?'

A few feet distant Sol Burke sniggered. 'Ain't no reason to be afeared of shit, it stinks but it can be cleared.'

'Like them two cleared it? Does it be that Sol Burke be no night soil man, or is it he be so much the coward he must send others to do his dirty work?'

Zeph's soft-spoken words were a direct taunt and the sharp hiss of breath that met them showed they had found their mark.

'I needs no man's 'elp to clear you into hell!' Sol Burke stepped forward, pausing as a knife blade glinted in the frosty light of the moon.

'I be glad to 'ear it. Wouldn't fancy a wait while you fetches some other poor bugger to fight for you, it be too cold a night.' Zeph lifted the knife holding it in front of him.

'It be warm where you be going.'

Sol Burke reached a hand into his jacket pocket, the explosion as he withdrew it rocking Zeph on his feet.

'Nobody walks away with Sol Burke's money.'

The barrel of the pistol gleamed as he aimed it again. 'I said I needed no man's 'elp to clear you into hell and that be where you're going.'

Pain such as he had never known burned in Zeph's chest but the knife in his hand remained steady.

'Ar, I reckon that be the way of it.' Beneath the shadows his mouth smiled but his eyes glittered their warning of death. 'And it be usual for Zeph Tullio to travel alone but this time I will make an exception.'

His arm absolutely still, only the wrist giving movement to the hand, he flicked the knife hearing the thud of it sinking into the other man's heart one second before the pistol fired again.

One foot dragging slowly behind the other Tamar walked away from the high-storied house. The answer there had been the same as at every other she had called at that day, we have no need of help. Pausing, she leaned against a railing, its decorative gold-painted tips rapidly losing their colour beneath the driving flakes of snow. She desperately needed to rest, to close her eyes if only for a few moments, but she had only to blink to see that ghastly scene again, the terrible scarred face smiling at her from a halo of fire. It had happened because of her, it had all been her fault.

A sob caught on her lips as she forced herself to move on. She had to find a place for the night or she could freeze to death.

Head bent before the increasing snow storm she

stumbled on. She must keep on the move, that much her brain told her but limbs almost paralysed from cold found it harder and harder to obey.

One last time, she must try one last time. Blinking snow from her lashes she glanced at a house stood alone at the end of a cul-de-sac. Large and square, tall windows closed off with curtains, it seemed to frown at her.

But she had to ask . . . and if they said no, if they too sent her away?

Trying to force the consequences from her mind she glanced at the highly polished door, its gleaming bell push not yet obliterated by snow. She could not go knocking on that door, that was not the entrance used by such as her. Turning away her eye caught a lighted window. She had not noticed the small gate set in the railings, or the short flight of steps leading down from the pavement. That must be the servants' entrance. Breathing a prayer she pushed open the gate.

'Employment . . . !'

The young woman who had opened the door to her knock rested both hands across the front of a frilled apron, its whiteness contrasting prettily against deep blue skirts and paler blue blouse.

'. . . you seem readier for the knacker's yard than you do for employment.'

Feeling the sting of yet another refusal bite into her throat, Tamar clenched her frozen fingers together. She wouldn't be able to walk much further, she hadn't the strength.

'Please, I will do anything.'

'The mistress isn't at 'ome and I can't set you up here off my own bat.'

Desperate at the thought of spending the night in the freezing cold of the streets Tamar begged. 'Please, if you can't give me work then might I shelter in an outhouse, it . . . it will only be for one night, I will be gone in the morning.'

The door already half closed the woman held it. Running a glance over the shivering girl, clothes soaked through, the wet shawl plastered to her head she seemed to be thinking quickly.

'Come in.' Pulling the door more widely open she stood aside for Tamar to step into the kitchen, inspecting her more closely beneath the light of several gas lamps. 'I could do with some help, but like I said the mistress don't be at home.'

The warmth of the kitchen melting flakes of snow caught on her skirts dripped tiny puddles at her feet. While those clinging to her shawl sent droplets coursing over her brow into her eyes and over her cheeks. The prayer more fervent in her heart Tamar brushed the moisture away.

Reaching a cloth from an airer strung above the large cooking range the woman held it out. 'Only the mistress can pay a wage, that means any work you do here would carry no payment other than board and keep.'

Board and keep! Tamar's spirit sang. Food and a bed, that was all she asked.

'And the work could be no more than a week or two at most,' the woman went on, 'the house and everything in it is to be sold, the mistress she be going abroad.'

Handing the cloth back Tamar felt the urge to say nothing of what she was doing here in this town, her reason for being in Bristol, but as soon as it came the feeling died away. She would not repay kindness with deceit. Honesty be the best policy had been her father's philosophy and she knew it was one she also must follow.

'Board and keep would be most acceptable and I would not shirk any work you gave me.' The words came firmly though her body trembled beneath its layer of sodden clothes. 'But before you offer it to me I would tell you why I came to Bristol, it could be that on hearing you will no longer wish me to be in this house.'

The cloth in her hand the woman stared at Tamar. The girl was soaked to the skin, looked as if the devil rode on her shoulders yet here she was speaking words that could have her thrown right back on the streets. Was it honesty or just plain stupidity? Nobody could be that daft! Flinging the cloth back over the airing rail she turned again to the half-frozen girl. It had to be honesty.

'You can tell me later, first you have to get out of those wet things and into some dry ones. Come you over to the fire while I see what I can find you out to wear while your own be drying.'

Watching the woman leave the kitchen Tamar felt a sharp tug at her nerves. This was too close to what had happened a few hours ago, a woman had offered a meal and a bed, but that was not all that she had in mind. Hadn't she learned anything from what had gone on in that house . . . was she willing to take the same risk again?

Pulling the shawl closer about her she turned towards the door that led to the street.

Lying on the bunk of his comfortable cabin, Nathan Burford stared at the ceiling. He had been restless since the *Verity* had left Bristol docks, unable to sleep yet a slight irritation gnawing at him whenever he had to leave his cabin. It could not be the prospect of another long voyage, the sea had given him his only true feeling of comfort since . . .

But he had vowed never to think of that. He closed his eyes trying to ban the memories, memories that brought shame and guilt, but try as he might they rose accusingly, staring at him, ghosts of yesterday, spectres of the past.

They had been engaged to be married, Louise and he. In a week they would be man and wife. Then he had caught them together, his brother Aiden and Louise locked in each other's arms. He had refused to listen when they tried to tell him they had loved each other for months, had tried to deny it, not seeing each other for weeks at a time but their love had simply grown the stronger.

Remembering his own fury he threw an arm over his face pressing it hard on his eyelids trying to drive away the picture beneath them, but still the faces stared back at him, faces that pleaded for understanding.

But he had not listened. He would not be made a fool of in front of their friends, the marriage would go ahead as planned, Louise would become his wife. He had made the statement flatly then turned and left them there; no show of emotion, none of the hurt fiancé, just a cold statement of fact.

Why? The sorrowful stare of his brother's eyes seemed to ask the question. Why no feeling of hurt or even of resentment?

Drawing a long breath Nathan faced the answer he had known five years before and still the owning of it lanced him like a surgeon's knife.

Because there had been none! He released the breath slowly. There had been no emotion, no feeling of bruised love because there *was* no love. He was not in love with Louise but he was in love with his own pride. That must not be tumbled, the world would not see him rejected for another man, not even his own brother.

They had left whilst he was on business to Gloucester. Eloped on a ship out of Bristol. Ten days later had come the news. The merchantman *Morning Star* had gone down in the Atlantic, no survivors had been found.

His brother and Louise had taken passage on that boat, both had lost their lives, and for what? For the sake of another man's pride. *He* had been his brother's executioner, except for pride Aiden and Louise would be alive today. And that was his guilt, guilt he would carry the rest of his life. He had left his home in Clifton the same day that terrible news had been brought to him. He had walked away from the beautiful Regency house where he and Aiden had been born and had never been back. Money was paid yearly for its upkeep but he had never been able to face going back. The *Verity* had become his home and he would never have any other.

It had taken a long time but he had eventually become settled, the pain of the couple's death, although always with him, becoming bearable, the restlessness fading to a quiet acceptance. So why its recurrence? Lowering his arm he opened his eyes to stare again at the ceiling. Why now after so long had the restlessness and irritation that had plagued him in those dreadful months following his brother's death returned to torment him again?

Swinging from the bunk he left the cabin climbing the companionway that gave on to the deck. Holding his balance easily despite the push of a strong wind he walked aft to stand at the ship's rail. Eyes half closed against driving flakes of snow he stared back along the line of white wake. The coast was long fallen behind, lost in the grey folds of sea and sky.

Suddenly he wanted to be back, back in Bristol, in the docks where he had met . . .

Was that the reason? Was that the reason he had thought so often of the girl he had met on the dock, the reason her face had haunted him?

The rush of wind-whipped waves sent spray flying high over the deck. Nathan blinked as it mixed with snowflakes stinging his eyes but still he stared land-ward.

Had fate tried to give him a chance at reparation? He could never completely exonerate himself but by helping that girl he might have righted a little of the wrong he had done.

Her plight had sounded so similar to his own; she had lost a brother who it appeared deserved no real blame just as Aiden had deserved none, a man could not be blamed for falling in love. Her brother had been forced from the country by the law, Aiden had been forced to leave because of his brother's pride. He had searched for Aiden and Louise, enquiring in every port he made call, having others enquire in those he did not, never believing his brother dead. But five years of search had brought no result and no peace. Would that girl search as long? She would never get to Australia but she might remain in Bristol enquiring of every boat that put in there.

Gazing out over the wind-tossed water it seemed among the spray the sea mist gathered itself, taking the shape of a beautiful face, a face whose lovely eyes pleaded, the face of the girl on the dock.

Had fate offered him a second chance and had he turned his back on it? But he had made enquiry, found out for her where the lad was bound, he could have done no more.

Before him the mist cleared taking the image with it but not before he saw again the look of pleading in those soft eyes.

What he told himself was not true. It was simply a

way of easing his own conscience as he had in the first days of his brother's disappearance, a self-justification. The real truth was he could have done more. He knew many seamen that sailed the Australia route, he could have asked them to watch for the boy, bring him word if they saw or heard of him so he could inform the girl; more than that he could have paid her passage, made it possible for her to follow after him . . .

Snow blinding his gaze Nathan turned toward the forecastle. When he returned to Bristol he would find her, do all he could to reunite her with her brother. Maybe that way he would find peace.

Chapter Fourteen

'These should fit . . .'

Coming back into the kitchen the woman halted. Tamar was already at the door that gave on to the street.

'. . . don't let me stop you if you want to go.' The woman dropped the clothes she was carrying on to a chair. 'The way be clear, there's only me in the house and as you see I've no wish to hold you; though this I will say, it be plain you must have suffered some nasty shock for you to be willing to face the storm that be brewing out there. It be a shock I can most likely guess at for I've heard the rumours that run around the docks. There be none of that here but then you can't be expected to believe that so take a bite of bread and ham with you and be away, only take care which doorway you chooses to sleep in.'

Was she being unfair to the woman? Unsure, Tamar turned to face her. Should she be judged against another woman's standards? As she watched the woman sliced a warm crusty loaf and spread it thickly with pale creamy butter. Placing two thick slices of juicy ham between she dropped the sandwich into a coarse brown paper bag that had once held lentils. Holding it out to Tamar, she smiled.

'There you be, that will keep the worms away 'til morning, and take my advice, as soon as you find a place to pass the night get yourself out of them wet clothes and into these.' She picked up the clothing she had dropped to the chair. 'Go on, take 'em, mistress don't want them and they be a pinch tight for me.'

Catching the hint of embarrassment in Tamar's eyes she turned to the shining black range busying herself with a kettle, steam rattling its lid.

'You don't have to feel bad about accepting them clothes, they will only go to the ragman's cart so you be robbing nobody save him and he'll never miss what they might bring, and even if he did it would serve him right, bloody old miser! He would give a babby a bladder with a hole in it if the mother didn't stand and watch him.'

'It is not the clothes has me feeling bad.' Tamar answered her cheeks pink. 'It is me, I . . . I should not distrust as I do.'

Remaining busy with kettle and teapot the woman did not turn around.

'Can I ask one question? Was it Lena Sampson's house you slept in last night?'

Hearing Tamar's swift intake of breath she went on.

'There be no need of answering, you've given that already though there was no need of it. I guessed it when first I offered you a meal and a bed, that makes your fears reason enough. She were a bad bundle were Lena Sampson, that fire has left Bristol a cleaner place for taking her.'

Teapot in hand the woman turned. 'Fire,' she nodded, 'not long after first light so I hear, the house went up in flames, nothing left of it nor of the two women who lived there, least not enough so as you would want to look at.'

'Corrie Fletcher is dead?' Tamar stared at the woman pouring tea into platter cups.

'She the one who got you away?' The dark head nodded. 'Well, that at least will count in her favour at the Judgement.'

'She . . . she told me to leave the house, to get away before Trader East . . .'

'I knows of Trader East!' The woman set the teapot aside with a thud, her face drawn into tight disgust. 'The whole dockyard knows of him and his filthy trade but nobody ain't ever caught him at it. I says it be a mortal pity nobody has set fire to him!'

Corrie was dead! Tamar's hands trembled. The poor scarred woman had saved her life only to take her own.

'I know what you be thinking. But I've been there when Corrie Fletcher has walked the street, heard the taunts of kids, the jibes and whispers of men and women who should have known better.' Taking the beaded cover from a jug taken from the larder the woman added milk to the cups. 'It be hard to say but to my mind the woman be better off dead; it was no life the one she led.'

'To have the same existence I've had since Lena Sampson gave me this . . .'

Staring at the woman yet not seeing her, Tamar listened to the words rushing into her mind.

*'Death will put an end to that whip . . . stop the rise and
fall of it . . .'*

A sob tumbling from her lips she dropped the food
and clothing, pressing both hands to her face.

'It were what she wanted, remember that.' The
woman was at her side a comforting arm about her
shoulders. 'Corrie Fletcher saved you from Trader
East then took her own release. She wanted free of the
torment that was her life. Try to understand and offer
a prayer then let her soul rest, don't plague it with
your tears.'

Pressing Tamar to a chair set beside a table covered
with a spotless cloth she placed one of the cups in front
of her before sitting down and drinking from the
other. Waiting for the spasm of tears to pass she spoke
gently.

'Drink that down while it be hot then if you still
wants to leave I'll bid you goodnight, though I say
before God, if it be you stay there will be none of the
likes of Lena Sampson will touch you.'

Shock and weariness draining the last of the
strength from her limbs Tamar stared at the white
cloth. She could not go on, she could not face the
bitter cold of the streets, run the gauntlet of the docks
at night, but staying here was also a risk.

Her own drink finished the woman carried teapot
and cup to the scullery. Returning she placed the
crockery on a large plain wooden dresser then looked
at the girl who had not moved a muscle.

'I know the thoughts you be having,' she said
kindly, 'and I know no words of mine can rid you

of them, but if you look you will see the door that gives on to the rest of the house has a bolt on this side as does the door to the street. If you want to bide here in the kitchen then you can slide the bolts across, can't nobody come in after that, not 'til you takes off the bolts.'

Tears not yet gone from her eyes Tamar lifted her glance.

Trust had to begin again somewhere, she had to have faith in someone. Her mouth trembling, she looked at the woman.

'Thank you,' she murmured, 'I . . . I would like to stay.'

All she had been told of the house being empty except for the woman who had taken her in had proved to be fact. Tamar placed the gown she had folded into the large travelling trunk. It had taken days for her nerves to quieten, jumping at her own shadow, always ready to dash for the street, but the woman had gone quietly about the business of closing the house, leaving her to work in the kitchen, to sleep at night the bolts shot into place.

'What do you think to this?'

Tamar glanced up pursing her lips as she looked at the gown of ruby velvet held for her inspection. Her nose wrinkling disapproval she shook her head.

'You are right,' the dress was dropped, 'a white veil over this and the guests would take me for Santa Claus.'

Joining in the laughter Tamar thanked her stars she had trusted Amy Williams, feeling a touch of guilt for the nights she had spent behind the locked kitchen door.

Amy had made no comment of that, simply wishing her goodnight as she left her alone. But that was over now, Amy had given her a small room on the same floor as her own.

Smiling at her now Tamar wondered how, the first night they had met, she could have taken Amy for anything other than the bubbly laughing-eyed girl cavorting before her a green taffeta gown held beneath her chin.

No? The wide blue eyes sparkled the question, the pretty mouth smiling at Tamar's unspoken answer.

She was to be married in a month's time, she had confided happily and was choosing a dress from her mistress's well stocked wardrobe.

Tamar had remarked on the kindness of Amy's mistress in allowing her to select a dress for her wedding but the girl had grinned mischievously admitting in a conspiratorial whisper, 'mistress don't know, besides she'll never miss one among this lot.'

It had seemed a trifle dishonest to Tamar, but Amy had dismissed it with a toss of her sherry-coloured hair.

'Why sell it to the ragman when I can make a wedding gown of it? He pays no more than a few pennies at most.'

Folding the green gown Amy tossed aside, Tamar

stroked a hand over the smooth shining cloth. She had often dreamed of velvets and silks, wondering how they must feel against the skin, but even in dreams it had never felt as soft as it did now. It must be wonderful to be able to dress in clothes like these. Placing it carefully with the others packed for dispatch she looked up as Amy giggled again.

Holding a bead-encrusted gown against her body the girl pranced and turned, the billowy folds of gossamer tulle spreading a pale pink cloud.

'What about this then?' She whirled. 'My Will would think I'd pinched it off the Princess of Wales herself, should I go up the aisle dressed in this.'

As quickly as the words were out Amy dropped the gown, her hands reaching out to Tamar.

'I'm sorry, I didn't mean . . . Oh Lord, me and my big mouth!'

Taking the hands outstretched to her Tamar smiled into the girl's stricken face. The words had bubbled out like the laughter bubbled, there was no snideness behind them, no hidden snub. She had shown real sympathy when hearing of Benjie's misfortune, dismissing the idea that because of it Tamar's presence in the house might be unwelcome.

'It be none of your doing.' Amy had told her. 'I only wish I could be of help, but there's no way I knows of getting you to Australia.'

But Amy had helped, not only in providing her with a place to eat and sleep but with her laughter and easy spirit.

'No way I know of getting you to Australia . . .'

Repeating her words Amy dropped the gown, her laughing eyes holding a serious question. Looking steadily at Tamar she put the look into words.

'. . . truthfully, how bad do you want to follow after your brother?'

How badly? Tamar's throat tightened as in her mind she remembered Benjie's frightened cry.

'Don't leave me Tam . . .'

Her eyes clouding she answered. 'If I could walk there I would.'

Extricating herself from the flood of pink tulle and catching Tamar's hand Amy started from the room. Once in the kitchen she smiled.

'You and me Tamar Hallam, are going to have ourselves a cup of tea and a serious talk. You make the tea while I fetch the cake.'

Minutes later watching the other girl spoon sugar into her cup as she bit into a thick slice of sultana cake Tamar pulled a wry face.

'Those gowns already need to be let out if you are to wear them . . .'

'Forget the gowns,' Amy said, her mouth full of cake. 'They never will fit me, trying them on was wishful thinking; beside I have other plans for them and for you if you be willing.'

Swallowing the last of her cake Amy went on. 'We have known each other less than two weeks but you must know I've told you nothing but truth.'

'Of course,' Tamar frowned, unsure of what Amy was about to say.

'Then trust me that what I be about to suggest be only with the thought of helping you find your brother.'

'Find Benjie . . . but how?'

'Drink your tea and listen.' Amy's vivid blue eyes were alight with enthusiasm. 'Don't interrupt 'til I be finished. I told you that the mistress be going abroad but I didn't say why. Her business be her own was what I told myself, but now I shall tell you. Three years ago the master, Edmond Bancroft, left England for the purpose of business. Least that was the story he gave to his wife. In all that time he has sent her no word nor a penny piece to live on. That is the reason for her leaving, she wants to search for him and it has to be now before the last of her money is gone. I am to accompany her.'

'But how can your going with your mistress help me find my brother?' Tamar asked confused.

'I said to listen 'til I were finished.' Amy sipped from her cup before adding. 'It can help because I don't be going. My Will has asked me to marry him and that be what I'm going to do; so you see you could go in my place.'

'How!' Tamar's exclamation was part laugh part incredulity. 'Your mistress would never allow . . .'

'My mistress need not know. Listen to me Tamar, the woman is ill she lies for days in a darkened room. Even now she is at Bath hoping the waters there will hold a cure. But there is no cure for the wasting disease. It has been arranged she will not come back to this house but go directly on board ship, and if my guess be correct she will be too sick to care who it is that tends her.'

It was a wild suggestion, mad! The woman would have to be sick indeed to accept what Amy suggested. Tamar shook her head.

'What if you are wrong, what if your mistress does not accept me.'

'Then she will travel without a maid, without a woman to nurse her when the sickness is bad. No, Odile Bancroft will not do that nor will she change her plans and wait until some other maid be found. She knows, deep in her heart, that she don't have the time to spare.'

'She is not going to die?' Tamar's incredulity changed swiftly into pity.

'Not 'til her time be due, that be so for all of us, ain't nothing can change that.' Amy's smile was philosophical. 'So it be up to each to make the best of their time while they be here, that's why I be marrying my Will and it be why you must decide whether wanting to find your brother be strong enough reason to take my place aboard that ship, but you need decide soon for the *Porpoise* sails in a week's time and passage has to be booked.'

'I can't.' Tamar shook her head. 'Even should your mistress accept me in place of you I cannot go with her. Benjie has been taken to Australia, that is where I must go.'

'Exactly.' Amy's eyes shone. 'And that is where the *Porpoise* is going.'

She could sail to Australia! Stunned, Tamar could

only stare at the other girl's smiling face. In a week she could be following Benjie, she would be with him.

'Isn't it a marvellous idea? This way we all get what we want. It isn't as though we intend harm to Odile Bancroft, just the opposite, all you have to do is act as maid until the voyage be over, it won't be strenuous work for like I said she keeps to her bed most of the time. Then once you arrives and she goes with her husband you will be free to go looking for your brother.'

It all sounded simple enough. More than that it sounded like a godsend. How else might she ever reach that country?

Tamar tried to rally the thoughts rocketing through her mind. Nathan Burford had talked of its being on the far side of the world, so far she may never have another chance of reaching it. But she knew nothing of being a lady's maid.

Saying the last out loud she watched the airy sweep of Amy's hand. Over the two weeks she had spent at this house she had become used to the other girl's easy dismissal of a problem.

'There be nothing to know, except how to speak respectful and you speaks that way natural, that were what led me to take you in that first night; anything else I can teach you. So . . . what do you say?'

Her smile hesitant, Tamar looked at the woman who had befriended her, who still seemed only to want to help her. 'Do you think I can do it?'

'I *know* you can.' Amy was on her feet grabbing Tamar's hands and whirling her about the kitchen. 'And we are going to start right now.'

'Injured in a fight you say?'

Philip Amory twiddled with the gold watch in his waistcoat pocket.

'Yes sir, four of them in a scrap outside of the Feathers, that be the public house . . . seems they had been playing cards and drinking in there earlier.'

'Something more than a scrap, Inspector; more of a drunken brawl one might say.'

'You might sir.' The man dressed in neat dark suit, a heavily starched collar of a white shirt pressed uncomfortably about a heavy neck, nodded agreement.

'So might he, you did say the fellow had been shot?'

'I did Mr Amory.' The police inspector touched a finger to the wealth of grey side whiskers adorning his sharply pointed jaw. 'Twice to be exact . . . I means he had been shot twice sir, not that I had told you twice . . .'

'Precisely.' Philip Amory's fingers worried at the watch. 'Please go on.'

Accepting a cigar from the box held out to him the inspector sniffed it appreciatively before placing it in his pocket. 'I'll keep it 'til I be off duty, that's if it's all the same to you.'

Nodding, Philip closed the box and waited. He had been told he might be able to assist the police in an enquiry when a constable had called to ask if he was willing to agree to an interview, but as yet he had no idea of the nature of the object of that request.

'There were four of them.' The inspector took up his explanation again. 'Three dead from knife wounds, one had the weapon still stuck in his heart, nasty business sir, nasty business.' The police inspector shook his head. 'The other, the man still alive had two bullets in him, one in the shoulder the other in the chest.'

'Is he still alive?'

'He is Mr Amory, though whether he will last be another question altogether. That be why I must ask if you would consent to coming to see this man.'

His fingers leaving the watch, Philip frowned. 'Come to see him?'

'If you wouldn't mind, sir.'

'But I do mind.' The answer sharp, Philip Amory stared at the man sat a little way from his desk. 'Are you implying I have something to do with this fellow?'

The inspector pulled at his whiskers. Amory was an important name in Birmingham, it wouldn't do to antagonise him, yet questions had to be asked.

'I had no intention of implying any such, but I had hoped you could perhaps identify the man. You see sir, he has so far refused to give his name.'

Rising to his feet Philip Amory looked coldly at the man who for some reason thought him to know something of a man shot almost to death.

His tone tight as his mouth he snapped, 'What gives you to think I can put a name to him; why come to me at all?'

'This, sir.'

Reaching into the pocket of his jacket the inspector laid a piece of brown paper on the desk.

His glance falling on the label neatly written in copperplate, Philip Amory frowned.

'Where did you get this?'

'Do you recognise it, Mr Amory?'

'Of course I do!' Philip snapped again. 'It is one of my labels, it says so here.' He jabbed a finger at the paper. 'The question is how did you come by it?'

'My questions first sir, if you don't mind.'

The authority in the policeman's voice was quiet but Philip recognised it. He also recognised the man would not put his employment on the line by questioning one of the city's more prominent businessmen were it not of real necessity. Holding his irritation in check he nodded.

Fingering his whiskers again the inspector watched the other man closely.

'Was something mislaid from your establishment some weeks ago sir, something of value?'

'Everything made at my establishment is valuable, they are made of gold; and if you mean stolen then say stolen!' Philip took out the pocket watch turning it over several times before returning it.

'Very well sir . . . stolen.' The inspector inclined his head. 'Was something stolen?'

Crossing to stand before the fire Philip stood with his back to the blue-tipped flames. That necklace had been wrapped in paper such as that, there had been nothing to mark it as special, nothing that set it apart from the other packages in the errand boy's basket; could it be this paper that had enfolded those fabulous gems?

'Yes.' He stared at the rug beneath his feet. 'Yes, there was something stolen; a necklace, a very costly necklace. One specially designed and created for Her Royal Highness the Princess of Wales. It was a diamond collet riviere . . .'

'Could you explain that more in layman's terms Mr Amory, I'm afraid I can't follow the goldsmith's language.'

'Of course. It is a necklace with each of the diamonds set in coronet-shaped claws. The stones increase in size as they come gradually to the largest of all, the centre stone. These stones are all flawless and as perfect a match as we could find; the whole thing is priceless.'

Glancing at the black bowler hat resting on his knee the inspector was silent as if digesting the information he had just been given. Then, looking up his glance gave away none of the thoughts behind it.

'You say the trinket that was stolen was priceless and yet it was sent through the streets in a basket pushed by an errand boy.'

Disbelief or sarcasm? Philip Amory was not certain of what he heard underlying the man's words but he felt the irritation of it. Allowing every particle of his sudden annoyance to reflect in his answer he looked up from the rug to stare coldly at the man seated in his study.

'First of all Inspector, it is no trinket. That necklace was especially designed and crafted for the future queen of England, the gold alone is worth a small fortune disregarding the diamonds. It is, and will most definitely remain, one of a kind. No craftsman in Hockley would set his hand to making another and a copy made anywhere else can never imitate their skills. It would be just that, a copy, and no doubt a poor one! As for it being transported in an errand boy's basket, that is the usual practice of the Gold Quarter, to have it delivered any other way would have served only to draw attention to it.'

'This errand boy, can you tell me his name?'

Irritation becoming anger, Philip released a breath short and sharp between his teeth.

'Surely you ascertained that before coming here. The case must have been recorded, and all details were given at the time!'

'The boy's name sir, if you please.'

The even calm of the policeman's reply curdling his irascibility Philip kicked at a log burning in the grate, sending a shower of brilliant sparks shooting into the chimney.

'His name is Benjie . . . Benjamin Hallam. He is thirteen years old. He has a sister Tamar Hallam, she I believe is eighteen years old. The boy was tried on a charge of theft and murder at Stafford Crown Court. A verdict of not proven was returned on the charge of murder but the charge of theft stood. He is to serve thirty years of hard labour unless . . .'

Looking up sharply Philip Amory glanced at the crumpled brown paper still lying on his desk. Then looking at the inspector he went on.

'. . . unless you have recovered that necklace. Is that it Inspector, have you found the Alexandra Stone? Have you, Inspector?' Philip asked anxiously. 'Have you recovered that necklace? If so the Hallam boy must be set free.'

'It is not quite so easy as that Mr Amory sir . . .'

The police inspector flicked an imaginary hair from his immaculately brushed bowler hat.

'. . . I did not say that there paper had anything wrapped in it, but supposing it did hold what you seems to think it might the lad can't be let go just like that. Just because the goods weren't found on his person don't mean he didn't steal them in the first place; could be he had an accomplice who he passed them on to . . . maybe his sister . . .'

'Rubbish!' Philip's hard held temper exploded. 'That girl had nothing to do with it.'

'Nothing that came out at the trial, but the fact remains the girl is no longer here in Hockley, that she left immediately the boy was sent to Stafford and has not returned since; therefore the suspicion must remain that the stolen property was taken by her to some other person who would pay for it and take it off her hands.'

'Suspicion!' Philip glared. 'Maybe suspicion must remain but take care it remains unspoken outside of this room Inspector, there are such charges as defamation of character and I would be prepared to see such a charge brought against your department. Those young people have suffered enough.'

Very much the gallant goldsmith! Police Inspector Titus Simeon smiled inwardly. Would he have been so quick to defend had there been no girl involved? Could the employer be interested in his employee in ways other than her work in his workshop?

'Your idea of civic duty is to be commended, the girl is fortunate in her employer.'

Philip saw the clearly defined sarcasm in the eyes returning his stare. Irritation flaring he snatched the watch from his pocket turning it furiously between his fingers.

'You came here to ask if I could identify a man you have in your custody, a man I have no doubt was found with that paper in his possession. That I trust is the only cause of your reasoning though quite why that should be is beyond my own; I do not rate thieves and killers among my associates.'

'There was no such thought behind our contacting you sir, but please realise even the most unlikely lead must be investigated.' Encased by whiskers the inspector's fox-like jaw tightened. 'However, if you feel you cannot see the man then perhaps you would allow one of your workmen to do the job instead.'

Furiously calm Philip Amory glared at his visitor. 'Do I take that to imply that my employees also are deemed to mix with thieves and murderers?'

Bowler hat in hand Titus Simeon stood up. The man glaring at him was a prominent figure but then when had that deterred him from an investigation.

Cynicism now openly apparent both in look and tone he answered quietly.

'You are free to imply whatever you wish, just as I am free to imply your answers, or evasions, in the same way. Thank you for seeing me Mr Amory, I will say good evening to you.'

'Tomorrow at eleven, the station at Hockley Brook!'

Turning to leave, the inspector looked across his shoulder as the words rapped at his back.

'Eleven o'clock Mr Amory.' He set the bowler on his head giving it a tap. 'At *Edgbaston* station . . . if you don't mind.'

Chapter Fifteen

'That isn't a soup spoon, it's a dessert spoon and this is a cake fork. Give the mistress that to eat her spuds with and she be like to take a fit of the hab dabs.' Amy laughed as she rearranged cutlery Tamar had set on the dining table.

'Amy, I am never going to remember.' Tamar looked dejectedly at the display of china stands and dishes. She had never thought a meal could require so many; and the array of knives and forks! Folk in Hockley only ever used one, in fact many used their fingers.

'Of course you will remember.' Amy glanced at the bemused face. 'You've only been at the learning of it a few days, you can't expect to grasp everything at one go.'

'I didn't think being a lady's maid would include having to know how to lay a dinner table.'

'Nor it don't.' Amy returned briskly. 'But you need to know how to set out a tray or at least a table setting for one, for like as not the mistress will take most of her meals in bed or in her cabin and for that you must have knowledge of which dish to use and which utensils to set out. But let's forget that for now, let's go sort out some more of the dresses she be wanting and those she don't.'

Full of misgivings about the whole thing Tamar followed the other girl up the curved stairway and along a corridor, its furniture shrouded in dust-sheets to the room usually occupied by Odile Bancroft.

Since the inception of the plan for her to replace Amy as lady's maid the girl had told her a great deal about the unfortunate mistress. It seemed she had often been left alone, her husband spending weeks at a time in London or some other distant city. Even when he was here in Bristol he spent every night away from the house, not returning until well after dawn and sometimes not even then.

That, Amy declared, was what had brought on her mistress's illness, the disease that was slowly wasting her body, the unhappiness of having an uncaring husband, one who preferred to spend his time in any house other than his own. And with any woman other than his wife, she had added darkly. Then, seeing Tamar's questioning look had gone on. Being a lady's maid has its advantages, one of them being you get to become privy to a lot of things the nobs think you don't know, and I heard plenty concerning Edmond Bancroft and his doings; gambling and womanising were all he were interested in, that and his wife's money! Amy had spat deprecatingly on the last. Then when he knew it to be almost gone he ups and sails off with his latest doxy on his arm. Business, he told his wife, well it were business alright, dirty business. The callous swine sold everything of value in the house and buggered off with the proceeds! Not a penny did he give to the mistress . . . and that three year ago.

'Here, try this on.'

A gown pushed into her hands broke the thoughts filling her mind.

'That one should suit you, your colouring is perfect for that shade of green. Go on, try it, you be the same size as the mistress when I first came here.'

'No.' Tamar held the gown away from her. 'It is not right, we . . . I should not . . .'

'Oh, stop being so strait-laced, I swear a corset couldn't be much tighter strung!' Amy grabbed the gown. 'Get them skirts and blouse off and try this, what harm will it do, ain't as if you be going to keep it.'

Fastening the row of tiny buttons that reached a line to the waist at the back of the dress, Amy looked at the face reflected in the dressing mirror. Eyes wide and green as summer grass stared out of a delicate waif-like face, while above them gently arched brows painted a dark line on clear magnolia skin. Tamar Hallam had all the hallmarks of beauty, with that thick auburn hair . . .

The idea coming quickly Amy grabbed the other girl's hand pulling her over to the dressing table.

'Sit there,' she ordered curtly, pressing Tamar to the stool, 'and watch.'

'What are you doing?' Tamar tried to prevent the pins being taken out of her hair but Amy brushed her hands brusquely aside.

Letting the rich folds of hair fall about Tamar's shoulders, Amy grinned delightedly.

'A lady's maid must know not only how to dress her mistress but how to complete her toilette. Have you ever used cosmetics?'

Tamar shook her head.

Amy took up a small jar from among several on the dressing table screwing off the gilt lid. 'Nothing to it, a dab of cream and a touch of rouge.'

'But surely your mistress doesn't . . . I mean . . . I thought just women of the streets painted their faces.'

'Don't you believe it.' Amy changed one pot for another tracing a feather touch of pink over each cheek-bone.

'But Vinny says only loose women paint their faces.'

'Your Vinny Marsh might be an expert at gold finishing but she doesn't know everything. The sort of women she talked about do paint their faces and most of 'em overdoes it. But used properly cosmetics can enhance a woman's looks. There,' she stepped back, 'what do you think?'

Glancing in the mirror Tamar caught her breath. That reflection . . . it could not be her! A slight shadow of pink highlighted the contours of her cheeks, the shape of her eyebrows was accentuated by the touch of a beauty stick while her mouth gleamed soft and supple with lip rouge.

'Well?' Amy's grin was wide.

'I can't believe it.' Tamar continued to stare. 'I can't believe that is me!'

'That is only half. Now we start on the hair.'

Grabbing a brush Amy drew it deftly through the folds resting on Tamar's shoulders, then with quick sure movements piled it high, securing its weight with pins – each adorned with a glittering green stone – before teasing strands into a line of soft curls fringing the heart-shaped face.

'There, all done.'

Looking at the face staring back at her Tamar could only gasp.

'I know.' Amy laughed delightedly. 'You're beautiful.'

Beautiful! Tamar shifted her glance to the smiling face watching over her shoulder and in that instant it seemed to change to another that had looked at her as intently, a face edged with a thin line of dark beard. Had Nathan Burford thought her beautiful?

'I am sorry I cannot help you. I do not know the man.'

Philip Amory turned away from the door with its tiny glass-paned window.

'He is not one of my employees and I do not recall ever having seen him, but then it is not my practice to frequent the local taverns.'

Titus Simeon nodded as he accompanied the goldsmith from the room. 'It was worth a try sir. Thank you for giving us your time.'

His aggravation of the previous evening sated, Philip Amory paused. With his label on that wrapping paper it was to be expected the police would call on him, also asking him to view the man held in their custody was not extraordinary, chances were the fellow could have been an employee.

'A pity my visit brought no positive result. However, as you remarked last evening, perhaps one of my workmen might recognise him. The Gold Quarter is a close-knit community, if the man you are holding has his home there then it would be known to the others. I will send Cal Perry along, he is chargehand at Amory's and if that fellow in there belongs in Hockley then Cal Perry will know of him.'

The police inspector nodded briefly. 'That would be most helpful, Mr Amory.'

'In the meantime what of the boy, what of Benjie Hallam? If the necklace has been recovered then you have the true culprit locked in that cell. The boy must be reprieved at once.'

Watching the other man draw on a beaver-lined glove Titus Simeon led the way from the cell built at the rear of Edgbaston Police Station.

'Things are not quite that simple . . .'

'What is not simple?' Philip Amory looked at him sharply. 'You have the real thief.'

Coming into the one room that was the body of the station Titus Simeon glared at a young constable who turned swiftly to the papers piled on a tall desk.

'We have a man who may have been found to be in possession of stolen goods,' he answered levelly, 'that does not prove him to be the initial thief. He may be an accomplice of Hallam, in which case the boy remains guilty and will serve his sentence; until we can ascertain how the stolen property was come by then things must remain as they are.'

Smoothing the gloves separately over each finger Philip took up the silk top hat he had laid aside on entering the police station.

'And once that man confesses?'

'*If* he confesses.' Titus Simeon emphasised the word.

'But he is guilty man, just look at the fellow!'

Guilty because of his appearance or because you want him to be? Why be so bothered about the boy unless the sister has taken your fancy? The thought raising an inward smile the inspector covered it by raising a hand to his whiskers.

'As I said, Mr Amory. If he confesses, or if evidence is found to prove him guilty or that shows Hallam to be innocent, then the boy will be brought back.'

Beneath the top hat Philip Amory's face took on a questioning look. 'Brought back? Brought back from where?'

'Australia sir. The boy chose to serve his sentence in Australia.'

'Australia!'

Philip Amory stopped short a look of incredulity sweeping the former question from his eyes.

'You mean the boy has been transported? That procedure was ended some time ago, the practice is no longer legal!'

'I did not say he was transported.' Titus Simeon noted the anger behind the incredulity. 'However, if the convicted person chooses to serve out their sentence in one of Her Majesty's colonies . . .'

'One of Her Majesty's colonies!' Philip Amory made no effort to hide the scorn in his reply. 'That was a choice given to a boy who can have no idea of the reality behind it, no possible knowledge of the distance between that country and his home. Just as he can have no true concept of how long thirty years can prove to be, a child to whom next week can be a lifetime away. How can this be justice! The practice is nothing short of revolting! I shall have words to say about this when next I speak to the city's representative in parliament.'

His sideways glance once more reminding the constable that his nose should be in the papers he was holding rather than in the business of his superior the inspector cleared his throat.

'You must do as conscience directs sir, same as others of us does as duty directs.'

'But how your duty directed you to discovering that necklace . . . you have recovered it?'

'That too remains to be seen sir. We do have a certain property in our possession which I will ask you to look at. However, I must inform you that others of your associates might also be asked the same.'

'And if it proves to be the Alexandra Stone?'

'Then it will be returned to its rightful owner.'

'And the boy, will he be returned to England?'

Uncomfortable beneath the goldsmith's stare the inspector took refuge in pulling his whiskers.

'As I have said Mr Amory, the lad's innocence must be proved beyond all shadow of doubt, the justices would have to be completely certain he had no hand in that robbery, he would need to be exonerated totally before they would agree to his being returned. That might be achieved when that fellow in the cells decides to tell his part in the affair, that is if he talks at all; or even if he recovers consciousness. Either way it looks likely to be a long drawn out process, Australia isn't exactly next door.'

Nor would the wheels of justice grind any the quicker because of a young boy. Talk to a Member of Parliament or not Benjamin Hallam would not be like to see these shores again for many a moon.

Adjusting the beaver collar of his overcoat Philip Amory nodded briefly before leaving the police station. Climbing into his carriage he leaned back as his coachman took up the rein.

It might be just as many moons before Tamar Hallam returned to Hockley.

Tomorrow Odile Bancroft would be returning to Bristol. Nerves banishing any attempt at sleep Tamar stared at the shadowed ceiling of the small bedroom. Amy was convinced their changing places would work but with every thought of it her own heart missed its beat. There was more, much more, to being a lady's maid than was obvious, and with the illness Amy said the woman suffered.

Tamar turned restlessly. She had never nursed anything more serious than a head cold, Benjie had fallen into the brook . . .

Benjie!.Her thoughts took a new turn. She had to go through with this for his sake, she could not leave him to live his life in a strange country, among people he did not know. If living a lie, if deceiving that woman was what it took to get her to her brother then, God forgive her, that was what she would do.

'I will do my best . . .' she whispered into the darkness '. . . I will look after her I promise, do whatever she asks, only please, please don't let her refuse to take me.'

Maybe she should tell Amy's mistress everything, tell the reason she so desperately wanted to get to Australia and ask her openly to give her the other girl's position as lady's maid. And if she refused?

The breath in Tamar's lungs tightened.

If Odile Bancroft refused then how else would she ever get to that country?

The other side of the world. That was what Nathan Burford had said. How many miles was that, how many days, and how could she ever earn enough money to take herself there?

Who had really stolen that necklace, who could have been callous enough to place the blame on a young boy?

Her mind turned this way and then that adding to the anxiety of the coming prospect of meeting Odile Bancroft.

She had asked the Mullin family to try to get word of her to Vinny as they passed through Birmingham. They had been so kind to her, as Vinny had been to her and Benjie. She wanted Vinny to know she was alright, that she was carrying on the search until she found her brother.

Australia! Tamar stared into the darkness imagining the look on the woman's face as she heard of the intention. Vinny would shake her head slowly, pull a wry face and declare, 'The wench must be ninepence short of a shillin'! How on earth does her expect to get herself clear across the sea? Bloody daft idea if you asks me!'

Vinny was probably right, it might well be a senseless idea, but what other way was there? She could not wait those thirty years, leaving Benjie alone for what could well be a lifetime. If Odile Bancroft refused to employ her she would find some other way to earn the passage money.

But how . . . where . . . would she stay in Bristol or leave for some other town?

Question pushing question from her mind Tamar closed her eyes but when at last sleep came it was peopled with scarred faces staring out from haloes of fire while hands grabbed at her pulling her down into darkness.

'Really Amy, I don't think I should take them, your mistress might have other plans for them.'

'Odile Bancroft's plans will go just so far as chucking 'em out for rubbish, far better you have them, a lady's maid can't go around dressed worse than a scarecrow; besides having to look decent while you be on that boat you'll need to look the same once you be in Australia unless you want to be mistaken for one of them convicts.'

'But it's like stealing.' Tamar protested as several dresses were pushed into her hands.

'Stealing, course it ain't stealing!' Amy's answer was sharp. 'You are going to have to work while you are with Odile Bancroft, you will likely have to be nurse as well as maid and there will be no pay. That husband of hers will reckon the cost of your journey will more than account for any wages you might claim so you can look on those dresses as payment.'

'I would not ask for any wage . . .'

'You wouldn't get any if you did!' Amy interrupted. 'In any case, the mistress always gives me choice of any clothes she no longer has use for . . .'

She broke off abruptly, her face thoughtful as she turned to the wardrobes still waiting to be emptied.

'. . . speaking of wages, how much money do you have to live on 'til you finds work in Australia . . . supposing you find any at all?'

Putting the dresses aside, Tamar withdrew the sixpence from her pocket, holding it on the flat of her palm.

'This is the sixpence you told me about?' Amy glanced back at the small silver coin. 'That won't buy much in this country and I doubt it will buy more in the one you are going to; so you needs to give a bit of thought as to how you are going to manage once you have left the Bancrofts. Might not be much call for ladies' maids out there in Australia.'

She had not given much thought to that. Tamar

watched the other girl run a hand over the gowns still hanging in the wardrobe. In fact, she had thought of very little except finding Benjie, but if the finding took some time, then a means of making a living was crucial.

'The mistress always gives me choice of any clothes she no longer has use for . . .' Amy turned, a smile spreading across her face '. . . that means most of these and I choose to take them all.'

'But you said they would not fit you.'

'Nor will they,' the girl laughed, 'but they aren't for me, I'm giving them to you.'

'Me. But . . .'

'Listen!' Grabbing Tamar's hands and shaking her into silence Amy went on. 'You will need to earn money if you are going to search any place, and that country can't be no different; folk don't do anything for nothing, not these days they don't.'

'But dresses.' Tamar was puzzled.

'Dresses are money . . . when you sells 'em. I don't know if there be any fancy frock shops where you are going but there will be women and where there's women there's sale for a decent frock. It's a way of being sure Tamar, a way to feed yourself while you look for your brother.'

Still puzzled Tamar shook her head. 'But you could sell them yourself and use the money to help set up your home once you are married.'

'I could.' Again Amy's face became thoughtful. 'But I won't. You see, like you I made a promise. Two years ago my Will was lost at sea. Everyone reckoned him to be drowned, but I prayed. I prayed so hard I reckon the Lord got tired of listening, for six months ago He brought Will home. I vowed then that if I could ever help another as the Lord helped me then I would, and I think this is the way He has chosen. Take these dresses and the bits and pieces that go with 'em and p'raps the Lord in His wisdom will see they help you as He did me.'

Tears welling in her eyes Tamar threw her arms about the other girl. 'Amy, Amy I will miss you so much.'

'We'll be here, me and Will when you bring your brother home. You will find us at the little chandler's shop across from the docks, that be Will's now.' Her answer husky Amy hugged the girl she had befriended and for a moment she was tempted to tell her to forget going to Australia, that the whole thing was useless from the start. From the talk she had heard among sailors on the dock that lad would never survive such a journey. But she kept the words inside her as she released Tamar.

'That's settled then.' Amy turned again to the wardrobes, 'Let's get this lot packed.' But as she reached for the dresses she could not shake off the feeling that rubbed cold along her spine. All would not go well for Tamar Hallam.

'She's returning today.' Amy read the letter through again before looking at Tamar. 'The mistress is coming back sooner than planned.'

Tamar felt the breath choke in her throat. She could not go through with it, she was not ready. Amy had tried but there was so much to learn, so many things to remember.

'She will be going on board about three, you will have to be there to meet her.'

'I can't!' Tamar's eyes reflected the panic inside her. 'I can't do it Amy . . . I tried to learn . . .'

'Stop that!' Amy's voice cracked across the room. 'You have learned, you've done wonders given the time you've had. You are ready Tamar, this is just nerves. Once you are on your way . . .'

'No.' Tamar answered quickly, 'I can't do it Amy, I can't.'

Slipping the letter into the pocket of her apron, Amy looked into the panic-stricken face. If this girl held any hope at all of getting to Australia then this was it, for heaven knew she would never be given another chance. She should tell her this, make her realise what she was throwing to the winds. Instead, her smile reassuring, Amy took the shaking hands in her own.

'Then you are not going to. I will go see the mistress and explain she will need to employ a new maid.'

'I'm sorry Amy, sorry I let you down.'

Leading the way to the kitchen Amy felt a touch of sympathy.

Hopefully that was all this girl would have to be sorry for.

Chapter Sixteen

'It was obviously a case of self-defence, there can be no doubting that, them three were after Tullio's blood and anything else he might have had, and they would have got it too had not that constable arrived when he did.'

'That was very fortunate, Inspector.'

'Fortunate, we could say that Mr Amory, though I doubt Tullio will.' Titus Simeon touched a hand to his carefully brushed side whiskers.

'Has he said anything apart from his name?'

'Not intentional.' The inspector glanced up from the bowler hat balanced on his knee. 'But the man I posted at his bedside in that 'ospital heard plenty. A man close to dying don't always have control of his tongue.'

'Then you have your confession.'

'The ramblings of a sick man heard only by a policeman don't always count for a lot with a jury, not to say we might never get that one into court; the doctors ain't holding out much hope.'

'But the Alexandra Stone was found on him!' Philip Amory fiddled with his pocket watch, his irritation with the whole business mounting rapidly.

'That be true enough, each of your business colleagues identified it separately; it's a blessing my man were on the scene of the murder as quick as he was, otherwise Tullio might have stashed it somewhere where it wouldn't never be found. We ourselves didn't know of it 'til he was stripped down at the 'ospital, and there it was, a neat little bundle fastened into his armpit. Crafty was that, your run-of-the-mill thief wouldn't have felt for anything there.'

'It is a great relief to have the necklace recovered.' Philip twirled the watch into place in his waistcoat pocket. 'It will I am sure be as much relief to the Hallam girl to hear it has been found. You have I presume informed her.'

The Hallam girl. Titus Simeon slid his fingers through his whiskers. It seemed his first impression was proving correct. Philip Amory was interested in the girl; more than interested judging by the tone in his voice. Carefully guarding the look in his eyes he watched the goldsmith, seeing irritation turn to anger as he answered.

'My officer tells me the girl is not at her home nor has she returned to her employment, but then you would know that for yourself, sir. But rest assured, she will be told just as soon as she comes back to Hockley.'

'Comes back!' Philip Amory snapped. 'That could take weeks and during all of that time she is to be left wondering whether that necklace has been found? Left with that to torment her mind? That is utterly preposterous; it is worse than that, it is cruel. You must send word to her at once!'

Drawing his fingers slowly to the tips of his side whiskers Titus Simeon kept the smile from his eyes. Leaving a moment's space he glanced at the man staring at him across the warm study.

'Edgbaston station don't have the men to spare to send traipsing the country after non-essential witnesses Mr Amory, but even were that not the case where would we send a man, do you know where the Hallam girl is to be found?'

'No.' Breaking off his glance Philip turned away, his fingers reaching absently for his pocket watch. 'I know only the rumours that pass around my work-shop, rumours that say the girl is in Bristol and may possibly try to get a boat to take her to Australia.' He rounded quickly his next words coming rapidly. 'But she must be told that is no longer necessary, she must be told her brother will be returned to England.'

'That last part could not be said even should she return tomorrow.' Titus Simeon took the hat from its precarious position balanced on his knee and stood up. 'As was said at our previous meeting the decision of the courts will stipulate what must be done regarding Benjamin Hallam. Until then there is no more I can do, and with respect sir, there ain't very much you can do either. Take my advice and leave the business of the culprits to the justices; you will have your property back just as soon as the court allows, that is all that need concern you.'

'That is your advice, is it?' Philip Amory's glance was withering. 'That is all that need concern me . . . and you too, eh? You need have no more thought for a boy sent thousands of miles from his home, from all he knows and loves, from those that love him. You have your property back so to hell with what happens to the lad . . . my God, what a creed! How in God's name do you live with yourself?'

Placing the bowler on his head the police inspector turned to the door his quiet reply resting on the sudden silence. 'I often ask myself that question, I ask it very often.'

'You wait here 'til I get back.' Amy Williams fastened the line of buttons on the jacket that matched her maroon wool skirt. Setting a jet-beaded pin to her pert bonnet she glanced at the girl stood with her in the kitchen of the Bancroft house. 'Could take a bit of time so don't you go flitting, this house will be closed but we will find you somewhere else, somewhere close to Will and me. You'll be safer with friends and I can go with you to the docks to enquire of any ships that come in from Australia.'

'Amy.' Tamar's eyes showed the guilt that had plagued her in those sleepless hours and plagued her still, guilt at having prevented the girl from trying to find a replacement maid for Odile Bancroft, then letting her down at the last moment. 'Amy, I hope I have not got you into trouble with your mistress.'

'She isn't my mistress any more.' Amy drew on grey woollen gloves. 'And there won't be no trouble, I can't hardly be gaoled for giving notice.'

'But she will want to know why you did not find her some other maid.'

Taking up her purse Amy checked it held a freshly laundered handkerchief. 'Then I will have to remind her that it isn't the duty of a lady's maid to hire a replacement, only the lady herself can do that. Look Tamar,' she smiled sympathetically, 'you thought you could go through with it but when it came to the push you couldn't, that's nothing to feel badly about. It happens to everybody at one time in their life; but at least you found your limit afore you jumped; that's something to be thankful for.'

Turning her head towards the sound of a knock to the kitchen door Amy walked to open it.

'That be the last of the trunks.'

A thickset man wearing a heavy worsted jacket over moleskin trousers fastened about the ankles with string touched a finger to a flat cap, its colour long ago stolen by sun and weather.

'Do you want to check them 'ere or along at the docks?'

'I'll count them on to the boat . . .' Amy answered, a slight emphasis on the word count. 'But while you are here you can carry those upstairs.' She pointed to several boxes stood just inside the kitchen. 'There will be sixpence added to the price agreed just so long as you go carefully in the carrying.'

'You sure you don't want them on the cart an' all?'

Catching the other girl's glance Tamar let her own fall.

'No.' Amy's reply was sure. 'They are not to go on the cart, they will not be wanted on the voyage.'

'There is something I wish to say to all of you. Telling it to you here in the workshop will mean each of you hearing the same thing and that way there can be no rumours.'

Vinny Marsh glanced nervously at the woman stood beside her, seeing a reflection of her own anxiety in Connie Harding's eyes. Was Amory about to give them each their tin? Talk said he was shutting down, giving up the gold working altogether and that were the cause of his long face and snappy answers whenever he were spoke to.

'It is concerning the item of jewellery that has come to be known by those of us involved in its making as the Alexandra Stone. I do not need to expound upon the reason for this nor upon the fact that it was stolen. It was suspected that Benjamin Hallam was the thief. However, it transpires that the robbery was planned between Charles Selby and Zeph Tullio and when Joby Turner discovered the plan he was killed by Selby.

That is not all,' he raised his voice slightly as angry murmurs sped from mouth to mouth. 'Tullio died yesterday evening . . .'

'Bloody good job.' Dinah Edwards gave vent to her feelings. 'That's saved we the job of finishing the gypsy swine!'

Raising a hand Philip Amory waited for the buzz of voices to die away.

'. . . due to the seriousness of an injury he had suffered in a tavern brawl it was not possible to bring him into court, therefore because it was feared he was near to death the magistrate and myself along with the police inspector of Edgbaston went to his hospital bed and heard him admit to both murders as well as to stealing the necklace with a view to selling it.'

'And what about the lad Mr Amory, what about young Benjie 'Allam?'

Taking the watch from his waistcoat Philip Amory twisted it between his fingers as his glance swung to the woman who had spoken.

'I asked the same question, Vinny,' he answered. 'I asked it on each of the occasions I met with the police and each time the answer was we must await the decision of the court.'

'In the meantime that poor little bugger is pushed off to Australia and we all know what that means! Benjie 'Allam will be the last one to be thought of by them legal folks.'

'Dinah be right.' Vinny added her voice to Dinah's. 'That lad might still serve thirty years afore anybody gets round to fetchin' him 'ome! It ain't good enough Mr Amory, it just ain't good enough!'

'The women say what we all of us think, Mr Amory.' Cal Perry stepped forward, standing a little apart from the cluster of work people. 'That lad were wrongly accused from the beginning, he's suffered for summat he ain't never done and it be right that suffering be put at an end. He should be fetched 'ome straight off . . .'

'I agree with you, Perry, I agree with the feelings of you all and believe me I will do all I can to achieve that. I have today arranged to meet with a lawyer. I shall instruct him to begin work at once on Benjamin Hallam's behalf, more than that I cannot do.'

'We thanks you serious for that.' Vinny spoke again. 'But what of the lad's sister, 'ave the bobbies told her that her brother were falsely accused, that the Alexandra Stone were found never to 'ave been pinched by him at all?'

Cal caught the glint of the gold watch twisting between long fingers. Amory was not used to being questioned by employees. Any second now he could turn awkward and that might result in one or two getting their tin.

'Your thoughts match my own, Vinny, and your questions are the same as those I asked . . .'

Cal Perry eased the breath slowly from tight lungs as the goldsmith answered patiently.

'. . . and the answer to your last one will bring you the same feeling it brought me. The answer I received was this. Tamar Hallam would be informed of her brother's innocence when she returns to Hockley.'

'When her returns!' Vinny's brow creased deepening the lines already there. 'But her won't come back, not 'til her's found her brother, her be set on following after him to that Australia . . . God alone knows how and only He knows how the wench could ever get back. The bobbies 'ave to send to Bristol, Mr Amory, they has to let her know it were Zeph Tullio were to blame, they 'ave to bring the wench home!'

Philip Amory's mouth lifted in a smile but on the instant it had gone, leaving one hand twiddling the watch with heightened intensity a touch of colour resting on his cheeks, and when he answered a faint quaver sounded beneath the words.

'That was my decision also. To that end I have this morning dispatched a man to Bristol to bring Ta – to bring Miss Hallam home.'

'I can't be saying it surprised me any, I never 'eld no trust for that one, Gypsy blood pah . . . ! No good never come of it.'

Vinny Marsh bit decisively into the bread and pork dripping that was her daily lunch.

'D'ain't take no thinkin' on.' Dinah Edwards replied, her own mouth filled with bread and dripping. 'When they found the Juggler with his throat cut I had me suspicions as to who it was had done him the service, then when they comes across Charlie Selby done in and lying back of the Temple of Relief . . . well!' She snorted disparagingly, 'Even the youngest babby in 'Ockley could 'ave told them bobbies who it was had slit *his* throat but it weren't 'til Zeph Tullio croaked that that lot had any idea.'

Nodding agreement Vinny stirred sugar into her mug of freshly brewed tea. 'You'll find more brain in a 'ead of cabbage than you'll find in that lot, they couldn't find a pot of ale in a brewery! If Tullio hadn't up and told the truth afore kickin' the bucket then like as not young Benjie 'Allam would 'ave carried the blame the 'ole of his life.'

'Which mightn't be more much longer lessen he be brought out of that 'eathen land!' Dinah sank her few remaining teeth into a fresh slice of bread and dripping.

'How come you knows it be a 'eathen place, 'ave you had kin sent there?'

Still smarting from Dinah's telling the lie of her husband's having the clap and from the hiding received when accusing him of infecting her, Connie Harding saw her advantage and took it.

'Not kin of mine Connie.' Dinah chewed contentedly. 'It was your father told me all about it when he was brought back after serving ten years in a penal colony. Pinchin', weren't it? Stole money from the bloke he worked for . . . was that why Amory wouldn't never give him a job along of this place?'

'My father weren't never deported!' Connie Harding's face flushed an angry red.

'Weren't he?' Dinah was calm as the younger woman was irate. 'Be you sure of that Connie, or is it that you was never told? It be wicked of him that, leavin' you to find out from some other body; still, you knows now.'

'And so does the rest of 'Ockley . . . or they soon will.' Vinny said as the younger woman ran from the small finishing shop. 'But I must say Dinah, what you just told her be a surprise to me, I never knowed Harding had done time in the colonies.'

'Nor he ain't, least not as I knows of.' Dinah

swallowed a mouthful of tea. 'Neither will Connie seein' as he ain't alive to ask.'

'Then why say he was?'

'That wench be thicker than shit!' Dinah's eyes lost their amusement, her mouth tightening. ''Er don't learn easy then her'll learn hard, but learn her will. No woman in 'Ockley smart mouths Dinah Edwards and gets away wi' it, no . . . and no man neither! Connie 'Arding tries it on wi' me then her gets trouble back, right in the face.'

'There do be some as deserves it.' Vinny took her mug and sat beside her friend. 'Not like that poor 'Allam wench. Eeh Dinah, I feels for her I really does.'

'We all does Vinny, though I was taken aback by Amory sayin' he had sent a man to bring her back; I wouldn't have taken the gaffer to be the sentimental sort.'

Chewing on her bread and dripping Vinny made no answer but thoughts tripped through her mind. She had sometimes caught Philip Amory's look as it had followed the figure of Tamar Hallam, caught it and wondered at its cause. Now she had those same wonderings again.

Stood alone in the silent kitchen Tamar wrestled with her thoughts. Would Amy be in trouble with Odile Bancroft? Had the girl been shielding her from feeling guilty when she had denied that she would?

And what of Odile Bancroft herself? The woman was sick, she would need someone to care for her on a voyage she had learned took months rather than days; and then there was Benjie, he was little more than a child. She had promised she would take care of him, promised their father before he had died; and Amy had given her the chance to at least try to follow up on that promise, to sail with Odile Bancroft to Australia to find him and be close to him. Now she had thrown away that chance, and by doing so had thrown the girl's kindness back at her.

Slowly, her fingers seeming to act of their own accord, Tamar unbuttoned the dark green coat Amy had given her. She would make it up to Amy, somehow she would repay that kindness.

Out in the street a carter rang his handbell following it up with a call that resounded on the stillness of the kitchen.

And how would she repay the rest? Guilt, strong and warm, rose to her cheeks. How would she repay that carter who had fetched her to Stafford, the Mullins who had made room for her on their narrow-boat, and Vinny. Was backing out now the way to thank all of those people?

'Promise me you'll come . . . promise me Tam . . . promise me . . .'

In the quiet stillness Benjie's frightened cry rang against her brain. Breath catching on a sob she caught up her skirts and ran from the house.

Chapter Seventeen

Tears half blinding her eyes, skirts flapping against her ankles Tamar ignored the stares of people as she raced through narrow cobbled streets.

The *Porpoise*, that was the name Amy had read out to her, the name of the ship on which Odile Bancroft had booked passage. Coming to the docks she stared at the vessels moored against its length, great masts rising like warning fingers against a sky the colour of lead, some with bow and aft painted in blues, yellows and reds, others plain and sea worn, their names hardly distinguishable.

It could not have sailed yet, there had hardly been time! Tamar stared at the ships, their wooden hulls rising sheer above her head, the smell of tar and wet hemp thick in her nostrils. Which one was the *Porpoise*?

Elbowed aside by a man balancing several baskets stacked on his head Tamar felt the wet stones of the quayside slide beneath her feet a cry pushed from her as she fell awkwardly against a pile of crates.

'Ain't no need for you to go lying there.'

One wrist caught in a tight grip she flipped like a rag doll. Hauled to her feet she stared into a leathery pock-marked face.

'We can find a better berth than the dockside for a pretty little package like you . . .' the blubbery mouth stretched in a grin '. . . you can keep Josh Taylor warm on a long trip.'

'Let me go!'

Tamar tried to shake free of the grimy hand but it held like steel.

'Now you don't mean that . . .'

Wet with spittle the thick-lipped mouth grinned again '. . . you wants to be with Josh Taylor right enough, but you thinks to be coaxed a little afore admitting to it. Well I don't mind accommodating you on that score. I be just about ready for a little game or two meself afore going aboard, 'sides it'll give you a taste of the games we'll play on them long nights at sea.'

A quick jerk pulling her against him a brawny arm almost lifting her off her feet he dragged her from the quayside, then pushing her before him into a narrow alley unbuckled the wide leather belt circling his waist.

Memories of Zeph Tullio and that night he had seen her home filling her mind, Tamar screamed.

'Stow that!'

A sharp blow to the side of her face sent her reeling backward striking a second blow to the back of her head. Her senses reeling she slid to the floor.

Vinny . . . Vinny would come, she would see Zeph off . . .

Half unconscious Tamar tried to ward off the hands drawing down her bloomers, the fingers touching the bare flesh of her thighs.

'That'll be enough of that Taylor . . .'

'Vinny . . .' Voice throbbing with fright Tamar clutched at her skirts, 'Vinny . . . thank God you came.'

'I don't be no Vinny miss, but I thought as how you hadn't gone willing with this vermin when I were told he'd half dragged you away.'

Blinking hard Tamar forced her eyes to focus and her swirling senses to calm. The man who had forced her into this alley was held firm, one arm twisted behind his back by a younger, cleaner looking man, his face drawn tight with anger.

'I never dragged her!' The wet lips caught the dreary light filtering into the alley. 'Her said her would for a shilling.'

'You made a bargain?'

'Aye, we did.' The first man twisted but could not break the hold on him.

'And you were to pay her a shilling?'

'Aye, a shilling.'

'Then you had best honour your bargain Taylor, pay the lady what you promised.'

'I'll see the slut in hell first . . . ar, an' you there along wi' her!'

'Hell.' The second man answered softly. 'A terrible place or so we was told as children. But believe me Taylor, it will prove infinitely more desirable to the place you'll find yourself sent to if Captain Short be informed of this escapade. Rape be a serious offence . . . combined with your existing record it will mean life in the penal colonies and you've seen for yourself what that can do to a man. Now I tells you once again, pay the lady what you agreed.'

'I don't pay for what I ain't 'ad!' Taylor kicked back violently with one foot but his captor was too quick. Side-stepping the blow he pressed viciously on the upturned arm.

'Then pay for what the lady has had,' he said, as a cry of pain broke from the other man.

' 'Ad?' Taylor gasped. ' 'Er ain't 'ad nothin'. If I ain't 'ad nothin' then 'er ain't neither.'

'I wouldn't call a blow to the face nothing. You took the privilege of striking her now you have the privilege of paying her. I calls that only fair.'

'God damn you, Allen . . .'

'Make that God damn you, *sir* . . .'

His voice losing the faintest essence of softness the second man tightened his grip forcing the twisted arm higher '. . . and well He might, but not before I see you damned first. Now pay the lady and get yourself aboard, and before you think of running let me tell you there be two of the crew waiting beyond the alley.'

'No . . . please. There was no mention of money and no bargain.' Her clothing adjusted Tamar turned to face the two men, stepping backward away from the grimy hand that held out a shilling. 'I did not agree to come here with this man, I did not agree to . . . to anything.'

Retaining his hold the younger of the two men glanced at her.

'Then take it in payment for his rough handling of you.'

Fright and tears mixing potently in her throat Tamar shook her head.

'I don't want his money; please, I came here to find a ship . . . I . . . I have to go before it sails.'

Releasing his hold, a foot to the seat of the trousers sending Taylor stumbling towards the entrance of the alley the younger man touched a hand to his forehead.

'First mate James Allen, miss. I be familiar with most of the ships as puts into Bristol. If you would allow I'll be happy to take you to whichever it be you 'as passage on.'

Glancing the way she had been pushed into the alley Tamar saw the figure of Taylor grabbed by two others. James Allen had spoken the truth when he told the man who had assaulted her that he was being waited for. Please God he was speaking the truth now.

'This be the *Porpoise* miss.'

Stood beside the gangplank James Allen smiled.

'You'll find the captain on deck, he be the sort of man who likes to see things being done, that way he knows all be as he ordered.'

'Thank you, Mr Allen.' Tamar returned the smile, a tinge of guilt touching colour to her cheeks as she thought of her doubts of minutes ago. He had made no move to touch her, keeping several paces distance between them as he conducted her back to the quayside.

'Be no need of thanks.' James Allen touched his forehead in quick salute before walking away towards a group of men carrying sacks across their shoulders.

No need of thanks! Tamar repressed a shudder as she went aboard the ship. That was not the way she saw it.

Listening to her request to speak to Mrs Bancroft the captain's eyes watched every movement of men carrying supplies on board. Giving instruction for her to be conducted to the woman's cabin he added that the ship would leave on the evening tide and she must be ashore by then.

Following the sailor down the narrow companionway reminded her of the Mullins' barge and the steps that led down to the small space that was home to the family.

'This be the cabin you wants.'

The words spoken the sailor was off up the companionway to the deck his feet making little sound on the timbers.

'Tamar?'

Answering the knock Tamar made on the cabin door Amy glanced quizzically at the face that still bore traces of Taylor's blow.

'I . . . I came to speak to Mrs Bancroft.'

'And got yourself knocked about in the process. I told you to stay away from the docks, now you've learned the reason for it. But now you're here you best come in, I'll ask the mistress if she'll see you.'

Inside the cabin Tamar looked at the small round

window, the bed built into an alcove, a table and two chairs and a wooden cupboard taking up most of the remaining space. It seemed not a deal larger than the narrowboat, but then this cabin was for the use of one woman not an entire family.

On the further side of the cabin a door opened and a pale looking woman, dark hair streaked with grey, entered.

'You wished to see me, Miss Hallam?'

Tamar dropped a curtsy as the woman lowered tiredly to one of the chairs.

'I . . . I came to apologise for the trouble I have caused.'

Tamar caught the shadow of a frown as it flicked across the woman's brow. Amy had told her nothing of the past couple of weeks, of giving her shelter in this woman's house or of the plan whereby she would take the girl's place.

Odile Bancroft's brown eyes regarded her questioningly.

'Trouble . . . I fear you must explain Miss Hallam, I know of no trouble.'

'It is concerning being your lady's maid . . .'

The first sentence out Tamar rushed on, the whole story pouring from her until Odile Bancroft had heard it all.

'. . . so you see ma'am, it is not Amy to blame for you having no replacement, what she did she did from kindness to me, she wanted only to help in my finding my brother.'

Odile Bancroft's smile broke slowly across her thin,

pallid face and when she answered her voice was cushioned in a soft understanding.

'I think I know Amy well enough to believe all you have said. It might not have been the most practical way to have handled the situation but then a woman about to be parted from the man she loves is not always the most practical minded creature. I admire your coming on board to tell me of what has gone on, no doubt it took more than a little courage. It is a pity that same courage failed you a while earlier, or is it that you have found some other way of reaching Australia?'

'No ma'am, I have not.' Tamar answered, surprised at the quiet way in which the woman had listened; not once interrupting or showing displeasure.

Taking a handkerchief from the pocket of a pale blue velvet travelling skirt Odile Bancroft pressed it to her lips trying to stem the cough that shook her thin body. The spasm passed she looked at Tamar with watery eyes.

'Forgive me, Miss Hallam, I have been somewhat unwell with a cough. I was asking if you intend some other method of travel to Australia, though I know of no way to reach that country without at some stage going by sea, or is it you have given up the idea altogether?'

'I . . . I will get there ma'am. I have to, I gave Benjie my word I would go to him; I know I thought at the time of saying it that it would be wherever he was placed in England but a promise is a promise no matter where the country I intend to keep it.'

'Amy.' Odile Bancroft switched her glance to the girl standing to one side of her. 'You did not have any length of time to instruct Miss Hallam in the duties of a lady's maid but how would you warrant her success?'

'Very highly, ma'am.' Amy smiled. 'I think Tamar would make a very satisfactory lady's maid.'

Pressing the handkerchief to her mouth the woman coughed for several seconds.

'You say you still intend to go to find your brother and Amy vouches for your satisfaction as a lady's maid.' She spoke again the second bout of coughing having passed. 'That being so, together with my need for a maid are you willing to accept that post?'

'But . . . but I was prepared to trick you!'

'Were you?' Odile Bancroft looked into eyes widened by surprise and once again her thin features were softened by a smile. 'Were you really? But you did not. Have you asked yourself why that is? I feel it is because lying and cheating are foreign to your nature. You were not forced to come here to defend Amy or to confess to me, you came because your heart would not allow you not to come. Honesty is a quality rare in the world we live in and it is one I would like beside me. If you will accept my service then I would be happy for you to travel with me as my maid.'

'You won't regret it, ma'am.' Amy smiled delightedly.

'Thank you, Mrs Bancroft ma'am. I promise I will do my best.'

'Then we will both be satisfied. But there is little time before we sail so if there is anything you need . . .'

'The boxes!' Amy's exclamation cut the woman short.

'Boxes?'

'Yes, ma'am. We . . . I packed the dresses you said I might keep. They were going to be brought on board with the others but when Tamar said she couldn't go through with what we talked of then they was put back upstairs at the house.'

'So the dresses were intended for use by Tamar.'

Amy glanced at Tamar before answering defensively.

'I thought seeing as you had said I might keep them . . .'

'That you could give them to someone else.' Odile Bancroft nodded. 'And so you may of course. Have them brought to the ship at once and Amy . . . please accept the dressing chest in my room as a wedding gift.'

'I told you everything would be alright.' Saying goodbye on deck Amy hugged the girl she had come to think of as a friend. 'Odile Bancroft is a good mistress, you will come to no harm with her. God keep you both Tamar, and remember Will and me will be here when you return.'

When you return.

Watching the shoreline fade into the distance Tamar thought of the words Amy had said earlier and her heart stopped painfully.

Would she ever return . . . would she ever see her home again?

'You are certain of that . . . certain you have the right girl?'

Philip Amory looked across his desk at the man he had hired to go to Bristol.

'I wrote down your description of the girl word for word as you told it to me Mr Amory. Several people I spoke to remembered seeing a young red-haired woman . . .'

'Then how come she is not with you, why have you not brought her back to Hockley?'

Waiting for the interruption to finish the private investigator watched the other man closely. This was the second time he had been hired to track the Hallams but clearly it was the girl interested Amory the most; it was also clear enough a blind man could see that interest went far further than an employer for an employee.

'I couldn't bring her back,' he continued, as Philip Amory's outburst subsided. 'Seems the wench . . . Miss Hallam be no longer in Bristol, seems her sailed a week since bound for Australia.'

Australia! Twiddling the pocket watch in his fingers he hardly heard the remainder of the detective's words. There had been talk of Tamar Hallam sending a message by way of a narrowboatman, a message saying she was to follow her brother to Australia but he, Amory, had discounted it. He had told himself the whole idea was an impossibility, that she would never have the means of travelling so far, yet she had seemingly found some way.

'The woman said a girl of the name Tamar Hallam and fitting the description you gave had lodged with her in Bristol for a fortnight and that she had taken a position as lady's maid to a Mrs Bancroft. Seems the woman was going to join her husband in Australia.'

'Did this . . . this . . . ?'

'Amy Williams, sir.'

'This Amy Williams, did she say when it was expected the Bancrofts were to return to England?'

Seeing the agitation in Amory's movements the detective held his own thoughts on a tight rein answering simply.

'There was no mention made of that but from what the Williams woman did say it was clear that Miss Hallam had no intention of returning without her brother; so it is a case of how long it takes to find him, and supposing he is made to serve his sentence in full . . .'

'Yes, yes I know all of that!' Philip swung the watch irritably back into the pocket of his waistcoat at the same time rising to his feet. Why the hell had he waited, why hadn't he sent to Bristol when he first heard of Tamar being there?

'If there is anything more you wish me to do Mr Amory?'

'What!' Philip Amory forced his attention back to the man he had hired. 'No, no there is nothing more. Thank you, you have done well.'

Thirty years! The detective gone he walked slowly upstairs to his room. The full sentence was thirty years, half a lifetime. He could send to Australia – go himself. But that was impossible, he had the business to run. Yet even should he make the journey he was not certain to find Tamar. He had looked at Australia on a map. The country must be vast, compared to it Great Britain was no more than a dot.

Slowly removing his jacket he unfastened the gold albert looped across his waistcoat placing watch and chain on the table in his dressing room.

He had often watched the girl from the window of his office, admiring the thick auburn hair, the creamy complexion and neat way she had of keeping herself dressed, though her clothes were worn and patched. She was so very different to the rest of the women in his employ, so very different from any women he knew. But he had not recognised that interest changing to attraction and attraction becoming . . .

Becoming what? Dressing-gown half on half off his shoulders he stared at himself in the full-length mirror. Love . . . was that it? Was he in love with Tamar Hallam? Enough in love with a workshop girl to marry her, was that what he wanted?

Pulling on the silk robe he returned to the bedroom, standing before the fire gazing at pictures in the flames, pictures that showed a lovely auburn-haired woman, while behind her others talked behind raised fans.

Was that how it would have been? As his wife would Tamar have been rejected by the social élite of

Birmingham, would he have been ridiculed for marrying a girl from the slums? And if so, what effect would it have had on his business?

The Ides of March!

The remembered phrase slipping into his mind as the pictures died he turned towards the bed.

Caesar had been warned but ignored it, consequently he had paid for his mistake. Had those pictures in the flames been his Ides of March, his warning of an impending disaster? Was it meant to tell him that marriage to Tamar Hallam would in some way destroy him?

Turning off the gasoliere, leaving the one solitary lamp burning beside his bed, Philip Amory stared at the pale yellow glow. Tamar Hallam was gone, maybe it were better left that way.

Chapter Eighteen

They would be going ashore at the next port. He had heard the lieutenant say the captain thought it good for the two passengers to stretch their legs on land for a few hours while the ship took on fresh water and a supply of fruit.

Ezra Payne let the huge wheel slide between his hands bringing the ship to the course shouted from the poop deck. He would wait until the women had gone ashore and then go below to their cabin, but he would need to be careful and watch out for Allen, that one had eyes up his arse! There was almost nothing got past him. But only almost. Ezra smiled showing yellowed teeth. Smart was Lieutenant Mr James Allen, but he didn't see everything.

And he wouldn't see him go below. Ezra listened to the crisp sharp orders issuing from the officers and the laconic answers of the crew. Many of them had been pressed into service, taken like himself from taverns or from the streets, forced to take the Queen's shilling; and bloody poor pay that was, but there were ways to bolster that pay, yes and ways to compensate the hardness of an ordinary seaman's life, provided the gold braid didn't get wind of it.

The wheel secured and the ship tied up alongside the dock Ezra listened to the names being called for shore duty. If his proved to be one of them he would have to delay his plan. But there might not be the same chance again, certainly not while the women were aboard, for the older one rarely left the cabin and the younger was on deck for no more than a few minutes at a time. She was pretty. That auburn hair that shone like living fire, the delicate face. As a boy he had imagined angels to look as she looked, so slender and beautiful. Would she be an angel in bed, naked with a man's nakedness across the top of her? Jos Taylor had thought to find that out for himself back in Bristol town but the lieutenant had been a mite too quick.

From the corner of his eye Ezra caught a flash of dark blue touched with the glint of gold and quickly moved to assist in checking the knots holding sail ropes were properly tied. Lieutenant James Allen! He swallowed, dislike acrid on his tongue. One day that bloke would be wearing his gold braid in a very different place!

'It would be very welcome after so long at sea, but I am not sure Mrs Bancroft will agree.'

'There is a much longer time at sea before we reach Australia.' James Allen looked at the girl stood at his side, the offshore breeze teasing tendrils of hair across a face pale from spending long hours below.

'How long does the voyage take?'

He smiled at Tamar's question. 'Two months, if the wind is fair.'

'Two months!' Surprise obvious in her answer Tamar glanced up at the handsome face; bronzed and lean it was so like the one that frequented her dreams, but that one had steel grey eyes and a pencil line beard.

'It still takes seven if you go by way of the Indies but this trip is taking us through the new canal of Suez, that is in Egypt.'

Tamar's memory showed her the books shared with Isaac Cohen flicking pages until it showed three huge pyramids. They were in Egypt. Would she see them from the new canal?

'The captain asks if you can be ready within the hour.'

It was not a question of being ready, but of whether Odile Bancroft would be able to go ashore. Tamar watched the lieutenant stride away towards the poop deck before making her way to the cabins that had been allotted to Odile and herself. They had both suffered from seasickness which made every hour a nightmare, but worse for her had been the leer and the touching hands of the man sent to them with food and water to wash in. Regular washing had been necessary in order to avoid other illness arising from the endless vomiting, Tamar acknowledged to herself, but had there been a real need of his hands on her breasts? Even now she felt a shiver of horror run along her spine whenever she remembered the man's leering face bending over her, a fear that returned each time she caught him watching her on deck. Were it not for the suffering of Odile Bancroft she would be thankful that so much of her time was spent below.

'It is very thoughtful of Captain Jones, but I really do not feel I want to go ashore.' Odile Bancroft wiped a limp hand across her brow as Tamar delivered the lieutenant's message.

'The air would do you good, ma'am. It is very mild and quite warm, so different from the weather we left behind in England. I never thought to see so much of a change in so short a time.'

Tamar tried to keep the eagerness from her voice. What she had seen from the deck of the city of Al Bayda with its high walls looked intriguing.

'Perhaps you are right, maybe a little time ashore would revive us both; you have been looking a little pale, are you sure you have recovered from your *mal de mer?*'

'Quite recovered, ma'am.'

'Then we will take Captain Jones' advice and both go ashore.'

Reaching a pair of white silk gloves from the chest Tamar tried hard not to show her delight. Just an hour from the confines of these stuffy cabins would be a godsend.

'Will it be warm in Australia do you think? I hope not for I find the warmer weather difficult to cope with.' Odile drew on the gloves adjusting each lace-edged cuff.

'I have no idea of that country's climate, ma'am.

None of the books Mr Cohen used to show to Benjie and myself contained anything of Australia.'

'No doubt we will find out for ourselves soon enough.'

Taking the silk-fringed parasol Tamar held out to her, Odile Bancroft turned towards the cabin door, weariness evident in every line of her body.

'We should not go if you feel you are not up to it. I will tell Lieutenant Allen . . .' Tamar felt a prick of guilt for her own eagerness. She should not have pressed this woman so her own pleasure could be satisfied.

'No.' Odile shook her head. 'We must not give in to our small weaknesses, nor must we deprive the handsome lieutenant of your company. I fear you have an admirer in that young man.'

Blushing furiously Tamar closed the door of the cabin behind them. Had she done the right thing in persuading this woman to go ashore? They were only three weeks into the journey and already it was telling on her; and the coughing sickness seemed to be worsening. She heard the wracking sounds of it long after retiring to her own cabin and often it was interspersed with the sound of weeping. The first few times of hearing those long-drawn sobs through the connecting door she had gone into the other room but had soon learned that by trying to hide her unhappiness Odile Bancroft simply added to her own stress; now she simply lay in her own bunk and listened.

Reaching the wooden companionway that gave on

to the deck, Tamar took the parasol leaving her mistress with both hands free to steady herself as she climbed the narrow stairs.

Life was being as unfair to this woman as it was to Benjie, neither of them deserved the cruelty fate was dishing out to them.

Destiny child . . . that is something money cannot buy and man cannot avoid . . .

Following on to the deck Tamar seemed to hear again the words of the old jeweller.

What was to be her destiny . . . life lived out in the shadows of some gaol?

Stepping on to the deck Tamar breathed the warm air, heavy with the scents of spices and ringing with the calls in language she could not even begin to understand.

Glancing across a jetty alive with figures scurrying like ants in every direction she could not help but feel the race of her blood as she caught the lavender line of distant mountains and closer the rise of huge walls that closed off all but four pencil-slim towers placed one each side of a great blue dome.

'The Mosque of Suleiman.'

Tamar turned as the voice spoke quietly at her side.

'Mosque . . . what is that?'

James Allen smiled. 'It is a place of worship.'

'You mean a church?'

'We might call it that, however, the correct name is mosque. It was built by the Ottomans when they first invaded this part of Africa.'

Tamar looked again at the dome glistening like a

great sapphire orb. 'It is really very beautiful, it looks like some huge magnificent jewel.'

'Ladies . . .'

James Allen snapped to attention as the captain joined them.

'. . . If you are ready we will go ashore . . . the temperature climbs very quickly here in the Mediterranean so I suggest we make our time ashore brief.'

Feeling the plank move beneath the brisk accustomed tread of the ship's captain Tamar quenched the quick surge through her veins. She must show no fear before Odile Bancroft, the woman was already on the verge of giving up the whole idea of their expedition ashore.

'Lieutenant Allen will escort you both. I would like to accompany you myself ma'am, but I must present my credentials to the Emir . . . you understand?'

'Of course, Captain Jones.' Opening the parasol Tamar had handed to her as they stepped onto the jetty, Odile raised it shading her face from the sun.

'Until later then, ma'am.'

Touching a hand to his smart gold-trimmed cap the captain left. Watching him stride into the mêlée of figures pushing or carrying a variety of baskets and carts Tamar had a sudden vision of another blue-uniformed figure; a tall well-muscled figure with a pencil-line beard following a narrow line along a strong jaw, steel-grey eyes piercing beneath eyebrows blacker than coal.

'Where would you like to go? Might I suggest you avoid the souk, it will be rather crowded and the spice market especially might be a little overpowering; the odours can be heady when you are not used to them.'

'Tactfully put, Mr Allen.' Odile held a handkerchief to her nostrils as they skirted a flock of black goats, flies buzzing over their backs and about their short bobbing tails.

'The street of goldsmiths perhaps.'

Shaking her head at the suggestion Odile Bancroft coughed into the handkerchief.

'I do not think Tamar would find anything new there, she has spent her life in the gold district of Birmingham.'

'Believe me ma'am, it can be nothing compared to an Arab gold market, they are . . .'

He broke off at Odile's exclamation following her glance to where a line of camels came towards them heading in the direction of a huge arched gateway set in tall sandstone walls and guarded by men with long curved swords.

'How magnificent!'

Her cough momentarily forgotten Odile stared at the richly garbed riders; pale lemon silk bolero jackets gleamed against shining ebony torsos, matching baggy trousers caught at ankle and waist with wide bands of gold set with green stones flashing in the sun, while a matching kaffiyeh protected their heads.

'They are a sight, ma'am.' James Allen agreed watching the riders clear a swathe through the crowded thoroughfare. 'They are the Emir's personal attendants.'

'Does he always travel in such style?'

'No ma'am. He only shows such paucity when he attends the mosque. It would be considered unworthy to display magnificence before Allah.'

'Paucity!' Odile exclaimed again. 'If that is a display of paucity then what would a display of wealth be like!'

Shaking his head James Allen watched the white stallion being ridden by a man dressed in a plain white robe and unadorned burnoose on his head.

'Trust me Mrs Bancroft, ma'am,' he murmured, 'it has to be seen to be believed and even then it takes some believing.'

'Why does one man ride a horse when others ride camels?'

Eyes bright with delight at the unexpected sight Tamar watched the rider. Tall in the saddle, three bare-topped men, black skins gleaming, scimitars flashing, walking each side and four more of the same at the rear, he seemed as one with his mount, a part of the animal.

'That is the Emir.' The lieutenant answered as the cavalcade drew almost level.

'But he is dressed so . . . so plain in comparison to the others, why is that?'

'The reason is a simple one . . .'

Blushing furiously Tamar bobbed a curtsy as the horse came to a stop. She would not have thought her words to have been heard by any but Odile and the lieutenant yet this man had heard them. Above her head he smiled.

'. . . it is the beauty of a man's soul which pleases Allah, not the beauty of his robe.'

'I beg pardon, sir.' Tamar's colour burned as eyes sharp as a hawk's probed deep into her own. 'I did not mean to be rude.'

'There is no pardon needed as there was no rudeness spoken. At the evening prayer I shall thank Allah for His goodness in bringing two such beautiful ladies to my country.'

'Phew!' James Allen breathed out slowly as the rider moved on. 'Thank the Lord for his mercy!'

Dabbing her cheeks with the slip of handkerchief Odile Bancroft stared at a group of passing women only their eyes visible among enveloping black robes.

'What do you mean by that, Mr Allen?'

'I mean ma'am, had the Emir taken offence we would not be standing here right now. Those scimitars his escort carried were by no means simply for ceremony.'

'You mean . . .'

'I do ma'am. In Libya that man's word is absolute.'

Holding her skirts as the press of the crowd closed behind the departing procession Odile looked shocked.

'But . . . but we are British, he could not have harmed us!'

Taking an elbow of each of the women James Allen guided them through the milling crowd towards the gate leading out of the city.

'He could and he would had he taken Miss Hallam's remark the other way.'

'Surely not!' Odile was emphatic. 'It would have brought retribution down upon him, the daughter of a member of Her Majesty's government.'

'The trouble with retribution ma'am is it often comes *after* the crime.'

'I never thought my words would be misconstrued, I truly meant no offence,' Tamar apologised.

'Of course you did not, and that . . . that Emir person had the sense to see that. I think Mr Allen is trying to frighten us poor women.'

Over the top of Tamar's bent head James Allen caught the flare of warning in Odile's eyes.

Taking his cue he laughed lightly. 'Discovered again, I see I cannot fool you Mrs Bancroft.'

'Tamar, my dear.' Odile raised her parasol as they emerged from the relatively shaded street on to the broad area giving on to the jetty. 'I am sorry to foreshorten our visit but I am very tired. Would you mind if I ask Mr Allen to return us to the ship?'

'Of course not.' Tamar was immediately solicitous, but as they boarded the ship she looked back towards the huge walls skirting the city, the beautiful blue dome and its mosque rising above them and could not help but feel a stab of disappointment that she could not see more of its fascination. Or was it the fascination of gleaming brown eyes gazing down at her?

The blush returning to her cheeks she followed silently behind her mistress, relieved the shadowed cabin helped to mask her sudden colour.

Nathan Burford flipped on to his back, floating effortlessly in the warm tropical waters of the estuary of the River Rokel. They had been here in Sierra

Leone almost a week loading cocoa beans and taking on stores and water for the return trip to England.

Closing his eyes to the brilliant sunlight he fought the disappointment in his heart. He had used much of the time since arriving here asking for news of Aiden and Louise describing his brother and the girl who had eloped with him, but at every turn he had met a blank wall. Every trip he told himself he would make no more search but like a steel drawn to a magnet he was drawn to look for Aiden.

'Cargo stowed, Captain.'

Raising a hand to the call Nathan turned on to his stomach, a few easy strokes bringing him to the rope ladder dangling from the lee side of the *Verity*.

On deck he glanced at the man stood beside the first mate, then nodded for him to follow below.

'So Douglas, how goes the business?'

Dried and dressed in uniform Nathan poured two glasses of wine offering one to his guest.

'Very well, Mr Burford. The crop is as fine as any we have had before.'

'And the estate workers, they are all well?'

'And proving it.' Douglas Coates sipped the cool wine, a slight nod indicating approval. 'There have been five babies born since your last visit and two more expected within the month.'

'Not yours I trust.'

'No, not mine.' Coates returned the grin. 'But you never know . . . one of these days.'

'Best get yourself married first you rogue.'

'Now you have to go and spoil things.'

'A habit of mine I'm afraid.' Nathan smiled again at the man who was as much his friend as his estate manager, then his look becoming more serious he asked, 'Has there been anyone in from the interior?'

His own smile fading Douglas Coates watched the face of the man who trusted him to manage a plantation worth thousands and one he would gladly give his life for. Nathan Burford had given him the chance no other man would. He had taken a penniless clerk and sailed him across the sea into a new life, a life that held respect as well as authority, but it was the man's trust in him that he most appreciated. That he would never violate.

'No one with any news.' Douglas shook his head. 'You cannot really expect anything, not after such a length of time.'

'I know.' Nathan turned to the small-paned window his eyes seeing nothing of the palms fringing the coast. 'But a man hopes nevertheless.'

'You have my word sir, even the slightest hint is investigated.'

'I never doubt that Douglas, but hope is all I have and I must hold on to it. I had thought to be over the loss, in fact I have all but given up making enquiries, but here . . . here I always feel somehow . . .'

Opening a ledger he had brought with him Douglas Coates gave time for Nathan to swallow the feelings that showed in every line of his fine face.

'I brought the accounts with me in case you did not intend visiting the plantation. You will see they are all healthy and showing a profit.'

'And that is due to you.' Nathan turned, his composure restored. 'You are a fine manager Douglas, and more than that you are a good friend.'

'Then allow one friend to show another a second line of business.'

Taking a small cloth bag from his pocket Douglas Coates tipped its contents on to the table.

'They were brought by a native in from the interior. He was almost starving when he came to the plantation. He offered those in exchange for a meal and a place to rest.'

'Good Lord!' Nathan breathed. 'I hope you fed the fellow.'

'Like a king.' Douglas spread the contents of the bag as he grinned. 'But more than that I went with him to the place he said he found those, a spot he stopped to take a drink. They must have been washed down with river gravel.'

Taking up what looked like a small pebble Nathan rubbed it between finger and thumb. 'But how come the fellow was in such a bad state?'

'He had done something that annoyed the chief . . . something to do with asking for the man's favourite daughter and that resulted in being kicked out of the village. He didn't want to go back there but eventually I persuaded him. The outcome is I bought the land around the spot where those were found; the chief was very pleased with the deal we struck. I hope I did right for you, sir.'

'And the man who brought these to you?'

Douglas Coates smiled. The question was no more

than he expected from Nathan Burford, he was ever careful that others were treated fairly.

'He was welcomed back, especially after I said that only a man of their tribe would have the courage to face again the wrath of a great chief against which no other danger was worthy of account.'

'Ever the smooth talker, Douglas. I only hope the man is still safely alive.'

'That, and the chief's daughter to grace the re-conciliation. I also asked that such a brave tribe provide a guard for the place and for him to be the fellow in charge.'

Tossing the pebble-like objects and catching them in his hand, Nathan smiled. 'I begin to think I underestimated you Mr Coates. Perhaps you would be more at home in Her Majesty's diplomatic service.'

'I prefer yours.'

The simple answer quietly spoken had Nathan silent for a moment, then equally quietly he replied.

'In what name did you register the land?'

A brief frown flicked across Douglas Coates' brow. 'Nathan Burford, the same as the plantation.'

'Then change it!' Nathan slapped the objects he was holding back on to the table. 'Register it in the names of Burford and Coates. From this moment we are equal partners in the diamond business.'

Diamonds! Douglas Coates having returned ashore Nathan took up one of the rough stones. He would gladly give them all to find Aiden and Louise alive. But then perhaps he would keep one.

Staring out through his cabin window he remembered a girl with gleaming auburn hair, green eyes smiling shyly back at him; and in his daydream he took her hand, slipping a glittering diamond ring on to the third finger.

Chapter Nineteen

Halfway up the companionway James Allen heard the stifled scream. He had escorted the women to their cabins leaving them at the door. Had one of them seen a rat? Vermin sometimes ran along the mooring ropes and got into the hold. Behind him he heard the sound of breaking glass and a woman's cry. Clearing the steps in a jump he raced back along the narrow corridor; not all vermin came aboard from a port of call, some were already aboard!

'Say a word, one bloody word and I'll kill ya, you 'ear me . . . I'll slit the throats of the pair of ya!'

The words came clearly from Tamar's cabin and James Allen halted abruptly. The door was still ajar but to rush in might have serious results. He knew that voice and knew the man behind it was not one to make idle threats. Like others of the crew this one had been press-ganged into the Navy years before and resentment had lived in him ever since.

'Remember, one word and you be dead, Ezra Payne don't be a man to go back on his word.'

At the door James Allen's body was deceptively loose. He had recognised the voice correctly. Payne was a nasty piece of work who would not hesitate to harm those women should he try to take him now.

Taking a few steps backward into a pool of dark shadow he carefully unbuckled the sword that hung at his side lowering it silently at his feet. He would not take the man with any weapon other than his hands.

Across the narrow space a line of light signalled the opening of the cabin door. Among the shadows Allen tensed. Payne was not a man to be played with and surprise was a brief element, it would afford him only one chance.

The band of sunlight widening he drew a breath holding it in his throat. The man would not risk being seen using this companionway, he would make his way aft and then amidships to the crew's quarters.

'Keep you in the cabin 'less you want more than this!'

At his sides the lieutenant's hands clenched as the sound of a hand striking flesh and a woman's terrified cry followed the words.

'. . . and you says nothin' to that bastard Allen . . . you 'ear what I says . . . you breathe a word of what you 'ave seen and that fancy man you been castin' sheep's eyes at will disappear over the side the first night we sails, you 'ave Ezra Payne's word on it!'

Hearing the man slide from the cabin, guessing the quick glance he cast the way of the narrow flight of steps that led to the deck James Allen kept the breath he was holding. He had known the man Payne was a vile character, but this . . . to strike a woman!

Stepping from the shadows the breath was snatched from him and though soft, was caught by Payne. Instantly alert he whirled towards it.

'Who be there . . . ?'

'That bastard Allen, the man you be going to throw overboard the first night we sail.'

Stepping further into the corridor James Allen hesitated. But the seconds when surprise held him in its grip was enough. Lunging forward Payne caught him a blow to the temple, a vicious heavy blow with a truncheon that sent him sprawling senseless to the floor.

'You are sure there was no intruder in your cabin when Lieutenant Allen returned you here?'

Glad for once of the bout of coughing that erupted from the cabin adjoining hers Tamar turned towards the sound, freeing herself momentarily from the hawk-like scrutiny of the captain's sharp eyes. James Allen had been found by one of the crew and Captain Jones was enquiring personally as to the safety of his passengers.

'I . . . I did not see anyone.' The lie trembled on her tongue.

'You could not help but see another person in here.' The captain sent a quick glance about the cramped room. 'So I must accept that no one *was* here . . . and Mrs Bancroft's cabin?'

'There was no one in there.'

This time it was not a lie. Tamar turned again to

face the man she guessed could all the time have read the truth in her eyes.

'I see. Then I must accept what Lieutenant Allen has said. He caught his head against a timber, though for so experienced a seaman I find it difficult to comprehend.'

'Is Mr Allen seriously injured?'

'Thankfully not.' The captain gave a slight bow before turning to leave. 'My compliments to Mrs Bancroft, with her permission I will call upon her this evening.'

They had heard the scuffle outside in the corridor, but they had been too terrified to leave the cabin. If only she had . . . Guilt riding through her Tamar went in to her mistress. If she had found the courage to throw open that door then maybe James Allen would not have been injured. It had to be that awful man who had struck him. She could tell the captain of her suspicion, but then Odile Bancroft's life and that of James Allen would be forfeit as well as her own.

The pleasure of the afternoon destroyed, Tamar measured a dose of laudanum, handing the tiny glass to Odile. Watching her swallow the medicine she felt a new niggle of worry. The woman turned more and more to the drug for relief but each time she awoke she seemed more listless and tired than before. If only the *Porpoise* carried a doctor. But James Allen had explained that first time she had requested one visit Odile, only ships of war carry a medical officer and the *Porpoise* was not on a mission of war.

Removing the glass she covered the other woman

with a light sheet, smiling down at her as she closed her eyes. How could any man have left such a kind, gentle woman? Pray God when Odile Bancroft found her husband he would be a changed man, pray God she would find her happiness.

Standing at the ship's rail Tamar breathed the hot dry air of evening. Daytime was a furnace heat, an almost intolerable beating down of a burning pitiless sun that had the land on both sides of the canal a vast endless waste of empty desert. Looking out over it now Tamar remembered the fantasies she had woven on the nights sleep eluded her, dreams of wonderful buildings and busy ports like the one they had called at for fresh water and stores.

Across the rising sand dunes the hot shimmering air danced in patterns and shapes, weaving into a cavalcade of camel riders dressed in lemon silk followed by a great horse, its rider dressed simply in white, the mirage fading as the man's eyes reached for hers.

A fantasy that died as soon as it was born, an empty teasing of her brain. Was that what this whole journey would prove to be, an endless chase after a dream . . . would her search for Benjie prove to have as little substance?

'Taking the evening air.'

The sound of the thick voice taking her unawares Tamar started. She had not heard the quiet tread of Josiah Taylor come to stand beside her.

'I knows a place where a body would be cool,

where folk can lie undisturbed; you come with Jos Taylor and he will ease those daydreams from your mind, he will give you pleasures that are real, give you what that trim little body of your'n be cryin' out for.'

'Leave me alone!' Tamar made to move away but a rough hand closed quickly over hers.

Thick lips wet with saliva, small eyes gleaming he grinned evily. 'Why deny yourself a bit of pleasure? This be a long voyage and it ain't near 'alf done yet, but that could be all to the good. Come, let me show you the way a man and a woman pass the long nights together. Have a taste of what Jos Taylor has atwixt his legs and you'll be longing for each nightfall.'

'You are disgusting!' Tamar snatched her hand free.

'Maybe.' Josiah Taylor's eyes hooded dangerously. 'So you best remembers what it is I've just told you; this be a long voyage and it ain't near 'alf done yet!'

'You there . . . look lively!'

A sob of relief breaking from her Tamar leaned heavily against the rail as the crisp command from the poop deck had Taylor move quickly away. She knew how he and a few of the others watched her when she came on to the deck, that was the reason she came just for a few minutes before night closed in, the rest of the time was spent in the cabin. Odile Bancroft's health had steadily deteriorated since the day they had found an intruder in their quarters. Even the laudanum, which was almost gone, seemed to have no effect any more, the woman coughing away the long night hours, her days spent lying worn out in her bed.

Perhaps once the Gulf of Suez was passed, maybe

then they would be in a cooler climate and Odile would recover.

'Was that man bothering you, Miss Hallam?'

'No, no Captain Jones, he wished me good evening, no more than that.' Tamar forced a smile to support the lie.

The captain ran an eagle eye over the knots of the sail ropes secured to the ship's side. The girl would not readily give a man over to punishment, that was a mark in her favour but one that could prove a danger in the long run.

'How is Mrs Bancroft this evening?'

'Sleeping at the moment.'

'Then I will not presume upon her. Perhaps before dinner?'

'I think she would like that.'

Tamar watched the straight figure walk along the deck checking every detail of the ship's accoutrements as he went, every man snapping to attention as he approached. She could so easily have asked that the man Taylor be kept away from her, she would be given the protection she prayed nightly for; but at what price? It was one she was not willing to pay.

Gathering her skirts she walked slowly back to the cabin.

'Tamar, why do you think that man took the things he did?'

Washed and dressed in a fresh cambric nightgown, hair more grey than black, neatly plaited and tied with blue satin ribbon, Odile Bancroft watched the girl she had taken on as lady's maid tidy away brushes and comb.

Tamar hesitated. This was the first time since its occurrence the question had been openly asked, both of them refusing to broach the subject of the robbery, neither wanting to hurt the other by bringing the painful episode up. Odile Bancroft had refused to have it reported to the captain or to James Allen; the things stolen were trivial, she had said, not worth the fuss reporting their loss would create. But Tamar knew, like herself, the woman kept silent to protect others.

'I can't say, ma'am.' She answered, not meeting the other woman's eyes.

'But they were such strange things for a man to steal, do you not think?'

Taking the hand mirror from the bed Tamar replaced it on the dressing chest.

'They cannot possibly be of use to him.'

'He probably intends to sell them at whichever port we put into next; but I could ask for their return if you wish.'

'No.' Odile Bancroft's quick answer brought on a bout of coughing that left her fighting for breath.

If only it were cooler. Tamar wrung out a cloth in water already warmed by the heat of the cabin, placing it on the woman's hot brow.

'They . . . they are of little consequence.' Odile went on as the coughing eased. 'But there is one matter I deem to be of great consequence.'

'Is there something I can do, ma'am? Have I forgotten . . . ?'

'No Tamar, you have not forgotten anything. Amy was correct in saying you would make a splendid lady's maid and I am grateful you came with me.' She paused, each quick shallow breath hard fought for. Tapping a limp hand on the bed cover she went on. 'Will you sit with me a while, I have something I wish to say to you.'

Looking at the flushed face, the normally lacklustre eyes brilliant now with the threat of fever, Tamar felt her heart quicken. Odile Bancroft was more sick than she had imagined. Going to the bed she sat beside her and flouting the rules of her station took the other woman's hand holding it between her own.

'Tamar, I have been thinking . . . in the event of my not reaching Australia . . .'

'Please ma'am, that is nonsense, of course you will reach Australia!'

Odile Bancroft smiled at the quick interruption, knowing the concern flooding the girl's eyes was genuine.

'No my dear, it is not nonsense, the possibility is, I fear, a very real one and must be faced. Listen to me Tamar . . .' she shook her head as Tamar went to speak again '. . . I have no more illusions. I know coming to Australia is a futile act. Even should I find my husband I know he will not return to me . . .' she broke off as the cough wracked through her '. . . with that and the possibility I have spoken of it is my wish you have the property left to me. Unfortunately it consists only of the clothes in these trunks and the few bits of cheap jewellery.'

'Don't say any more!' Tamar lifted the hand holding it against her cheek. 'You are going to reach that country and your husband will be delighted you are together again.'

'That will not be the way of it, Tamar. I faced the pain of knowing so long ago but a woman fools herself with dreams. But now the dreaming is done.'

Releasing the woman's hand Tamar refreshed the cloth, returning it gently to the heated brow.

'You have been more than a maid.' Odile pressed a handkerchief to her lips but the cough refused to be stemmed, then as it eventually passed she smiled wearily up from her pillows. 'More than a maid, you have been a friend, and as my friend I ask you to take the only gift I have to give you.'

'But I don't need any gift,' Tamar protested. 'You have already done enough by allowing me to take Amy's place.'

'It will please me for you to agree.' Odile Bancroft's eyes flared like newly lit torches. 'Say you will accept Tamar, say you will take what I offer. If the Lord wills I do not reach Australia then take what little there is, sell it and use the money to search for your brother, say you will.'

Looking into the flushed face Tamar felt that to discuss the matter further may aggravate the fever burning in the gentle face. Tomorrow would be time enough to tell Odile she wanted nothing but the woman's friendship.

'Please rest now, ma'am.' She rose, still looking down at the tired features, lids closed over fever drenched eyes.

'Promise me, Tamar.'

The whisper was soft as breath on the wind.

'I promise, ma'am. But please rest while I will get a jug of lime juice, it will help cool you.'

She hated leaving the cabin at night. The narrow corridors between decks were filled with shadows during the daytime but night peopled the shadows with frightening illusions. But a cooling drink would help settle Odile to sleep.

Closing the cabin door softly behind her Tamar moved towards the flight of steep narrow stairs, her senses leaping at every creak of the ship's timbers. If she should meet Taylor now! Her flesh creeping she forced herself not to turn back, not to run to the safety of her cabin and lock herself in. There would be no escape from him here in this narrow passage, nor would he be seen in this inky darkness. Feeling the breath tight in her throat Tamar almost cried out at a sound from ahead. There was someone there in the shadows. She listened to the quick footfall. It was someone who knew his way, someone confident he would not be apprehended.

Maybe if she pressed close to the bulkhead, kept absolutely still he would pass by without realising she was there. But that was futile, she stared ahead her own fears giving the shadows a life . . . movement . . . there was hardly room in these corridors for one person to pass another without touching.

There was still time for her to get back to her cabin. She could wait there in the hope of Lieutenant Allen calling, but if he did not . . .

Fear and indecision combined while Tamar stared ahead, a scream rising to her lips as a figure emerged from the blackness.

'Eh, I be sorry I startled you miss.' The young cabin boy who had been assigned the duty of bringing meals to the women's quarters came to an abrupt halt, a scare echoing in his usually chirpy voice. 'I never expected to see you outside of your cabin.'

'I was hoping to find the kitchen.' Tamar said, weak with relief.

' 'T ain't the kitchen miss, you means the galley. You don't find kitchens 'cept in an 'ouse, a ship 'as a galley.' The boy took pride in his explanation. 'Do you want I take you there or be there summat as I can fetch to your quarters?'

'I was hoping I could have some fresh limes to make Mrs Bancroft a cooling drink. I would be grateful if you would see to it.' Tamar accepted the boy's suggestion gratefully.

'Just you let me see you safe to your quarters miss, it be darker than the devil's soul below decks. You might easily knock yourself against summat you not bein' used to the ways of a ship, then I'll be along to the galley an' get the drink you asks for.'

Breathing a prayer of thanks Tamar followed the lad, thanking him as he opened the door for her. Standing for a moment in the humid stillness the thought of home and the people she had known from childhood returned with a vivid intensity, the pain of homesickness sharp in her breast. Would she see them again, her and Benjie together?

Pushing the longing to the back of her mind she passed into the adjoining cabin.

'I met the cabin boy in the corridor. He is going to bring some fresh lime juice.'

Looking down at the face free now of the flush of heat, closed eyelids blanking out the gleam of fever, Tamar dropped to her knees beside the bed. Odile Bancroft had not answered, she would never answer again.

Chapter Twenty

It was truly magnificent. Philip Amory looked at the jewellery laid out on a table in his sitting room. Nestled against purple velvet the necklace sparked a myriad tiny iridescent flames echoed in the matching earrings. Two square-cut diamonds underslung by a large teardrop, each stone perfectly matched and expertly cut, they gleamed in their heavy gold setting. Isaac Cohen was indeed an artist with stones, the whole suite was a masterpiece and worthy of the nickname it had among the workfolk of Hockley.

'There you are, gentlemen.' Philip cast a glance at the assembled goldsmiths. 'The Alexandra Stone. What do you think, is it worthy of a princess?'

'It be worthy of the Queen Empress herself!' Matthew Summers breathed his appreciation.

'That be right enough,' Saul Fisher nodded, 'but would giving it to the Queen serve the same purpose? Remember the reason it were made, to bring industry back into the Gold Quarter, industry follows fashion and it be the Princess of Wales sets the fashion not her mother-in-law.'

'Are we all still agreed on that, it goes to Alexandra?'

Philip Amory paused giving the men time to disagree if they wished, then as each nodded accordance went on. 'Then it remains for us to decide which man will accompany the pieces to Kensington Palace.'

'It should be you, Amory my friend.' Isaac Cohen looked over the top of steel-rimmed spectacles.

'Ar, it should be you, it were your idea in the first place. Make the Princess of Wales a piece of fancy jewellery and the whole world would be clamouring for the same was what you said.'

'Yes Fisher, that was what I said and it is what I still believe; but it does not automatically give me the right to make the presentation. You all reinvested your money in the venture after the necklace was recovered therefore each of you has the right to hand it to the Princess.'

'We cannot all go, my friend.' Isaac Cohen raised his shoulders in his peculiar shrug. 'They might take it as an invasion, who knows already!'

'A friendly invasion I hope.' Philip smiled.

'The world has already seen too many of the other sort, the Almighty forbid this island should ever see the like.'

'Amen to that,' Summers put in as the old Jew shook his head. 'But let's deal with one business before talking of another. I agree with Cohen, it should be Amory takes that jewellery to London . . . anybody who don't?'

Once again a pause in conversation gave each man time to register his opinion, but as before no man raised an objection.

'There you have it, Amory my friend. We are all of the same opinion, the honour must fall to you. Now this old man hears his bed calling.' Isaac stood up, a sound of discomfort slipping quietly from his lips as he straightened. 'My bones are not as young as they once were, they need their rest. I wish you all the shelter of the mantle of the Lord of Hosts.'

'I must be off as well.' Matthew Summers followed the others to the hall. Taking his overcoat and hat from Philip's manservant he nodded. 'Goodnight to you Amory, be sure you lock that jewellery away in your safe, it wouldn't do to 'ave it pinched a second time. By the way,' pulling gloves over his hands he turned as he reached the open front door, 'has there been any word from Edgbaston? That Tullio fellow said the boy had not stolen the Alexandra Stone, surely the law has acted upon that.'

Unconsciously drawing his watch from its pocket Philip Amory twirled it between his fingers.

'The lawyer I instructed has not as yet had any definite answer as to the boy being fetched home, but I have talked to a friend who is in the House, he has promised to raise the question with the Home Secretary. I have every hope that will settle the matter and the boy can be transported back to Britain.'

'Very good of you, Amory. I knew we could depend on you.'

Closing the door after his departing guests Philip

felt the old sting of guilt. Who could Tamar Hallam depend on . . . why had he not been there for her?

James Allen touched the arm of the girl sat staring at the narrow bed set in an alcove of the cabin. He had heard her cry even on deck and calling to the bosun had raced below. Now with that officer to take charge he tried to get Tamar to return to her own cabin.

'I think you should leave,' he said quietly, 'there is no more you can do for her.'

But the words went unheard, his touch unrecognised. Still as stone, her thoughts pounding like waves against her brain Tamar watched two crewmen lift the wasted body of Odile Bancroft and place it on a length of sail cloth.

It was as if the woman had known she was about to die, as if she had known she would have no further need of the things she had insisted Tamar promise to take.

'Come away now.'

James Allen's fingers pressed gently against her arm but numb with shock it made no impression on her mind.

Why had she decided to go fetch that drink herself, why could she not have waited? The cabin boy would have come to see if they needed anything before they retired. If she had waited she would have been with Odile when . . .

A soft cry breaking from her lips James Allen drew

her gently to her feet a supporting arm about her waist.

'I should have stayed with her.' Eyes wide with self-reproach looked up as he quietly urged her away, 'I should have stayed.'

'You were not to know. Even had you been with her you could not have prevented what has happened, you must not blame yourself.'

He was trying to be kind but the words had no solace. Inside her the feeling of guilt, of letting down the woman who had been so good to her, cut like a razor. Please God let her find her happiness . . . that had been her prayer for Odile Bancroft . . . now she would never find it.

Pausing at the doorway she turned to look back, the shock of what she saw taking the last remaining strength from her body. Trembling in every limb, clinging to the lieutenant's arm she stared at the scene before her, stared at the man sewing the body of Odile Bancroft into its canvas shroud.

If he could be with her, hold her, whisper away the pain he had seen in those lovely eyes . . . but he could not.

James Allen stared out over the dark waters. For the first time since signing his name at Deptford he resented being in the navy, resented the regulations that tied him to his duties as lieutenant.

He had ordered that the cabin boy spend the night in the corridor, sleeping at Tamar's door. The boy would be snug enough, he had slept in worse places and there was no crew member other than the bosun he could trust to stay there. But like himself the bosun had duties that could not be neglected.

But was it only the fact of duty keeping him that plagued him now? Not if he was honest. The slap of canvas in a rising breeze drew his glance upward. Ever since seeing her in that alleyway in Bristol trying to fight off the advances of Taylor he had felt drawn to Tamar Hallam, had wanted to be with her, and as the voyage had progressed so had his feelings, until now he knew he loved her.

He had first realised the truth of that when he had caught the look that emir had cast at her, the appreciation that had glinted in the man's eyes. He had wanted to tell her then but knew he must not. As an officer of the Royal Navy he must not be thought to be taking advantage of a woman's loneliness or of his position. But when the voyage was done, once they reached Australia and she was no longer in the care of the *Porpoise* . . .

Allowing his eyes to travel over the velvet blackness of a sky strewn with a million jewel-like stars he breathed deeply.

. . . When she was no longer a passenger on this ship then he would speak.

The continued slap of canvas breaking his thoughts he turned from the rail of the poop his glance raking the darkness of the main deck. Fore and aft lanterns spread a negligible glow, another strung above the wheel adding little more.

Why was that sail not being secured?

The darkness no match for experience his glance went immediately to the spot the sail rope was secured, then back to the deck his mouth tightening.

Unhurried, deliberately controlling the anger surging up in him he cleared the short flight of steps his tread making no sound on the planking as he made his way to the crew's quarters.

Stopping at the space set apart from the rest he bent towards the man, who was on his feet before the hand reached his shoulder.

Alert as ever! James Allen admired the man who, like himself, had pulled himself up from nothing, sheer hard work and dedication the path that had led him to becoming more than an able seaman. Touching a finger to his lips, the other man's nod saying he understood the need for silence James led the way aloft.

'Who is taking the dog watch?'

All trace of sleep leaving his brain clear the bosun frowned as he answered.

'Taylor be taking second dog watch sir, he took over from Payne, he stood first dog.'

'Then where is he?' The question was crisp.

'He be there at his station, sir.'

'I see. Then perhaps you will show him to me!'

His own sight keen as that of the man beside him, experience honing it the bosun shot a glance across the space of the deck his voice gritting through closed teeth.

'He were there when I made the night rounds but he'll wish himself anywheres *but* there when I finds 'im!'

'Wait!' James Allen spoke quietly. 'We don't want to rouse the ship, remember we have a passenger aboard, and the captain . . . it will go easier with everybody if we can keep this from him.'

'That can't be done Mr Allen, begging your pardon. A man missing from his watch be a serious offence, even more so when it be a night watch, and it also be an offence to keep a matter such as that from the captain. It will 'ave to be reported, sir.'

'Yes, of course.' James agreed quickly. 'But not now, there will be time for that later, first we must secure the watch. I will take it while you get a man to replace me, then we will look for Taylor.'

Taking up position as the bosun returned below James Allen let out a slow breath.

When they did find Taylor it would be well for him to be nowhere near Tamar Hallam!

A bewildered sailor set to the watch the bosun handed over a truncheon, keeping a second one for himself.

'Thought we best 'ave these handy sir, Taylor be a nasty piece of work, 'specially if he's been drinking.'

'Is this necessary?'

'The men knows the ruling sir, the only alcohol they be allowed while at sea be the daily ration of grog, but they don't always abide by rules.'

If the man did prove to be drunk then that would

be one more regret he would have. Taking the lead James Allen once more made his way below.

Another voyage that had proved fruitless.

Naked against the heat of the tropic night Nathan Burford lay in his bunk. It was always this way. Returning to England with no word of his brother, disappointment barring the sleep that would for a few hours at least ease the ache in his heart. He had known deep within himself that it was futile to hope, but somehow hope was always there only to be killed again.

But on this voyage there had been a new barb probing him, driving the dart of restlessness deeper, allowing him no respite.

Flinging from the bunk he crossed to the window opening it to the sultry night that drew almost no relief from the harmattan, a cool breeze that blew during the dry season.

Breathing deeply he tasted the soft air that even now carried a faint aroma of perfume. An echo of ginger mingling faintly with the perfumes of moist grasslands and exquisite tropical flowers. That was what he told himself. That was what he had told himself every night. But it was no truth!

Impatient with the admission he returned to his bed closing his eyes against the satin softness of the night; but still he could not block out the teasing perfume that played relentlessly on his senses, nor the truth that underlay it.

It was no perfume of a tropical night, no exotic fragrance of spice or flowers that tormented him. It was the warm scent of a creamy skin, of auburn hair washed in fresh rainwater, it was the scent of Tamar Hallam!

But why? Why should that girl have this effect on him? He had spoken no more than a dozen words to her, a cup of coffee in a Bristol coffee house.

'. . . I have never had that . . .'

The words she had spoken when he had asked were coffee not to her taste returned to him now their soft candour adding to the restless feel inside him.

She had looked so vulnerable sitting there, a thread-bare shawl her only protection against the bitter February cold, her eyes bright with the promise of tears. Such lovely eyes.

A groan escaping his lips he laid an arm across his face but the eyes still looked at him.

He had been abrupt with her, sharp to the point of ridicule when she had spoken of going to Australia. Was it because even then, regardless of his not realising it until now, he had felt himself drawn to her but at the same time felt guilty at being so?

He had objected to Aiden's being just as drawn to Louise, rejected their pleas to be forgiven, denied his brother the right to love. So why should he have that right? He could not.

Lowering his arm he opened his eyes, staring out of the window at the canopy of huge low-slung stars.

He could never allow himself that which he tried to take from Aiden, he could never allow himself to love.

He would keep the word he had given himself, he would give that girl any help he could to find her brother. Once they reached Bristol he would seek her out, offer what help she would accept.

Closing his eyes he listened to the gentle slap of waves against the hull, the lazy flapping of canvas sails but his thoughts remained stubbornly centred on a slender auburn-haired girl whose lovely sea-green eyes seemed to plead with him.

From the quarter deck the clear sound of a bell being struck signalled the changeover of the morning watch: 4 a.m. Nathan had no need of a clock to recognise the time. He had lain awake all night, but then he had followed that pattern for five years past and was like to follow it for the rest of his life . . . a life that would be as empty as those years had been.

From the blackness behind closed eyes the lovely face smiled hauntingly.

They could have settled their differences. Aiden and he could have worked things out, Aiden and Louise could still be alive if only he . . . but instead he had allowed pride to rule his head, he had written his own ticket to hell, one which carried a life sentence.

Swinging his legs over the side of the bunk he got to his feet. Leaving the candle lantern that swung from a beam in the centre of the cabin unlit he reached for his clothes.

He had made his future and in it there would be no woman, no love, no marriage; those were luxuries his own pride had robbed him of, luxuries Nathan Burford would never know.

Chapter Twenty-One

They would take no lantern, the years spent serving aboard the *Porpoise* must be his guide now.

James Allen moved carefully down the steps that gave on to the bottom hold. He wanted no flicker of light to warn of their coming, whatever thievery Josiah Taylor was up to the man must be caught red-handed.

Standing for a few seconds at the base of the ladder that gave on to the bowels of the ship he allowed his sight to accustom to the darkness, for black as the night was on deck, here the blackness was thicker.

A touch from the bosun indicated they move on. They had searched each level in turn, head and shoulders bent as the corridors became narrower, each giving less and less headroom. But once past the crew's quarters with its snores of sleeping men behind them the ship had become near silent, the creak of timbers her only song.

But each level had proved a blank. James Allen stepped carefully, every sense vitally alive. Should this, the bottom hold, prove the same then there was no place left to look except . . . but he would not hide his takings there, surely the man would have more sense than to go to the women's quarters . . . unless it was not the hiding of stolen property he went for!

The thought burning like acid in his brain he misplaced his step catching a boot against a barrel. Instantly the bosun's hand was on his arm steadying him, then a double tug to his sleeve alerting him he stared ahead. There, yards from where they stood, the faint gleam of a candle lantern spilled into the darkness.

They must go carefully now, who could tell what manner of weapon the man might have?

No shout of challenge or sudden flurry of movement telling his slip had been heard James Allen moved slowly, the truncheon gripped tight in one hand, the other already lifted defensively across his chest.

Ahead, the candle lantern swayed with the roll of the ship, its pale light momentarily chasing the stifling shadows from the bulwarks.

What was there down here worth the stealing? Only sailcloth and twine were stored in the lower hold; food, if food it was the man was bent on stealing, was kept in separate storerooms and those were amidships.

Thoughts arrested by a low moan James Allen resisted the urge to hurry forward. The man sounded to be injured, that moan suggested as much, but even injured, Josiah Taylor was a threat.

The moan louder and more regular, its own masking the soft tread of their feet, the two officers pressed forward then as they came to the pool of light both stopped abruptly.

'What in the name of God . . . !'

James Allen gasped at the sight that met his eyes. Ezra Payne, a blue-stoned necklace about his throat, a matching silk gown thrown back to his waist lay sprawled on a pile of canvas, eyes tight shut, low groans issuing intermittently from his partly open mouth while between his widespread legs a second man lay face down, two broad hands caressing and stroking Payne's stomach while his mouth nuzzled hard flesh.

'Christ!'

Ezra Payne's closed eyes flew open his legs imprisoning Taylor's head as he tried to snap them shut.

'What the hell do you think you are doing?'

'Seems clear what they be doing sir.' The bosun's laconic answer held no humour.

'Aye it be clear what we be doing.' Unlike his partner Josiah Taylor showed no sign of fear as he rolled slowly on to his back.

'How long has this been going on?' The lieutenant's voice was low with anger and disgust.

Taylor sniggered. 'What . . . buggery? I'd say just as long as men been making long voyages.'

'Don't make things worse for yourself Taylor, answer the lieutenant.' The bosun lifted the truncheon tapping it lightly against a rib of the ship.

'Answer the lieutenant, kiss the lieutenant's arse!' Taylor spat viciously, 'Well *you* answer it, you kiss his arse and lick his balls for Jos Taylor won't.'

'Then you will answer to the captain.'

A leap as agile as a mountain cat had Taylor on his

feet the light of the lantern spilling over a body streaking with perspiration.

'Aye, I'll answer to the captain,' he breathed, both hands curving into claws, 'but not afore you 'ave answered to me.'

A pistol he had stuck in the waistband of his trousers gleaming in the candlelight the bosun raised it slowly the barrel aimed directly at Taylor's heart.

'I'd be 'aving me a second think about that were I in your shoes,' he smiled grimly, 'a good second think Taylor, for you knows I never misses what I aims at.'

Keeping his eyes on one man he kicked out at the other.

'You,' the smile became grimmer, 'smooth your skirts, we wants you looking pretty when we brings you afore the captain.'

Scrabbling to his feet, fear strong on his narrow face sweat-soaked hair plastered to his head like a coat of brown paint, Ezra Payne babbled furiously.

'Not the captain, bosun please . . . lieutenant . . . !'

'Stow that!' The truncheon striking hard against the wooden rib reinforced the bosun's snapped command. 'You knowed what you was about when you stole that frock together wi' them beads. No . . . leave them be,' he tapped the truncheon menacingly, 'like I says we wants you looking pretty for the captain!'

Though tense in every fibre, his body one with the ship James Allen compensated her roll on the swell keeping his stance with the ease of long years at sea.

Glancing at the man struggling with his woman's skirts he gritted his teeth, words having to push to clear them.

'I will ask you Payne, how long has this been going on and do not give me any tripe about long voyages, your friend here has tried that already.'

'It . . . we . . . I ain't never . . .' Illuminated by the pallid shifting light Ezra Payne's sallow skin shone with an anaemic sickly yellowness.

A thick laugh erupted from Taylor's throat. 'It'll be time for the dog watch afore he spits it out!'

In the gloom the tap of the bosun's truncheon gave impetus to the snap of his reply.

'Then you spit it out forrim, you seems to do other things 'appy enough for the scum!'

Taylor sniggered at the bosun's words, his eyes still riveted on the lean figure of his superior officer.

'Aye, I'll do that, I'll answer forrim. It be simple Mr Allen *sir*, ask yourself 'ow long you've served aboard the *Porpoise*, that'll give you the answer you be seeking; and while you be about it ask yourself this an' all. What will Captain Jones 'ave to say when he 'ears, when he sees what efficient officers serves under 'im?'

'Captain won't be interested in your lies, the way you pair look now will be interest enough for him.'

Eyes as keen as a hawk cut through the gloom, the barrel of the pistol pointing steadily the bosun went on.

'Leave your trousers Taylor and before you think to swipe out let me tell you I would get more pleasure from putting a hole atween your eyes than I would from striking gold.'

The endless wastes of desert had become endless wastes of empty sea but stood on the deck Tamar was unaware of the change. Standing a little apart from the silent crew she stared with aching eyes at the canvas-wrapped bundle laid on a rough plank of wood placed on two barrels.

Odile Bancroft was dead.

The quiet woman was dead and no family to mourn her, no coffin to lie in, only a rough canvas shroud to hold her body.

'Are you sure you wish to go through with this Miss Hallam?' Beside her James Allen was concerned. 'You can go back to your cabin, no one will see any disrespect in that.'

'No.' Tamar's reply was low, almost lost among the sound of waves beginning to slap harshly against the hull of the ship. 'I . . . I must be here, I am all she had, I cannot leave her now.'

Glancing at the face that tears seemed only to have made more enchanting James Allen felt an almost overwhelming desire to hold her in his arms, to whisper comfort against her soft mouth. He had felt this way almost from the beginning, wondering how it would feel to hold her, to feel her lips beneath his own, to tell her . . .

'Captain on deck!'

The curt words sliced through the thick humid air

and James reluctantly forced away the thoughts leaving his mind clear as the figure of Captain Jones strode through the line of assembled men to stand beside the shroud-wrapped body.

'In the name of the Almighty . . .'

At her side Tamar felt the brisk movement as the lieutenant followed the suit of crew and officers, removing his braided cap as the captain opened a small prayer book.

The cabin boy had returned with the promised lime juice. Tamar glanced at the blinding sun feeling the glare of it bite at her eyes. She had been kneeling beside Odile's bed when he entered the cabin. She had not told him of the woman's death but he knew. A frightened cry leaving his lips he had turned and fled returning with Lieutenant Allen. He had been so kind, a strong gentleness beneath the efficiency, he had taken immediate control.

It was impossible to keep the body on board until they reached Australia he had told her, the heat of the tropics would not allow that, and then there was the superstition of the men, keeping the dead aboard was like inviting the devil to sail with them, it could bode nothing but evil.

She had listened but not understood. She glanced again at the brazen sky dancing with heat. Not understood that this was what he tried to prepare her for.

'. . . we commit the body of Odile Bancroft to the deep . . .'

The sombre voice floated across the bent heads of the crew.

'. . . in the knowledge that on that last glorious day, at the sound of the final trump the sea shall be called upon to give up its dead . . .'

The glare of the sun beating against her face Tamar stared through the brilliance to where two seamen stepped forward.

'No!' She reached both hands towards them as they tipped the plank upward. 'No . . . you can't . . . you can't . . .'

Catching her to him James Allen held her back, feeling the shudder wrack her as the body of Odile Bancroft slid into the sea.

Tamar stared at the trunks that had been moved into her own small cabin. She had folded and packed each item of clothing, every last thing that spoke of Odile Bancroft having been on this ship, it was all put out of sight. But memories of that woman would never be put from her heart.

'. . . *you have been more than a lady's maid, you have been a friend* . . .'

It seemed the quiet gentle voice spoke in the silence. But that friend was gone. Tamar felt the rise of tears that were never far below the surface. Odile was gone and she was alone. She had known that she would be left on her own once they reached their destination, that the woman would be with her husband while she must search for Benjie, but she had not reckoned on the desperate emptiness that parting would leave behind.

She had been desolated on losing her brother but beneath that awful feeling had been the flicker of hope, the knowledge that she could find him, that they could be together again, but there was no such hope for Odile. Closing her eyes against the bitterness she caught a hand to her throat as the picture of that canvas-shrouded body sliding downwards into the sea flashed into her mind.

'Beg pardon miss . . .'

She had not heard the tap against her door. A startled gasp breaking from her she jumped to her feet turning towards the sound.

'. . . begging pardon miss, the captain said to present his compliments and would you kindly join him on the quarter deck.'

She had never been summoned before. Tamar followed the boy, his nimble steps taking him ahead so he had to wait at the foot of the companionway. Was it something to do with the business of this morning? It could not be anything else, the captain must need to know the whereabouts of Edmond Bancroft, the address at which to send notification of his wife's death. But she could not furnish such information, if Odile knew that herself she had not confided the same.

Reaching the main deck Tamar hesitated. The whole of the ship's company were assembled as before, but the burial service was over, it had ended hours ago!

'Allow me to escort you, Miss Hallam.'

One of the ship's officers, resplendent in dark blue

uniform trimmed with gold appeared at her side.

'Why are the crew assembled, is it something to do with the funeral?'

Taking her elbow the officer urged her towards the steps that led up to the quarter deck his lips barely moving as he murmured. 'Please Miss Hallam, the captain is waiting.'

Holding her skirts against a rising wind Tamar climbed the short flight of steps casting a querying glance at James Allen as she came to stand beside the captain.

'I regret having to disturb you at such a time, Miss Hallam.'

Dropping a small curtsy Tamar acknowledged the brief inclination of the man's head. He and his officers were nothing if not courteous, it seemed to make no difference to them that she was no more than a lady's maid.

'I know the events of this morning were painful for you but I ask you to bear with me in this matter. I feel your assurance, if witnessed by my crew, will give my action deservance in their eyes.'

'Assurance, I don't understand . . . what . . . ?'

From the quarter deck the clang of the ship's bell striking the end of the forenoon watch drowned the remainder of her words and she stood silent watching one seaman replace another.

The sound dying away in the brisk swirl of the wind, Tamar turned to speak but the captain was already addressing the officer who had escorted her to the poop deck. Sliding her glance behind him to where James Allen stood her eyes were questioning but the merest shake of his head said he could not answer.

Below her the slight murmur of voices increased, added to by the clink of chains and as the press of bodies parted Tamar's hand fled to her throat.

Two men, both chained at the ankles, followed by four armed with pistols, shambled forward to stand immediately below the officer deck, their guards taking up a stance that brought them face on to the muttering crew.

'Mr Price.'

The captain's call had immediate effect and in the silence it created the bosun stepped smartly forward.

'Is this the way the prisoners were attired on being discovered?'

'Aye, Captain.' The bosun's reply, equally loud, reached every ear. 'That be how Payne were dressed, Taylor was naked as the day he were born, but for the lady's sake I thought it best he wear that cloth.'

'Lieutenant Allen, is this the way you found these men dressed, all except for the loincloth?'

'Aye sir, it is.'

Anger tightly controlled the captain touched Tamar's elbow edging her a little closer to the deck rail before asking.

'Can you, Miss Hallam, identify the gown and necklace the man Payne is wearing?'

Unable to look at the man dressed in Odile's gown and necklace she could only nod.

'Will you tell us when last you saw that dress?'

The question repeated, Tamar felt a sickness fill her throat, the fear she had felt that night she and Odile had come upon that man in their quarters, the man who stood now as he had stood then, in Odile Bancroft's gown.

'I . . . I last saw it . . .'

Tamar sensed the sudden holding of breath as each of the assembled men seemed to strain to catch her words.

Her own breath tight in her chest she went on.

'. . . I last saw the gown and necklace several days ago when Mrs Bancroft and I returned from going ashore, they . . . they were being worn by that man.'

'And were either of you threatened?'

To answer might add to the man's punishment but she knew the captain would not be satisfied with silence, that would only service to prolong the discomfort of men made to stand in the merciless sun and to the shame of the two held in shackles.

'Yes.' She gave her answer, regret painting every word.

'The words Miss Hallam, the very words if you please.'

Glancing at the figure beside her Tamar's eyes begged for release, begged to be excused reliving the horror of that moment, but the captain's eyes were fixed firmly on the scene below.

'He . . .' She swallowed but the dryness in her throat would not be eased. 'He said he would kill us, slit the throats of the pair of us.'

'Was that all he said?'

Why was he forcing her to speak, what difference would words make now? The man was caught. Realising there was no option but to speak she answered.

'He warned us to say nothing to Lieutenant Allen, he said to do so would result in Mr Allen's disappearing over the side the first night we sailed.'

Still keeping his gaze on the crew the captain spoke again, this time to James Allen.

'Do you verify that this man was in the late Mrs Bancroft's cabin and that he was wearing that dress?'

'Aye sir, I do.'

Hearing the ripple run among the men below him Captain Jones raised a hand, lowering it as silence returned.

'Mr Price, who had the first watch the night we sailed out of El–Bayda?'

'Ezra Payne sir.'

'And who was it took over the middle watch?'

'Josiah Taylor was duty for that watch.'

'Mr Allen.' The captain asked as the bosun saluted and stepped back to the ranks. 'Was the middle watch manned when you went up on deck?'

'It was not my usual practice . . .'

'No excuses Mr Allen, was the watch manned?'

Tamar flinched at the ferocity of the command. James had once said the captain was no man to be played with, now she saw why.

'No sir.'

Below her she heard the man Payne give a quiet desperate cry. Stealing a dress was an offence yes, but not one to warrant being dealt with in such a fashion, to be humiliated in front of the whole ship. Glancing again at the figure stood beside her she opened her mouth to say as much but again the captain was speaking.

'Did you look for the man whose duty it was?'

'Aye, sir.'

'And where did you find him?'

Heat from the sun-baked wind seared across the sweltering decks grabbing at Tamar, burning in her throat. If only this were all over!

'Mr Price and myself found Taylor in the bottom hold . . .' James Allen's reply seemed to pound against her temples.

'. . . he and Payne were together sir, both as you see them now.'

'Doing?'

The question was sharp and clear, a note of judgement already in it.

'They . . .' James Allen hesitated, his glance going to Tamar. 'Miss Hallam sir, must she hear this?'

'Aye sir, she must!' The answer rapped out. 'They all must, I will have no cover up aboard my ship. Now, answer my question, what were these two men doing?'

Giving one more glance in Tamar's direction James Allen drew a long breath. 'They were involved in an act of a sexual nature.'

That man she had seen on the way into Stafford town, the man with a half naked boy pinned beneath him flashed into her mind. This was why those two men had been paraded as they were, they were doing the very thing she had saved Davy Mullin from. A gasp breaking from her, her senses swimming amid the blinding glare of the midday sun, Tamar swayed. Joe Mullin's revenge had been dreadful to see, the man who had assaulted his son had paid a terrible price . . . would these two pay the same?

Chapter Twenty-Two

'I was most graciously received . . .'

Philip Amory addressed his workers. He had given his fellow goldsmiths an account of his visit to the palace to deliver the recovered necklace, but these were the people who had turned an idea into reality, theirs the skills that had created that beautiful diamond ensemble, these as much as anybody deserved to hear of its acceptance. Twirling his pocket watch he smiled.

'. . . the princess herself took them from my hands.'

'Oooh! Did her 'ave a crown and a long train stretching right back behind like a fairy princess?'

A young girl of ten years old, eyes wide and lips apart stared from her own private dream world.

'I wouldn't reckon to that Ginny wench, nor to 'er 'aving wings neither.' Dinah Edwards laughed.

'But I bet as 'er was beautiful, Ginny, beautiful as the fairy queen herself.' Glaring over the girl's head at Dinah, Vinny Marsh laid a kindly hand on the girl's shoulder.

'Be that right Mr Amory, do the princess be beautiful as the queen of the fairies?'

He looked down into the child's soft eyes, into a face alight with her own imaginings and for a moment he could not help but contrast her life in the slums of Birmingham with the indescribable splendour he had seen at every turn of the head in that palace. The child could dream but not in the wildest of them would she know the luxury and the beauty that surrounded that woman.

'Yes Ginny.' He nodded. 'The Princess of Wales is beautiful, she has wide brown eyes and a pretty mouth, just like yours, and when she smiles it makes you feel like the sun has just come out, and her hair, her hair was a lovely shade of auburn . . .'

He broke off remembering the thoughts that had burst into his mind the moment of seeing that hair, thoughts of another very different girl but one just as beautiful.

'What colour be auburn?'

Smiling at the child's question Vinny glanced at the owner of the workshop seeing the look that sometimes lingered deep in his eyes.

'It be the colour of Tamar Hallam's and that of her brother both, they 'ave hair that be auburn.'

'Did 'er 'ave on a gold frock?'

Thankful for the amusement that swept over his workers, Philip Amory took the moment to clear his mind, to brush away the thoughts ever ready to plague him.

Replacing the watch he glanced again at the young girl the pleasure of fantasy so vibrant on her thin little face.

'I see I shall have no peace until Ginny here has a full description, but it will be brief, gold does not work itself. A footman dressed in pale blue velvet with gold buttons and lace at his throat and wrists showed me to what he called the small ante-room even though it had six sofas and as many chairs, not to mention the rest of the furniture.'

Ignoring the long drawn breaths of the women he went on.

'A lady-in-waiting . . . her frock was lavender, Ginny, came to say Her Royal Highness wished to speak to me herself and that she would join us presently. A few minutes later two more women came into the room and the taller one was the princess. She was very elegant and regal. Her gown was cream with sprays of tiny butter yellow rose-buds and her only jewellery was a rope of pearls, her hair was dressed high on her head and when she smiled . . . but then I have told you of when she smiled.'

'Ohh!' The child heaved a long sigh. 'I wish I could 'ave seen 'er.'

'You will one day Ginny, we all will.' Vinny's hand pressed the thin shoulder. 'When 'er husband be made king they'll come visit Brummagem, a new king visits all over his country; then you'll see the princess only by that time 'er will be Queen of England.'

'And will 'er wear the Alexandra Stone, when 'er comes to Brummagem I means?'

'I think she will, Ginny.' Philip Amory answered. 'Judging by the reception she gave it I think she will wear it often. She was delighted with it and I think I detected a little touch of pride when I told her we had named it the Alexandra Stone, she smiled and said

then that was how it would be known and she asked
me to thank you all from her.'

'Well we all 'ope it 'as the effect you aimed for Mr
Amory sir,' Cal Perry put in. 'We 'opes it brings
business back to the Gold Quarter.'

'I think it will.' Philip Amory nodded. 'I really
think it will.'

'Are you unwell Miss Hallam?'

Captain Jones glanced sideways as his lieutenant
moved to catch Tamar's arm.

'No . . . no, it . . . I am not accustomed to the
heat.'

'Do you wish to retire for a little while?'

If she had to be witness to this then it were far better
done now. Shaking her head she freed her arm. 'That
will not be necessary, Captain Jones.'

'Then we will proceed.' Taking one step forward
he raised his voice.

'I have had these men paraded before you in the
exact state in which they were arrested so all may
know the crime of which they stand accused. Payne,'
he paused, 'for the crime of theft and threatening the
lives of passengers and an officer of this ship, you are
sentenced to twenty lashes; for the act of buggery,
twenty-four lashes more, the flogging to take place
immediately.'

Waiting for the murmurs of the crew to die away
he spoke again.

'Josiah Taylor. You are guilty of the crime of

buggery for which filthiness you will receive twenty-four strokes of the whip. In addition to that crime you are charged with one far more serious – dereliction of duty. By deserting the watch you put the safety of this ship and the life of every man aboard her in peril. You let your own perverted pleasures come before the well-being of your shipmates. The sentence for that is death. You will be hanged from the yard arm at sunset.'

'No!' Tamar pushed to the rail staring over it at the dirty pock-marked face turned upward its grin mocking as Taylor looked at her.

''Ow would you like to share a man's last hours? You could give 'im a right send-off I'll be bound.'

'Close your dirty mouth!'

Below the rail the bosun raised a closed fist jabbing it hard into Taylor's face but still the man grinned.

'What you say to lying with Jos Taylor? He'd open that tight little belly of your'n . . . he'd make this trip one you wouldn't forget.'

Lifting her face to a sky hotter than Amory's furnace, to a sun infinitely more brilliant than polished gold, Tamar felt the world floating away.

'. . . one you wouldn't forget.'

Followed by the man's coarse laughter the words dropped with her into blackness.

She would not forget any of the horrors that had happened to her since leaving Hockley.

Tamar took the cool damp cloth the cabin boy

wrung out. Holding it against her forehead she tried
not to think of what had just passed on deck.

'You be feeling better now, miss?'

'Yes . . . thank you.' She tried to smile at the
anxious enquiry. 'It was the heat, nothing more.'

But it was more, it was the thought of the punishment those men would suffer. True they had both
threatened; Taylor in that alley in Bristol and Payne
right here in this cabin, but terrifying as each of those
events had been she would not want such a dreadful
punishment for either of them and neither would
Odile have wanted that.

A sound from what had been her mistress's cabin
catching her ear she held her breath staring at the
communicating door with frightened eyes.

'It be alright miss, 'tain't nothing to fear over. The
captain be 'aving a bolt fixed to both sides of that door,
says it might 'elp you feel easier.'

Releasing the breath held in her throat Tamar
relaxed against the pillows.

'These two was the captain's quarters, this'n was his
day cabin and next door his night cabin.'

The boy volunteered the information cheerfully.
'They was give to you and Mrs Bancroft for your use
'til we reaches Australia, but seein' as yonder one be
empty the captain be takin' it back to his own use.'

'Is the captain there now?'

Bowl of water in hand, the young boy glanced first
at the communicating door then back to Tamar.

'I seen he were not on deck when Mr Allen bid me
tend you, so like as not he could be in there.'

The boy left for the galley and Tamar laid aside the damp cloth. Perhaps he might listen to her, James Allen had said he was a fair man. At least she had to try.

Running her hands over her hair smoothing a few stray strands into place she glanced at the door, its heavy oak echoing the noise of hammer and chisel, then walked out into the corridor.

Dismissing the carpenter as she tapped the open door Captain Jones indicated a chair drawn to a table covered with an array of maps.

'Be seated, Miss Hallam. How may I be of service?'

Did this man know her background, know she was a penniless girl from the back streets, that she had never owned a decent dress in her life until Amy Williams gave her the clothes she wore, that a meal of faggots and peas was a banquet to her? And would he treat her any different if he did know? Taking the chair Tamar felt that somehow none of those things would matter, that this man would behave no differently to pauper as to princess.

'I . . . I would like to speak to you regarding the two men.'

Across the table the captain's eyes hardened. 'I take it you mean Taylor and Payne?'

Tamar felt a quiver of nerves. She could leave now, make some excuse and leave. Instead she nodded keeping her glance firm as she answered.

'Yes, it is Mr Taylor and Mr Payne I would speak to you about.'

'Go on.'

It was as hard as the stone in his eyes but Tamar did not flinch.

'I know that stealing and threatening the lives of others is wrong and cannot go unpunished, but they did no actual harm, no person was hurt and it was only a dress and a cheap necklace that was taken; neither Mrs Bancroft nor myself would want so cruel a punishment as the lash and certainly not a death sentence.'

'No actual harm . . . no person was harmed! And by whose grace was that? You think my sentence harsh but I hold the lives of many men in my hands. Allow a desertion of the watch to go unpunished once and it will happen again and who knows with what consequence. The sea is a dangerous place Miss Hallam, and a jealous mistress. Take your eyes from her for a moment and you can easily forfeit your life and that of others. A captain of any ship cannot take that risk. It gives me no pleasure to take another man's life.' He paused and for a fleeting moment Tamar saw real pain etched on his sharp features. 'I do not do so with impunity, but the *Porpoise* is not a pleasure boat, it is a ship of the line, a ship of Her Majesty's Royal Navy and punishment for whatever crime must be swift and it must be seen. That way discipline and duty remain observed. I realise that what you witnessed today was both strange and painful to you. Seeing Payne in that gown. But I will not dwell upon that crime, suffice it to say it is one not tolerated in Her Majesty's Navy and as such may not be excused.'

Taylor had endangered the ship and every soul

aboard it and for that his own life would be taken. Was such a price necessary? Slowly Tamar walked the short length of the quarter deck impervious to the looks and murmurs of men appreciating her trim figure and pretty face. But then she could see the captain's point of view, see the fairness behind his decision. He had others to protect. But what of the fairness behind Benjie's sentence? His life had in a way been taken. For thirty years he would not know freedom, would not be allowed to walk where he willed or do the things he wished to do. For thirty years he would live in a foreign land with no hope of return, and all for a crime he did not commit.

Pausing at the ship's rail she stared over the vast stretch of ocean, quiet now the quickening wind had faded.

Where was the fairness in that?

'Tomorrow we shall berth in Geelong.'

It was over. Tamar breathed a mixture of relief and apprehension. The long sea voyage was almost done but the search for her brother must go on. Where would she look, who could she ask for news of him?

'Miss Hallam . . . Tamar.'

She glanced at the man standing at her side. In the weeks since the hanging of Josiah Taylor and the flogging of Ezra Payne she had made a practice of coming aloft only once in the evening and then keeping only to the quarter deck as Captain Jones had requested.

'The day we went ashore at El-Bayda, Mrs Bancroft said something of you having spent your whole life surrounded in gold . . .'

'Hardly, Mr Allen.' Tamar smiled. 'But I am quite used to the handling of it though I must tell you none of it was my own. I worked for Philip Amory, he is a goldsmith with a workshop in Hockley; the place holds so many premises working in gold that the people who live there call it the Gold Quarter.'

'And you . . .'

'I worked at the polisher's bench, not a very important job . . .'

'I'm glad!' James Allen broke in quickly. 'I . . . I mean I'm glad your family do not own that work-shop.'

'No, it does not belong to us, and as for family I have only a brother and . . . and he is in Australia.'

'He is here?'

Returning her glance to the sea she stared out over the dark stretches. Tomorrow they would see land, tomorrow . . .

'That is why I came, to find him and be with him. You see Mr Allen, my brother is a convict.'

'Tamar, you don't have to . . .'

But quietly, determinedly, she carried on speaking, not stopping until he had heard the entire story.

'It makes no difference.' He touched a hand to hers resting on the deck rail. 'It makes no difference to what I feel for you. I love you Tamar, I want you to marry me. Return to England and I will give up the navy . . .'

'No.' Her smile gentle Tamar removed her hand from his. 'I will marry no one until I have found my brother.'

'Then I will wait . . .'

'No.' She shook her head. 'Who knows how long the search might last? It could take years. I do not want you to wait that long, I do not want another life to be wasted.'

'Ours need not be wasted. I love you Tamar and I will wait if you will only promise one day to marry me.'

Looking up into his face Tamar felt a sharp kick against her heart. There, for just a moment, the fair hair turned to black, shadows touching against his chin gave it the line of a neat clipped beard and turned blue eyes to steel grey.

I love you, Tamar. The strong mouth seemed to say the words but then the illusion was gone. Blinking against the suddenness of it she struggled for an answer but against the sharp breathlessness in her chest could only shake her head.

'I won't press you Tamar, but if you should change your mind . . .'

Her answer a whisper she smiled shyly. 'I know James, I know.'

Lifting her face to the cooling evening breeze she glanced at the setting sun, its rays gilding the purpling sky with gold-edged crimson.

'It is so beautiful, so like the skies at home, they turn crimson when the furnace gates are lifted.'

'You've seen that?'

'Many times, and each time the beauty of it takes my breath away. I don't think even that emir for all his wealth can match the splendour of it.'

'You too!' He laughed softly. 'I used to dream as a lad that the gold edging would fall to earth and land at my feet and I would be rich as a king, but now I know that no king on earth could possess anything near as magnificent or as beautiful.'

'Where did you dream?'

Turning his face to hers James Allen took her hand.

'In a town not many miles from Birmingham. I was born in Wednesbury and lived there with my folks until I was sixteen. By that time I had realised the only gold I might find would not be in that town. Oh there is gold there. But only for the mine owners, black gold wrenched from the bowels of the earth, coal that gives men a living but takes their lungs in return.'

'So you left.'

'Aye.' He nodded. 'I left and eventually took the Queen's shilling. Not gold I grant you, but it was a regular wage going to my mother and my lungs are filled with nothing but sea air, not counting the stink of the occasional port.'

'She must miss you very much.'

'As I will miss you Tamar . . . please say you will marry me, if not now then some day.'

Her fingers squeezing gently on his Tamar smiled against a sudden film of tears.

'No, James, I cannot say that. You have been a good friend to me, but I . . .'

Raising her hand to his lips he kissed her fingers.

'No more, Tamar,' he said quietly, 'no more; a man knows when a woman loves another.'

When a woman loves another.

Watching him stride from the deck Tamar felt the same jerk to her emotions as she had minutes before. Then it had not been the face of James Allen that looked back at her or his voice she had heard but the face and voice of the man who had bought her coffee. But that had been simply illusion.

But the kick of her heart was no illusion.

When a woman loves another.

Could she be in love with another?

Chapter Twenty-Three

The last of the cargo unloaded, Nathan Burford stood looking out over the docks in Bristol. He had not visited his childhood home, but then he had not done that in five years so it was not that could account for the restless churning in his stomach, a restlessness he had felt the whole of this voyage.

'The narrowboat be ready to leave, Captain.'

Glancing at the man come to report Nathan nodded briefly, then as the man turned to leave asked, 'What boat is she?'

'The *Brummagem Maid*, the same as we have used before, she takes the cocoa bean right up to the chocolate works. If there is anything you don't like about it I'll have the lot off . . .'

'No.' Nathan shook his head briefly. 'Let it stay but ask the bargee to wait, I would like to speak with him.'

He had told himself that on his return to Bristol he would give that girl any help he could to reach her brother, now he would hold to that promise; maybe that way he might know a little peace.

Several minutes later Joseph Mullin watched a tall figure stride towards his moorings. He had more than half expected this man and now he was here.

'Ar, I knows the wench you speak of.'

It would have been pointless to deny it, this man had an eye like a hawk and doubtless a mind as sharp. The very fact of his being here told he remembered their meeting that day on the dockside. His answer given Joseph stood in silence.

'Then perhaps you can tell me where she might be found.'

'P'raps I will, p'raps I won't.'

The man could lose his cargo for answering in such a manner, but that was to his credit, he was not willing to sell a friendship short.

'I promised the girl my help in tracing her brother, that is the only reason I ask after her, but to give help I need to speak to her.'

Joseph looked at the strong face tanned to the colour of fine leather. Nathan Burford was known as a man who kept his word. But he and his family had seen no sign of Tamar since she had left the barge, he could tell the man no more than that.

'We sailed for Brummagem the day you spoke to the girl on yonder dock. Tamar Hallam refused to sail with us, she said only that she couldn't go 'ome to Hockley 'til her brother were found; we've had no word from her since.'

'But that was weeks ago! Have you looked for her?' Nathan let his chagrin show.

'Me and my lad both, but it seems nobody knowed of her.'

It was the truth he had told. Joseph watched the other man stride away. There had been an anger in his voice, but it had held something else besides, something that smacked of disappointment.

Would she have made her way to Liverpool, or even to London? It was possible . . . but then it was possible the girl had made her way to any port with ships sailing to the colonies, to search them all would take months, and in that time . . .

The thought stirring emotions and fears he found difficult to deal with he turned into the chandler's, there were several things the *Verity* needed to stock up on.

Stepping in from the bright May sunlight, Nathan peered toward a shadowed counter almost lost beneath a deluge of boxes and packages.

Ordering candles, oakum and a roll of sailcloth, he counted out a number of coins.

'I'll get them sent out to the *Verity* within the hour, Captain Burford.'

Standing in the small living room at the rear of the shop, Amy dropped the duster she was holding. The *Verity*! That was the name of the ship Tamar had mentioned, the one Nathan Burford commanded; she had blushed as she had said his name. They had talked a lot that last night before she had left and Amy had felt there was more than a passing interest in Tamar's voice when she spoke of that man.

Touching a hand to her already neat hair she walked into the shop. Pretending surprise at seeing her husband with a customer she apologised, at the same time turning back towards the living room.

'No need to leave on my account ma'am. My business is finished. Good day to you both.'

'Good day to you Captain Burford, and like I says I'll have your order delivered to the *Verity* within the hour.'

'Captain Burford?' Again Amy injected just the right amount of surprise into the words.

'The same, ma'am.' Glancing at the smiling face, hair that despite the gloom of the shop shone with a hint of gold and eyes whose brightness gleamed like port beacons, Nathan searched his memory coming up with no recognition.

'Forgive my forwardness.' Amy dropped a small curtsy. 'But when I heard the *Verity* mentioned and then your name I felt you were probably the same man my friend mentioned. Tamar said you were very kind to her.'

'Tamar?' Every nerve suddenly alert Nathan looked more keenly at the smiling face.

'Tamar Hallam. She said you told her that her brother Benjie had been put aboard the *Swallow* and when she said she would follow after him you answered she must be prepared for a long journey, for Australia was on the other side of the world.'

Those had been his very words. The friend this woman spoke of had to be the girl he could not keep from his mind, the one that stared back at him from his dreams. It had to be the same Tamar Hallam.

'The girl you speak of, she was about your height with green eyes and hair of deep auburn?'

He remembered a good deal for someone who had met a girl just once. Amy hid her smile.

'That description fits Tamar, she is as you describe.'

'Where is she now . . . will you take me to her?'

Shaking her head the bright smile dying on her lips Amy looked into the handsome face.

'That is something I can't do Captain Burford, though I truly wish I could. You see, Tamar sailed for Australia some two months ago aboard the *Porpoise*.'

Two months ago! In his cabin aboard the *Verity* Nathan checked the facts he had weaned from the port authority. The *Porpoise* had indeed sailed for Australia almost two months before, and, though a royal naval vessel, had carried two passengers; one the daughter of a Member of Parliament, the other her maid.

Anything could happen to her out there. Why on earth could she not have waited . . . what had driven her to go careering off to the ends of the earth?

'Of all the stupid things!' He drove an angry fist into his palm. 'Didn't she know I would help her.'

But how could she? Reaching for a roll of parchment he spread it open on the cabin table then stared at it without seeing it. How could she know he would help when he had not told her so?

The last of her boxes had been carried on deck. Tamar took a deep nervous breath. This was what she had aimed to do and now that aim was achieved, she was here in the land of Australia. A few hours and she would be with Benjie.

'The captain be ready to go ashore miss, if you wants to go with 'im you best come now.'

Following the cabin boy Tamar felt her nervousness increase. This ship had become her world and now she was leaving it.

Looking towards the shore a shock of surprise ran through her. Where was the town she had expected? The large important looking buildings such as the centre of Birmingham held?

There were none. She ran a glance around the curvature of a wide bay lined with tall trees. There were no trees in Hockley save for the few that grew in the churchyard.

'This is Geelong Miss Hallam, such as it is.'

Her own glance, following that of the captain's, swept the muddle of wooden buildings growing together in a clearing scooped from the treeline, most of them from this distance appeared to be little more than shacks. Was one of them where she would find Benjie?

'If you are ready Miss Hallam?'

'Yes, yes I'm ready.'

Turning to follow the man who had spoken to her Tamar's glanced lifted to the quarter deck meeting that of James Allen. They had said their goodbyes the evening before, but now with the actual moment of leaving came a sting of regret. Why did she always have to part from people she came to love? James Allen, like the Mullins and Amy, had become someone she could rely on, someone she knew would never harm her and now he too would be lost to her.

'Do you have someone meeting you?'

Taking the hand held out to steady her from the

longboat Tamar glanced at the flurry of people further up the beach sorting boxes and bales unloaded from the ship.

'I expect Mr Bancroft will be here to meet his wife . . . he will not know . . .' She broke off, the rest still too raw in her to speak of it.

'Of course.' Eyes squinting against the brilliant sunlight Captain Jones scanned the milling people. 'It will be my duty to inform him; if you would be so good as to point him out.'

This was something she had not counted on. She had never expected to arrive without Odile. She had no idea what the woman's husband looked like.

'I . . . I can't do that,' she faltered, conscious now of how foolish it must sound, 'I have never seen him, and Odile – Mrs Bancroft – was not certain which part of the country he might be in.'

'Not certain!' He turned an incredulous look on her. 'Are you telling me the woman was making the journey on the off-chance her husband *might* be here?'

'It was not an off-chance. Mrs Bancroft knew he had come to Australia.'

'She knew he had come to Australia.' Half-raised hands falling back to his sides he glanced along the tree-fringed skyline with its distant backing of purple mountains before looking back at her. 'Good God, this isn't England, this isn't a pocket-sized island you can cover in a week! Australia is a vast country, most of it as yet unknown to us, you can't go *hoping* someone is in any part of it. You have to *know*.'

'But he has to be here.'

'The man does not *have* to be anywhere. Best thing will be to ask the commanding officer of the penal stockade, he will know if anyone does.'

The heat of the sun-drenched sky already draining her energy Tamar struggled to keep up as the captain strode towards one of the larger wooden houses that stood a little beyond a tall fence above which she could see a watch-tower manned by a uniformed soldier, a rifle held in his hands. Was that the prison to which Benjie had been brought . . . where he was to spend the next thirty years of his life? But he would never survive in this, how could anyone survive? Pressing a handkerchief to her nose she tried to blot out the stink of poorly dug cesspits, of drainage channels leading down across the open beach and swimming with refuse of every kind, the odour of them choking with each hint of breeze. She could not let her brother stay in this hell, there had to be something better.

'I assure you there is no one of that name in Geelong nor has there been in the three years I have been in charge here.'

Tamar pulled her thoughts together. She had hardly been aware the man was speaking, now she looked into a hard face flushed an unhealthy red.

'Are you sure Mrs Bancroft said Geelong?'

'Mrs Bancroft simply said her husband had sailed to Australia.'

His business with the captain of the *Porpoise* over and that man gone the camp commander was eager for the entertainment he could see waiting for him.

His tone betraying an interest that did not lie in the direction of Odile Bancroft he asked.

'What of the letters she received from him, they must carry an address?'

Looking across at him, almost sensing the feeling beneath his open stare Tamar rose to her feet. She could not tell him that according to Amy there had never been any letter. Instead she said quietly. 'I only joined Mrs Bancroft's service the day she sailed for this country, that being so I am not aware of any communication between them.'

'Then you don't know for sure Bancroft ever did come here. For all you know he could have been dropped off in almost any country in the world.'

'But Mrs Bancroft . . .'

'Yes, yes, you told me, the woman says he came to Australia.' He stepped forward his glance sweeping her. 'But all I can say is that he must be in some other part of it. . . now you and I can find better to talk of than the Bancroft woman.'

Despite the shade of woven grass window blinds the room was filled with a stifling heat. Two steps away from her he lifted his hand brushing it across her breast bringing a wave of sickness to Tamar's throat.

Trying to move backward she caught against the chair toppling into it as he bent over her. Months of travelling, of searching, of continued disappointment suddenly spiralling together, she struck out at the flushed face.

For a moment he hovered over her his eyes glaring

revenge. 'You are going to be sorry you did that,' he hissed, 'very sorry indeed.'

'I am sorry I struck you, but I have no wish to be mauled like some animal.'

'You have no wish . . . !' Laughing low in his throat the commander straightened but he did not step away. 'Let me tell you Miss Hallam, you have nothing here in Geelong, neither wish nor hope except that which I allow. You want news of that woman's husband . . .'

Hands locked tightly together Tamar knew she had to speak now or she would lose the courage.

'No sir, I do not want news of Mr Bancroft. His wife is beyond any help I might give her so for me the matter ends there.'

His wife! Turning away Henry Forbes stared at the shutters shrouding the windows of the stuffy room. She had not referred to the woman as her mistress, nor was she herself a convict, in fact this girl was different to any that had arrived in Geelong for many a bright day; but she would be treated no different from any who had come with any semblance of looks, and here in Australia there was nobody would bother with those.

'There is another matter I wish to speak to you about.' She paused waiting for him to turn around but he remained with his back towards her. At home in Hockley a man would have his backside kicked for showing such rudeness, but as she had seen already this was not Hockley. Drawing a long breath she went on determinedly.

'I wish to speak to you about a young boy . . .'

Lips drawn back from a row of discoloured teeth the speed of his movement belying the corpulence of his body the man whirled about.

'You wish . . .' he snarled '. . . I've already told you that here you have no wish!'

Nerves jangling like bells Tamar held on. She must not give up now, she must not let this man's bullying deter her. She had come too far for that. Fighting the fluttering in her stomach she looked at him with an even stare.

'Very well, I will put it another way. I believe a thirteen-year-old boy was recently transported here and I require you give me his whereabouts.'

'Another belief!' This time the man's laugh was loud and openly derisive. 'Another maybe! Well I don't care for maybe's any more than I care for a chit of a girl telling me what she *requires*. This is a penal settlement not a bloody Salvationist meeting house.'

'That is only too painfully obvious as is the fact that you are no man of God!' Weariness flared to sudden anger bringing Tamar to her feet. 'You are the commander given charge of this settlement and as such have a responsibility towards those unfortunate enough to have been placed here, as it is your responsibility to provide information regarding the welfare of a convict when requested to do so by a relative!'

She had no idea if what she said was correct but as it came pouring out the look in those puffy eyes

changed, looking at her with a new intentness. Almost
warily, with a softness that was sibilant he asked.

'A relative?'

Reading the animosity in his puffy eyes, the threat
contained in the very softness of his voice it was all
Tamar could do not to turn and run; but if she were to
have any hope of finding Benjie she must face up to
this man.

'That is what I said.' She lifted her chin challen-
gingly. 'I am enquiring after my brother. His name is
Benjamin Hallam. He was sentenced to serve thirty
years in Australia and was brought her on the *Swallow*.'

'When was he brought here?'

Nerves still clanging Tamar did not detect the hint
of amusement in the man's eyes.

'I cannot answer exactly not knowing how long his
journey lasted . . .'

'Another don't know!'

Set in folds of flushed flesh small eyes gleamed
mockingly.

All around, the heat of the room seemed to bear in
upon her robbing her lungs of air. Desperately fighting
against the urge to run, to leave this house, this man,
Tamar dug her nails into her palms using the pain of it
to hold her senses together. To give way to her
feelings now would result in her every effort being
wasted; more than that this man would have the
satisfaction of knowing he had driven her away.
But it would take more than rudeness and threats
to do that. Gathering her diminishing strength she
stared back at those sneering eyes.

'The *Swallow* sailed in mid-February, therefore given the opinion of Captain Jones of the *Porpoise*, it must have arrived here very recently.'

'I see you are well informed.' He lowered his glance letting it slide arrogantly over the length of her then holding it for long seconds on her breasts. 'But not as well informed as I. You want my help . . .' he lifted his glance to meet hers full on '. . . then you must be prepared to pay for it.'

'I have a little money.'

Tamar's mind flashed to the coins she had found among Odile Bancroft's effects. Surely she was entitled to a little of it as the woman's maid, and if not she would pay it back from the first money she might earn.

'I'm not talking of money.'

He stepped closer the smell of his perspiring flesh in her nostrils adding to the nausea of the overheated room. The urge to run still strong in her, Tamar had to hold herself rigid to stay still.

'A man likes a little change now and again . . .'

He raised a hand brushing it first across her cheek then dropping it to her breast.

'. . . a little variety in his bed, you understand?'

Fingers tightening, his eyes gleamed as he squeezed.

'You want the whereabouts of your brother I have them. You give me what I want and I will give you what you want; a little exchange . . . what could be more simple?'

It could not be what she thought . . . he was an officer in Her Majesty's army!

The shock of what she thought he was proposing together with the touch of his hand on her breast left Tamar unprepared for the swift move that pinned her close against him, a saliva-drooling mouth trailing along her face and down her neck to her throat.

'You pleasure me good and you'll get your information,' he slobbered against her mouth. 'Colonel Henry Forbes knows how to show his appreciation.'

Stunned by her own disbelief that what was happening was real her limbs held as though bound by ropes Tamar felt the blood pound in her temples.

'You bring this delicious little body to me each night and you'll . . .'

The touch of his hand now beneath her skirts, the trailing of his fingers over her bare thigh, the tugging at her bloomers brought Tamar suddenly to life. Every ounce of her energy in one push she sent him tumbling away, crashing into a small table that collapsed beneath his bulk.

'Don't you dare touch me!' Livid with anger and repulsed by the sight of that fat scarlet face Tamar's anger turned to pure disgust.

'You fool.' He scrambled to his feet the look he gave her one of pure venom. 'Don't you realise who I am? I *am* Geelong, nothing and nobody gets past me. Mine is the only authority here, folk live or die by my say so regardless of whether they be serving convicts or those who have done their time.' His lips curved in a smile but there was only cruelty in his eyes.

Stabbing a hand on a bell stood near him, not even glancing at the man who stepped immediately into the room, he continued to smile malevolently at Tamar.

'Live or die.' He hissed. 'You have just decided which it is to be for that brother of yours.'

Chapter Twenty-Four

Nathan Burford rolled the parchment into a tube, shoving it back among a pile of others. What the hell was the matter with him? He couldn't concentrate, he couldn't hold his mind to anything except . . .

Refusing to accept what his brain offered, he slammed from his cabin. On deck he breathed deeply, the smell of wet canvas, of oakum and boiling tar filling his nostrils.

It would require only a few days to take on fresh cargo and supplies. In days he could be at sea bound for the Sugar Islands.

'The stuff you ordered from the chandler has arrived, will you be checking it yourself, Captain?'

Relieved by the interruption Nathan Burford gave a brief smile. 'No need, not while you serve as first mate.'

'I've got the list of galley supplies from the cook, they all appear reasonable enough.'

'The usual brandy?'

'Aye, sir.' The seaman grinned. 'Requested by him and crossed off by me.'

'Oh well. You don't hang a man for trying but

maybe one day we will shock him to death by letting a keg or two get through.'

'That would be a shock for more than just the cook and good seamen be 'ard to find; so mebbe I'll just keep a close eye on the list like always.'

As his officer turned away Nathan stared out across the dock. This was the life he had condemned himself to, a life that held no rest, no peace; his only solace lying in the hope that the next voyage might bring news of Aiden and Louise. But for how many years could he hold on to that hope? How long before the constant despair of never finding a trace of them destroyed his life?

Across the dock a woman's skirts fluttered in the warm breeze of early summer.

Her skirts had been patched and patched again, *her* ringlets showing beneath a blue bonnet she seemed to look straight at him.

But it was no blue bonnet Nathan Burford saw nor any pale ringlets. The hair was a deep shining auburn half veiled by a worn shawl, the eyes gleaming like meadows of spring grass and the face . . . it was *her* face . . . Tamar Hallam's face.

Instantly his thoughts were back to that day. She had watched the last sight of the *Swallow* as it cleared the estuary, watched it carry away her brother but there had been no despair in her voice when she spoke, only a determination. Now she had succeeded in getting herself passage to Australia but how far would that take her if the Bancrofts dismissed her?

Returning to his cabin he paused for a moment. It was a gamble. Reaching for pen and paper he wrote rapidly.

Standing on the low wooden veranda that circled the house, the man who had answered the summons of the bell glanced behind him at the closed door.

'Wait there.' He pointed to where a group of trees stood edging the close huddled houses before returning indoors.

Wait for what? Cheeks still flaming from her recent encounter Tamar walked quickly back to the spot where her box and those of Odile Bancroft sat on the blinding white sand just clear of the rolling surf. Wait to be insulted again, did he intend trying what that commander had tried? So many assaults, why was the world so dangerous?

'You want them boxes carried?'

She turned to where a swarthy man stripped to the waist stood watching her.

Carried to where? Realisation seeming only now to dawn on her she glanced to where the *Porpoise* rode at anchor. She had nowhere to go.

'No,' she shook her head. 'I . . . I don't want them carried.'

'Suit yourself.' He turned away adding over his shoulder. 'But you best get 'em shifted afore the tide, that is if you wants ever to see 'em agen.'

Maybe she should have accepted James Allen's offer of marriage, returned to England.

'. . . *don't ever leave me Tam, don't leave me, I be feared* . . .'

The words her brother had cried seemed to dance across the glittering water and Tamar knew she could never return, never leave off her search until she found him.

I won't leave, Benjie. Her lips moving silently she stared at the graceful lines of the ship. I won't leave.

'I said to wait over by the trees.'

She turned to the half-whispering voice.

'Go up to them now, I'll join you there; it don't be safe to be seen talking.'

He was gone almost to the top of the beach leaving his hurried words to drift back to her.

What was unsafe about being seen to speak to her? A frown drawing across her brows Tamar stared after the disappearing figure of the man from the house. Was what he said a lie, a ruse to get her to the cover of those trees?

She must risk it, he might have news of Benjie and if not she could always scream.

Dragging cool sea air into her lungs she made her way towards the spot he had indicated, every step a marathon in the exhausting heat.

'I'm the colonel's batman.' The man spoke, drawing her hurriedly into the shelter of the trees. 'You need 'ave no fear of me. I'll do you no harm, I mean only to help you.'

'Why . . . why should you help me?'

'I can understand your doubting after the colonel . . . well let's just say not every man in Geelong be like him, this place could grow to be a nice little town were it not for that man. There's many a one of us prays he won't go on much longer. But while he be 'ere it might be better if you ain't; you stay and you could be inviting trouble.'

'But he is an officer . . .'

'And a gentleman?' The man laughed mirthlessly. 'Not with the likes of you . . . young, pretty and alone . . . you are just fair game to him. You do like I say and get yourself away.'

'I can't. I came here to search for my brother and that is what I must do.'

'That be partly why I be 'ere now.' He threw an anxious look toward the palisade fence of the stockade. 'Your brother ain't in Geelong.'

'But . . .'

'Listen!' He caught her hand. 'There be something else the colonel didn't tell you. You said the lad were aboard the *Swallow*. Well that ship ain't put into Geelong recently nor any of the years I've served 'ere.'

Staring at him as he let her hand drop Tamar felt the world spin. Benjie had not been brought here!

'You be certain it were the *Swallow* . . . and that it were Australia she were bound for?'

Fatigue and disappointment giving way to tears that glinted on her lashes she nodded.

'Then it must be some other penal settlement it were bound for, they be sprung up in many parts 'long the coast, seems like the government back 'ome 'ave found a dumping ground for them they don't want.'

Seeing another nervous glance sweep to the stockade Tamar asked quickly. 'These other places, where are they, what are the names?'

'I knows only one or two by name, but there be many as I don't. I overhear the colonel when he be speaking with men from the supply ships that be how I know. One be Cairns and another be Cooktown, p'raps Sydney.'

'Wait please.'

He had already begun to leave, weaving his way through the trees so as not to be spotted by the watch.

'These towns, are they far?'

'Can't answer that, miss.' He glanced back at her. 'I 'ave no idea as to distance but I reckon a fair few 'undred miles.'

Hundreds of miles and even then Benjie might not be there.

Her hopes in a thousand pieces she walked slowly back towards her boxes.

'You want all of this, Captain?'

The first mate of the *Verity* read through the list he had been handed.

'It be some two or three times what we normally use. As for cargo, since when 'ave we took the like to the Sugar Islands or to Sierra Leone?'

'We haven't.' Nathan Burford smiled.

'Then why now?'

'The answer is simple, we are not sailing for the West Indies nor for Africa. I am taking the *Verity* to Australia.'

'Australia!'

Meeting the astounded look Nathan nodded.

'Aye, Mr Brooks, Australia.'

Shaking his head slowly for several moments, bewilderment still evident in his voice, the seaman glanced again at the papers Nathan had handed to him.

'I don't understand. You said to take on supplies and cargo for the run to the West Indies . . .'

'And now I have changed my mind.'

'Aye sir, but that don't be the surprise of it, the surprise lies in where you changed your mind for. You vowed that were one country you would never take the *Verity*.'

'Not quite what I vowed, Tom.' Nathan stood up, his tall figure seeming to fill the small cabin. 'I vowed never to carry human cargo and that vow still stands. I will carry no convicts there or to any other penal colony.'

'So, begging your pardon Captain, why go?'

'Assemble the crew on deck, every last one. I will tell you and them the reason for my decision.'

Still puzzled but knowing not to press more questions, Tom Brooks returned to the deck. Nathan Burford was as much friend as he was captain but where the *Verity* was concerned that friendship came second.

Standing alone in his cabin Nathan stared at the window, its small glass panes glistening like jewels where the sun slanted across them. Why had he decided to do this, why had he changed his mind?

From somewhere deep within him a faced pinched with cold, snowflakes gleaming on auburn hair, green eyes wide and pleading superimposed itself upon the window. Taking his cap from the table he left the cabin. He knew why this trip would not be to the West Indies.

From the quarter deck he scanned the faces of the men stood below, each showing its measure of enquiry.

Raising a hand he stilled the quiet murmurs yet had almost to shout to be heard above the rattle and clamour of the dockside.

'I want each man to know the *Verity* will not be sailing for the West Indies as you thought. Instead she will be going to Australia . . .'

He paused, waiting for the ripple of disbelief to die away.

'. . . No doubt this will come as something of a shock for you all know well my feelings concerning the transportation of convicts; but true to my word there will be no soul on board who has not chosen to be there. That includes her crew. No one of you will be pressed into this voyage, any man wishing for his ticket will be given it along with the pay due him and my thanks for the service he has given me. As for any who choose to stay I make no bones about what lies ahead. The journey is double any we have made before, even by taking the route of the new Suez Canal we are looking at two or three months . . .'

'What be in Australia we can't be finding in the Sugar Islands?'

'Good question.' Nathan's keen glance landed at once on the sailor who spoke. 'But not the right question. You should ask what be in the Sugar Islands that can't be found in Australia?'

'Then what do that be, Cap'n?'

Glancing towards the second enquirer Nathan smiled before answering. 'Sugar . . . molasses, wheat, fine cloth . . . the lists are endless and each speaks of trade. There are people living there whose time has been served, some with wives and families that joined them, God only knows by what means. But those the government sends across so gladly they don't pay to bring back and from what I hear from ships that carry regular cargo of convicts they have no chance in hell to earn the means of getting themselves home so they are forced to stay in Australia. Those people need food and goods every bit as much as do the prisons they had to build; the *Verity* will take some of that food.'

'And bring back what . . . what do that country hold not counting convicts, will the *Verity* be bringing back such men as 'ave paid their dues?'

'If need be.' Nathan answered. 'Though it is my aim to trade goods for goods not for men. As to what those goods may be we must wait and see. Now I say again, those among you taking their ticket my thanks and God speed, for I would take no man so far from his home against his will. For any man who signs for this trip, his pay will reflect the length of time served aboard plus a token of goodwill.'

It had always been a practice with him to tell his crew the truth of any voyage.

Once more in his cabin, Nathan closed his eyes against the face that stared from its shadowed corners.

But this time he had only spoken part of that truth. Of the real reason he had said not a word.

'How many do we need to sign on?' He turned as the first mate entered the cabin.

'None.' The answer rode a wide smile. 'Not one man took his ticket. They all appreciates fair dealing and they be with you to a man.'

'What about you Tom, do you think I'm being fair? After all, it was my word said the *Verity* would never make that run.'

Tom Brooks' smile lessened but remained touching the corners of his mouth.

'There be many things a man reckons never to do in life but as many times fate steps in to change that and he be left to accept it.'

'This isn't fate Tom, this is my doing.'

'Is it, Nathan? You and me we've seen too many unusual occurrences to accept this as less.'

'Unusual.' Nathan nodded. 'Yes, I grant that. But not unavoidable; fate has no hand in this.'

'Then change it Nathan. Reverse the decision, throw these lists overboard and give the order to make sail for the Indies.'

From the dockside shouts of porters and stevedores busy with the business of loading and unloading ships invaded the silence that dropped between the two men, but out of the mêlée came one solitary voice.

. . . *when you love someone no distance is too far.*

Reaching again for the parchment he had studied earlier, Nathan spread it open. Touching one finger to the continent of Australia he spoke quietly.

'Fill out those lists, Mr Brooks.'

That Colonel had as good as threatened Benjie's life.

Tamar sat on one of the boxes that held all that was left of her hopes and Odile Bancroft's life.

But Benjie was not here in Geelong so that threat was empty. Yet that by no means ended her problems. Her brother was not here and that meant she must look elsewhere for him . . . but how did she do that without money?

For the first time since he had been taken from her she felt the true helplessness of her situation. Covering her face with both hands she gave way to the fears and emotions that tore at her, letting her hot tears fall over her fingers.

'You made up your mind yet about them boxes?'

His tread soundless on the soft sand Tamar started at the unexpectedness of his voice. Squinting against the glare of the sun she looked into the unshaven face of the man who had spoken to her earlier on the beach.

Brushing one hand across her cheeks she shook her head.

'Well, you best do it quick if you be going to do anything at all,' he said, glancing at the rolling surf, 'tide be turning. A few more minutes then you and them will be floatin' out to sea.'

'I can't move them.' Tamar sniffed biting back a

fresh flood of tears locking them in her throat as he turned his glance again to her.

'It be a certain fact you can't go leavin' 'em 'ere, not lessen you wants to lose 'em.'

Her lips tight, afraid that to soften them would allow the tears to flow again, Tamar stood up.

'I have no choice but to leave them here, I have nowhere else to take them.'

'But you 'ave folk, why else would you come to Geelong?'

The words stirring the brew of emotions swirling inside her Tamar pressed a hand to her mouth.

'I . . . I have a brother,' she managed after a few moments, 'I thought to find him here but . . .'

His sun-darkened face creasing with sympathy the man nodded. 'Your brother be a convict, another poor bugger invited to spend years in Her Majesty's tropical paradise! I could see it wasn't you for the stockade when you come ashore wi' that sea captain. That proved a bit of a disappointment for the colonel I'll be bound.' He glanced towards the fenced enclosure. 'But you 'ave to get off this beach or you will still find yourself a guest in his house and that you would regret, you take George Cooper's word on that.'

'But I don't have . . .'

'I know, I know. That much I gleaned for myself. You best come along wi' me.'

Grabbing one of the larger trunks he dragged it towards the line of small wooden houses. Watching him Tamar wrestled with her thoughts. There had been so many people seemingly willing to help her while in truth they wanted only to use her for their own ends.

Zeph Tullio had tried to rape her, Lena Sampson had wanted to sell her to Trader East for heaven knew what purpose, then there had been Josiah Taylor and his assault on her in that dockside alley and now the commander of this penal settlement. But to be fair there had been others who had truly helped her, people she could trust, the Mullins, Amy and . . .

She blinked as a trick of the sun playing over the man calling to her from the top of the beach turned him into a tall, dark-haired uniformed figure with a trace of beard etching his strong face.

. . . and Captain Nathan Burford.

She had spent less than an hour with him, but she could so easily have given her whole life.

The last thought bringing a burning to her cheeks she swiftly picked up a box. Day-dreaming would do her no good and she had already learned the hard way that wishes didn't come true, not for the likes of a Hockley wench.

Chapter Twenty-Five

'It were the right thing my man did in bringing you 'ere, 'tain't safe to be out there at night.'

Tamar watched the woman who had welcomed her into her home bustle about the room, its sparse furnishings fashioned from the same trees that had formed its walls. The houses of the work people of the Gold Quarter, poor as they were, held more than this, yet it seemed to contain a warmth that was not due simply to the fire that burned on the open hearth.

'You wouldn't last long sleeping in the open.' The woman stirred the contents of an iron pot set directly on to the glowing fire. 'The dingoes would make short shrift of you.'

Perched awkwardly on one of the boxes George Cooper had brought into the house, Tamar itched to help with the woman's chores but felt too shy to offer. She asked simply, 'Dingoes?'

Millie Cooper looked up from stirring the pot.

'Wild dogs,' she answered. 'They've taken to the 'abit of comin' down from the bush at night . . . the bush be what we knows as forest and scrub in England . . . anyway, them dogs comes scavenging around the settlement once darkness settles. Might be the smell of mean cookin' that draws 'em, but whatever it be a body be best off indoors once the sun goes down; dogs they might be but they be vicious creatures. Some says they ain't agin carryin' away a babby and devouring it, every bone and sinew.'

'But surely the soldiers patrol . . .'

'Patrol . . . them!' The woman's laugh was short and cold. 'The only time they patrols is when Colonel Henry Forbes' loins is itching and there be no comely woman to scratch them and when that 'appens a closed door don't be much use.'

'They . . . the soldiers . . . they would not just knock on someone's door.'

'Knock . . . no.' Millie returned the ladle to the pot. 'At least not 'til after they kicked it down.'

'But the people here, surely they . . .'

'They does nothing.' The woman set three bowls on the rough table. 'Except what they be told by Henry Forbes. This be a penal settlement and even them as 'ave served their time be still under his hand.'

Her eyes on the woman's thin face Tamar caught the sudden flash of fear that swept over it as the door swung open and the long breath of relief as her husband walked in.

'So why do people stay . . . I mean, once their sentence is served why don't they move to a different town?'

'I asked myself the same question when I arrived ten years since, but I soon learned the answer.'

Taking her husband's jacket Millie hung it on a wooden peg hammered into the wall. He took his place on the one chair which he drew to the table.

'Folk fresh out from England allus asks that question,' George Cooper answered. 'But they 'as to learn same as you going to 'ave to learn, this don't be England. A body can't up and walk to the next town even supposin' they knowed in which direction that town be. It be said this country has deserts that could hold a hundred Englands and still not be pushed for space; and then there be the bush with its Abboes, they be black men as some reckon eats white folk. Then there be wild animals; nobody survives the bush that be why the convicts be free of ankle chain while they be working beyond the palisade. The bush or the sea, them two be the only way out of Geelong and both be impossible to survive.'

Impossible to survive! Tamar watched the woman ladle broth into the bowls. But she had to leave Geelong, she had to continue her search.

Accepting the stool the woman placed for her she spooned dispiritedly at the broth. There had to be a way, she needed only to think calmly.

'I fetched in the last of those boxes you brought from that ship.'

Ship! Tamar looked up quickly. The *Porpoise*! It may have other ports of call along the coast, perhaps Captain Jones would take her to one of them. Tomorrow she would ask him, somehow she would find a way of reaching that ship. Tomorrow she would leave Geelong.

'It were as well I got them when I did.' He spooned a lump of meat into his mouth. 'Or they would be well into the bay by this time, followin' after that boat.'

Her own spoon idle in her hand Tamar looked at him with hope-filled eyes. If there was a boat going out then the same boat could be hired to sail her across in the morning.

'Could I hire this boat?'

George Cooper stared across the table before laughing out loud. 'Hire, you says. Not lessen you 'ave as much money as be in the purse of the Queen of England 'erself! That boat you speaks of hiring be a ship of the line, a vessel of the Royal Navy, but you knows that already for you sailed 'ere in 'er.'

The *Porpoise*! Tamar's hand trembled, rattling the spoon against the bowl. He had said the boxes would be following *after* . . .

'But even should you 'ave that much money you be too late, she be naught but a speck on the 'orizon by now.'

Her voice little more than a whisper Tamar dropped her glance to the table. 'The *Porpoise* has left?'

Glancing at his wife, catching the brief shake of her head he answered gently. 'Ar wench, the *Porpoise* be gone, her took the evening tide.'

The *Porpoise* had sailed. Tamar lay on the heap of skins Millie had spread in a corner of the tiny living room.

Her one means of leaving this place had gone and she was trapped here. She too was now under the hand of Henry Forbes.

Remembering what Millie had told her of the

patrols and the wild dogs she caught her breath as a blood-chilling howl rent the silence of the night. But it was not the cries of dingoes set her limbs trembling.

'It belonged to a woman sent down along of me.'

Millie Cooper opened the door of a timber building set a little way nearer the edge of the great half-moon swathe that had eaten into the tree line overlooking the broad bay.

Her head throbbing from a sleepless night and heightened by a temperature already unbreathably hot Tamar stepped after her into a room that smelled of dust.

'We served one time together behind that fence.' The older woman jerked her head in the direction of the prison compound. 'We cooked for the convicts, if you could say that some of the muck we were given to serve up could be said to be cooking; then, our time done, we both took ourselves a man from among the same convicts, that way we was safe from others with a roving eye and an urge to bed a woman.'

'But why do they no longer want this house?' Tamar looked quickly at her companion. 'Have they found a better one?'

'Some folk in Geelong think they 'ave.' Millie Cooper nodded slowly.

'Where . . . have they left . . . ?'

'No, they ain't left, not in the way you means it.' Her eyes showing their sadness, even in the shadowed gloom of the shuttered house, Millie half smiled.

'They still be 'ere but at least they be free of that swine sitting up there in the governor's 'ouse. It were the patrol. Seems Henry Forbes had seen Mary washin' 'erself 'neath the the little waterfall that drops into the lake set beyond the trees and took a fancy to 'avin' 'er warm his bed. That night the soldiers came and when 'er man tried to fight them off they clubbed him to death with the butt end of their rifles and laughed as they dragged Mary away. She come back a week later, Forbes had tired of her by then and was looking for new game. Her man was already lying in his grave out there beyond the hill and that very day Mary joined 'im; she set a rope around 'er neck and hung herself from a tree.'

'And no one did anything?'

'That be summat else you best learn sharpish.' Millie swung back the shutter, letting the strong sunlight pour in through the window. 'There be nothing any man can do against Henry Forbes, he commands the soldiers and soldiers 'ave guns. Sticks be little use against guns and sticks be all the weapons we 'ave. Women get taken and men get shot or beaten to death, that be the way of it 'ere.'

'But surely the authorities back in England should be told!'

'Ar, wench, they should. But who is there that be going to tell 'em? Forbes be civil enough when any naval ship calls. As for the others their captains gets too good a price for the run they brings than to risk their trade by saying anything back 'ome of what goes on 'ere. No, I reckons the only way we will get relief from Henry Forbes will be when he be carried to the same place Mary and her man lies; and then we runs the risk of gettin' another that be equal as bad. We can only trust to the Lord to guard us from that. But I be thinkin' it will take more than trust to keep you from that man, he's set his sights on you already. You be ready to leave should that naval ship drops anchor again at Geelong for I doubt there will be a merchant boat will take you off; 'til that time try to stay as much out of sight as be possible, and remember to bar the shutters and door at night. My man and me will do all we can to 'elp you.' Taking Tamar in her arms the woman held her close. 'God keep you girl,' she whispered, 'God keep you.'

Watching her leave the house Tamar felt the tears rush into her throat. Who would have dreamed things could have turned out this way? Dropping to her knees she pressed her hands to her lips, murmuring against her fingers. 'Please Lord, help me, help me find Benjie. Help me to leave this place.'

'Now isn't that a picture to warm a man's heart, a woman praying for him to come to her!'

Opening her eyes Tamar looked to the figure standing at the doorway, its silhouette black against the golden sunlight, then bit back a scream as Colonel Henry Forbes strode into the room kicking the door closed behind him.

From the shadows of her husband's chandler's shop Amy listened to the flow of conversation. His ship was fresh in from Cyprus, the man in thick sweater and heavy boots was saying, and he wished he were back there where the weather was kinder to a man's bones.

She knew where Cyprus was and that it was an island set in a long inland sea. That were the Mediterranean Sea William had told her. But the maps he showed her told it was nowhere near Australia.

Listening now to the men talking she thought of the evenings since Tamar had left, of the long hours she had thought of the girl who had so quickly become a friend. The fears of thinking maybe she was dead, drowned in that long stretch of water.

William had laughed at that, telling her that should that have happened then word would have reached Bristol by now. But there had been no news of Tamar so why should there be news of a sunken ship.

'The *Porpoise* . . .'

Amy's senses tightened as she heard the reply to the question William always put on her behalf.

'. . . no, we saw no sight of any ship of that name, but then if it took route through the new canal then we wouldn't have sight of her.'

The new canal. Amy turned away going quietly into the kitchen set behind the shop. William said it was called Suez and that it cut the journey to the East Indies by half. Had Tamar gone that way? Had she ever reached Australia?

Taking the pie she had made earlier from the oven she set it on the table, already laid with a spotless white cloth and pretty blue flowered china.

If anything had gone wrong, if Tamar were drowned or taken captive in some awful foreign land it would be her fault.

'I ought never to have done it.'

'Done what?' William stepped into the kitchen.

Guilt turning to tears Amy flung herself into her husband's arms.

'Oh Will, it's all my fault. I shouldn't have pushed her into it . . .'

His arms closing about her William frowned.

'Shouldn't have pushed who into what?'

'Tamar.' Amy sobbed. 'She didn't want to be Odile Bancroft's maid it was me made her do it. I talked her into it, I said it were the best chance she might ever get of going to Australia, of finding her brother, and now if she be dead it's my fault.'

'Who says Tamar be dead?'

'Well if she were living she would have written, she would have let me know she was safe.'

Lowering his wife gently into a chair William pushed aside the plates before reaching a large book from a table set beneath the window.

'Look.' He opened the book as Amy wiped her eyes on a corner of her large apron. 'Here be England and here be Australia. Whichever way a ship might sail, either to the east or to the west, there be a world between them. Word must travel thousands of miles before it can reach us and ships anchor in many ports before they come home. You have to allow time Amy, I've told you so often enough; it don't be like the post here in this country, a couple of days on horseback or in a wagon. It can take months for a letter to get here from so far away.'

'I know.' Amy sniffed. 'But that doesn't help me feel any less guilty. If I hadn't been so keen to get married . . .'

'You were not the only one keen for that.' William kissed his wife's damp cheek. 'And as for Tamar, she would have found a way to get to Australia even without your help. As it is, going with Odile Bancroft aboard a Royal Navy ship was much the best, the crew aboard those ships are well disciplined, they know where not to put their hands.'

'Not like you eh, Will Granger?' Amy smiled through the last of her tears.

Closing the atlas, Will chuckled. 'You cut me a wedge of that pie woman, then I'll show you where my hands should be.'

'Do you honestly think Tamar is safe?'

The meal finished Amy placed the washed dishes back on the dresser that was her pride and joy.

'I honestly think she is.' William Granger tapped his long-stemmed clay pipe against the palm of one hand. 'Added to which I think somebody else believes the same thing.'

Pushing the last of the cutlery into a drawer Amy went to sit on a cushion at his feet.

'Who, Will?' She turned vivid blue eyes eagerly to his. 'Who else thinks Tamar is safe?'

Teasingly William filled the bowl of his pipe with slivers of tobacco sliced from a block, pressing it down until his wife pinched his knee in aggravation.

'Tell me, William Granger, who else thinks Tamar be safe, tell me at once or I'll be showing you where a woman's hands can be!'

Reaching a taper to the flames William tried not to smile as he held it to the bowl of his pipe.

'You should have stayed in the shop a little longer,' he said between sucks on the long stem, 'you would have heard for yourself.'

'Heard what? I'm warning you Will Granger!'

Replacing the taper in a small jug set in the fireplace William caught the hand reaching for his shirt collar.

'Heard the rest of what that seaman had to say. They had not sighted the *Porpoise* . . .'

'So!' Amy almost shouted.

'So they could bring no news of her, but they had sighted the *Verity*, not only that but he had spoken to her first mate when they dropped anchor in the same port.'

'The *Verity*.' Amy frowned, searching for the ship in her mind.

'Aye, the *Verity*.' William puffed contentedly. 'That be Nathan Burford's ship and it seems that what I heard the last time her were here in Bristol is true.'

Memory returning Amy nodded. Nathan Burford . . . She and Tamar had spoken of him and the girl's cheeks had blushed. Was Tamar's the only interest? She looked up quickly.

'What was said the last time he was here?'

'That Nathan Burford was thinking of breaking a vow he took years ago when his brother were lost at sea; a vow to sail none but the route that led to Africa or the West Indies.'

'And you think that now he has broken with that vow.'

Taking several puffs from his pipe William watched the trail of lavender-grey smoke curl into the up-draught of the chimney.

'I had my thoughts he might be pondering on doing that when I filled his last list of supplies. There were things asked for he had never carried before, not according that is to the record books kept before we took on the chandler business. They spoke of a much longer voyage and of a trade in goods that were unusual for the *Verity*, goods that might be valuable in a colony less settled than the Sugar Islands.'

'Are you saying that Nathan Burford has gone to Australia?'

'I don't be saying as he hasn't.' William blew smoke over his wife's head.

'Could he be looking for Tamar?'

'Mebbe he is, mebbe he ain't.' William grinned mischievously as Amy jumped to her feet her mouth drawn tight with impatience.

'William Granger you are the most aggravating husband a woman ever had to deal with!'

'But one you wouldn't change.'

'I wouldn't go putting too much store on that. There be others easier to handle.'

Still smiling William set his pipe in the hearth before drawing Amy on to his knee.

'Easier to handle but not so satisfying.' He kissed

her lips. 'But I'll tease you no more. That seaman told me the *Verity* was taking on a heavy supply of fresh water when they berthed alongside her on the coast of North Africa and talk had it bound for Australia.'

'Then he has gone to Australia and that can only mean he is looking to find Tamar and bring her back.'

Touching a hand to the head resting on his shoulder the teasing gleam faded from William's eyes. 'Looking be one thing Amy, finding be another. From what I've seen of that country in the atlas, together with the stories seamen tell, its true size be beyond imagining. Burford might well search for years only to find what he's found of his brother . . . nothing.'

Sitting in the quiet warmth of her cosy kitchen Amy closed her eyes. Guide him to her, she prayed silently, let him find her . . .

Her eyes flicking open she stared at the fire while the feeling that came each time she prayed surged inside her. Was she praying for Tamar's safety or was it for relief of her own guilt?

Chapter Twenty-Six

Every nerve a needle end pricking her skin Tamar scrambled to her knees.

'It's funny.' Henry Forbes' flabby mouth spread in a wet smile. 'I had not thought of myself that way before . . . as the answer to a maiden's prayer.'

Fingers clutching her skirts Tamar tried to halt the ring of fear in her voice.

'What do you want?'

'Want . . . ?' He moved towards her his tread light for such a heavy man. 'I thought I had made that obvious yesterday. I want you.'

Light from the window spread over the small room enhancing its bareness. Seeing her glance he laughed.

'There's nothing here you can hit me with . . . and don't bother to call of Millie Cooper; oh yes, I know where you spent the night and you know what will happen to that pair if you don't co-operate, and it will be neither pleasant nor healthy.'

'Co-operate!' Her back already against the wooden wall Tamar stared, dislike and fear darkening her eyes. 'You call physical assault co-operation?'

The smile widening pushed the fat of his face upward enclosing his small eyes even deeper in their folds.

'I don't call it anything but then I don't have to. You call it what you like it will make no difference, I take what I will when I will, just as I intend taking you.'

He was so close she could smell the stale sweat of his body, the brandy on his breath. She could not scream even should the muscles of her throat relax, he had made clear enough the danger to the Coopers should they try to help her.

Eyelids pressed hard down, teeth clenched tight together she shuddered as his fingers slid the buttons of her gown undone then pulled it down along her arms.

'Nice . . . very nice.'

It was muttered on a short gasping breath that carried its foulness to her nostrils. Her stomach heaving she caught a sob, holding it in her mouth as he dragged away her chemise lowering his slobbering mouth to her breasts.

The touch of his tongue rolling her nipples galvanised her. Weaving her fingers in his pomaded hair she snatched his head backward on his neck, glaring into his puffy eyes.

'I don't need the Coopers to fight my battles, Colonel Forbes, I am well able to deal with a swine of my own accord.'

Shoving him away she ran for the door snatching it open. 'Will you leave now or do I show everyone why you came here, what type of man you are?'

Running both hands through his rumpled hair he smiled blandly. 'You wouldn't be telling anything that shit out there didn't know already but they would enjoy the sight of a pretty pair of tits, some of the convicts ain't seen tits for more years than you've lived and would willingly kill to get their hands on yours, and that goes not only for the men . . . so you see you will be better off with me, at least only one pair of hands a night would fondle you.'

'I would rather die!'

Pausing at the door his bulk filling its frame he reached forward grabbing one breast he squeezed hard.

'Oh you will do that . . . ' Digging fingernails into the soft flesh his smile cold and evil as a serpent he squeezed again '. . . you *will* do that . . . after I have finished with you!'

The words ringing in her mind her whole body trembling Tamar leaned against the closed door. The man was an animal . . . a filthy animal. She had to leave, surely there was someone other than that man who could help her trace Benjie . . . and if not . . . ? Sobs rattling in her throat Tamar faced the answer.

'There be nothing you can do wench . . .'

Millie Cooper looked with pity at the lovely auburn-haired girl, lifting a cornflower-strewn dress from one of the boxes her husband had brought into the house.

'. . . you've already shown more nerve than any other woman he's tried it on with but it don't do to try being too brave; far better let him have what he

hankers for and get it over with. That way his ego will
be satisfied and he'll let you alone.'

'I couldn't do that, Millie.' Tamar looked up from
the box. 'I could never live with myself if I did that.'

'You'll like not live long if you don't!' Millie
Cooper's mouth tightened.

'That is something I am willing to risk.'

Her mouth softening Millie nodded. 'Ar wench, I
can see that and I'd stake a sovereign fat Forbes sees it
also, that is if I 'ad a sovereign; but I'd 'ave given more
still to 'ave watched him squirm in your 'ands. That
would be a treat a body wouldn't forget in ten life
sentences.'

Holding another of the gowns against her face
Tamar gave way to the sudden amusement bubbling
inside her.

'I must have looked like Vinny Marsh,' she giggled,
'I would sometimes see her grab her sons by the hair
when they went too far.'

'Who be Vinny Marsh?'

'She was a neighbour of ours in Hockley – a very
good friend.' Sat on the floor beside the box Tamar
gave way to the flood of memories that had helped
sustain her through the long empty nights since
leaving the Gold Quarter, and there, the sunlight
slanting through the window Millie Cooper listened
to the whole story.

'So who do you think took this Alexandra Stone
then?' she asked as Tamar finished.

'I couldn't say.' Tamar looked back at the dresses
she had been unpacking. 'I only know it could not

have been Benjie, my brother never stole anything in his life. He wouldn't, Millie. I tried telling them that but no one in that court would listen. They simply took him down to the cells. I was supposed to see him next day but as I told you he had already been taken off to Stafford and . . . and I have never seen him since.'

'Lying buggers!' Millie clicked her tongue disparagingly. 'The law be all the same for folk as don't 'ave money. But for gentry it be a different tale. Speaking of gentry it seems to be that employer of your'n, what did you say his name was? – Philip Amory – seems he could 'ave helped more'n he did if as you says he believed your brother innocent.'

'Mr Amory was always quite kindly spoken to Benjie and to myself, perhaps had I stayed in Hockley he would have done something more.'

'Ar wench, p'raps he would, and p'raps that diamond 'as been found and your brother's innocence established.'

'It is not his innocence I am looking to find, it is him, but how do I go about it Millie? How can I leave this place with Colonel Forbes watching my every movement?'

'God knows!' Millie shook her head sending darts of sunlight shimmering from hair that years of suffering had long since turned grey. 'When I were a child in Sunday school the vicar used to tell us how the Lord had a plan of all our lives and that nothing 'appened to us 'cept by His will; but when I was deported for no more than answering back to the squire I began to think p'raps the vicar were wrong or the Lord's plan had gone somewhat adrift. Now with the years I knows they both was wrong. I could tell you what the church rammed down our young throats, adversity comes through the evil of one's own actions and the only help was God's: I could tell you to pray to him and that your prayer would bring restitution but that would be lying for I 'ave no faith left in anything save what I can do for myself, and that be my advice to you. Watch out for yourself, do what you can for yourself, that is the only way to survive . . .'

A loud rap to the door halted her in mid-sentence. Millie shot a warning glance as Tamar rose to her feet. The door flew open before either of them could reach it. A uniformed soldier with rifle in hand swaggered into the room.

'The colonel sends to tell you that you be ockipyin' crown propery and that you pay the reckizite amount due or out you goes.'

'Crown property!' Millie's eyes blazed. 'This were Mary Daly's 'ouse and Forbes knows it, same as 'e knows 'er wrote a note leavin' it to me.'

'I ain't claimin' to know what the colonel do or don't know, but mebbe's you'd like to put him straight, eh Millie Cooper . . . I think he'd like that.'

'Wait!' Tamar stepped forward a hand clasping the other woman's arm. 'Did Colonel Forbes say how much is due?'

'He sent this.' Drawing a sheet of paper from the cross-belts on his chest the man flung it on to the rough wood table George Cooper had managed to find.

Reading the paper Tamar's face blanched. Five guineas, he was demanding five guineas payable immediately! But how in the world was she to find so much money?

'The colonel said to pay now or to get out.'

'You be enjoyin' this don't you, you scum!' Millie spat, 'but then, that be all you ever 'as to enjoy ain't it? Tormenting women be the only pleasure you gets from 'em cos even them wi' the pox wouldn't play with your dangler!'

'Bitch!' His face distorted with rage the man raised his rifle bringing the butt hard down on Millie's chest following it with a savage boot to the stomach as she fell to the floor.

'Stop it! Stop that . . .' Tamar threw herself between Millie and the foot drawn back to strike again '. . . strike again and Colonel Forbes will hear of it, and be sure . . . he will be more than ready to listen to me.'

His hands gripping the rifle the soldier grimaced then stepped back a pace. The wench was more than right in what her said, every bloke in the unit knew the colonel had an urge for this one.

'The money . . . now,' he growled, his eyes on Millie as Tamar helped her stand.

Pay it and he would go. But how, she had no money except that which had belonged to Odile Bancroft and now rightfully belonged to her husband.

But Edmond Bancroft was not here and possibly might never be. Wrestling with the rights and wrongs of using the dead woman's money Tamar reached for the purse she herself had placed at the bottom of the box. Tipping out the contents she counted out five guineas, replacing the two pennies that remained. Together with the silver sixpence she had sewn into the lining of the jacket Amy had given her that was every penny she had.

Shutting the door behind the departing soldier she crumpled into a ball, trembling in every limb.

'It's alright, wench.' Millie gathered her in her arms rocking back and forth. 'He be gone and it's all over.'

But for how long? Comforting the trembling girl Millie kept the rest to herself. How long before that swine sent for the next five guineas or even ten? He knew the girl had virtually nothing, knew that sooner or later she would break.

'I don't have any more, even that I gave did not belong to me. It was Odile Bancroft's money.'

'Well that one won't be needing it.' Millie answered practically as she dished up the meal she had cooked.

'But what of Edmond Bancroft?' Tamar's eyes showed the worry that had plagued her in the hours since handing over those guineas. 'What if he should come for it, what do I tell him?'

'Tell him there was no money. He won't be knowing any different. After all, its been a good few months since he provided any . . . if he ever did.'

That would be lying and she had already committed a terrible enough crime without compounding it; theft was a dreadful crime and she had stolen Odile's money. There was no other way of describing what she had done. Should she be found out she would be imprisoned. Benjie had been sentenced to thirty years . . . what would her punishment be, how long would she be sentenced to? How long here in this colony, in the prison controlled by Henry Forbes?

Glancing at the food Millie and her husband had shared with her Tamar recognised there was an even more pressing need for money than she had realised. The Coopers could not go on providing her with food. Somehow she needed to find a way of making her own living.

'What do you think you'll be doing wi' all them frocks?'

'What?' Tamar looked up taken by surprise at the question.

'Them frocks.' Millie swallowed the bread she had dipped into the remains of yesterday's broth. 'There be a fair few of 'em and right pretty they be judging by what I've seen.'

'I . . . I don't know. Amy insisted I bring them, she said I might get sale for them.'

'Amy and me both. They would fetch more than enough to keep you fed and housed.'

'But any money I make the colonel will take.'

'The wench be right.' George Cooper looked up from his plate. 'There be as much chance of hiding money from him as there be of flying back to England.'

'There be more to making a livin' than the getting

of money.' Millie answered tersely. 'There be ways and means and one of them be barter. Tamar can exchange them frocks for other things; like my mother always said fair exchange be no robbery, swap a frock for a sack of wheat or a few joints of meat . . . fat Forbes would find little to interest him in that.'

'Millie 'as summat there.' George nodded. 'It bears thinking on, wench.'

Looking at the faces of the two people trying so hard to help her Tamar wished herself anywhere but here. They had suffered so much already and by setting themselves with her were placing themselves in danger of Henry Forbes' vicious spite.

'I could not lie to Edmond Bancroft,' she said at last, 'the man may have been a philanderer but I doubt he was a fool. He would need only to see one of those dresses to know they were not mine and I can't see him accepting corn or meat as payment for them, no it would have to be money.'

'Then money it'll be.' Mopping up the last of her broth Millie chewed the scrap of bread with alacrity. Only when it was swallowed did she glance at her husband. 'There be plenty of folk in Geelong hates fat Forbes as much as we do and they be as eager to put one over on him. You knows the procedure – half and half – exchange goods paid in the open where all can see and money paid in private away from prying eyes. Spread the word, and mind you tell them anyone chewing the cud with Forbes will have their bed made up at the cemetery!'

'Won't be nobody in Geelong daft enough to tell

Forbes anything they shouldn't,' George answered, 'but do you really think folk 'ere will pay good money for a frock?'

Resting her elbows on the table Millie grinned at him. 'George Cooper, if you thinks a woman starved of a chance to wear summat pretty after years of nothing but prison yellow wouldn't give 'er eye teeth to do it then it be plain you don't know women.'

'Then they will buy those dresses?'

'Ar Tamar wench, they'll buy 'em.' Millie's eyes gleamed. 'They'll buy every last one, 'specially when George 'as one put on the coast trader.'

Gathering the used dishes Tamar frowned questioningly.

'Coast trader?'

'It be summat of a packet boat.' George reached for his pipe. 'Travels around the coast selling stuff from one settlement to another. Like Millie says, put one of them frocks on that boat an' it'll be back for more.'

So there *was* a way out of Geelong. Outside, the same chilling howl she had heard before split the silent night. Lying on the pile of skins Tamar suppressed a shudder, glad she accepted the Cooper's offer to stay the night at their house, the thought of Henry Forbes visiting her churning her stomach. But now there was a way of escaping him. The packet boat would take her dresses . . . somehow it must be persuaded to take her.

There was no telling whether she would still be in Australia. Maybe she had sailed on with the *Porpoise*.

Nathan Burford lifted his face to the windless sky. The days had been hot as Hades and the nights little cooler. How in God's name did men and women chained below decks of those prison ships ever live to reach port? But it was not just prisoners who died in these climes, paying passengers did too, dysentery was rife among ships not to speak of typhoid. Had either of those diseases struck Tamar Hallam? Had she died during the long sea voyage? But she had sailed on a ship of the Royal Navy, conditions aboard those were better than on most merchantmen, chances were she was alive. She *had* to be alive!

'How much longer do you think this will last?'

Nathan shook his head as the first mate came to stand beside him at the forecastle rail.

'You have as much idea of that as I have Tom. I've heard of the doldrums, of ships being trapped for days without wind to fill a sail but this is the first experience I've ever had of it.'

'Aye, and let's hope it's the last.' Wetting a finger against his tongue Thomas Brooks held it above his head before lowering it. 'No sign of wind . . . except that coming from the bosun's arse, I say we strap him to the spar and he'll blow the *Verity* the rest of the way.'

Their laughter dying away Nathan stared at the sky, each star as big as a pigeon's egg. It was a magical sight, one that never failed to stir him; nature could be so beautiful but it could also be dangerous.

'How are the men taking it?'

In tune with his crew as he was he knew he had no cause to ask but he voiced the question anyway.

'One or two ripe suggestions.' Thomas Brooks grinned. 'But that's as it should be, shows the men still be of good heart.'

'But for how long Tom? We've already been stuck in this bit of ocean for near a week. I've got the best crew any man could wish for but even they won't be able to take much more of this.'

'Luckily you had more water put aboard at that last port than was thought necessary, we would have been in right fettle without it.'

'You would have done the same, Tom.' Nathan paused watching a shooting star trail a fiery arc to the horizon. 'You are every bit the seaman I am, probably more so.'

'In that case p'raps the suggestion I be about to put won't sound so daft.'

Glancing at his first mate, the stern light illuminating his face, Nathan Burford smiled. 'I hope it is Tom. It will be a first and I'm not a man to spurn a new experience.'

A nod acknowledging a captain's compliment to his seamanship Tom Brooks stared into the jet black night.

'I've been thinking of what you said a minute since. The men be the best crew afloat but even the best need to see that them above 'em be doing something to ease a sticky situation.'

'But how Tom? We can't control the wind.'

Thomas Brooks kept his stare buried in the velvet darkness. 'No, we can't control the wind, but we can control the ship.'

Beside him Nathan Burford stood silent. His first mate was not given to making idle conversation, somewhere in that tow head was an idea, give it birth and it might get them out of this devil-ridden spot.

'I've been to thinking . . .' Thomas went on '. . . set a line, one end to the prow, the other to the longboat and we could tow the *Verity*.'

'Tow her!'

'Aye, tow her.'

'In this heat?' Nathan frowned. 'How long do you think they could keep that up?'

His own unsmiling face lit by the glow of the stern lamp Thomas Brooks turned to face his captain.

'As long as you or me Nathan, and that be as long as it takes to get the *Verity* to safety.'

'Very pretty. You should buy that Sarah, p'raps it'll put life into your Samuel.'

Shoving the dress she had been holding into Tamar's hands the woman looked once at Henry Forbes before scuttling from the house.

Heart pounding, Tamar forced herself to calmly replace the dress on one of the crude hangers George Cooper had fashioned for her. It had been more than a month since word had gone round the settlement that there were dresses fresh out from England for the buying and almost every woman not serving a sentence had bought one. No one of them had spoken of what payment was given, but Henry Forbes had come several times to this house and each time was a threat.

He had not given up the idea of taking her. That was obvious in the way his eyes roved her, but in them she had detected a new gleam, a new amusement. He had seen the fear on her face with his every visit, seen the trembling she could not control and he was baiting that fear, feeding on it like a vulture fed on rotting flesh. Henry Forbes was enjoying his new entertainment, spreading it from day to day and week to week, exulting in the terror he knew he aroused; but one day he would tire of the game.

At her back she felt the heat of his breath on her neck. What if he were tired of it already?

'You must be making a nice little pile from this business, mebbe the Crown should have asked more than five guineas for this house.'

Clenching her nails into her palm Tamar felt the hand trace her neck then ride over her shoulder towards her breast. Twisting away she went to stand on the opposite side of the table.

'I . . . I take no money!' It was only a half truth, George Cooper was given the half of any bargain struck but it was money being paid to her.

'I'm no fool, girl . . . !'

Beads of moisture on his brow trickling down between the rolls of flesh beneath his jaw. The smell of brandy on his breath drenching the stifling hot air of the tiny room.

'There's nothing takes place in Geelong as I don't get to hear, and what I don't make a man pay for.'

Was that another of his threats or did he really know of those payments?

Catching the doubt that flicked across her face he laughed. 'I see I was told right.' He came towards her. 'But there be a way a man might be released payment . . . a woman could pay for him.'

Pushing hard with his body he threw her backward across the table, one hand stifling her screams, the other flinging her skirts over her face.

Chapter Twenty-Seven

'You were right Amory, that jewellery be going to bring new life to Hockley, I'd say the gold trade be set for a revival.'

'I reckon what Fisher says be true enough.' Matthew Summers smiled at his host. 'I've already had a dozen enquiries from people wanting the same thing since the princess wore it to that state do.'

'So where do you get stones so perfect as that one, mebbe you should ask yourself already.'

Irritated by the old Jew's caution Saul Fisher frowned. 'Trust you to chuck a spanner in the works, Cohen!'

'It is a spanner we must watch for.' Philip Amory intervened. 'There can be only one Alexandra Stone as there can be only one suite of jewellery of that particular design, to sell exact copies would displease the royal family and that we cannot afford to do.'

'So what do you propose, that we kiss this opportunity goodbye?' Fisher banged an angry hand to the table.

'We will have done that should we disregard what Philip says. The royal family have overwhelming influence on the people who have the sort of money good stones and fine gold can fetch. We must have thought for that at all times if the trade is to prosper.'

'There be money enough abroad.' Saul Fisher answered, his tone still sour.

'And also discriminating eyes. Foreign aristocracy is as old as that of this country my friend, some even older, with a heritage of handling and owning the world's most exquisite gems,' the Jew raised both shoulders in his familiar shrug, 'they will not be easily duped.'

'Who the bloody hell mentioned duping them!' Fisher's short temper bubbled near the surface. 'Any goods from my workshop be the real thing.'

'True my friend, true,' Isaac Cohen smoothed the other man's ruffled feathers, 'as it is from the workshop of every man here. What I meant to convey, and what I should have said, is that by using stones other than diamonds . . .'

'Tcha!' Saul Fisher flung a look at his associates. 'Some men prefer diamonds and there be women won't take less, to refuse to give what they asks is to throw business away.'

'Business does not have to be refused if it is handled properly.'

'Damn you Cohen, be you saying . . . ?'

'We might all hear what Cohen be saying if you stay quiet long enough Fisher.' Matthew Summers intervened. 'Give the man a chance to say his piece then if you don't like it you don't have to bide by it.'

'Amory my friend,' the Jew began again as all eyes turned to him, 'you said that to produce exact copies of the Alexandra Stone would be displeasing to the royal family and I agree it must remain unique, and therein lies the answer. Design several suites, each one different, each one perfect in its own way, every piece unique; that very word will add immeasurably to its value; and named for the woman or family . . .'

'Cohen has something there.' Matthew Summers broke in excitedly. 'There be women would give anything to have a piece such as nobody else has got and men willing to pay for it. I vote we do as Cohen says.'

'A word of caution.' Isaac Cohen raised a hand. 'Do not let enthusiasm override your common sense. To over produce would reduce the uniqueness, remember the vanity of some people, they want to be one alone who owns a thing. Keep that always in mind and vary your product, maybe one day the man in the street may be able to buy your jewellery and then will be the time to reproduce an item in its hundreds.'

'The man in the street . . . afford to buy jewellery! Tcha, pigs might fly!' Fisher laughed coarsely.

'Even that my friend . . . even that.' Isaac shrugged. 'This world we live in has seen many changes and there are changes yet to come, maybe that of the man in the street buying your jewellery will be the least of them.'

'That would be no change, it would be a miracle.'

Looking across at Matthew Summers the Jew smiled. 'But Christians believe in miracles do they not my friend?'

'Aye Cohen, we do.' Summers laughed. 'Trouble

be they take a long time in coming. But until that happens I for one intend taking your advice.'

'One more word then. Make one piece, a very fine piece and let it do your talking for you. Use the finest stones you can buy and once seen adorning a pretty neck the commissions will come.'

'An Alexandra Stone in its own right!' Philip Amory nodded. 'I too shall follow Isaac's advice. All I ask is he select and cut my stones.'

'He did not mislead us over the Alexandra,' Summers smiled, 'so I say what about a consortium, a partnership with the four of us working together?'

For several moments Saul Fisher stared at his companions then raised his glass. 'A partnership . . . and who knows, it might one day become jewellers to the Crown.'

'Colonel . . . Colonel sir, there be a man up at the lodge asking to see you.'

His hand tearing at Tamar's underwear Henry Forbes grunted.

'Colonel sir . . .' The voice came clearly through the door.

'Whoever it be tell him to bugger off, I be busy.'

'I said for him to come back later but he insisted I call you sir, he says he be something to do with the government, he's just come down from Sydney on the coastal packet . . .'

Lifting himself off Tamar, Henry Forbes kept his hand pressed hard down across her mouth, his eyes gleaming among the flushed folds of his sweat-soaked face.

'I'll be back,' he grunted. 'I've waited long enough for a taste of your little belly, but it won't be so little by the time Henry Forbes be satisfied.'

At the door he glanced back at Tamar struggling with her torn bloomers.

'Don't bother putting them back,' he laughed, 'I told you I'll be back, meantime you ain't going nowhere.'

Humiliation and despair flooding her eyes with hot tears she caught her breath as the door he had banged shut opened again.

'It be me miss . . .'

Shrouded by the mist of her tears the colonel's batman stood in the doorway.

'. . . the coastal packet . . . get yourself on it, I'll spread the word to say you ran off into the bush.'

The coastal packet. The words shouted at her though the man was gone, but Tamar's mind stayed with the happenings of a moment ago.

'The packet be in.' Millie Cooper burst into the room. 'But it ain't staying, it just called to drop a man off. You 'ave to be quick.'

Seeing the state of Tamar's dress, the tears clouding her eyes telling their own vivid story Millie grasped her, shaking her until the wild panic cleared from her brain.

'Tamar,' she whispered urgently, 'the coastal packet be in the bay but it will be leaving when that man be finished his business. You 'ave to get yourself on it now afore Forbes realises what you be about. Here, I brought this . . .' She shoved a cloth bag into Tamar's hands '. . . it be the money my man were 'olding for you; pay it to the captain of that boat, give him every penny if you 'ave to only get yourself on it, it be your one chance wench, for Forbes won't be took in a second time.'

'But this money is not mine!'

Grabbing a pair of bloomers from a chest and Tamar's jacket from a cupboard she pushed them on to the trembling girl.

'I don't care if it belongs to the devil 'isself, I only know it be your one way out of Geelong. Now get yourself into them clothes quick and I'll get George, he'll find a way of getting you to that longboat without the tower guard spotting you.'

Buttons made the more awkward by the trembling of her fingers Tamar replaced the torn underwear. How would George cover her going to the beach, what if he were caught helping her? Bundling the jacket in her arms she hesitated. The Coopers had been kind to her, she could not repay them by putting them in danger of the colonel's wrath.

'Millie I can't . . .'

She looked up as the door opened, but it was not Millie who stepped inside. Sunlight glinting on fair hair, a small neatly clipped moustache adorning his upper lip a man swept her with a swift all-encompassing glance.

'Miss Hallam?'

Tamar nodded then caught her breath as the colonel followed after him into the room.

'You were acquainted with my late wife? Oh yes I have heard of her death, Captain Jones of the *Porpoise* informed me of the sad news when we met in Sydney. Sad . . . very sad . . . but not for all of us I see.'

Crossing to where the gown still hung from a peg on the wall he fingered the soft green tulle.

'This is Odile's gown, is it not? I remember she wore it for our second wedding anniversary along with some rather good emeralds . . . might I ask you to get them for me along with the rest of her jewellery.'

Across the room Henry Forbes' heated face broke into an evil smile and Tamar felt fear return, cold and almost paralysing. What had he told this man?

'You do have my wife's jewellery?'

Dragging her glance from that malevolent smile Tamar stammered. 'Odile . . . Mrs Bancroft did not have any jewellery apart from a necklace with blue stones and . . . and her wedding ring which Captain Jones left in my care.'

Beneath the moustache the somewhat weak mouth tightened. 'One necklace! You expect me to believe my wife brought just one piece of jewellery with her?'

'It is the truth. If she had more then it is back in England.'

'Is it?' He flung the dress aside. 'Is it really? Or is the truth of it that you have sold it off along the way just as you have been selling her dresses almost from the moment you came here?'

Only Colonel Forbes could have told him that. Tamar's glance swung again to that red, perspiring face and suddenly it felt like the bars of some invisible cage were closing in on her.

'I told you wench, nothing goes on in this settlement, in or out of that compound, that Henry Forbes doesn't know about, and as for your leaving on that packet boat you can forget it. Mr Bancroft has a charge to bring against you.'

'A charge!' Tamar's eyes widened.

Throwing up the lids of several chests Edmond Bancroft turned a cold insipid glare at the girl trembling from head to foot.

'The colonel tells me you have for several weeks made a business of selling my wife's effects. From what I see of her boxes that appears to be correct, unless of course you have them stored elsewhere against my calling for them. Do you have them so stored?'

Her tongue cleaving to the roof of her mouth Tamar could only shake her head.

'I see.' He loosed the lid of a chest the sound of its falling echoing loudly from the bare walls. 'Then I bring a charge of theft both against my late wife and against myself. You stole her jewellery and her clothes then attempted to make off with the proceeds.'

'No!' Tamar gasped. 'No . . . I did not . . . I did not intend to rob you . . .'

'You were not about to run away . . . to take passage on that packet boat hoping to evade me?'

'No, I . . .'

'No?' He reached forward, 'Then why this? It is hardly the weather for wearing a coat indoors.' Snatching the jacket from her arms he glanced first at her stricken face then at the cloth bag that jingled as it hit the floor.

Picking up the bag he turned to the man watching from the doorway. 'Colonel, I accuse this woman of . . .'

He broke off as shouts and cries suddenly erupted outside. Throwing the jacket aside but holding on to the bag he followed the colonel into the sunshine.

Breath leaving her in a series of shudders Tamar held on to the table to prevent herself falling. A few moments more, just a few moments and she would have been free, now she would never find Benjie, maybe never see him again.

'Now, quick, while Forbes and his visitor be occupied.' Millie was somehow at her side. 'Run now, make for the bush and wait 'til dark, George will come . . .'

Afraid as she was, common sense was stronger. Involving the couple deeper in her affairs, leaving them to face the consequences would be more painful than any prison sentence. Holding back as the woman made to pull towards the door she shook her head.

'No Millie, it is no use my running away and I will not have you risk your safety for me. I did sell those dresses . . . but there is no time for that now. Please promise me should you hear of my brother's whereabouts you will try to send word to him . . . tell him I tried to find him.'

'You know we'll do that wench, but you 'as to go from 'ere, Lord knows it be your final chance, even the bush be better to deal with than that swine . . .'

A high-pitched scream rising over the hubbub still sounding outside drowned out Millie's frantic whisper.

'What is happening?'

'Pay no heed to that.' Millie pushed her towards the door.

'But that is a woman's scream.'

Millie jerked her arm fearful that Tamar's hesitation might rob her of her one chance to run. 'It be an Abbo girl, a couple of the men caught her and a lad over against the waterfall; but you 'ave no time to worry about that.'

'A girl. But why is she screaming . . . what has she done?'

'Abbos don't 'ave to do anything for some swines to hurt them. Forbes makes a hobby of it.'

As he had made a hobby of frightening her! Tamar took the last steps to the door. On the tree line yellow uniformed convicts stood with axes and saws, the felling of trees and building of houses temporarily forgotten as they gazed at the spectacle below them. Following suit Tamar caught her breath.

Two black figures both totally naked roped together at wrist and ankle were caught in a circle of men and women. What on earth had they done to be so humiliated?

Her glance riveted on the two stumbling figures she asked. 'Why have they been stripped?'

Anxious for Tamar to get away Millie answered tersely. 'They ain't been stripped, Abbos don't wear no clothes . . .'

'Leave 'em alone!'

A woman's shout rose followed by another. On the edge of the gathering Tamar saw Forbes and Edmond Bancroft elbow their way forward.

Why had they been captured? Turning to ask the question of Millie she looked quickly back at the scene below as again the black woman screamed.

Edmond Bancroft had grabbed the dark fuzzy hair dragging the woman's head back on her shoulders, the other hand squeezing her breasts.

Millie's warning already behind her Tamar was running down the slope pushing her way through the assembled crowd. Eyes wide and filled with disgust she slapped Bancroft's hand from the girl.

'Leave her alone!' she panted. 'Do you think she is some animal you can sport with.'

'Got it in one.' The weak mouth parted in a sneer. 'That is all they are, black pigs useful for no more than sport.' His pale eyes mocking he grabbed the girl again swearing loudly as the boy roped to her bit into his arm.

'Why you black swine . . . ! Cut him loose!'

Pushing Tamar roughly aside he snatched a whip from the hand of the man holding the rope.

'I'll teach the vermin it doesn't do to touch a white man!'

Pushing the boy forward the man who had cut the rope stepped clear as Edmond Bancroft cracked the long strip of plaited leather.

'Take his balls, Bancroft.' Henry Forbes laughed. 'Make sure he produces no more black shit; the men on that packet can have the girl, some of them have a taste for black meat. At sixpence a go she will earn you your fare back to Sydney and when you be done with her chuck her over the side, she'll make food for the fish.'

The boy was no older than Benjie. Tamar looked at the coal-black face, eyes rolling in fear. Was this the sort of treatment her brother was going through? Was he ever threatened with a whip as this terrified child was being threatened?

'Well, go on Bancroft.' Forbes urged, excitement thick in his voice. 'Give us a show. A bit of sport sets a man's appetite up, not to mention other parts of him, take his balls now or by Christ I will!'

Ignoring the coarse laugh that followed, Tamar stared at the girl, her skin gleaming like polished jet in the sunlight.

'Leave the lad be, he's no more'n a babby!'

Again a woman's shout rose over the heads of the watching crowd.

'Well Bancroft, are you going to let the black rat go?'

Glancing once at the fat face red beneath its film of moisture the other man nodded.

'Yes, I'll let him go when I be finished with him, just have your men ready to clean away the pieces.'

Cracking the whip once more, the smile that edged his mouth one of pure pleasure, he flicked it forward slicing leather into the boy's thigh.

Blood spurting from the blow trailed crimson ribbons over the black satiny skin and as the child screamed in agony the whip lanced again catching the girl across the shoulders as she threw herself in front of him.

'Stop it . . . stop it!' Her own scream mingling with that of the girl Tamar lunged forward both hands outstretched knocking Bancroft off balance. Snatching the fallen whip she held it defiantly.

'Let them go,' she breathed, glaring at Bancroft, 'let them go or I swear I will use this on you!'

Piggy eyes folding back into pudgy cheeks Forbes' smile was evil. This was going to be more amusing than he thought. 'She won't use that Bancroft,' he laughed. 'She wouldn't dare. Take it back, give her a taste of it. No? Then I'll do it for you!'

Seeing him reach for the whip Tamar instinctively raised it and as he lunged for her struck at him, the leather cutting across his face.

'Take her,' he screamed, 'and take the black dung with her.'

'Then you'll need tek me as well.' The voice that had shouted before rose again.

'Ar, an' me an' all . . .'

'And me!'

'And me.'

On every side the shouts rose in chorus.

'Tek one and you teks we all . . .' Millie Cooper stepped to Tamar's side '. . . we've seen enough of your torturing them Abbos, they be God's creatures same as all o' we.'

'God's creatures!' The piggy eyes swung to her. 'You call that excrement one of God's creatures?'

'I don't rightly know the meaning of that word,' Millie snapped, 'but if it means shit then this be what I answer. If the Lord made the pile of it known as 'Enry Forbes then yes He made the Abbo, and when it comes to the reckoning I can take a fair guess as to which of His creatures will find favour.'

His slashed face distorting with rage Forbes glared at the watching guard. 'Take them!' he screamed. 'Take them!'

'You've teken the last Abbo you be going to tek.' A woman's shout acting as if a signal, the crowd surged forward swallowing the dark-skinned pair.

'Tamar!' Millie's shout drifted behind her as she was swept away by the tide of moving bodies. 'Tamar!' She called again. But caught beneath Henry Forbes Tamar did not answer.

Chapter Twenty-Eight

'I want her flogged, I want her . . .'

One hand clutched to his bleeding cheek Henry Forbes looked at the fair-haired man whose grey insipid eyes blazed now with fury.

'It doesn't matter what you want, you got what you came for and if you wish to keep that and your own skin intact you'll get back on that boat and leave with the tide; what happens to this bitch is my concern.'

Nodding to the batman who had been the only one of his men with nerve enough to approach him he watched the man pull Tamar after him towards the prison compound.

'But she is guilty . . .'

'I'll be the one to say yea or nay to that.' Blood oozing between his fingers he glared back at Bancroft. 'As I'll be the one to clap you in irons if you aren't gone within five seconds, and *I* don't have to file charges!'

Turning on his heel he stared at the crowds of people disappearing beneath the tree line. They would pay for defying him, every last jack of them would pay . . . but the Hallam girl would be the first.

At the gate of the compound the batman halted.

'I'll do what I can to see you be housed decent,' he whispered, 'but by the saints you should 'ave legged it while you had the chance.'

'I'll give her over to the officer in charge sir. Which wing will I tell him you wants her put in?'

His face streaked with blood Forbes puffed up to them.

'No wing.' He glared at Tamar, rage spitting from the very soul of him. 'Miss Hallam is used to having a room of her own. We must show her that hospitality endures here in Geelong as in any other place. We must find her a room at the Lodge.'

The essence of a frown his only reaction the batman propelled Tamar towards the low-framed veranda that surrounded the house she and Captain Jones had been shown to the first day she had arrived.

'Which of the guest rooms, sir?'

'Oh, the best.' Holding his lacerated cheek Forbes' face twisted in a grotesque smile. 'We must make sure Miss Hallam is comfortable.'

'Right sir.' The batman swung open the fly-screen that kept insects from the house.

'No, not that way. I think our guest will be more comfortable at the rear of the house, it gets most of the sun. Put her in the cage!'

'But Colonel Forbes . . .'

His tone venomous Henry Forbes stared at Tamar.

'The cage,' he repeated softly, 'a night or two in there will cool her temper. That is my dear, if you last that long . . . dingoes have an acute sense of smell, one whiff of that blood on your pretty mouth will have them howling down on that cage and it will take them only moments to rip it apart and you with it, Oh . . . ! and watch out for snakes, the back of the house be a favourite place for them.'

'Sorry miss, but I 'ave to do it or the colonel will have my hide.' Setting the heavy bar that locked the door of the wooden structure in place he added quietly, 'I'll bring you some water and something to eat as soon as the colonel be quieted down.'

Unable to stand upright in the close-barred cage Tamar peered out but all she could see was a bare patch of ground edged around by trees. She could see none of the settlers but would they see her? Yet supposing they could it would be madness for them to attempt to rescue her, Forbes was bound to have set a watch.

Her back painful from being thrown beneath Forbes and now from bending almost double she sank to the ground. On all four sides the wooden bars touched against her, if those wild dogs came there would be no way of avoiding their teeth and claws.

Trying to put the thought from her mind she rested her forehead on her knees. How that colonel must be enjoying this, locking her in a cage like an animal; how many more men and women before her sat here like this . . . and for how long? Was it a regular form of punishment, did every other penal colony have its cage?

Despite the close set of the bars they were too narrow to afford shelter from the sun. Like a boiling cauldron set in a blazing fire of cloudless sky it screamed its assault on her bare head, biting at arms and shoulders where her dress had been torn.

In the distance the chop chop of axe against tree thudded dully, the rhythm of it matching the pain in her temples.

It seemed she had been penned in this one position for hours when she became aware the chopping had stopped. Overhead the sun blazed as fiercely as ever. That meant it was one o'clock. The convicts and settlers had finished work for the afternoon, they would be resting beneath the trees or in the shade of their houses while the heat of the day was at its highest. But there was no shade for her, no respite from the cruel sting of the sun.

Panting like an exhausted dog, the hot air bringing no relief to the tightness in her chest she laid her head against the bars. She had heard tales of men dying in the heat. Her body on fire she closed her eyes. If God were merciful she would die quickly.

'Miss, miss . . .'

The sound whispered like a soft breeze, but there was no breeze only heat, a dreadful consuming heat.

'Miss! It be me . . . I've brought you some water . . . Miss!'

The bars moved beneath her cheek. Seeming to drag herself from a pit of flame Tamar opened her eyes.

'I brought you some water . . .'

Standing with hand outstretched a figure danced as her eyes struggled to focus.

'. . . take it quick for the colonel don't be asleep

yet. If he should cop what I be at it could mean curtains for me.'

Limbs tingling from so long in one position, unaware that she cried out at the pain of moving, Tamar pushed herself as straight as her prison allowed.

'That's it, miss.' The batman encouraged. 'That's it, take the cup.'

Her vision still hazy she lifted a hand through the bars feeling him press the cup in her fingers.

'Now, drink it down, it will help until . . .'

'There'll be no water . . .'

The words cracked almost as sharp as the whip that curled about her wrist jerking the cup from her.

'You know the rules . . . break them again and I'll have you shot!' Waiting until the man had disappeared indoors he spoke again.

'More blood, tut tut.' The cut, red and angry on his cheek, he stared at the whimpering girl holding her wrist against her breast. 'Don't you remember what I told you of the dingo? One whiff of blood . . . But then perhaps if we wash it away.'

Pain smarting from the cut on her wrist, her body feeling like it was being mangled through rollers of molten steel, Tamar slumped against the bars of the cage as he walked away.

'Miss Hallam . . .'

Her torment was not ended, he had not gone away. But he could do nothing else to her, nothing except let her die.

'Miss Hallam!' The whip cracked snapping the silence and bringing her eyes jerking open. 'I really do advise you wash away that blood; but there, I would not force a woman against her will.'

Folds of florid flesh crept upwards, twisting the cut like a small red snake, folding away small, evil glinting eyes. He smiled as he lifted a ladle he had fetched from a barrel set against the wall of the house. The smile never leaving his face he tipped the ladle sending a stream of water trickling slowly to the ground.

Tamar . . . Tamar wench, I've made a nice cup o' tea . . .

Tamar smiled at the knock, knock. Vinny always made a drink before banking the fire at bedtime and always she knocked on the door for her neighbour to come share it . . .

Tam, watch me Tam, watch me swim . . . Benjie called jumping up and down on the parapet of the little bridge that spanned Hockley Brook . . . she would swim with him, there was no one to see. She smiled down at the glistening water. Come on Tam, come in with me . . . Benjie's feet drummed rhythmically on the stone of the bridge.

'Asleep are we, Miss Hallam?'

The bars of the cage dug sharply into her cheek as Henry Forbes shook them viciously. Moaning softly Tamar opened her eyes.

'Benjie . . .'

'No, it ain't your brother.'

The bars banging against her face roused Tamar

from the dreams she had drifted in and out of through the afternoon. Painfully her eyes opened.

'I see you have caught the sun. Really, you should take more care my dear, you have such delicate skin.'

Dry lips cracking, her tongue swollen against the roof of her mouth she tried to focus on the man looking down on her. 'Water,' she whispered, 'please give me some water.'

'But of course, my dear.'

Once more fetching the ladle Henry Forbes looked at Tamar, her eyes closed, slumped against the cage.

'Too sleepy to drink it? Then I will not disturb you. Goodnight my dear, I will see you in the morning, or what is left of you after the dingoes are finished. This?' He raised an eyebrow as Tamar forced open her eyes. 'Not to worry over a little wasted water, there is plenty more.'

Tipping the ladle he watched her cry out as the water trickled to the ground. Then, laughing in his throat, he walked back into the house.

Tamar . . . Tamar wench. Out of the torrid heat, the agony that was her tortured body Tamar heard the voice that called to her again, heard the knock . . . knock. But as the hallucination dragged her to itself she knew the voice was unreal, the knocking not on the door of her home in Hockley, but the sound of men resuming the work of their own imprisonment.

It was dark and a cool breeze fanned her swollen face. Another dream . . . another hallucination? If so it was welcome. Overhead the moon, huge and silver floated among drifting clouds. So stiff only her eyelids would move she watched the great shining orb then caught her breath. Somewhere something moved, rustled as if sliding over dry grass.

Snakes! Henry Forbes had said they had a preference for the rear of the house. Fear overcoming pain she drew her knees close up to her chest, holding her skirts tight about her ankles. But that was no protection . . . Oh God, that was no protection.

Holding her breath she listened for the sound. There . . . ! There it was again, a slither across baked earth! She peered from the cage but, her sight still blurred from the heat of the day, she saw nothing save the dark fringe of the trees.

Would its poison work quickly . . . would she die in seconds or fall slowly into unconsciousness? Fear trembling along every nerve she shivered as the moon drew a cloak of thick cloud over its bright body plunging the cage into darkness. She screamed as something dry brushed against her arm.

Henry Forbes had not lied. There was a snake moving along her arm. Too terrified to even try to scream again she sat frozen as the moon emerged spilling light on her closed lids.

Sss . . . sss . . . the soft hiss touched against her ears. How long before the creature's fangs sank into her? Her eyes tight shut Tamar fought her rising terror then cried out as something tapped against the bars of the cage.

Its tail? Despite her efforts to remain immobile she shuddered violently.

The sound came again, the tapping regular, a

pattern of sound, but no fangs and no more brushing along her arm; and that pattern, it was being repeated by a whispering voice . . . a human voice.

Opening her eyes she screamed, pushing the cry back into her throat with balled fists. Beside the cage the silver glow of moonlight illuminated bands of white on a darker ground. Pressing both hands hard against her mouth Tamar stared at the figure of a naked man.

It was one of those black people Millie had called Abbos; one of those people said to eat white folk.

Pressing as far back as the bars of the cage would allow she stared at eyes showing white against black skin.

Lifting the bar that locked the cage, he placed it on the ground, then swung the door open, neither movement displacing the silence by so much as a breath.

Bending forward, he stretched a hand towards her and as she loosed her hands to cry out she saw a second figure step from the trees. It was the woman she had saved from Edmond Bancroft and as if to prove the fact she pushed forward a young child, the boy she had protected from the whip.

They wanted to help her. Tamar reached for the hand, suffocating the groan of pain from her tortured limbs as he gently eased her out.

Touching a finger first to her chest and then his own, the man pointed to where the trees swayed in the quickening breeze.

'Yes, please . . .' Tamar nodded. 'Yes . . . please!'

Ignoring the waiting pair she saw the flash of white teeth as they smiled, then her hand tight in the woman's she followed into the bush.

Jewellers to the Crown! Philip Amory took up the newspaper looking again at the photograph displayed on its front page.

'The Princess of Wales honours Hockley.' He read the caption slowly.

'Wearing a necklace which she graciously named the Alexandra Stone, Her Royal Highness accompanied the Prince of Wales . . .'

His eyes ran over the words he had read several times during the day. The article said it all, how the jewellery designed especially for her had been graciously received, how the stones had been painstakingly chosen, their perfection meticulously matched. But of the story behind its beauty there was no mention, the princess must not hear of the deaths arising from its theft, nor of the child banished to the far side of the world upon being accused of that theft. Royalty must not be placed in the compromising position that the revelation might bring.

Nor would he wish them to be. The fault was in no way theirs. Sighing, he laid the paper aside. Nor was the fact the child had not been brought home due to any fault of his. He had done all a man could do, even written to the Prime Minister, yet still young Benjie Hallam made no appearance.

The reply had been terse but polite. The matter would be referred to the appropriate department.

The appropriate department! He dropped into a chair and stared into the fire. And once there his letter would do what, lie with a pile of others until dust hid it from view?

And the boy's sister, was she lost to the world the same as he?

A flicker of draught caught the flames, fanning them into the chimney.

So beautiful! Philip watched the streamers of copper red. Her hair was beautiful, it had shone like beaten copper whenever she carried a piece to the glow of the forge, beautiful, as her face was beautiful! But like her brother, Tamar Hallam was gone.

Maybe he should have continued the search for her, paid that man to go abroad, to look for her in Australia. But what could a venture of that sort result in. Even should the man have agreed to go, there was no way he could search the whole country.

'*No, thank you Mr Philip . . .*'

From the quietness of his heart the words returned echoing softly in his mind.

'*. . . I have no need of it, though I thank you again for the kindness of the thought behind the offer.*'

With the refusal of his money the girl's head had come up, a quiet pride in every line of her and remembering, he felt again the touch of something that had left him the poorer, the remnant of that need he had felt for her.

Tamar Hallam had been an employee, a workgirl

from the slums of Hockley. That had been his defence, his answer to the pull he had felt so often since her leaving. But the defence had failed. He knew now what he had refused to recognise at the time. Tamar Hallam was from the run-down back streets of Hockley but she was not *of* them; she was different to the rest of the people living in the squalid houses tumbling in on one another. She had an air of refinement, a quiet finesse that set her apart. She would have been no embarrassment but an asset. As a wife she would have brought credit to his house and joy to his bed.

'. . . *I can only say what my heart tells me* . . .'

More of the words she had spoken in his office on that last day returned, haunting him as they had done so often. But he had not said what his heart told him. He had held on to silence and that silence had repaid him with sadness, a sadness he would experience for the rest of his life.

Beware the Ides of March!

Regret like a weight pressing on his heart Philip Amory closed his eyes.

He had not ignored the warning, he had misconstrued it. His senses had tried to tell him that making Tamar Hallam his wife would not end his dreams, but that not making her his wife would end his happiness!

Staring again into the flames he smiled at the irony of it. And now she was on the other side of the world.

Chances were he would never see her again.

Chapter Twenty-Nine

Sunlight pressing once more on her eyelids Tamar lay perfectly still. She was in a wooden cage, locked behind its bars a snake brushing along her arm.

But the brushing had ceased . . . Trying to gather her thoughts, to put them together in some semblance of recognition she kept her eyes tightly shut.

Water, she had asked for water and Forbes had brought it to her . . . but she had not drunk it. Why? She frowned inwardly, raking up the dry ashes of memory. Why had she not drunk the water? A picture of Henry Forbes flashed across her closed eyes. He had not given it to her but poured it into the ground. Then had come darkness and with it the snake! No, she held her breath, it had not been a snake had touched her arm but a twig, a twig with dried leaves and it had been held by . . .

Lids flying open she sat bolt upright. It had been a man, a man with white stripes painted on his black face and body.

Glancing about the tiny clearing panic faded only to return at once. Those three had not harmed her but they had left her here. Where was here . . . how far was any settlement . . . which direction did she take?

Questions raced around in her brain but none found an answer. She must find water. She tried to think logically. There were trees and plants all around her so somewhere there must be water.

Moaning from the bite of cramped limbs she stood up. Which way should she go? Half turning she froze. From the edge of the clearing the dark-skinned man was watching her.

He had not harmed her last night, but now . . . these people ate white folk . . . Teeth clamped together holding back a scream she backed away. The man watched but did not move.

How far would she get . . . how far would he let her go before attacking her?

Although the day was just yet born she felt a film of perspiration form on her brow. In that wooden cage or here in the bush, either way she was going to die.

At her back a tree branch caught her arm. Unable to hold her fears any longer she cried out as she sank to the ground covering her face with her hands.

Moments later the same tapping sound she had heard the night before sounded from across the clearing. Parting her fingers she peeped through them.

A few yards away the woman was urging the boy forward. Hesitantly, his eyes showing much the same fear as her own, he came to where she huddled against the tree.

Glancing back at the woman who flapped a hand at him he held out the huge curled leaf he carried in his hands.

Hands still pressed against her cheeks Tamar made

no move to take it. Across the clearing the woman called and the boy raised the leaf to his mouth swallowing a little then trickling a few drops of liquid on to the ground.

Watching the droplets glisten like diamonds as they fell, seeing them flatten and spread damp spots on the dry earth she almost sobbed. It was water, the boy had brought her water!

Taking the leaf she drank deeply, the water cool and soothing against her parched throat and as she held the leaf back to him the boy grinned.

Seeing her answering smile the woman came to stand beside the boy. Pointing to Tamar she proceeded to dip both hands into the shallow bowl the leaf then made as if washing her face. The charade finished she signed to Tamar to follow.

Her fears somehow melted, she rose. Following the pair through the close-packed trees she smiled at the boy who turned several times, his own hand eventually reaching shyly for hers.

At the fringe of the trees Tamar stopped with a jolt. As if a line of demarcation had been drawn by a giant hand the lush greenery gave way dramatically to a vast, unending stretch of desert dotted with clumps of dry twisted scrub. Yet its bareness held a strange beauty.

Pale red, it stretched away, folding itself into a violet grey horizon while the rim of the earth was edged with the peaks of purple mountains that seemed to float in the crystal clear brightness of dawn. To Tamar, gazing at it for the first time, she felt it catch at her heart; it was the most beautiful sight she had ever seen.

A tug at her hand recalling her attention, she allowed herself to be drawn along while all she wanted was to go on gazing at the breathtaking grandeur all around her.

Leading her to a water-hole, its contents sparkling clear despite its location, the boy giggled as she washed but the slight frown on the woman's face showed sympathy as Tamar gasped at touching the blistered skin of her arms.

Sending the boy scampering back to the trees with a few rapid words, the woman took the fern-like plants he brought back. Crumpling them until they oozed green oily sap she handed them to Tamar signing for her to rub them over her burned arms.

Doing as she was bid Tamar smiled her thanks. The juice of the plant was cool and pleasantly scented, but better still it immediately soothed the stinging of her skin.

Returning to the clearing she hung back. At its centre the man had lit a fire and threaded on twigs suspended above the flames were several fish.

Motioning her to sit the woman placed each of the cooked fish on a separate leaf. Giving one to the boy she pointed to Tamar.

Unbelieving, she took the food. These people were sharing their meal with her, far from doing her harm they were caring for her. Meeting the man's eyes the look in them seemed to show he knew her thoughts yet he simply signed that she eat.

Their meal finished, she watched the man carefully extinguish the fire while the woman and boy buried the debris at the mossy base of a tree. She had heard one or two people at the settlement refer to such as these as black heathens no better than beasts. Henry Forbes had called this boy a black rat, the woman black shit, while Edmond Bancroft had named them vermin, black pigs useful for no more than sport. But they were neither. They were cultured people caring of their environment, they did not throw waste into open channels waiting for rain water to flush it into the sea. This man had not tried to abuse her, they were decent, caring human beings and from what little she had seen of them they were far above the like of Forbes or Bancroft.

Taking the hand the boy held to her she joined the man and woman, their brown eyes gleaming friendly smiles.

The settlement had held fear of rape and imprisonment at the hands of Henry Forbes, and though she might face worse by following these people, at least that would be her own choice.

For a week they walked, always in scrubland, the pale red earth giving no ground to the lushness of pine forest. They could move more quickly without her but Tamar knew instinctively they would not leave her. By late morning of each day the man brought them to a water-hole skirted by a few acacia trees that brought her memories of those shading the Baskerville mausoleum back home in Warstone Lane cemetery. And each day he managed to find food either snaring a wild hare or tickling fish that thrived in the water-holes.

Watching him now divide a roasted hare, taking care to divide it equally into four parts, she thought again of the man who had charge of both the penal institution and the free men and women forced to settle beside it, of his cruelty and licentiousness; and Edmond Bancroft, what had he shared with Odile? He had shown her nothing but lies and deceit; yet they called themselves gentlemen. Smiling at the boy as he brought a share of the meat to her she glanced at the man and woman he returned to. These were the truly gentle folk. How could white people treat them so despicably, but then how could they treat their own kind the same way?

Perspiration trickling into her eyes Tamar blinked trying to clear the hallucination that danced on the horizon but hard as she blinked the smudge of green remained, and as she forced one weary foot to follow the other the smudge heightened into trees, desert scrub giving way to ferns and sweet-smelling grass. Breathing the cooler shaded air she murmured a prayer of thanks. Beautiful as she had found that vast empty land she realised the danger it held.

Smiling at the child who had walked the whole time beside her she longed to ask if this place was where they lived, if it was their home. But the language they used was unintelligible to her, she would simply have to wait before finding out; and if this sheltered green spot was their home would they share it with her?

A few yards ahead the man and woman stopped. Gratefully Tamar sank to the ground. A short rest and a cool drink of water, the man always found water. Leaning her head against the bole of a tree she closed her eyes. When she was stronger she would find ways to help . . . gather wood for the fire . . .

It was so much cooler here among the trees sheltered from the fierce heat of the day; perhaps they had reached home. Opening her eyes she looked for the child. He was not here, neither of them were here. Startled she sat up. They had not left her alone before, always the woman or the boy remained with her. Her throat suddenly tightening she scrambled to her feet. They would not abandon her . . . lead her so far from the settlement then leave her here in the middle of nowhere.

Perhaps she was worrying over nothing, perhaps they were simply hunting for the next meal. A flurry overhead causing her to look up she saw the multi-coloured flash of tiny wings as a flock of small birds settled noisily on the branches; but it was not their exquisite plumage she stared at.

That was the reason it was so much more cool and shaded! The sun was no longer a brazier of burning gold. It was crimson, a half-drowned crimson orb in a sea of purple-edged turquoise. It was evening! In a short while it would be night . . . night with its blackness and noises of wild animals.

Tightness in her throat becoming panic she called but the sound was a croak that set the birds chattering their own alarm.

'Please, please come back . . . don't leave me here alone, please . . .' She called again, but again only the birds answered. Why had they done this to her, was it their way of taking revenge for what had happened to the woman and the boy? Had they taken her from that cage simply to have her die alone in some unknown place? That made no sense, they could have done that days ago out there among that dry desolation of a desert. No, those people would not leave her, she was simply letting her imagination run away with her, they would be back soon . . . they would be back.

Trying desperately to hold on to both common sense and courage she stood listening to the whisperings and shufflings of the undergrowth until the distant howl of a wild dog broke her nerve sending her running blindly through the trees.

Branches clutching at her arms, twining into her hair dragging at her as she passed were unfelt in the panic that returned fastening her firmly in a grip of blind terror.

Unseeing, unhearing, her body bumping against tree trunks, their twigs scratching at her face, her only thought that she was alone she stumbled on, then one last cry erupting from her throat she felt the weight of something against her shoulders, heard the heavy growl that followed her into blackness.

Tom Brooks' idea was good in theory but in practice . . . !

Awake in his bunk Nathan stared at the candle lantern swinging from the low ceiling of his cabin.

His crew *were* the best men afloat but how long before they became exhausted, and to what end? Strong as they were they could not row across an ocean. He could try whistling for a wind. Remembering the old superstition, still popular among some seamen he smiled, yes he would even whistle if he had to.

And if that did not work? His smile fading he closed his eyes. If the *Verity* were becalmed then any other ship in the area would be suffering the same, he could not hope for help in that direction. Tom had said they had water, but that would last only days . . . how long would this damned calm last? Had he brought these men to a lingering end? Had putting his own desires first driven them to their death as it had driven Aiden and Louise? God it couldn't happen . . . it mustn't happen, not again.

Flinging from his bed he strode to the window looking into the thick darkness of night.

He had been so arrogant, so stupidly self-centred! Why had he not seen things for what they were . . . seen that those two were in love? But he had seen none of that; blinded by his own pride he had seen none of it. Now they were dead, the man he loved most in the world was gone and it was his doing; just as it would be his doing if the men with him now should die.

He would never sail the Australia route! Hadn't that been what he had said, the vow he had made? Resting his brow against the glass he listened to the silence of the airless night. But he had broken that vow, reneged on the promise of his word and for what? For the purpose of trade? No that was not true; for the purpose of bringing ex-convicts home to Britain? That too was a lie as was that of keeping a promise to a girl he had met just once. The truth was as before, he was satisfying his own desire, he had placed these men in danger of their lives for the sake of himself just as he had done with Aiden.

Hands clenched he brought them hard against the glass. 'Forgive me Aiden,' he murmured, 'forgive me, both of you.'

On deck the ship's bell sounded the morning watch.

Four o'clock. In the furthest reaches of darkness Nathan saw a pink greyness impeach upon the velvet black of the sky. A new day, more long hours of hopelessness.

Behind him the lantern swung gently on its chain.

Should he try Tom's idea, let the men row the ship? The swing of the lantern sent fingers of light dancing over the walls of the cabin exciting the shadows, but eyes closed against the window their pale ballet went unseen.

. . . Should he launch the longboat, row with them?

The lantern chain rattled.

. . . Would it be as Tom said, would it give the crew spirit if they could see something tangible being done?

His body slipping forward to press against the woodwork he took the weight against his knees. Half upright he paused . . . the lantern was dancing on its chain . . . the ship's timbers were creaking . . . God Almighty could it be?

Swinging round he stared at the lantern. It was a wind, by all that was holy they had a wind!

Shouting with relief he ran for the deck laughing with the men. Tom Brooks already had them unfurling the sails.

They were over the worst. Exchanging grins with his first mate Nathan grabbed at the thick rope, hauling with the others. Thank God, they were over the worst.

'It be a blessing old Sampson there found the wench, another ten minutes and it would 'ave been too dark for me to follow him.'

Lying in the dark still comfort of the pit she had dropped into Tamar listened to the voices somewhere above her head. If she lay still they would go away, leave her to the lovely peace.

'But what do you reckon a young wench to be doing out there in the bush and be you certain her be alone?'

'Certain as I can be, were there more then Sampson would 'ave let us know.'

'Ar, that be so, Sampson ain't one to miss anything.'

Above her the conversation went on, but she would not join in. Semi-conscious Tamar smiled in her darkness. She would not let them know she was here.

'You see that, you see the smile touch her mouth? Her be coming back, praise be her be coming back!'

Who was coming back? Tamar listened disinterestedly then irritably as something touched against her shoulder.

'Wake up! Wake up!'

The strong voice beat at her brain driving away the darkness, disturbing the pleasantness of her silent world. Despite her efforts to stay locked within it she felt herself float upward, float towards the light, back into a world of pain.

'Wake up!'

Eyes closed the world of memory opened up. There had been a man, he had snatched her jacket, the jacket with her sixpence sewn into it, he had called her a thief . . . Like patterns in a kaleidoscope the pictures flicked from one to another . . . he said she had stolen Odile's jewellery. Bancroft! It was Edmond Bancroft and he was whipping a child, a black child . . . and there was a black woman . . .

'Open your eyes!'

Tamar ignored the voice the scenes in her memory too vividly painful.

Forbes . . . Henry Forbes had locked her in a cage but a black man had released her and the three of them had led her . . .

'Wake up. You have to wake up.'

The voice was loud and strong.

. . . had led her in circles . . . A sob gathering in her

throat she opened her eyes . . . they had led her back
to Henry Forbes.

'That's better wench, you be alright now, you be
safe.'

Eyes misty with tears Tamar blinked against the
shadows.

'We thought you was a goner, seemed you might
never pull out of that sleep.'

Why should Forbes care whether she woke or not?
Unless it was to put her back into that cage.

'You go warm the soup and leave the wench to
me.'

That was a softer voice, a woman's voice. Blinking
away the tears collected in her eyes Tamar peered into
the gloom, 'Millie?'

'No, I don't be Millie.' A brief pause accompanied a
rustle of movement and a stronger light revealed a
smiling face. 'I don't be Millie though I thinks I knows
the one you speaks of, that is if you speaks of Millie
Cooper.'

'Yes.' Tamar pushed up from the soft pillows at her
back. 'Millie Cooper and her husband George. Are they
here . . . are they alright . . . has Henry Forbes . . . ?'

'Steady girl, steady.' The woman set the candle in a
holder. 'One question at a time be all a body can
answer and we will answer all we can but first you has
to eat, the strength must be near spent in you, thank
the good Lord He guided your steps here.'

'That be enough of tongue wagging Esther, let the
girl eat and then sleep, there be time enough to talk
tomorrow.'

Accepting the bowl an elderly man held out to her Tamar swallowed a little of the tasty liquid.

The Lord had not guided her steps here . . . a black man had. But where was here? The voice she had thought to be that of Henry Forbes was not; but how long before he came for her?

Chapter Thirty

'These be old-fashioned but they be clean and presentable.'

Tamar took the clothes, they were so different from the pretty dresses Amy Williams had given her but they were no less welcome.

'I will try to mend these but I doubt they'll ever be as good as they was.'

Gathering dress and petticoats draped over a chair, the woman smiled as she left the bedroom.

Rinsing herself with water the woman had poured into an enamelled bowl, Tamar pulled on the flower-sprigged muslin gown, fastening first the self-covered buttons of the bodice then the thin green satin ribbons threaded high beneath her breasts. Fashions may have changed, she smoothed the delicate cloth, but the pleasure such a pretty gown gave must have been the same for that woman as it was for her.

Running a comb through her hair she glanced about for something with which to tie it back, finding nothing she left it loose.

'There now, don't you look better!'

The woman looked up as Tamar came hesitantly into a room a quick glance showed to be so like the

Coopers' living room. Table, chairs, a cupboard set against one wall, all were rough hewn but well scrubbed and like the Cooper home the floor boasted no rug, but the fire in the hearth glowed beneath a black-bottomed kettle.

Black! Instantly Tamar's mind turned to the people who had left her among those trees.

'My Obed and me, we both thanked the Lord for bringing you safe here last night.'

'It was not the Lord.'

'What?'

Watching the frown settled on the other woman's brow Tamar answered tersely as before.

'It was not the Lord brought me here, it was a black man.'

Glancing at the door as her husband stepped inside the woman's frown dissolved giving way to a beaming smile.

'You hear that Obed, her were fetched here not by God but by an Aboriginal.'

Putting the logs he carried into the hearth he ran a hand over shabby moleskin trousers as he looked at Tamar with eyes that smiled through a film of sadness.

'And who do you think guided an Aboriginal to bring you to us? The Lord's ways are not always easy to understand,' he glanced at his wife, 'nor is a man's stomach when it be empty. Supper first and then we can discuss the methods of the Almighty.'

'Last night you spoke of Millie Cooper.' The woman ladled boiled potatoes on to a plate. 'Does that mean you be from the settlement out at Gee-long?'

Tamar looked up sharply. 'Is . . . is this not Gee-long?'

'No, child, this be Bendigo. Was you hoping it to be Geelong?'

'Enough now Esther . . . let the girl at least swallow her meal before you go barraging her with questions.'

'A man and his stomach, they always has to take precedence.' Returning the pot to the hearth the woman's face creased into a smile as she took her place at the table.

'We might at least introduce ourselves Obed, the wench will be wondering just whose laps the good Lord has dropped her into.'

Not waiting for his answer the woman touched a hand to his. 'This be my husband Obadiah Wesson and I be Esther.'

'My name is Tamar, Tamar Hallam and I have come from Geelong.'

Obadiah's reprimand not to question disregarded, Esther Wesson's brown eyes held a sudden worry.

'Geelong.' She forked potatoes but lifted none to her mouth. 'You be out here from Geelong . . . then where be the others that be with you, why be you alone, what happened to your escort?'

His own faded blue eyes echoing the worry of his wife's Obed took the hand that had instinctively reached for him. Folding the fingers between rough-ened palms he looked steadily at Tamar.

'You said you were left in the bush by an Aboriginal. Were you attacked by them . . . were those with you killed?'

'No!' Tamar shook her head. 'It was the boy who was to be killed . . .'

'Not the Simmons boy? Oh Lord, that will finish his mother!'

'It was not the Simmons boy they tried to kill, it was a young lad, they said he was an Abbo.'

'An Aboriginal,' Esther pushed her plate aside. 'When will it ever end, when will the killing stop?'

'It will Esther, it will. One day in the Lord's own time all of this will end and this country will live in peace, Aboriginal and settler both.'

'The boy was not killed, no one was.'

Both hands still holding that of his wife Obed looked across the table as Tamar spoke.

'Then where are the men Henry Forbes sent with you?'

A puzzled frown settling between her brows Tamar glanced at the worried faces.

'No men came with me . . .'

'Henry Forbes did . . . did he send you to Bendigo?'

Esther's query was tremulous, the voice emulating the fear stark in her brown eyes. Tamar felt her heart twist. This woman was as afraid of the army commander as she herself. But why . . . did his influence spread so far, if so what had he done to these kind people?

'I was not sent here by Henry Forbes.' She answered quietly. 'I was brought here to get away from him.'

Esther cast a quick glance at her husband before drawing her hand from his and reaching it to Tamar.

'Has he . . . has he touched you, child?'

The full meaning of the question clear to her Tamar gave a quick shake of the head.

'Praise be for that!' Esther sighed. 'But he tried, of that you have no need to tell me, but to get away from him . . . how, when everyone at the settlement be feared of the man?'

'It . . . was the man I spoke of . . . the Aboriginal man, he took me from the cage . . .'

'Cage!' Esther breathed. 'He wouldn't . . . not even Forbes would put a girl in there!'

'Hush, Esther. Let the girl speak. But mind,' Obed moved to the fireplace reaching for a clay pipe, 'you say only what you wants us to know child, your business be your own.'

In the quiet of the little room, an orange sun slanting rays through a window Esther had dressed with pretty blue curtain Tamar began to speak and when she finally ceased the whole of her story had come out.

'That swine.' Esther swung her head slowly from side to side. 'He be no better now than when he took my boys.'

That was the cause of the sorrow always visible in the eyes of this couple. Tamar felt a stab of guilt at adding the burden of her own troubles.

'I'm sorry. I did not know your sons were in that prison.'

'How could you know, wench? Lord, how I wish

you had killed Henry Forbes 'stead of just slicing him once with a whip.'

Coming to his wife Obed took her in his arms whispering quietly to her until her sobs died. Then signing to Tamar to follow he led them out on to a veranda draped with sweet smelling blossom.

'My wife and myself, we like to sit here of an evening if chores allow, we likes to watch the sun go down.'

Was this a way of telling her to touch no more on the subject of their sons?

Slipping back into the house Tamar picked up the pipe he had laid aside. Her father had owned a pipe like this, she had so many times packed it with shavings of tobacco he sliced from a block. There by the fireside of their damp little house in Hockley he would smoke his pipe while telling stories to her and Benjamin. Her favourites were tales of St George slaying the dragon, but Benjie would bury his face in their father's lap saying he were feared of dragons, then her father would stop and take the boy on his lap . . .

Tears grasping her throat Tamar clutched the delicate stem of the pipe.

'I'll find you Benjie,' she whispered. 'I'll find you and then there will be no more dragons, nothing will ever frighten you again.'

'I must ask you to give me passage, Captain Burford. I have important government business that will not wait until the next Royal Navy ship puts into harbour.'

Nathan Burford looked at the man seated in his cabin. Dressed in sober black jacket and trousers, a white wing collar holding his throat in a starched grip, he was the epitome of the English gentleman, his apparel giving no quarter to the heat of a semi-tropical sun.

'My business here is not yet done, I have trade to complete.'

'I appreciate that, Captain,' the man fingered a black top hat balanced on his knee, 'perhaps I might facilitate in the selling of your cargo.'

No doubt he could. Nathan turned to the window looking out across the waters of the bay. So incredibly beautiful, yet all it encompassed was misery, the misery of men sentenced to serve their lives on a foreign shore. There was no more enforced deportation to Botany Bay, but the people brought here were no less prisoners of that same government that this man now asked his assistance in serving.

'I have business other than that of trade, business that will likely take more time than you wish to spend waiting.'

His glance on the top hat the man stroked it with a slow finger. Apart from trade there was only one thing brought folk voluntarily to Botany Bay, the search for family, loved ones who had broken Her Majesty's laws, or maybe fallen foul of those in whose hands the ordering of those laws rested. It amounted to the same thing. But who was this man looking for; parent . . . brother . . . or was it a woman?

'Business?' He answered quietly. 'Her Majesty's representatives have shall we say . . . influence . . . perhaps I might help with whatever other than trade has you here.'

His glance travelling over the sparkling waters to the wooden buildings following the curve of the bay Nathan thought of the week he had been anchored here. He had enquired after Tamar but no one seemed to have seen her; he had enquired of her brother but again had drawn a blank. The commander had answered politely enough. No one of the name of Hallam had been brought here. So where was he . . . and where was she?

Damn! He had sailed hundreds of miles of this coast, for days at a stretch seeing nothing but trees, just how big was this country?

'Thank you but no.' He brought a closed hand against the glass.

'Forgive what may appear to be impertinence Captain Burford, but should it be that this other matter of which you speak involves searching for . . . an acquaintance . . . then perhaps I might remind you of the vastness of the country we are in. Should a person choose to go inland then one might spend a lifetime looking for them.'

'A person might count that a lifetime well spent!'

'Or foolishly spent, when help may be forthcoming.'

Grey sideburns immaculately shaped to the edge of his chin, light blue eyes unsmiling beneath well-defined brows, the man rose.

'Think about it Captain Burford. I will be at the Governor's Lodge should you wish to contact me.'

Might the man know anything of Tamar? Nathan remained unmoving as his visitor left. He obviously had contacts as an envoy of the British government and as such would no doubt have influence. It might serve a purpose to take advantage of that influence. And if the man came up with no more than he had himself? Then he would still have to take him where he wished to go, a bargain must be kept even if he himself gained nothing as a result of it.

'So what will you have lost, Nathan?' Murmuring the last to himself he reached for one of the maps rolled and pigeon-holed in a heavy oak bureau.

Tracing a finger along the painted line of the Australian coast he looked up as his first mate tapped his door before entering.

'Everything stowed and ready for sail.'

'Thanks, Tom.'

'Where to next?'

'I'd thought of making for home.'

'Be that why you got your finger on this coast?' Tom Brooks smiled as he glanced at the map.

'God help me I don't know what to do! We've bought and sold, done what we came to do.'

'No, you haven't . . .' Tom Brooks watched his friend turn away from the table holding the spread map. 'You've sold and bought with that I don't argue but you haven't touched on the real cause that brought the *Verity* to this continent. I don't know what that cause be Nathan but I know it be eating into the very soul of you and it has to be got out if you are to be the man you was.'

The man he was! Nathan drew a long slow breath. He would never be that. He had caused the death of his brother and the woman that brother had loved, how then could he ever be the man he was?

'I came here to look for a woman.'

Staring from the window of his cabin Nathan gave an account of his meeting with Tamar and of his promise to help her.

Holding his silence Tom listened. He had known there was more behind this voyage than trade, but a girl! Nathan must have been well and truly struck.

'We should go home, Tom.' Nathan turned. 'It isn't fair to the men to put it off any longer.'

'They'll stay as long as you asks 'em to.'

'I know that.' Nathan's smile was brief. 'That is why I must not ask. We sail for home, Tom.'

But Nathan Burford's search would not be ended. Tom Brooks glanced again at the map. He would be back, he would be back as many times as he found that girl not returned to her home and Tom Brooks would be with him.

'Do we carry a passenger?'

'You mean him?' Nathan flicked a sideways nod towards the door. 'He's on some government business and you know how long drawn out that can be. No Tom, the *Verity* will carry no passenger, that man is not bound for England and we are going home.'

'Could be repercussions should you refuse.'

His brows pulling sharply together Nathan frowned. 'This is my ship and she goes where I say and the government can go hang!'

His reaction a smile, Tom Brooks nodded. 'If that be your verdict then I'll pull on the rope.'

The frown gone instantly, Nathan touched a friendly hand to the other's shoulder. 'You be a good friend Tom; so tell me, what is your counsel?'

'That be according to where the fellow asked to be set down, do it be forward or back to where we've been already?'

Turning to the map Nathan bent over it. 'Does that matter?'

Joining him the first mate touched a finger to the spot marked Botany Bay. 'Course it do, we be here. To go here, here and here,' he jabbed a finger to a different spot with each word, 'would be of little benefit to you for you've gone over that ground already, but should it be that government chap be bound for somewheres we haven't called then you can kill an extra bird with the same shot. You can put him ashore and make enquiries regarding . . . what did you say her name be?'

'You know full well what I said her name is, you rogue!' Nathan laughed.

His own eyes bright Tom Brooks tapped the map. 'So I'll ask again . . . where to next?'

'Give me an hour, Tom . . .' Grabbing his cap Nathan swung from the cabin, the rest of his words floating back across his shoulder as he skipped lightly up the narrow companionway that gave on to the main deck '. . . I'll have the answer to that when I get back.'

'Thank you, child.'

Obadiah Wesson took the pipe Tamar handed to him. Pulling gently on it he breathed out a cloud of grey-blue smoke that spiralled, searching for a breeze that would carry it towards the glowing sky.

'The three that brought you to Bendigo,' he asked as she took a chair beside Esther's, 'could you describe them?'

'I . . . I didn't look too closely . . . they . . .'

'I understand.' He puffed quietly. 'Nakedness be hard for us to come to terms with, but was there anything other than that?'

'Their features were quite different to any I have seen before and of course I could not understand their language, but their actions were very gentle and they seemed to understand I could not keep going the same way they could. In fact, I think they recognised my needs before I did myself.'

'The Aboriginals are a gentle intelligent people,' he replied, 'and one day the white settlers will regret what is happening now. They will realise the black man is not some game animal to be hunted and shot for sport.'

'But who would do such a terrible thing?'

'Men like Henry Forbes, men such as Bancroft, you have seen for yourself what they can do.'

'Yes Obed, the wench has seen.' Esther interrupted

her husband. 'But she also spoke of something else she has seen. The ordinary folk of Geelong, she saw them rise up against Forbes, saw them spirit the black folk away, heard them shout there had been enough of their being killed. The Lord's hand is moving, Obed. He has stirred the settlers and they outnumber the like of Forbes a thousand times over, with His help they will put an end to cruelty against the Aboriginals. There are decent people living in this land, people who, given the chance, will make it a great and prosperous country, one where men can be free and where black and white will live in peace, and men like Forbes will no longer be able to take life and limb as it suits him, no nor imprison a woman's son for defending his mother.'

Hearing the tremble of fresh tears in the woman's voice Tamar wondered what it was had taken Esther Wesson's sons from her but out of respect for her husband's unspoken request she retained her curiosity and her silence. Had they wished her to know they would have said.

'How come the black woman and the boy were in Geelong?' He switched the talk back as Esther dabbed at her eyes with a handkerchief.

Still curious yet glad the topic was changed, the older woman's sadness finding an echo in her own heart Tamar answered. 'I know only that they were caught by some of the men out hunting, they were taken by the little lake at the foot of the waterfall and brought up to the settlement.'

'The men who took them, were they settlers?'

Tamar frowned, concentrating on recalling the incident. 'No . . . no they were no one I recognise from there though I had seen them before but they were in uniform.'

'I guessed as much!' He blew a stream of smoke skyward. 'Soldiers . . . Pah, call themselves men! They took that woman and the boy so as to make money, they knew somebody would buy them.'

She did not ask for what; she already knew.

'But why did they not capture the man also.'

Taking the pipe from his mouth Obadiah Wesson tapped the bowl against his palm returning it before speaking.

'You say his body were streaked with paint?'

Tamar nodded. 'Yes, white paint, it was quite distinctive against the shadows. He washed it off at one of the places we stayed overnight.'

Obed chewed the clay stem thoughtfully. 'Sounds like there's been a gathering, these folk sometimes comes together for a ritual of some kind. Esther and me have heard them once or twice in the distance making their music. Sounds like they be blowing down some hollowed-out branch, least it don't be the sort of music as we know it. That would be the only reason for his leaving the woman and her boy, them not being included in such.'

'It almost cost the lad his life, and even worse for the woman . . . poor soul!'

It was the first note of censure Tamar had heard in Esther's voice but her husband took it up quickly.

'We has no right to judge a man's beliefs Esther nor

427

the way he worships his God. We have our ways, the Aboriginals have theirs, who's to say he be wrong. He has lived on this continent for countless years and sees the hand and the power of the Creator in every living thing, every plant and tree, we cannot deem such people savages.'

'You be right Obadiah, I wasn't thinking.'

Reaching a hand to hers he patted it gently. 'You were thinking of the woman and the boy, you can be forgiven for that.'

'But he must have known what might happen had he been caught that night he rescued me, so why take the risk? The woman and child were safe away so why come back?'

Staring at the sky, a glorious burst of gold-trimmed scarlet and mauve-edged purple he took a moment before answering.

'Who can read a man's mind, child, or give reason for his actions, but it be my guess he would not move far before seeing you also were safe.'

'But I am white, why would he save me?'

'Had you not saved his wife and son, what better reason would any man have?'

But he had taken such a terrible gamble. Breathing the soft perfume of blossom trailed along the fence of the veranda, Tamar tried to shut the consequence from her mind leaving only her gratitude to linger. She was free of Geelong, free to resume her search for Benjie.

Chapter Thirty-One

Folding the pretty sprigged gown Tamar stroked a hand over the delicate muslin. The dress felt wonderful and it was kind of the woman to offer it to her but she could not accept it.

Hoping not to sound ungrateful she held the dress to the older woman whose eyes showed uncertainty.

'It is a lovely gown Mrs Wesson but you must not give it to me. Your son will come home and one day he will take a wife and I am sure she would want to be married in this; it is so pretty any girl would love to wear it as her bridal gown.'

'My son come home . . . ! He should have come home two years gone . . .'

Her lined face crumpling, Esther Wesson dropped to a chair holding her apron to her eyes.

Laying the dress aside Tamar knelt beside the woman. 'I'm sorry, Mrs Wesson,' she touched the woman's hand, 'I did not mean to upset you.'

'It don't be you upset me.' Esther sniffed behind her apron. 'It be that Forbes.'

Henry Forbes. It seemed at every turn the man's name cropped up, whenever there was pain and misery his was the name on people's lips.

Loth to speak lest sympathy be mistaken for curiosity Tamar squeezed the work-worn hand. Rising to her feet she set about making a cup of tea. Whenever Vinny Marsh or one of the women back home were upset a cup of tea was the first line of comfort.

Listening to the heart-broken sobs echo in the quiet room she felt so helpless. Whatever Forbes had done to Esther Wesson there was no reparation, no one to bring him to book.

Wiping her eyes Esther smiled apologetically as she took the cup from Tamar.

'Them tears have wanted to come for a long time now, I be sorry they had to be shed in your presence.'

Tamar smiled more definitely. 'Better out than in was what my mother used to say.'

Balancing her cup with one hand, dabbing a corner of her apron to her eyes with the other, Esther looked at the girl whose lovely face was suddenly shadowed with the kind of pain she thought only her own heart could hold. Reaching for her hand she pulled Tamar to a chair beside her own. 'You no longer have your mother?'

Shaking her head as she fought the tears in her own heart, Tamar answered. 'My mother died several years ago and my father not long afterward, there is just Benjie and me.'

'Ah, yes, your brother. You told us he was the reason for your coming to this country . . . God give him back to you soon.'

'I have to find him, Mrs Wesson, I promised him . . .'

'There now, wench, getting yourself all upset won't do no good.'

'But he's so young and he gets frightened.'

'That be understandable. But you have to hold faith that you'll find him.'

'I see little chance of that. They said in Geelong there was no way to reach any place except by the coastal packet.'

' 'Twere no packet boat brought you to Bendigo and . . .' The woman broke off, her hand tightening reassuringly over Tamar's as the girl started in fear.

'Pay that no mind . . .'

'But horses . . .' Tamar stared towards the door '. . . it must be men from the colony . . . Forbes . . . !'

'That don't be Forbes.' Esther glanced at the sun-filled doorway. 'That just be old Salome.' Catching the querying look she chuckled. 'An old woman's fancy. We already had a Luke and a Matthew and what with each of the family's names being took from the Bible we figured why break with it when the animals came along so it were Sampson for the dog and Salome for the mare.'

'Salome . . . that is an unusual name for a horse.'

Releasing Tamar's hand the older woman smiled. 'It ain't often you hears it, but Obed and me thought it apt enough. Seems she had flapped her tail at a stallion for she dropped a foal some months after we bought her. But once weren't enough for her for she flapped it again whenever chance presented itself, throwing it about like Salome with her veils, hence the name. But Shadrach be the last of her foals, old Salome only flaps her tail at flies these days.'

Luke and Matthew, were they the sons Esther Wesson had spoken of? Gathering the cups Tamar let them lie when the woman touched her hand.

'Luke and Matthew be my boys,' she said quietly, 'Luke be eight and twenty this Michaelmass and Matthew, well he would be two and thirty were he living.'

'Mrs Wesson, I . . . I didn't know.'

'That one of my boys be dead? Of course you didn't, but Henry Forbes knows . . . and well he should for he were the cause of it!'

That name again! Tamar felt her heart twist as she saw the pain on the older woman's face.

'Matthew, my eldest, were walking home from the fields when he heard a cry from the track that ran alongside the hedge. He were in time to see two men drag a third from his horse. He shouted and as he ran up to them one struck him in the face with a willow branch. It blinded him for a few seconds so he stumbled and fell into the ditch. By the time he climbed out the rider had been joined by men from the nearby farm. They claimed my Matthew were in on the robbery and pointed out the weal across his face as having been done by the fellow's whip striking out. The top and bottom of it being my son were sent to Geelong for fifteen years servitude in the penal colony. He were just fifteen years old, little more than a child.

'Obed and me we couldn't take being so far from

him so we sold up all we had and came out here. We hoped that just knowing we were here would some-how help him to bear being locked up.' Getting up from her chair she crossed to the open doorway and stood staring out towards the trees fringing neatly sown fields.

'Things were bearable at first,' she went on softly, 'we were allowed one hour a week to visit with our son, and from time to time we would see him work-ing with other convicts set to clearing the trees or building houses. Then one day I saw him close to the house we had taken. I should not have gone to him. I know that but I didn't think . . . he was my son and I needed to hold him if only for a moment. I had my arms about him when the guard shouted. I should have let him go then but the feel of him in my arms his head against my breast was too sweet. The guard called again and as Matthew took my arms from round him I felt the rifle butt against my back. As I fell I saw my son's face, his dear young face so twisted with a rage and hate such as I had never seen in him, I heard his cry as he leapt at the guard. That was when Luke ran to help his brother. I managed to drag Luke away, that was when Henry Forbes and several of his men came up. They pulled their own man free then set about beating my boy . . .'

She paused. One hand against the door-jamb she breathed a long trembling breath as she gazed at a scene only she could see.

'. . . and Henry Forbes stood by watching . . . watching while they beat my son to death.'

Horrified Tamar moved towards the woman but her story was not yet done.

'They dragged Luke from me and took him into that prison. Obed and me we tried to see him but Forbes would not allow it. Then word were sent, brought as we sprinkled soil into Matthew's grave. Luke had been found guilty of affray and of striking a member of Her Majesty's forces engaged in carrying out his duty.'

Esther's fingers tightened on the door-jamb and her voice trembled. 'Was that what Her Majesty calls duty, to have a lad beaten to death for defending his mother and to have an eleven-year-old boy condemned to ten years for going to his brother's aid? No!' The word shuddered through her pent-up agony and pain shaking her like a leaf in the breeze. 'That don't be no woman's justice, no nor a man's neither 'cept a man like Henry Forbes.'

Her quick brain calculating the numbers Tamar found herself at a loss. Luke, the Wessons' son, had served that time he had to have done if he was twenty-eight years old.

'I had learned my lesson with Luke.' Esther continued to gaze at the drama playing for her eyes only. 'I spoke to him only during that hour we were given to visit. Then came the day of his release. We waited at the gate, Obed and me but the hours came and went. At last Forbes sent to say we was to go to the Lodge. He came to us on the veranda. Luke had been disorderly, his punishment would be two years added to his sentence. There was no why or wherefore, no explanation of what he called disorderly. In the days that followed I thought I should go mad, I asked every guard I saw but none would speak of Luke. Then I saw him digging a ditch and God help me I did as I had done before, I took him in my arms. Oh Lord, how many times have I damned myself for that! How many times I have wished it were me in that prison!

'It were no more than a moment, one moment of holding a son I had not held since his childhood, the sweet touch of my hands against his face, a kiss I had been denied for so long . . .'

Her voice fading to a whisper Tamar only just caught the rest of her words.

'. . . and all over in a moment . . . in one small moment but that moment added five years to my son's torment. From that time we were to be denied all contact with Luke, visiting rights were withdrawn and he would not be part of any work detail allowed beyond the palisade so long as we, his parents, were in Geelong.'

'Is that why you came to Bendigo?' Touching a hand gently to the woman's shoulder Tamar felt the shudders running through her.

'We could not condemn Luke to that, never to step beyond that fence, to spend his days isolated from others to prevent his at least seeing the trees and the sea and his home, the place he knew we would be waiting for him. Take all that from a man and his heart shrivels, his soul begins to die. So we left Geelong and made a new start here.'

'But Luke, does he know?'

'Yes, he knows, he knows we would die before leaving him completely. It was too risky to ask any of the convicts to pass word to him. It was Millie Cooper did that, he will know where to come.'

Swallowing the tears that clogged her throat Esther gazed out over the small field sown with wheat, the neat vegetable garden closer to the house.

'Luke loved this place,' she murmured, 'as a child he would say that one day he and Matthew and their father would have a sheep-holding that would take in the whole valley, but now one is dead and the other is an old man . . .'

'It isn't too late, Mrs Wesson.'

Dropping her hand from the door-jamb the older woman turned, catching Tamar's hand.

'It will always be too late for us, as long as Forbes be in Geelong. It takes more than hard work to build a farm of sheep-holding, it takes money and he would see to it that the Wessons never made more than it takes to live.'

'But he does not bother you here.'

'How long do you think that will last once Luke is free? Henry Forbes does not let go easily, he holds the devil's sword and takes pleasure from the using of it; I fear he isn't done stabbing the Wessons yet.'

'Then I have to leave, to be found here would surely bring down more of Henry Forbes' spite and that is one thing I will not risk.'

Her fingers tightening over Tamar's, her faded eyes showing a spark of light, Esther drew her from the doorway.

'Would you risk the bush, make a journey such as you did with the Aboriginals?'

Could she face the heat of the desert again, lie in the darkness of the night trembling with fear at the rustlings in the undergrowth, at the howling of wild dogs? But then there was Benjie!

'Yes,' she nodded, 'yes, Mrs Wesson, I could.'

'I thank you for calling, Captain Burford.'

Still dressed in dark suit and heavily starched collar that reached his jaw line Paul Tern handed a glass to his visitor.

'May I hope you have come to offer me passage aboard your ship?'

'That depends upon where it is you wish to go; my crew have been away from home long enough and it is several weeks sail before they will sight the coast of Britain. That being so I will not take them a longer voyage around this country.'

'I applaud your concern Captain, but I think I shall prove correct in saying a long detour will not be necessary. There is a map in the study. If you would be good enough to accompany me there.'

Setting the glass aside Nathan rose to his feet and as he did so his eye fell on a folded newspaper. Below a photograph he read the caption.

Their Royal Highnesses the Prince and Princess of Wales attend the opening of La Traviata.

'A beautiful woman, His Highness and England are both blessed.'

'My sentiments exactly,' Nathan replied, his eye still grabbing at the printed words.

Picking up the newspaper Paul Tern held it out. 'Take it if you wish, Captain. It is already several weeks old but out here news of home is welcome no matter its age.'

'Thank you.' Folding the paper once again Nathan slipped it into his pocket. 'As you say, news of home is welcome whatever its age.'

Poring over a map in the comfortably furnished study, Paul Tern traced a finger from Botany Bay along the south-eastern coast to Geelong.

'That is where I must go. I am no sailor Captain, nor do I make any claims to knowing the ways of winds and currents, but to my layman's eyes it might be less of a journey to travel home via the Indian Ocean than to go north and sail more than halfway around the country . . . that is if you intend to take the Indian Ocean route.'

'I do and you are correct Mr Tern, we would be better served that way.'

Paul Tern's handsome face creased in a brief smile as he led the way back to the sitting room.

Replenishing both glasses with Madeira he settled into a leather wing chair.

'How soon can you expect your vessel to be re-victualled and any new cargo stored?'

'If what you are asking is when can the *Verity* be made ready to sail the answer is she was ready when you came aboard this morning.'

'I see you are not given to wasting time, Captain.'

Staring into the rich red depth of the wine Nathan's face betrayed the emotion that surged like a rip tide along his veins. He had wasted time once before. He could have gone to Aiden, told him that it was stupid pride that had caused him to lose his temper. He could have wished his brother happiness with the girl he loved; instead he had done none of those things and his brother had died as a result.

Swallowing the wine he looked at the man seated across from him. 'Life is time Mr Tern, and it is too great a gift to waste. Should you still require passage on the *Verity* then have your luggage aboard before the morning tide on the day after tomorrow.'

'The fee . . .'

Cap in hand Nathan cut in sharply. 'There will be no fee, the *Verity* serves the Queen's business so you say, then that is fee enough.'

The diplomat rose, his height matching almost exactly that of his visitor, a smile resting on his mouth.

'Well said, Captain, but if you will not accept one offer then accept another.'

A quick frown drawing his own brows together Nathan slapped his cap irritably against his thigh. 'I have said already . . .'

'I know what you have said already.' The other man's smile remained steady. 'But remember what *I* said when we talked this morning, Her Majesty's representatives have influence. Well I have used that influence to learn that the *Porpoise* made a call at another settlement before coming here. That is the ship you have been enquiring after is it not? I also found that though it is a Royal Navy vessel she carried a private passenger, a Mrs Odile Bancroft, daughter of the Foreign Secretary.'

Bancroft! Odile Bancroft! That was the name the chandler's wife had used. That woman had taken the *Porpoise* and Tamar Hallam had sailed with her.

His throat tight Nathan forced the drumming inside him to stop. 'Where did the *Porpoise* call?'

He had not been wrong. Paul Tern watched the other man struggle to smother his feelings. Lifting a silver bell set on an elegantly small rosewood table he rang it before answering. 'The *Porpoise* made a brief stop-over at Geelong, just long enough to disembark its passenger. A bargain is a bargain when it is kept, eh, Captain Burford? I hope yours proves a fruitful one.'

She had put down at Geelong. Arrangements made for the taking on board of his passenger, Nathan lay on his bunk. Paul Tern was no man's fool, he had seen the effect his words had created. But he had made no mention of Tamar nor of her brother though both had been mentioned by name during his own enquiries made around the penal settlement and at the prison itself. Did that mean the two had not been heard of here in Botany or was Tern withholding something?

The sound of the ship's bell ringing the middle watch he turned restlessly, thoughts he couldn't hold running free in his mind.

She must have disembarked when Odile Bancroft did. She must be at Geelong . . . or maybe not! Maybe she had moved on, maybe her brother had not been taken to the prison there but to some other place? With so many convicts still peddled out to Australia prisons were sure to get filled up, perhaps there had been no room for the lad at Geelong.

Perhaps . . . perhaps . . . it was always perhaps. So many times the word in his heart he had followed up a tale of a man being found here or picked up there, always with hope of finding Aiden but that hope was always dashed. This time he must not expect anything, that way he could not be disappointed. But when sleep eventually came the hope was still in his heart.

'You know what travelling through the bush be like, you know it be no Sunday school outing.'

Esther Wesson looked keenly at the girl sat in her kitchen. She had already trod a path to hell's door but there was further yet to go if she was to find her brother.

'I know that, Mrs Wesson.'

The answer was quiet but it held no trace of a quiver. Holding her gaze for a moment Esther seemed to go over the question in her mind, then her reasoning done she stood up.

'Obed and me talked of this last night. We knowed we couldn't look to keep you for long. When he comes in we will see how best to . . .' She glanced towards the veranda as the sound of boots echoed on its wooden boards.

'Speak of the devil . . .'

'You'll say that one of these days woman and it

really will be Old Nick and he'll frighten the stays off you!'

'Then I must be sure and buy a new pair for these be worn to a thread.'

Joining in the smiles of the other two Tamar reached a cup as Esther lifted the teapot from the side of the stove.

'I was telling Tamar that we talked last night of the possibility she would want to move on, and it seems she don't be feared of another trek through the bush but it has to be soon . . .'

Obed's raised hand halting her in mid-sentence. Esther frowned, then replaced the teapot beside the stove.

'What is it Obed?' The frown gone she sounded suddenly fearful. 'What be wrong?'

'I took this from the fence that hems the vegetable patch.'

Taking a loose rolled leaf from his pocket he spread it on the table taking care his fingers touched only its edges then motioned both women to look at it.

But what was she looking at, what was she supposed to see? There were marks on the leaf but they were simply veining, no more than that.

'See here, this be hills.' Obed traced a mark with his finger outlining its shape to Esther who bent closer.

Why did they both look so serious? They were scrutinising the leaf as though it were some important document. Watching them, heads drawn close together, she wondered that such stable sensible people could become so intent over an ordinary leaf.

'And this.' Obed's finger moved carefully avoiding contact with the leaf. 'This here be a man.'

'You be right Obed, that do be a man!'

It was the same game she used to play with Benjie. Tamar smiled at the woman's answer. They would watch the flames dance in the grate and turn them into knights and ladies, unicorns and dragons. Pictures in the fire or pictures on a leaf they were no different; they were simply that, pictures and nothing else.

'It were in the usual place?' Esther straightened.

'Like I said, placed on the fence with a stone to hold it. Weren't there when I went out this morning but it were there when I come by just now.'

'So what do you think it to mean?'

Passing his hand through his thinning hair Obed looked again at the broad leaf taking his time before looking up. 'What would you say girl, what is it you think these marks to mean?'

They did not mean anything, they were simply the natural marks of the leaf's growth. Tamar glanced from one face to the other. Had these two people lived so long apart from others, lived with the pain of the loss of their sons until to ease it they had begun to believe their own fantasies, to see what they wanted to see rather than what was really there? Reluctant to hurt either of them she glanced down at the leaf hiding the thoughts that showed in her eyes.

'I . . . I have no idea . . . they seem . . .'

'It be unfair to ask the wench what meaning she

sees.' Nothing lost on her, Esther came quickly to Tamar's aid. 'One leaf be like another when you don't be knowing the ways of the bush.'

'Then look carefully, girl.' Obed's finger retraced the marks slowly and as he spoke the scratches did indeed come to resemble the description he gave to each.

'The veining is unusual.' Tamar said as he finished.

'That be no veining girl.'

'Then what caused those marks?'

'Not what child, but who . . . who made those marks?'

'That be enough Obed, the wench be confused by your talk, tell her plain what that be about.'

'The Aboriginal family that showed you the way to Bendigo, they drew these marks and left this leaf where I would be sure to find it.' Obed explained patiently. 'When that lad of theirs were nobbut two years old he were copying the ways of his father hunting a Joey . . .'

'A Joey?'

'It be an animal, a kangaroo. They be hunted for meat by black and white folk alike, most like you've seen one brought into the settlement at Geelong.' Seeing her nod he went on with his explanation. 'Well that lad were toddling along after a Joey when it stopped sudden and he went headlong over its tail the outcome being the little 'un's arm were broke. My Esther came upon 'em by the stream and some-how got them to understand the boy needed to have the bone held by a splint. Anyway they allowed it and camped here 'til the boy were mended. Ever since then we have left food from time to time on the fence and they have replaced it with a fish or a hare. Neither family needs what the other gives but it is a thread of trust and friendship, one that God willing will grow and spread throughout the entire country.'

'And the leaf, that is a gift from them?'

'Not a gift child, but a message. See . . .'

Bending over the table, Tamar watched the scratches being explained yet again.

'. . . hills, they'll be the ones you can see from the doorway,' he glanced towards the open door then back to the leaf, 'while this . . . this represents a man.'

She could see a resemblance, but a message! Not wanting to appear sceptical Tamar remained silent.

'It be telling that there be a man over in them hills, a man they ain't see afore.'

Lifting his glance Obadiah Wesson looked deep into Tamar's eyes as she straightened. 'Don't you see child, they've come across a stranger . . . a white stranger!'

A white stranger! Tamar's heart leaped violently. But how could Obed know the stick picture he saw as a man be meant not as another black man?

'I see what you're thinking.' Obed smiled. 'But look again child, the legs be seen only from the calf, that means whoever be in them hills be wearing trousers and as you've seen for yourself, the Aboriginal wears no trousers, therefore this picture be telling of a white man.'

Her hands trembling, Tamàr touched the leaf.

Could her search be over . . . was the figure on the leaf a drawing of Benjie . . . was it her brother wandering those hills?

Chapter Thirty-Two

Glancing at the newspaper he had dropped on to the table in his cabin Nathan picked it up, his glance running over the words he had read several times before.

> . . . The princess was graciously pleased to
> wear the necklace that has become known
> as the Alexandra Stone.

There was no word of its history apart from its being specially crafted for the princess, no mention of the lad who had been sent down for thirty years for a crime he likely never committed.

Staring at the photograph a few moments longer, he folded the newspaper, slipping it into the pocket of his jacket as he left the cabin.

He had talked of that theft to Paul Tern during the run down to Geelong. The man had a quick wit and an agile tongue and made an excellent conversationalist but he had held out little hope of the boy.

Coming on to the deck Nathan breathed the fresh air of early morning his glance circling the great blue horizon until it came to the clearing where yellow-uniformed men and women were already busy with the labours of servitude.

No hope of the boy. He stared landward. But there was hope of Tamar. It was highly probable she had left the *Porpoise* at this settlement, but were the chances the same that she might still be here?

Spending several minutes speaking with Tom Brooks, assuring himself all was ready to take the tide, he went ashore, walking quickly up the stretch of beach fronting the wide half-circle clearing that held a clutch of wood-built houses, guessing they belonged to time-served prisoners denied the right to return to England. His glance sweeping a line in each direction as far as sight could reach, he felt again the swell of appreciation that had filled him so often since first sighting this land. It was a country a man could breathe in, be proud to be a part of, a place his children could grow in freedom. Only the penal colonies marred its beauty, but even now these were changing and one day they would be nothing but a memory, a shadow on the horizon of the past, and when that time came men would speak of being an Australian with dignity and respect.

'Beg pardon, sir . . .'

His thoughts interrupted, Nathan glanced at the man who spoke, who even now despite its change of command glanced towards the prison compound with nervous eyes.

'It was you was asking after Tamar Hallam?'

'What do you know of her?'

Seeing the other man flinch Nathan apologised for being so abrupt.

'I should not have spoken so roughly, it is just that you are the first person in months who might know of her.'

'Yes sir, I know of her.' George Cooper glanced again at the compound. 'But this be no place to talk. My house be over there if you would step inside.'

'My wife and me took the wench you be asking after and found her a place to sleep when her landed in Geelong, ain't that so, Millie?'

Slightly awed by her visitor, Millie nodded.

'Then she is here?'

'No sir, her ain't here.' George put his wife's shake of the head into words.

'But you said . . .'

'I said we took the wench under this roof and there her stayed until Henry Forbes stuck her in a cage.'

'Did you say a cage? By God, I'll break every bone in his miserable body!'

Watching the anger settle like a mask over Nathan's face Millie remembered the look that had been in the girl's eyes when she spoke of this man sitting now at her table. They had been a few words spoken only in passing, but the eyes had told a story of their own.

Pouring two glasses of cool ginger cordial she set one in front of each man but as she turned to leave the room George raised a hand.

'Nay love, you knows as much of this as me, and then more. You be the one to do the telling of it.'

'And that was the last you saw of her?' Nathan's

fingers showed white about the glass as Millie finished speaking.

'The very last,' George replied. 'We knows the wench were put in the cage . . . that be a favourite ploy of Forbes' . . . his batman don't be a bad sort, he told what had happened and that Forbes had denied her water . . .'

'God in heaven!' Flinging away from the table Nathan struck a palm with his fist.

'. . . I waited 'til after moonrise,' George went on, 'then I took a bottle of water to water to where I knew that cage were at the back of that lodge but Tamar was gone and we've heard no more of her from that day.'

'But you must have some idea where she went, which settlement she would head for!'

'There be no place for miles and certainly not one any woman could find for herself.' George shook his head. 'The outback be desert and bush and if the snakes and dingoes don't get you first then the sun and thirst surely does.'

Desolation replacing anger, Nathan took his cap from the back of the chair he had been sitting on and as he thanked them Millie caught the flash of anguish pass across his grey eyes.

'Wait!' She touched a hand to his arm. 'That don't be the all of it. Tell him George, tell him what you saw.'

'It be just my thinking woman, a trick of the moon.'

Removing her hand from Nathan's arm Millie set

both hands on her hips the look on her worn face saying she would not be denied. 'Tell him, George Cooper,' she said determinedly, 'you tell him this instant or you'll have me to deal with!'

'Is there more, Mr Cooper?'

Shifting uncomfortably from foot to foot George glanced first at Millie's set face then at Nathan.

'It be nothing but my imagination . . .'

'Were the door of that cage your imagination or that you say now was naught but shadow?' Millie's voice was sharp.

'You place too much on that Millie, the captain will take me for a fool.'

There was something more. Nathan glanced at the two faces, one determined the other sheepish. They had not told him all.

'Mr Cooper.' He turned towards the man. 'I take no man for a fool until he proves himself to be one. Judging by what I have heard you are far from being that. If there is more you can tell me, however much you may think it imagination, then I would appreciate the hearing of it; but should speaking of it cause you embarrassment then I would not press you.'

It had been many a long year since a man of authority had spoken to him with such politeness. George Cooper met the other man's look. There was honesty in that face and respect in those eyes. He would not think a man a fool for saying what he thought he saw.

'It was like I said Mr Burford,' George began slowly. 'I took water thinking to pass it to Tamar through the bars of that cage but when I got there it were empty. I thought first it were dingoes . . . they be wild dogs that comes to forage about the place after dark . . . I thought they had snatched her from the cage, she wouldn't be the first they had dragged off. But the bars were intact and the door was open on its hinges with no sign of attack.'

'Could the door have been opened from the inside?'

Shaking his head at the question George went on.

'There were no chance of that; the door were secured with a heavy bar, a woman forced to sit on her haunches wouldn't manage to lift it supposing her arms could pass between the bars. No, that door had been opened from the outside.'

'The batman?' Nathan asked, hope returning to his face.

'Not him sir, nor Forbes neither, judging by the hue and cry that went up the following morning.'

'Then how?'

Dropping her hands Millie went to stand beside her husband. 'Tell him, George,' she said gently, 'you've come this far it be only fair to speak the rest.'

Taking his wife's hand George Cooper hesitated for a moment, then taking a long breath continued his account.

'I was stood beside the cage, everything was silent. As I remember, it were that which struck me, the silence. It were strange . . . the bush ain't never truly silent and 'specially not at night, the sounds of animals can always be heard. But that night there was none.

That told me there was something not quite usual and I turned to look towards the tree line and as I did the moon threw off the cloud that covered it and it was then I saw . . . I thought I saw . . . a shadow.'

Giving him a moment Nathan asked. 'A shadow of what . . . could you recognise it?'

Millie's hand pressing gently on his arm George Cooper nodded. 'It were a man. His body were only an outline, black against the night shadow, but I seen him clear as clear and he was daubed with white stripes.'

'White stripes?' Nathan's brow creased.

'What my George thinks he seen was an Abbo, a black man,' Millie said, as her husband broke off. 'They be the natives we spoke of earlier. 'Twas one of them he thinks took Tamar from that cage.'

Concern thick in each syllable Nathan swallowed hard before asking. 'These Aboriginals, are they prone to taking white people captive, of harming them?'

'We would say the boot be on the other foot, especially Henry Forbes' foot.' George answered scathingly. 'That man has had the poor creatures hunted and shot since the day he came to Geelong, but there ain't been one time an Abbo has took a white, if it be that one has taken the wench, it could well be just imagining.'

'It ain't like him to go imagining.' Millie looked up at Nathan. 'If he says he seen a man then a man was what he seen.'

'I believe that too, Mrs Cooper. But given that I have to ask why, why would an Aboriginal abduct a white girl? It can only be revenge and in that case . . .'

'It be nothing of the kind!' Millie stamped her foot in exasperation. 'You men be all the same, you be so busy looking for the worst you never sees the best. That woman and the lad, the ones Tamar was protecting, they was like to be the man's family. He didn't abduct the wench, he rescued her. He was paying like for like, Tamar saved their lives and he was saving hers! It has to be that way, nothing else makes any sense. He has taken her to be with them, to keep her safe.'

'Mrs Cooper, do you have any idea where they could have gone?'

'No, Mr Burford, I ain't and that be the truth of it, but my heart tells me Tamar be safe and that one day her will come back.'

If only he had not told the crew they would sail for home once he had delivered Paul Tern to Geelong. He could change his mind, tell them the *Verity* would stay here until he had made a search of the hinterland. But his word to his crew was his bond. Fingers twisting his cap he looked at the couple who had done so much more for Tamar than he.

'I believe that too and I would stay to look further for her but my crew have been away from their homes too long already to ask them to stay longer. But I will be back. If Tamar should return before then would you tell her what I have said and will you show her this.'

Taking the newspaper from his pocket, Nathan smiled his thanks.

'That will tell her what she has always known. It was not her brother who stole that necklace.'

Would it be Benjie, was it him the leaf had said was hiding in the hills? She had wanted to go with Obed, begged him to take her but he had been adamant. The journey was no joyride, she must stay with Esther until he returned.

'Come you out on the porch and sit 'til the heat be gone, you be fair giving me a headache with all that moling about.'

She was restless it was true, but how could she rest not knowing. Picking up a dish she had dusted beneath ten times already Tamar glanced at the pebbles it held.

'They be Luke's and Matthew's . . .'

Esther took the yellow pottery bowl touching a finger to the colourful pieces of rock.

'. . . they would play hours with these, neither admitting the other the winner.'

Wrapped up in her own thoughts, her own needs Tamar had become unaware of that same need in the older woman, the need to ease the heartache inside her. Guilt flooding through her she laid the duster aside.

'I would like to hear of that if you will tell me.'

'I mustn't burden you with my sorrows.' Esther's quick glanced showed her understanding.

For the first time since Obed's refusing to take her with him Tamar smiled. 'It would lighten my burden

Mrs Wesson, it would remind me of talking with Vinny.'

'That woman were a real friend to you, wasn't she wench?'

'Yes.' Tamar's eyes took on a far-away look. 'She was a real friend, Benjie and I loved her very much.'

'Then you fetch us out a cool drink and we will both talk of loved ones.'

The gaudy bowl held against her chest Esther walked out on to the veranda settling herself into one of the crudely built armchairs.

Joining her, Tamar could not help but look across to the line of hills their tops misty with the haze of heat, her whole being crying out that it be Benjie they sheltered.

The chink of pebbles in the bowl recalling her she sat beside Esther. Both had their hopes and their dreams, pray soon both would come true.

'My boys would sit here after the day's chores were done and play jacks with these pebbles.'

Taking a handful of the small stones Esther placed them on the small table beside the glasses of ginger beer.

'We would play the same game, my brother and I, that is if it is the one where the pebbles were tossed in the air and caught on the back of the hand.'

'That be the one.' Esther smiled. 'Luke was always a bit cag-handed, he dropped more'n he catched but that didn't stop him from declaring himself the winner.'

'Benjie was quite good at the game to say he still had such small hands.' Her mind slipping back over the years she seemed to see again the young boy, his dark red hair gleaming in the sunlight as he sat cross-legged on the grassy sides of Hockley Brook laughing up at her that he had won yet again. They had spent so many Sunday afternoons there or beneath the trees of Warstone Lane cemetery. She had taught him little singing rhymes and his numbers. He would bring the biggest daisy he could find and together they would count the petals, then one by one he would pull them off shouting delightedly when he correctly said the number that was left; and each outing would end with his choosing a halfpenny worth of sweets from Mother Hartill's front-room shop. That had taken longer than the game but the touch of his small arms about her neck as he thanked her was worth the cost of the stale loaf the halfpenny would have bought.

'You'll find him wench, I knows that.' Touching the hand that held the pebbles, Esther too smiled. 'The Lord be good. Though He bide His time He'll send the lad home to you. Meantime you keep them stones, could be they'll help you think of him and remember the Wessons.'

'I won't need anything to help me remember you, you have both been so kind.'

'Well keep 'em anyway, I'd like to give you something of value but what bits and pieces we had went long since.'

Lifting the older woman's hand Tamar pressed it to her cheek. 'My father taught us to value friendship above all else,' she whispered, 'you have given me the finest gift of all and I will treasure it forever.'

Faded eyes moist with emotion Esther touched a free hand to the shining hair. This was the girl she would have dearly loved to see married to her son but it was a girl instinct told her already loved another.

Releasing her hand as Tamar's head lifted she glanced at the pebbles, hiding the look she knew must show.

'They are so very pretty, such lovely colours, surely Luke will want them once he comes home.'

'My Luke be eight and twenty, could be he be grown out of such games but should be ain't then there be a hillside full of such stones over yonder. Him and Matthew would often fetch themselves a new batch and sit arguing who had the finest.'

'They are pretty . . .'

She got no further, jumping to her feet she slipped them into her pocket her gaze following the line of Esther's pointing finger.

Coming out of the tree line that bordered their ploughed field was Obed. Tamar caught her breath, one hand flying to her throat.

Leaning heavily on Obed's arm was another figure, a figure whose hair gleamed in the sun.

'Benjie!' She cried softly. 'Benjie.'

The Aborigine had guided Obed to the hills and helped him home.

Tamar lay sleepless in the room that had been Luke's and Matthew's.

Tomorrow they would leave. Esther had complained it was too soon that they each needed to rest. But her husband would have none of it. The Aborigine had drawn a picture in the dust, the picture of a ship with sails hoisted and underneath he had marked four straight lines. That meant there was a ship in the harbour that would sail in four days time and it would take them all of that to reach it. She had not questioned how the black man would know that, like Obed she trusted his intelligence, knew that it equalled their own. But even he could not get them aboard without Forbes hearing of it and once he had they would never be allowed to leave.

Closing her eyes she watched the picture her mind recalled. One figure helping the other, one whose hair gleamed red in the lowering sun, heard herself cry her brother's name.

But it had not been her brother. The red gold of the dipping sun had touched grey hair lending it an illusion of colour, the face she saw as they came nearer was that of a man full grown; it was not Benjie.

That was why, even if the chance presented itself, she could not sail on that ship, she could not leave Australia.

But neither could she remain in this house to bring the danger of that man Forbes' anger down upon the Wessons. Esther had tried to make her change her mind but tomorrow she would go with Obed and the stranger back to Geelong.

Who was he . . . the man sleeping before the fire in the living room? He could not tell them, he knew only that he had been found by a tribe of black people and they had fed and cared for him, keeping him with them on their wanderings until at last they had brought him to a cave in some hills, and it was there Obed had found him.

Had he been a convict? Had he escaped some penal institution? Had others escaped with him? All of these questions Obed had wanted to put to him but fussing like a mother hen Esther had forbade them. They would wait she said, rest must come before questions.

But of all those questions Tamar wanted to ask only had he heard of her brother? Had he too escaped?

But if he had where was he now? Alone in the bush he would stand no chance. Remembering her own journey she threw an arm across her face closing out the moonlight silvering the room. She had been with the Aborigine family yet still there had been moments of heart-stopping fear, alone it would have been a nightmare!

'I be feared Tam . . .'

Across the space of memory the words cried in her brain and in her heart tears answered.

Chapter Thirty-Three

Obed glanced towards the nearing tree line a whisper of thanks in his heart. He had made this same trek several times since being shown the way to the Aborigine but he was always relieved and thankful when the arid desert was behind him. It was dangerous enough with only himself to look out for but with a girl and a man almost exhausted it was doubly so. But getting them there was only half the battle, how to get them aboard ship was the other half; getting them past Henry Forbes would be nothing if not a miracle.

The man had not apprehended him on those occasions he had come into Geelong to buy tea and sugar and those other things they could not grow for themselves, but that did not mean Forbes had not known he was there, it merely meant he was playing his war of nerves, like a cat plays a mouse.

They were moving slowly, too slowly. Worrying though that was Obed knew he could not travel any faster, he must keep the pace to one the man beside him could manage. The black people had fed him he had said, but the amount and type of food those people could live and thrive on, especially on long treks across ground such as they were on now, would leave most white men near to starvation. He glanced again at the figure stumbling along beside him. He was thin to the point of scrawny but that he felt would be due more to conditions of his journeyings than to lack of food; he seemed the wrong sort to turn his nose up at a few juicy ants and grubs. He was made of stronger stuff; yet how much longer could he force that thin body to go on, how long before he dropped from exhaustion?

Walking in their wake Tamar watched the younger man stumble then shake his head as Obed asked if he wanted a moment's rest. Humidity adding to her own breathlessness, every fibre of her screaming its weariness she forced one foot in front of the other. How could she ask to rest when that man could carry on?

How long had they been walking . . . how many days? She tried to think to pull her mind back from the edge of blackness it constantly walked but her mind did not wish to forgo the peace that darkness promised. How far had they come? She tried again to think but how to remember days, each surrounded by the eternal emptiness of scrub desert, days that melted into each other, the hours of night not enough of a division to mark them separate, for she woke as weary as when falling asleep.

Glancing behind to the girl stumbling along, her head slumped on her chest, Obed realised she was at the end of her strength. To stop now would risk losing that ship but to force her to go on might mean more of a risk. Lifting his glance to the sky he noted the sun already directly overhead. They would be unable to travel during the heat of the afternoon but they needed to reach the shade of the trees.

Dropping a few steps behind he put an arm around Tamar's waist taking her weight on himself.

'A few more yards, girl,' he encouraged, 'a little further then you can rest, the trees be just up ahead.'

Rest! It was the only word her brain seemed to recognise. Her legs folding in response, she sagged against Obed.

Knowing that, slight as she was he could not carry her and to let her lie in the open in the full glare of the midday sun would finish her, he shook her his voice sharp and deliberately angry.

'You was the one wanted to go back to Geelong, you was too, all knowing to take a telling from others, well now you'll bloody well walk, do you hear me!' He shook her again. 'Walk damn you! Or by Christ I'll leave you to the dingoes.'

It had gone against his nature to speak to the girl like he had but it had been the only way. Holding his own water bottle to her lips Obed felt a deep sympathy for the girl sat propped against a tree. She had proved stronger than many a man would under the same circumstances. Surely such determination deserved to be rewarded; she had to find that brother.

And the man that had trudged beside him without once asking or complaining, he too deserved more than to be taken by Henry Forbes. Giving the man the last of the water, receiving a smile of thanks in return,

Obed gathered the three bottles. They would need to be filled for the remainder of the journey.

Treading as quietly as he could, never sure of what might lie ahead he made for the water-hole the Aborigine had shown him. Coming to its edge he bent over its glistening waters dappled with the shade of acacia and eucalyptus. Holding the second bottle beneath the surface he started as a rustle among the thick undergrowth sent a flock of pink and grey galahs screeching into the air.

Scrambling to his feet the third water bottle forgotten on the ground he turned just as a uniformed man lifted a rifle butt above his head.

'It'll be a feather in our caps if nothing else, capturing a runaway.'

Senses swirling from the blow to his head Obed opened his eyes. A little way from him three men, each dressed alike in the uniform of the garrison, stood talking.

'What if he ain't no runaway?'

'What else would he be stuck out 'ere in the bush?'

One of the men turned to look at Obed. 'He ain't wearing convict's clothing.'

'What do that prove,' his mate sneered, 'only that he pinched what he has on from some settler's wash line and ditched his yellows somewhere along the way.'

'Mebbe you be right.' The one with three stripes stitched to the sleeve of his jacket seemed unconvinced. 'But I don't recall seeing him in the compound.'

'We all knows you don't miss much, Sarge,' the first man laughed, 'but even you can't remember every face you sees in that gaol, not unless it be a woman's.'

'I can remember a smart arse . . . and I knows 'ow to deal with him!'

Backing down beneath the sergeant's stare the man turned to where Obed lay on the ground, his wrists tied behind him.

'I could ask him, Sarge, mebbe he don't be one on his own, could be others along of him.'

Nodding agreement the sergeant took a drink from a leather bottle.

'Says he be on his own.'

Burping loudly as he refastened the bottle to his cross-belt he walked across to where Obed had struggled to sit up. Sharp eyes taking in the dust-caked boots and sweat-soaked lines of dirt on the face looking up at him he asked:

'What be you doing out here alone as you reckons?'

'I be on my way to Geelong.'

'Hah! And my arse be a lemon!'

His stare ice cold the sergeant ignored the other man's coarse laughter speaking again to Obed. 'On your way to Geelong? You be sure you ain't on your way *from* there?'

'I tell you I am on my way to Geelong, I go there two mebbe three times a year to pick up supplies.'

'And you be travelling alone?'

Blinking perspiration from his eyes Obed used the moment to think. Maybe the others would find their way to the settlement, far better for the girl to take her chances that way than to be found by these three.

'Yes, that's right.' He nodded. 'There be only me and my wife out at Bendigo and she be too frail to make the journey to Geelong.'

'Bendigo!' The first soldier glanced at his superior. 'There be no such place, there be no place other than Geelong. The old man be lying.'

Making no answer the sergeant kept his glance on the lined face. 'So you be coming from a place that don't exist and you be going to carry supplies back to this never never land all by yourself!'

'Bendigo does exist . . .'

'The man be a bloody liar! Let him 'ave another taste of old Betsy 'ere and he'll spit the truth out along of his teeth.'

'Hold it!' The sergeant touched a hand to the raised rifle. 'He'll be worth nothing dead. Get him on his feet.'

Hauling Obed upright the soldier's grip tightened and he grinned at his sergeant as a piercing scream rang through the trees, its sudden sound scattering the flock of small cockatoos like a cloud of pink and grey petals.

'Don't sound to me like he be alone Sarge, and that don't sound like no old woman neither.'

She had felt the movement against her arm, felt the warm slither against her neck. She was in a cage . . . in a cage with a snake sliding over her body . . .

Fear escaping in an agonised scream Tamar woke to see the frightened kangaroo bound away among the trees.

'I tried to scare it off but it seemed to like you, I don't blame him for that.'

Propped against an opposite tree the man from the cave smiled as he threw down a pebble he was holding.

'They be inquisitive brutes but harmless provided you give those forepaws a wide berth. Not scared you too much has he?'

Still trembling, Tamar shook her head. 'No, no . . . I was dreaming.'

'Well, nightmares are not allowed before one minute to midnight and they are banished at one minute past.'

He stopped suddenly, a shadow passing across his face as if trying to catch a memory that danced away before he could grasp it.

She had seen that look as he tried to answer the Wessons but their questions had brought no response. The man's memory was a blank from before being found half dead by the Aborigines. But his speech marked him as English, did it also mark him a convict?

'Obed should be back soon.' He glanced at the patches of sky visible among the overhead branches not telling her the man had been gone so long already it was causing him concern. The fellow was no longer young . . . a fall or an attack by a wild animal . . .

The crack of dead twigs underfoot ending the

thought he breathed a sigh of relief as Obed emerged from the trees but as quickly it became a gasp as he saw the man's hands were fastened at his back.

'Stay you there if you know what's good for you.' Behind Obed the sergeant raised his rifle as the other two dropped the kangaroo they carried slung beneath a pole.

'Mr Wesson!' The cry ringing around the tiny clearing, Tamar was on her feet, but before she reached Obed she was caught. One arm about her middle his other hand in her hair dragging her head backward on to his chest the soldier grinned.

'Well well! I've catched myself a prize, and one that be neither old nor so frail; you be going to give old Cobbler a good time.'

'Set her down.'

'What, so you gets to 'ave fust go? Not bloody likely, them stripes 'ave no say in this, Cobbler be fust to take a taste and you waits 'til he be finished same as Turley be 'aving to wait . . . and that might be some time.' Swinging Tamar about he fastened a hand in the neck of her blouse snatching it free of the buttons, then hooking one foot behind her ankle sent her sprawling on her back.

The soldier already unbuckling his cross-belts Obed thought quickly. Turning to the sergeant he spoke softly.

'That girl be Tamar Hallam . . .'

Excitement mounting in his blood the man Turley urged his companion on. His breathing becoming more rapid he knelt behind Tamar pinning both arms behind her head grinning as the other man threw aside his heavy leather belt, dropping his trousers to his ankles.

'. . . Tamar Hallam be the wench Colonel Forbes placed in that cage . . .'

He had caught the sergeant's attention but not so much the man did not see the thin figure make for the two men. Lifting the rifle butt he brought it crashing against the grey head sending the man senseless to the ground. Sickness lurching inside him at the sound of that body hitting the floor, a stronger fear curling his innards at Tamar's screams Obed did his best to remain calm.

'. . . the wench Forbes had a liking for. There'll be more than a feather for your caps if you returns her to Geelong used. There'll be an invitation to a party and you three will be guests of honour, so much so you will still be there when everybody else be gone, you'll be hanging from a gibbet, for Henry Forbes don't be a man who likes a prize snatched from beneath his nose.'

Seeing the interest on the man's face Obed pressed his point.

'Oh, you can use her, take your pleasure then slit her throat, slit all our throats. But when the thirst be slaked what be you left with? Take her to Forbes as you found her and tomorrow you'll be a sergeant-major and you can still ease your loins once he be finished with her.'

The wench in the cage. Forbes must have wanted her bad the furore he raised when he found her gone;

no man dared look at him for a week. Sergeant-major. He fingered the rifle. The old man was right; this was a chance for him to have his cake and eat it as well.

A few yards in front one man held the girl's arms the other, his bare flesh white in the shaded light, knelt between her spread legs.

'Go on Cobbler, shove it up her!'

'I wouldn't be doing that if I was you Cobbler, it be bad for you.'

'But bloody good for you, eh! Leave fust pickings for you . . . well you can kiss my arse, Sergeant!'

Lowering the rifle until the point of the bayonet touched the bare flesh the sergeant's smile was lethal. 'Oh, I'll do more than that, Cobbler, I won't tell you what but in two seconds this bayonet is going so far up it'll cut your throat from the inside!'

A jab from the blade sending him rolling from Tamar the sergeant glared at Turley.

'Let her up!' he growled. 'Give her a minute to tidy herself and then tie her hands. And you,' he stared at the furious face of Cobbler, 'get yourself into your trousers, then tie that one up as well. We don't want no rock on the back of the 'ead while walking to Geelong.'

Drawing in a long breath of air Obed sank to the ground. The girl was safe . . . at least for now.

'You reckon he meant it, that he would come back?'

Spooning meat and potatoes on to a plate, Millie Cooper nodded. 'That one be fair struck. He said he would be back and it be my guess you can count that be just what he'll do.'

Taking up knife and fork George popped a potato into his mouth, chewing it thoughtfully.

'Seemed like he meant it well enough but England be a far off from Geelong, it ain't like making a two-mile trip to the next village.'

Taking her own seat Millie glanced across the table.

'I knows how far away England be, George Cooper, I remembers that journey too well not to know. I also know that there Captain Burford be in love with Tamar Hallam and from the look that crossed his face when he heard her had been put in that cage, then I say distance or no distance God help Henry Forbes when he do.'

'If God do help Henry Forbes on that day then it will be the last day I offers prayer to heaven!'

Jabbing another potato on his fork George lifted it to his mouth holding it short of his tongue as the cry rang from outside.

'George . . . George . . . get you out here!'

Casting a questioning glance at his wife George Cooper set down his knife and fork signing for her to be still as he rose from the table.

'Be it the soldiers?'

Millie's frightened eyes met his, the cutlery slipping from suddenly shaking hands.

'That be no soldiers.' George shook his head. 'They don't call a man out they breaks his door down then drags him out. Stay there . . .' he cautioned her again '. . . I'll see what it be about.'

'Where you be, I be!' Slipping from her seat Millie moved to his side but George thrust her behind his back as he opened the door.

'Take a look at this.' Beyond the step a neighbour beckoned. 'Don't that be Obadiah Wesson? And the wench, ain't it the same one struck that Bancroft bloke with a whip? The same one Henry Forbes set in that cage?'

'Tamar?' Edging her husband aside, Millie darted into the open, her eyes opening wide as she saw the draggle of bodies walking towards the prison gates.

'Is it her?' She looked quickly at George, his sight had always been a shade keener than her own.

Shading his eyes from the setting sun be peered at the figures preceding the soldiers carrying the dead kangaroo and the sergeant bringing up the rear.

The skirts could be those of any woman but the hair could belong to only one as he knew. Glowing like rich Burgundy it flowed dark red about her shoulders.

'Yes.' He nodded. 'That be Tamar.'

'And the man?'

Screwing his eyes against the brilliant crimson of the sky he waited a moment, wanting to be sure of his answer.

'That be Obadiah Wesson,' he said lowering his hand, 'but the other one? I ain't never seen him afore.'

'But they be tied . . . their hands be tied, don't they?'

'Hush, woman.' George turned to his wife. 'We don't want no soldiers coming down on us.'

'Millie be right though George, they do be tied. Why be that you reckon?'

'Tamar Hallam made a break from that cage so it be likely her would be tied if recaptured, but Obadiah?' He glanced again at the small cavalcade. 'Why he be shackled I don't know nor the man with him, unless he be a convict.'

'Ain't none gone missing from 'ere.' The man who had called them from the house scratched a finger beneath his hat. 'And there be no other penal settlement I knows to be within walking distance, so where do you think that one be sprung from?'

'There can be no telling.' George Cooper answered quietly. 'Same as there can be no telling what be in store for that wench now her be back with Henry Forbes.'

Chapter Thirty-Four

'Why has he brought we 'ere?'

Millie Cooper stared with frightened eyes around a room dominated by the large desk set with silver inkstand.

'Can't be for no good, you knows the ways of Henry Forbes same as me; it be revenge he be after, revenge for our helpin' that wench. We be set for another spell in his gaol, all that needs to be said is 'ow long.'

'No, that ain't all as needs to be said.' Millie slipped her hand into that of her husband. 'I needs to say I love you George Cooper, the five years I've 'ad with you 'ave been the best of my whole life and if it is we ain't to be together no more, then I thank you now for all you've bin to me.'

Holding her close, George Cooper's eyes misted with love and hate. Hate for Henry Forbes and what he had done, what he was still doing to them.

They had watched those soldiers take their prisoners into the prison compound and an hour later had come the sound of a rifle butt to their door. They were wanted up at the Lodge. His arms tightening protectively around his wife George Cooper's teeth clamped hard together. Forbes would not have them put straight into cells, he had to torment them first . . . well, so sure the swine put a finger on Millie he would kill him and to hell with what the authorities could do after that!

Pressed close against him, Millie shuddered as the door behind them opened. Her fingers clutching tight at his jacket George kissed the top of her head. This could be the last time he would ever hold his wife. Resting his lips against her greying hair, he whispered, 'I love you, Millie, there ain't been a day since we wed that I ain't thanked God for love of you.'

'George and Millie Cooper . . .'

Her face hidden against her husband's chest Millie's eyes flew open. It had to be gone through and she wouldn't add to George's suffering by showing her own. Her hand seeking his, their fingers twined together, she turned to face the desk.

'. . . Good evening. My name is Paul Tern. I am the new Governor of Geelong.'

Already heavy with fear of what lay in store for Millie rather than himself, George's mind refused the words.

'Henry Forbes . . . he sent . . . he wanted we brought here.'

'No, Mr Cooper, it was I asked you be brought here and I must apologise for disturbing you at this hour.'

Apologise! Millie's faded glance lifted to the finely wrought features edged by neatly clipped sideburns, the eyes regarding her clear and blue. What game was this, what had Forbes dreamed up?

His voice shaky despite the self promise not to display the play of his nerves in front of Millie, George answered.

'If it be all the same to you, sir, it be Henry Forbes wanting Millie and me, 'twere his soldiers hammered on our door and it be best not to keep 'im waiting.'

'Colonel Forbes will not be seeing you.' Paul Tern signed for them to sit then took his own chair. 'The colonel has been relieved of his post and is to return to England. I am to take over the Governership of Geelong settlement and the penal institution.'

'Thank God!' Millie sank to her chair.

His face showing no indication he had heard the whisper Paul Tern went on. 'Mr Cooper, do you know a man by the name of Obadiah Wesson?'

This man could be no worse than Forbes and though first meetings were rarely anything to go on somehow he had the feeling this one would be no Henry Forbes. Relief adding to the tremble in his voice George replied, the other man listening as he gave a full account of the Wessons.

'So you would call Obadiah Wesson an honest man?'

'There be none more so, sir.'

'So it seems . . . so it seems.' Silvered hair catching the light of twin oil lamps set atop the empty fireplace, Paul Tern nodded. 'What you have said complies perfectly with his own account.'

'Do . . . do Obed be being sent down?' Millie's lip

quivered. 'Oh Lord, that'll see Esther under the sod.'

'No one will die of grief, Mrs Cooper.' Tern smiled. 'And Mr Wesson is not to be sent down as you put it, he is to be sent home and his son with him.'

A gasp breaking from her Millie made no move to wipe away the tears trickling down her cheeks, as he continued to ask next about Tamar.

As before, he listened in silence only nodding now and again but his lips tightened as George told of the whipping of the black boy and Tamar's imprisonment in the cage.

'You are no doubt aware the girl has been returned here to the prison?' he asked, when the explanation finished.

'We seen the soldiers bring 'er in, sir.'

Tern nodded again, noting the simple honesty of the couple sat before him. They had made to attempt to lie, simply stating what they knew with no varnishing of the truth.

'Mrs Cooper,' he turned to Millie, 'that girl has been through a terrible ordeal . . .'

Eyes widening with concern, Millie burst in. 'Her ain't been . . . ?'

'No, let us say those men did not go through with their intention.' Seeing the woman relax he went on. 'However, I feel she needs the comfort of a woman but not the discomfort of a prison cell and as there is no Mrs Tern at the Lodge, would you have her to stay with you until other arrangements can be made?'

Surprise trapping her tongue Millie needed a shove

from her husband before she could answer, then smiled. 'Ar sir, Tamar can come to George and me, we'll take her and gladly.'

'Tell me,' he said, as Millie beamed at George, 'do you know anything of the man brought in with them?'

George Cooper shook his head. 'We couldn't see his face from where we stood so I can't be saying definite, but what I did see of him rung no bell, though I would count myself on the winning side sir, were I to bet the man be a stranger to Geelong.'

The same quiet nod his answer, Paul Tern regarded his hands resting on the desk. Away to his left a clock ticked quietly.

'You have been first prisoners here and now settlers.' He looked up. 'In that time have you seen prisoners return after attempting to escape, after they have spent time in the bush?'

The question put he watched the other man closely but there was no hesitation, no few moments of working on an answer, it came instantly.

'Ar sir, I've seen men that 'ave spent a few days in the bush . . .'

'A few days?'

George understood the question behind the question and nodded. 'A few days be all it takes to drive a man mad from thirst.'

'But Obadiah Wesson did not die from thirst!'

'No, sir, he didn't. But then you see Obadiah tells he had help from the Abboes and Obadiah ain't a man to lie.'

Tapping his fingers against the desk Paul Tern watched them a moment then looked up.

'The man brought here earlier would benefit from careful nursing, that I cannot as yet guarantee will be given in the prison. It seems an infirmary was thought an unnecessary addition to a penitentiary.'

'Is he a convict, sir?' Millie leaned forward.

'I cannot say at this time . . . the man appears to have lost his memory.'

Her former fears gone Millie spoke quickly. 'If the man be weak as you say, sir, then he ain't likely to do no moonlight flit, so if you agrees I will nurse him.'

This was what he had expected. Hiding the smile behind calm eyes the new governor appeared to weigh his thoughts.

'Is your house large enough to house two more people?'

'No, sir, it ain't.' Millie smiled. 'But the 'ouse Tamar rented for to sell 'er frocks be empty. That man would be alright lodged there and during the day me and Tamar would take turns in the caring of him.'

'Then you have the caring of them both.'

Touching a small silver bell, Paul Tern smiled as the door opened and Millie flung herself at the girl who came in.

'He said he would return, come back just to search for me?'

Millie glanced at the pretty face still drawn despite her care, the fear of what had happened still plain in her eyes. It had been a week since both her and the stranger had been given over to them, a week since that new governor had taken over and already the entire settlement had taken on a new air. Folk went about their business with heads raised and even them still serving time seemed less downtrodden.

'Ar, wench, he said that and what's more he meant it. Believe Millie Cooper when her tells you Nathan Burford be a man to keep his word. He'll be back afore a twelve month be passed and meantime he said to give you this, that it would tell you summat you already knowed but to give it you anyway.'

Taking the newspaper from a drawer Millie handed it to Tamar. ' 'Twere a blessing his name cropped up or I might have forgot that paper for good it being of no use to George or me for most words in it we can't read.'

Why had Captain Burford left her a newspaper . . . and why had he come to Australia when he said it was one route he would never sail? Cheeks colouring Tamar looked down at the newspaper. Was it true what Millie said, had he really come only to search for her?

Turning the page her fingers shook as she read the report of the royal visit to the opera. The princess was wearing the Alexandra Stone!

Eyes glistening with tears she looked at the smiling Millie.

'Ar, wench,' the woman nodded, 'it be like it says and though it makes no mention of your brother's name or of that robbery it be my guess that when recovering that necklace the true culprit was also found.'

'Then Benjie . . . he could be set free.'

'Mebbe he already has.' Removing the clay pipe from his mouth George looked at the two women. 'I wasn't going to tell you this not until Tamar was set to go looking for 'im.'

'Tell what?' Millie rounded on her husband her brows already drawn together in accusation. 'What you be 'iding, George Cooper?'

Taking another pull at the pipe he blew a stream of smoke slowly into the air until Millie stamped her foot in irritation.

'A sailor on the packet, he told me.'

'Told you what?' Millie's voice rose.

'Told me a lad of fourteen or so, of slight build and with hair matching the colour of Tamar's was seen on a ship that put out from a place called Whyalla few days since and that the ship was bound for England.'

'Benjie,' Tamar whispered, 'he's going home.'

'Steady on, wench.' George cautioned. 'There were no name given and nothing said of the lad at all save what I've told you. Could be he ain't your brother . . .'

'The lad has hair the colour of Tamar's!' Millie answered sharply as if that were the only proof needed.

'So that sailor said, but them two don't be the only folk with red hair . . .'

'So how many more 'ave you seen?'

Laying aside his pipe George answered patiently,

knowing Millie's asperity to be no more than a wish for the lad's freedom and his sister's quietness of mind.

'Millie love, I don't be saying it ain't the lad, but you must own there has to be others filling such a description, after all we sees only them as be sent to Geelong. How many more such colonies must be set up in this country? All I means is for Tamar not to set her 'opes too high.'

. . . not to set her hopes too high.

Lying on the skins set out for her in the corner of the Cooper's tiny living room, Tamar hugged the newspaper to her chest. They had talked long after those words had been spoken, talked of the fact there must have been an enquiry into the stealing of the necklace and that enquiry had surely found her brother was not the guilty party, that he had had no part in that robbery.

That meant he must be freed, brought back to England. It had to be him that sailor had seen. Happy as that had made her, lying now looking at the window-framed patch of moonlight she felt her heart twist. She still could not be with him and if Nathan Burford did not keep his promise then she would never be with Benjie again for there was no way of earning the money passage to England would require.

Would that captain keep the word he had given to Millie? Behind her closed lids a pair of ice grey eyes stared back at her telling her nothing.

Carrying a cloth-wrapped basin filled with soup, Millie saw the flinch and the shudder of the girl beside her as a uniformed soldier walked towards them. The nightmares still came and there were nights she sat with the trembling girl, rocking her in her arms. The terrors would fade with time but even time would not erase them completely.

'John be gathering strength daily.' She used the name she and Tamar had chosen to call the man Obadiah Wesson had brought from the hills but the girl's eyes were fastened on the approaching soldier, a gasp breaking from her as he stopped directly in their path.

'Tamar Hallam, you be wanted at the Lodge.'

The soup spilling into the cloth Millie supported the slight figure that slumped against her. Finding the courage to speak she stared defiantly at the soldier.

'What be her wanted for?'

The man shrugged. 'The governor ain't told me that. All I knows is I was told to bring the wench to the Lodge.'

'It were Governor Tern told you?'

'Not direct, it was the batman, but you can count it the governor's direct word, won't nobody go against him. He be a different man to Henry Forbes but his word be just as strict.' Glancing at Tamar's face that had grown even paler he added kindly. 'I don't think you need to fear the governor miss and you'll come to no harm from that compound not while I be the man beside you.'

'Go along, wench.' Millie tried to hide the worry niggling inside her. 'I'll take the soup to John then I'll come wait for you at the gate.'

He had been so kind to her that evening she had been taken to the Lodge, so kind . . . so kind . . .

Fingers curled into a ball as she followed behind the soldier Tamar repeated the words in her mind willing this meeting to be the same but behind the words the cold shock of fear lingered.

Met by the batman who had tried to give her water she could not answer his smile or thank him for his reassurance as he showed her to the study.

Millie would be at the gate. Breath trembling into her lungs she moved towards the desk. But would she be allowed to leave this house?

Forbes had put her in a cage. Christ, he should have throttled the bastard!

The staccato ring of the second dog watch wafted over dawn washed waters while softly spoken words of men changing shift whispered quietly on the cool air. But none of it registered, just as the hours he had stood staring back across the silence of the ocean had not registered.

What if she should fall into his hands again . . . what if Forbes should . . . ? Nathan Burford's hands gripped tight to the ship's rail. He should have stayed, stayed in that settlement. Sent the *Verity* home with Tom Brooks. He could handle her as well as himself.

But it was too late for that now. A rogue breeze catching the spray, tossed cold droplets into his face but he made no move to wipe them away.

'You should get some rest, you've been here since the first dog watch.'

'I couldn't sleep, Tom.'

'You don't try.' Tom Brooks glanced at the man who had stood beside the rail since before midnight and now it was past four.

'I should have stayed, Tom. I did the wrong thing in leaving.'

'You did what you saw as right for the crew. That be what every ship's captain should do. You put their need before your own and that be as it should, you know that and so do I. Harbouring regret whether it be for what be right or for what be wrong never bought a man a new shirt.'

Regret would not bring him any good. Nathan stared at the dark waters emerging from the mists of dawn. But it could not be turned off like a tap.

Folding his arms along the rail Tom Brooks too stared at the dark sea jewelled with the first pearl light of morning. He knew the torment his friend was going through, knew the bitterness and futility of regret. He had followed the path Nathan Burford was treading. He had left a girl behind letting the call of the sea blind him to what he did not wish to see. That her need was greater than his. He had returned a year later to find her dead and buried, hounded to death by a father who could not face the disgrace of having a daughter bear a child out of wedlock. Since that day regret had been a constant companion, never far from his shoulder. God keep that same punishment from Nathan.

'It don't be too late,' he said, the spectres of yesterday still dancing in his mind. 'The *Verity* can be turned around in a matter of days and on her way back to Australia. You will find her Nathan, you'll find the girl.'

Would he? Nathan Burford breathed long and slow. Twice he had betrayed his own word . . . once to find Aiden and once to help Tamar Hallam.

'. . . *you will have betrayed me twice . . .*'

The words he had so often been told were spoken by the Lord and His last supper echoed in his brain.

Like that disciple he had broken his word. He too had the Judas touch.

'What did he want?'

Catching Tamar's arm Millie drew her quickly away from the Lodge.

'He . . . he wants to send me home.'

'What!' Millie stood stock still, mouth and eyes wide open with astonishment.

'It's true.' Her pale face smiling for the first time in days Tamar nodded. 'He wants to send me home to England.'

'Eh, wench!' Millie heaved a long sigh. 'That be good news.'

Returning the woman's delighted hug Tamar grabbed her hand pulling her towards the house occupied by the man Obed had rescued.

'That isn't all, he is having John sent back at the same time.'

Her own smile lighting her lined face Millie let herself be drawn along. Minutes later, sat beside the bed he lay in, she saw the tiny frowns chase across his forehead as he listened to Tamar. Memory had not returned to him and watching him now she wondered if it ever would.

'He said the colonel must come before something called a court martial and because of his treatment of me I would have to speak, that was why he must send me back.'

'He wants you to testify . . . to give evidence against Forbes . . . but is that wise? If the man should be found not guilty . . .'

'Mr Tern said that was not likely to happen, not with the son-in-law of the Foreign Secretary also attesting to his cruelty . . .'

'That one!' Millie interjected. 'He be no more to be trusted than a wounded dingo! You should 'ave told the governor you won't go.'

Glancing at Millie, Tamar shook her head. 'He said the authorities would demand my return, that the talk of Henry Forbes' treatment of settlers and prisoner by seamen and others returning to England could no longer be ignored.'

'But why should he send me also, for all he knows I could be an escaped convict.'

'It seems he talked to Obadiah Wesson and to my George about that and they both answered the same. Going on what they had seen of men come out of the bush you had not been there just a few days. You must 'ave been in the outback for many months. Given that time any report of missing convicts would 'ave reached Geelong but there ain't been any, so you see you ain't no convict.'

Confusion still darkening hazel eyes, he shook his head. 'But I might not be English.'

'What does that matter?' Millie asked sharply. 'What matters is the wench will be on her own against Henry Forbes, there should be somebody to watch out for her and that can't be me nor George but it can be you . . .'

'No, Millie.' Tamar smiled at the woman knowing she wanted only to protect her. 'John has done enough for me already, he could have got himself killed trying to prevent . . .'

'Ar, trying to prevent!' Millie was sharp as before. 'We all knows what he were trying to prevent and that the same thing can 'appen again to a young wench travelling alone.'

'Millie, please . . .'

'Millie is right, you should not be left to travel alone.'

His hand closing over hers, Tamar felt a sudden calming of her nerves. He had had this effect on her from the very first, an indefinable something . . . a feeling that with this man she was safe, but more than safe . . . she was happy.

Embarrassed by her own thoughts she dropped her glance, her voice a little unsteady as she answered.

'I must go, John. I have to take the chance it was my brother seen aboard that ship but I would not ask you to go with me.'

Raising the hand he still held he pressed it to his lips. 'You do not need to ask, Tamar.' He smiled over her fingertips, his eyes deep and warm. 'I could not refuse . . . I could never refuse you anything.'

Chapter Thirty-Five

'I would offer you a penny for those thoughts, if I had a penny.'

Tamar smiled at the man standing beside her. He looked fitter and stronger, the voyage to England was working wonders for his health, but his memory . . .

'I was remembering the last time I was in this port.' She smiled up at him. 'Mrs Bancroft and I went ashore and while we were there the most wonderful cavalcade went past and the emir spoke to us.'

'And what did the emir say?'

The teasing note bringing a blush to her cheeks she glanced away to the busy scene of the dock, the blush deepening as the words she had heard that day came quietly back.

'. . . *two such beautiful ladies* . . .'

Smiling at the colour flooding her face he touched a hand to her chin, tilting it upward.

'Tell the truth Tamar, what did that emir say?'

'He said it was the beauty of a man's soul pleases Allah, not the beauty of his robe.'

'And . . . ?'

'He would thank Allah for bringing two such . . . such beautiful ladies to his country.'

His hand staying for a moment beneath her chin, his deeply hazel eyes seemed to search the limits of her soul.

'I too thank God for bringing you to me, you are beautiful Tamar, very beautiful; as that memory is beautiful.'

'Yours will return John, you will remember everything. It just needs time.'

'Time!' The look in his eyes changing to one of yearning, long since becoming hopelessness, he turned his face towards the dock. 'Who knows how much time I have had already?'

The sadness of it twisting her heart Tamar touched a hand to his arm. 'It will come John, I'm sure of it.'

'Sometimes I feel so close, as if there is something there in the emptiness and that all I have to do is take it, but each time I reach out it slips away and there I am again, alone in a darkness that never lifts.'

Her answer threaded on a string of tears, Tamar answered softly. 'You are not alone John, I won't ever let you be alone.'

'Quite the touching little scene.'

The hated voice touching her like ice, Tamar turned.

'The nights must be quite something . . . are they spent in your cabin or his?'

He must have been watching them, seen John leave her and go below.

'Please . . . go away. I have no wish . . .'

'Do I have to tell you again . . .' his heavy jowled face perspiring with the heat, Henry Forbes laughed sneeringly '. . . it isn't what you wish but what *I* wish.'

'We are not supposed to be on deck at the same time, the captain . . .'

'But the captain isn't here, and neither is your lover.'

'John is not my lover!'

'Then John is a fool. Once we are back in England you will not find me wasting such an opportunity.'

Out of nowhere his hand seemed to touch her body, to stroke her flesh making it crawl now, as it had crawled before and with it came a sickness that filled her throat.

Half sobbing, she turned from him, going quickly to the opposite side of the ship.

'P'raps it don't be just that mindless fool you pleasures, p'raps the captain gets his share too. Is that why he lets you up on the deck any time you please while Henry Forbes is kept below? But mark this, I won't always be aboard this boat . . . and neither will you!'

Drawing a deep breath, forcing herself to look at his leering face, Tamar stepped to one side but he was quicker. A podgy hand grabbing her arm, swinging her hard against the ship's side. He smiled, an evil threatening smile.

'You think that hearing will condemn me, then you think wrong.'

Fear racing cold along her veins Tamar glanced about the deck but it was empty of sailors, they must all be ashore helping to take on fresh supplies. Defiance her only defence, she shook the hand from her arm, her eyes cold with dislike and disgust.

'Colonel Forbes. When Mr Tern said I would be called upon to speak against you I had doubt that I could do so. I wanted no part in sending a man to prison, no matter the harm he had done me. Now that doubt is gone. I will be glad to tell it all, not only what you did to me but what you did to the Wessons; how you stood by and watched their son beaten to death and how you keep the other son in prison for no reason at all. Yes Colonel Forbes, I will be very glad to speak against you!'

Rage screwing his eyes even smaller, despite the smile that curved his flabby mouth, Henry Forbes laughed softly.

'You have to get to England before you can do that, my dear.'

A forearm whipping across her throat, the other slipping instantly beneath her thighs, he tipped her over the side watching the dark waters snatch hungrily at her body, dragging it deep.

'My bed or that one.' He smiled. 'It makes no difference to Henry Forbes.'

'It was like some horrible nightmare, if John had not come back on deck when he did . . .'

'It's all over now Tamar, you have to try to forget it.' Amy Granger looked at the girl sat in her tiny back room, her hands shaking like leaves. 'That swine Forbes won't be bothering you no more, not from where he is.'

No, he would not be bothering her again, but the

memory of him might never leave her, as the cry John had given would never leave her. She had heard it as she sank beneath the waters but it was only days later she knew the cause.

He had come on deck as she had screamed, seen what Forbes had done and rushed to help her. Forbes had grabbed him and in the struggle they had both fallen backward over the rail. There had been insufficient time to save them both, the heavy boots and uniform Forbes had refused to give up had quickly dragged him under. He was already dead when John dived overboard a second time.

'So now there'll be no trial?' Amy's husband tapped a clay pipe against the chimney breast.

Tamar shook her head. 'No accused, no trial, was what the captain told us. He said he would be submitting a report of an accident at sea, that then would be the end of it.'

'So this man who saved you, he won't be charged with Forbes' death?'

'Will Granger, do you have to be so blunt!' Amy glared disparagingly.

'The captain said if John had not accidentally knocked Forbes overboard then he might have done so and quite deliberately.'

'Good for him.' Will Granger nodded. 'The man showed a deal of sense. Even so it was lucky for your friend a sailor came aboard and saw the whole thing.'

Turning to the teapot that had already been filled and emptied twice, Amy hid the thought that plagued her. Would the Justices think the same should this

John fellow be hauled in front of them? From the way Tamar had spoken of him, the tenderness in her voice mebbe she wouldn't be able to face more heartbreak.

'So where is this John, when do we get to meet him?'

Forcing a smile to her lips she set the freshly brewed pot on the table.

'That's just it, I don't know where he is. He became more and more withdrawn as we neared England. I would see this dreadful haunted look in his eyes and the terrible pain on his face. It was as if he didn't want to come to this country, as though something horrible was waiting for him here. Oh Amy . . . I never should have let him come!'

'The decision were his own to take,' Amy answered firmly. 'And if there is something will stir his memory then I say it will be a good thing; even bad memories must be better to live with than emptiness and doubt.'

Perhaps Amy was right. Tamar accepted the cup, staring into its milky depths. But where was he, why had he disappeared the moment the ship had berthed in Bristol?

'Did them folk in Australia say the name of the boat they thought your brother to be sailing on?'

Glancing across at him, Amy sighed with exasperation. Changing the subject were all well and good but did men always have to be so clumsy.

Resting her cup in its saucer as Tamar shook her head she said gently. 'That boat must be calling in at several ports; it'll make Bristol in a few days.'

'No, no it won't. If Benjie had been coming he would have been here by now. I have to face it Amy, the boy that sailor on the packet spoke of could not have been my brother. I have to go back.'

'You can't!'

'I have to Amy, I promised.'

'But how will you get there?'

'I don't know, but there will be a way . . .'

'Maybe Nathan Burford . . .'

'No.' Tamar set her cup aside. 'I cannot put that man to such a trouble, he owes me nothing. He attempted to help once and that is more than enough. If he should call here again please tell him what I have said and that I do not wish him to come to Australia.'

There was no way the man would accept that. Amy thought back to the day he had come into the shop, the look on his face as she had asked after Tamar. Nothing would hold him from following after her.

'Well, at least wait for him . . .'

'No.' Tamar stood up. 'I have to go now. Thank you both for giving me a place to stay.'

'You'll come back after you've been to Hockley?'

Her arms about her friend, Tamar smiled. 'Where else will I find a woman to turn me into a lady's maid?'

Huddled in the coat Amy had insisted she take, Tamar stared over fields and hedges white with winter frost. She had often heard Vinny say that given time a wheel comes full circle and hers surely had. She had first come to Bristol in a narrowboat with sixpence only to her name. Now, more than a year later, she was returning to Birmingham the same way.

They had been reluctant to take her. She glanced at the bargee's wife emptying a bowl of water into the canal, her thinness masked by layers of clothes caught around her middle with a length of string. She had told them of her return from Australia, saying only she was there in search of a brother but it was clear the woman and her husband had not believed her, only thieves and murderers went to the colonies. But her sixpence had swayed them. It would pay for her ride and one meal a day, they could afford no more.

She wanted no more. Tamar huddled deeper into the coat, the cold keen against a skin grown used to a semi-tropical heat. She wanted only to see her friends in Hockley then she would find a way to return to Australia.

Thrust deep in the pocket of her coat her fingers closed over the pretty, coloured pebbles Esther Wesson had given her. Millie had smiled on seeing them. Gazing at the silent shrouded landscape, Millie's words circled in her mind.

'. . . you won't need no pebbles to remember nor will you ever be truly alone. You carry friends with you in your heart same as this country will always be in your heart. I prays you finds your brother wench, but should it be the Lord don't allow that then ask him to return you to the friends that wait 'ere. You won't be turned away.'

They had both cried then, caught in each other's arms, they had sobbed and George had suddenly developed an acute sniffle.

'. . . you won't be turned away . . .'

Of that she was sure, but first she must find a way to

return. Amy had tried to persuade her to wait for Nathan Burford. But the ship had re-victualled and next morning the *Verity* had gone without his returning to the chandler's shop. He had sailed without saying where and Will Granger knew only that those supplies taken aboard would not last a voyage to the other side of the world.

Chiding herself for the prick of disappointment she blinked away the moisture whitening along her lashes. The man had a life to lead, he could not be expected to waste it chasing after someone else's problems. From now on she must not think of him.

Turning at the bargee's call she went below to stand at the front of the boat.

She must not think of him! But how did she stop her dreams?

'Gas Street Basin be not far past the next bend but if it be 'Ockley you wants then you'd do better set down 'ere for that place lies just yonder.'

One hand to the bridle of the horse towing the barge he pointed to where a church spire touched the grey sky.

Calling her thanks to them both Tamar jumped down on to the towpath. The hardness of frozen ground biting through the worn-out soles of her boots she set off across the heath the spectres of those last days in Hockley dancing at her side.

He had to come, to see his home once more.

Emotion thick in his throat Nathan Burford brushed aside the surprised welcome of his housekeeper, quick strides carrying him up the wide staircase to his own room.

He had enquired in every port they had dropped anchor but no one had seen or heard of the girl until Geelong. He sank to the bed, sitting with his head in his hands. The feeling as the Coopers had said they knew her had been one of elation but it had not lasted long. She was no longer at that settlement and they had no idea where she was, like some elusive will-o'-the-wisp she had vanished into the night; he had lost her as he had lost his brother. The years of searching had brought no word of Aiden or of Louise, would the rest of his years be spent the same way, searching for a girl he would never find?

He had thought his feelings due to his need to repay in some form the wrong he had done, that by helping the girl his own debt could be repaid. Then as thoughts and dreams of her persisted he had put them down to infatuation, a passing fancy for a pretty face.

But it had not been infatuation or fancy. The girl had haunted him, catching him every moment he was unaware. Smiling at him in his sleep, her gentle eyes gleaming like fresh grown meadow grass, her hair peeping out beneath a ragged shawl. They were dreams that told him he was in love with Tamar Hallam, dreams he had still. Only now he knew the truth of them. But that truth had come too late.

Along the landing, the sound of objects being moved drifted in to him. Damn that blasted housekeeper, did she have to clean now, couldn't she wait until he was gone!

Pushing angrily to his feet he crossed to the window, looking out over the well-tended garden, covered now in veils of white frost.

Would Tamar Hallam have loved these gardens as his mother had, loved the heady perfume of full blown roses, the regal beauty of the lilies? Somehow he felt she would. And would she have enjoyed hearing the laughter of children at play in them as he and Aiden had played?

His gaze reaching out into the distance he watched the mist-like figures of two young boys fall laughing to the ground, rolling together after some pretend sword fight.

Damn that woman!

The clink of china snatching him back he strode from the room.

He would tell her now the house was to be sold, pay them all a year's wages and have them out of this house in an hour!

Halfway along the landing he paused. The sounds were coming from his mother's room, well he could tell the woman there as easily as he could anywhere else.

His tread though firm and decisive was swallowed by thick Turkish carpet, so he came to the open door without a sound. Already half inside he stopped as if met by a hammer blow to the stomach.

It was not his housekeeper. It was a man, a man who held a small silver-framed photograph in his hand. Surprise holding him silent, Nathan watched as he slipped the frame into his pocket.

The man was a thief!

Years of wanting, of longing for his home and his brother, years of frustration and dying hope suddenly turned into a swamping wave of bitterness that screamed for revenge. Hands curling into balls of steel he stared at the man's back.

'You bloody thief!' he grated. 'I'm going to break your bloody back!'

Launching himself across the room he grabbed the man's jacket spinning him around. A red haze of rage clouding his senses he raised a fist but before it smashed into the startled face he paused. He was looking at a ghost . . . the same ghost of a child he had watched a moment ago rolling in a summer garden.

'Oh, God!' he breathed raggedly. 'Oh, God . . . Oh, God!'

Looking into a pair of slowly awakening hazel eyes, his own shamelessly spilling tears, he breathed again, a long juddering sob-wracked breath.

'Aiden! Oh, my God . . . Aiden!'

Chapter Thirty-Six

Nothing had changed. Tamar glanced at the narrow high-storied dingy houses bordering the busy streets of the Gold Quarter. Walking quickly along Newhall Street she made her way towards her home, averting her eyes as she passed the Temple of Relief.

No one would be there. Her steps slowing she came to the entry that gave access to the houses grouped together about a tiny yard. Vinny would be at work as would all the others.

The daylight was already as good as gone but the recent chime of the clock of St Paul's Church striking six meant there were two more hours yet to go before Vinny Marsh would be home, but Isaac Cohen worked from his own house.

It took only a matter of minutes to walk along Frederick Street and from there into Regent Place but at the door to the old man's home she halted shyly. He had welcomed her and Benjie so often into his home but would he welcome her now?

'. . . *friends be carried with you in your heart . . .*'

These had been Millie Cooper's last words to her, but would Isaac Cohen still reckon her a friend?

Her hand trembling, she pushed open the door,

hesitating as voices floated out into the dim little scullery. Isaac had a guest, she should leave. Turning quickly her coat caught against a metal bucket sending it tumbling with a clatter.

'It . . . it's only me, Mr Cohen.'

Righting the bucket she looked up at the tall figure staring at her.

'Tamar?' It was a question whispered in disbelief yet carried on the wings of hope.

'Tamar!'

The whisper came again but this time it was buried in her hair as Nathan Burford folded her in his arms.

Behind them the old Jew smiled as he went back to his work bench. The reason for that sea captain coming to Hockley had been to ask after young Benjie Hallam. He had said Tamar was still in Australia. Taking up his jeweller's glass he bent over a stone . . . questions could wait.

'I'm sorry.' Nathan's face clouded as eventually he released her. 'I should not have grabbed you like that, forgive me please, I was just so relieved to see you.'

This was the man she had thought about so often, the one she had not admitted meant so much to her when James Allen had asked her to marry him; and those moments of being in his arms, of feeling the touch of him hard and close against her had been moments she had dreamed of.

Ashamed of her own thoughts, Tamar turned away. 'Amy and Millie Cooper both told me of what you said to them but really Captain Burford you should not hold yourself responsible, you gave me no promise and even if you had I would not hold you to it.'

'It was no promise.' He caught her arm turning her until he could look into her face. 'I told myself that because at first I could not recognise the truth. Yes, I went to Australia only to search for you, and once my business in Hockley was finished, I intended to go there again. I intended to stay in that country until I found you. I love you Tamar, and finding you here I . . . I don't think I can carry on without you.'

Giving herself the sweetness of his kiss, Tamar knew he would never have to. This was what her dreams had been made of, being in the arms of the man she loved and of finding her brother.

But she had not found Benjie, and would Nathan still wish to return to Australia to look for him?

Sat in Isaac Cohen's living room Tamar related the happenings since first leaving Hockley, finishing with the same question.

'My wife's concerns will always be my concern.' He smiled. 'We shall search for your brother until we can bring him home, just as you brought my brother home.'

Tamar's brow creased. 'Nathan, I don't understand, I don't know your brother.'

Touching her lips with his, despite the old man's smile Nathan laughed, a joyous sound that filled the tiny room with softness.

'Oh, but you do, my darling, though his name is not John but Aiden.'

John was Nathan's brother! Listening to the brief account of his own searching she could not help the tinge of sadness that touched her heart, a sadness for her own lost brother.

'You must come with me to Cliveden. We have to tell Aiden our news.'

Pulling her gently to her feet, Nathan placed an arm about her as though fearing she would disappear again.

'I am sorry you did not find the boy, Tamar.' Isaac Cohen smiled at the girl he had known from childhood. 'But I thank the good Lord you have found a man that loves you and I know those good people in Australia would be glad also.'

'I almost forgot.' Reaching into her pocket, Tamar withdrew the coloured pebbles. 'Esther gave me these, I thought they looked very much like some of the pictures in your book.'

Taking them from her he placed them beneath the powerful jeweller's glass, studying them for some time in silence.

'Where did you get these?' he asked, as he looked up.

Repeating how she came to have them she glanced at Nathan as the old man raised his shoulders in the gesture she remembered so well.

'Well then, Tamar Hallam. Be it that these can be clipped from the walls of that cave, then you are a wealthy girl already. These pretty pebbles of yours be opal of the finest grade.'

'They are valuable?'

'Hasn't Isaac Cohen told you so already!' The old man's shoulders lifted again. 'These will buy you anything you want.'

'I have what I want.' Tamar smiled as she caught Nathan's free hand. 'But they will buy the Wessons the land Luke needs and the sheep to build his station.'

Leaving the stones with Isaac she looked up at Nathan as they walked together towards Vyse Street. She would say goodbye to Vinny and the others.

'. . . *you carry your friends in your heart.*'

She would always carry these friends with her.

'Tam?'

The call turning her to stone, her hand gripping Nathan's, she stood still.

'Tam . . . Tam, do that be you?'

Turning slowly, her gaze reaching to where a figure stood beneath a street lamp, she loosed a long trembling sigh.

'Benjie . . . Oh, Benjie!'

If you enjoyed THE JUDAS TOUCH, here's a
foretaste of another compelling Meg Hutchinson novel,
THE PEPPERCORN WOMAN.

Chapter One

'Throw it to the dogs!'

Drained of colour, Tyler Cadell stared at the woman watching him, horror etched deep on her face.

Livid with rage he struck out with a booted foot sending a small ebony table crashing against the wall, a crazed shout echoing after it.

'Do it . . . do it now!'

'You can't mean that . . .'

His eyes hard as blue granite, he lowered his voice to a menacing whisper. 'I mean every word. You feed that monstrosity to the dogs! Do as I say or by Christ I'll do it myself and throw you in after it!'

Huddled beneath a hedge, shawl drawn tight against the lancing rain, Garnet Cadell sobbed as memories trod relentlessly through her mind.

The letter had said Tyler would be home in one week's time. His business in India now finished he had a few things to settle in London and then he would be home.

Tall, fair-haired and blue-eyed he had swept her off her feet the night they had met at the Commissioner's Ball in Mariwhal. For a year he had paid court to her, calling at her parents' bungalow on the hill that overlooked the bustling Indian town, ever polite, ever the gentleman. There had been no hint at all at that time, no pointer to the cruelty that was the very core of Tyler Cadell. They had been married there in India and a few months later her parents were dead of typhus.

Her loving gentle parents. A long-drawn sob rattling through her chest drowned the sound of a snapping twig.

She had not been allowed to return to Mariwhal to bury the two people she had loved most in the world, to see where they would lie together, to whisper them a last goodbye. '*I cannot allow you to take the risk, my love, perhaps in a year or so, once I can be certain all danger of infection is passed.*'

Why couldn't he have let her return to that town while the infection was rife? That way would have been easier, that way he could have taken what he really wanted from her much sooner and she . . .? She would have been at peace with her beloved parents.

A sudden flurry of wind caught at the hurrying drops of rain flinging them needle sharp against her face, but deep in the misery of her thoughts she did not feel them, nor did she hear the soft tread of a boot.

Three days! Three days was all it had taken for Tyler to put her on a boat for England. He would follow as soon as he could, meantime Raschid would take care of her.

And he had taken care of her. A sob she could not hold back spilled into the dark silence, and once more the soft tread of feet was masked. Raschid, Tyler's Indian manservant, had cared for her as a father might, seeing to her every comfort on that long voyage back to England, then on to the Midlands and her father's childhood home. The home where her own child had been born, her beautiful dark-eyed child.

'You'll get nothing but the influenza sitting there in this weather.'

A foot hitting sharp against her thigh brought terror flooding back.

'No!' A scream piercing the rain-swept night, Garnet was on her feet, her thin frame hurling itself forwards. 'I won't let you . . . I won't let you kill my baby!'

'Tyler, my dear, you must try to forget, you cannot go on grieving this way, you are making yourself ill.'

'Mrs Benson is right, Cadell.' Arthur Benson nodded agreement with his plump wife. 'All the fretting in the world won't make no difference. The past be over and done with, heed what I says and let it go.'

'You are both very kind and I know you mean well . . .'

Rising quickly from his chair, Tyler Cadell strode to the window, his back turned to the industrialist and his wife, his shoulders holding just the right amount of tension.

'We knows what you 'ave been through, it was an ordeal would 'ave killed a lesser man, but you survived it and now 'ard as it is you must get on wi' life.'

'I have my business—'

'Oh ar, lad, you has that,' the older man inter-rupted, 'but you know what they say about all work and no play, they makes dull companions.'

His head lowering slightly, the taut shoulders drop-ping a little, Tyler smiled to himself as he caught the woman's sympathetic murmur.

'I apologise.' The huskiness in his voice reached that perfect level, just clear of heart-break. 'My com-pany is not fitting for kindness such as yourself and Mrs Benson have shown since—'

Breaking off, a dramatic half-stifled sob finishing the act, he was hard pressed to keep the smile hidden as Winifred Benson bustled to his side.

'You have no need of apology my dear, Mr Benson meant only that too much of one and too little of another don't be good for a man; work and grief be right, they have their place, but they needs be ba-lanced if a body is to keep his right mind. It has been two years, though to you it must seem forever since your wife and little one was took. But like Mr Benson says that be in the past and hard though it be you must pick up your life again.'

'I have no life without my loved ones . . .'

If the strangled swallow caught in his throat, Tyler Cadell congratulated himself. Each perfor-mance got better, he was as good an actor as Sir David Garrett.

Tears rolling down her ample cheeks Winifred sniffed loudly, fumbling in her pocket for a hand-kerchief.

This was the opportunity he had waited for, a God-given chance, but he must play it carefully.

Brows drawn together, a look of abject apology on his face, Tyler turned quickly taking the podgy hands between his own long-fingered ones.

'Forgive me, I didn't mean for my grief to touch you. I would not give unhappiness to so caring a person, to . . . to one who has been like my own dear mother. How can I tell you –' he raised the hands to his lips, kissing each one in turn, '– how can I show you the remorse I feel?'

'We ain't asking for no apology.' Arthur Benson's florid features broke into a smile as he watched his wife's hands being kissed. 'All we asks is that you picks yourself up and gets yourself out once in a while.'

Eyes glittering with a forced film of moisture, Tyler looked deep into the woman's eyes. She was a fool like her husband, but she could be a useful fool! Still holding one hand he lowered the other, releasing it against her skirts. Then, the faintest trace of a smile touching his mouth, he brushed a tear with his forefinger as he whispered, 'I will enter the world again . . . if you will guide my path.'

The evening had been a triumph. The exact amount of pathos. His smile broad and open, Tyler Cadell slipped the shirt free of his body, throwing it carelessly across the bed. Nothing worked so well with a woman as a man fighting to suppress his tears, to hide his emotions. Winifred Benson had reacted as he knew she would, she had fallen for his lies . . . and she would go on falling for them for just as long as it suited him! She would dance to his fiddle as others would, as his housekeeper must dance.

Undershirt following shirt across the bed he stared at himself in the long cheval mirror, at the tall lean body, muscles rippling in the fine shoulders and taut legs. He had cut a dashing figure in the regiment and on the polo field, there were times he almost wished he had not given up his commission, but retiring on the pittance of an Army pension, where every penny would need to do the work of two was not to the taste of Tyler Cadell. So when he had been introduced to the Wintons and their quite pretty daughter he had seen the chance of a vastly more acceptable way of life and had grabbed it with both hands. Garnet had been so easy to woo. Left in England at a school for young ladies, then joining her parents in Mariwhal and being introduced to a handsome Guards officer resplendent in scarlet and gold uniform who paid her the kind of attention she had never been paid before, she had been only too happy to accept his proposal of marriage. Her parents had gladly given their consent. But that was not all the Wintons had given. This house, their tea plantation, together with a thriving spice importing business and of course the lucrative business of supplying metal goods to the Armed Forces of the Crown.

Smiling at the reflection in the mirror he bowed slightly.

'Congratulations, Mr Cadell,' he said aloud, 'you have done well, you have done very well.'

But he was not finished. There were fresh fields to

conquer, fresh games to play; and the playing was about to begin.

Taking the freshly laundered night-shirt laid ready for him he slipped it over his head then touched a hand to the face that had months ago lost the last traces of the heat of the Indian sun. No, it showed no trace. He leaned nearer, peering closely in the mirror. A few lines at the corners of the eyes caused by the glare . . . but that could happen in any country, it was the colour of his skin, the deep tanning effect of constant sunlight he did not want; but it was gone . . . all gone and with it any fears.

But had the fears gone . . . truly gone? Throwing back the covers and slipping into bed he reached for the lamp stood on his night table turning the flame down until its dull gleam lit only the immediate area of his pillows, hesitated as he saw the shadows rush forward, their incandescent shapes hovering like dark phantoms. If the fears had gone why the nightly reluctance to extinguish the lamp completely, why this dread of what those circling shadows might hold?

They held nothing!

Annoyed with his thoughts he blew out the tiny flame killing the last of its light, but the thoughts clinging to the edges of consciousness were not so easily got rid of.

It had had to be done!

The child had had to die!

With his eyes shut hard against the menacing shadows he dismissed the threads of guilt trying to weave together in his mind.

To allow it to live would have meant the end of everything he hoped to have, no . . . everything he *intended* to have. It would have been a blight on his life, a drawback to all he had gained, to that which was yet to be gained. He had done the right thing, the child was better dead; that way it brought him sympathy, the kind that would open many doors.

Nobody knew, except for Florrie Wilkes and she would not tell, not unless she wanted to end her days on the gallows and that is how it would be by the time Tyler Cadell told the courts his story. A woman who had harboured her mistress in a love affair with her Indian manservant then deliberately destroyed the fruit of their union, had cold-bloodedly thrown the body of a child to the dogs.

There would be no question in the minds of the jurors, those twelve good men and true. Tyler's mouth curved in a cynical smile. They would not doubt the word of a man so devastated he could not bring himself to mingle in society, a man who despite the heart-break could not bring himself to have his wife's name blackened or the memory of an innocent child ostracised, but instead had lived with the misery of the knowledge of what she had done to him, lived in silence and in pain.

Yes, with the child dead his way was clear.

Gritting his teeth against the tortured scream echoing in his memory he turned his face into the pillows.

The child was gone, his wife had not been seen for

two years. Tomorrow he would consult a lawyer. It was time for Tyler Cadell to take a new wife.

'You shouldna' 'ave fetched 'er to the camp, the bringing trawls naught but trouble in its wake . . .!'

Loud and condemning the words carried on the damp night air reaching inside the gypsy caravan. Setting a blanket over the girl she had sponged then dressed in a rough calico night-gown, Hepzibah Kane rose to her feet, her black skirts rustling as she flung open the door. Standing on the uppermost of three steps that reached to the rain-sodden ground she stared at the men sitting around a blazing fire set between the grouped caravans, its dancing flames flickering over their wooden bodies giving life to painted roses, movement to carved leaves and branches.

'We welcomes no gaujo to our midst, to let one lay its head in a gypsy camp, an' that one a juval, be askin' for misfortune. We all be of the same mind.' The man cast a quick glance at the faces of the men listening in silence. 'Tek the woman to where you found 'er, tek 'er now afore the mornin' sun finds 'er 'ere.'

'I teks no warning from you, Lorcan Nash, if warning be the meaning of your words.'

Hepzibah listened to the answer come from her son, heard the quiet iron of his will and was proud.

'I was elected leader by the Kris, and while I be first man it will be done according to what I say and I say that woman or any other being, whether Romany or gaujo, that be in need of help will find it here in this camp.'

'Then it might be as you should no longer be first man!' Ringlets of dark hair highlighted by the leaping flames, Lorcan Nash stepped forward, a swagger in every line of his lean frame.

JOIN
MEG'S CLUB!

Become a part of the Meg Hutchinson story
today by joining the

* * * * * * * * * * *

Meg Hutchinson Readers' Club

* * * * * * * * * * *

Membership of the club is free and, once you join,
you will automatically receive each new edition of
the club newsletter *THE YARN*.
Inside you will find special messages from Meg,
exclusive extracts, fellow readers' letters, the
chance to obtain collectable Meg merchandise,
competitions galore and price promotions
available only to club members.

* * * * * * * * * * *

To join the Meg Hutchinson Readers' Club and receive
the first edition of the club newsletter *THE YARN*,
simply send a postcard with your name and address to:
Margaret Hutchinson, Kadocourt Ltd,
The Gateway, Gatehouse Road, Aylesbury,
Bucks, HP19 8ED.